THE DUNSTON BLADE

John Nelson Daines

ISBN-13: 978-1536983050

ISBN-10: 1536983055

"To Margaret, my wife, for her patience and help without which this story would not have been completed."

John stirred, he could feel the flickering light on his eyelids caused by the sun breaking through the leaves of the old oak tree under which he lay. His head ached and his left shoulder felt as though it had been severed. Gradually his mind recalled the fight and the blow that felled him. He tried to sit up but the ground whirled and he fell back, was he mortally wounded? His right hand explored his body and felt the cut on his shoulder. He remembered walking through the wood with his friend Roger when four men appeared in front of them, John could see that they were armed with bows and swords. Roger confronted them demanding to know what they were doing in his father's wood and accused them of poaching. The leader of the group glared at Roger. "That will be enough from you my lad, we are honest men and have no need to steal," he said.

"Then what is in that bag your friend is carrying?" responded Roger.

The man's reply was to draw his sword. "Methinks 'tis time you were taught some manners," he said as he advanced on Roger. The other three also drew weapons and a short melee ensued in which the two young men were easily defeated. John remembered a heavy blow to his shoulder and a shout from the leader, "No deaths," then a blow of a mailed fist to the side of his head followed by blackness.

Where was Roger? He managed to sit up at last and looked around, Roger lay six yards from him, on his back, not moving. "Roger!" John croaked. "Roger, are you hurt?" There was no answer and John shivered, perhaps his friend was dead. How was he to explain this to his and Roger's parents?

Jack Ivanson, the Smith of Dunston was wielding his hammer at the forge when four horsemen rode into the Village. They dismounted by the Village Cross and the tallest walked over to the Smithy and asked the direction to the house of Sir Walter de Brehalle. Jack pointed out the towers of the Castle showing above the tops of the trees.

"There, my lord, it is but a short ride, before you go can I offer any of my services for your animals?"

“No thank you, our horses were freshly shod before we left,” said the man as he looked into the Smithy.

Jack could see the man was of some wealth as shown by his richly embroidered blue cloak. The leader returned to his companions and the group mounted and thanking Jack rode off in the direction of the Castle. “I wonder what they want with Sir Brehalle, no good I warrant. ‘Tilda has the lad come back yet?”

Matilda looked at her husband. “ No he has not, chasing wenches with that no good Roger I’ll warrant, but he is late, they should have been home by now.”

John stood up and held on to the trunk of the tree until the world stopped spinning. Looking around he could see his sword lying in the grass. Tentatively he walked over to Roger who had begun to stir, he could see a large bruise and blood on the side of his head. “Can you hear me Roger, how do you feel?”

“Bloody awful,” oaned Roger. “I wish someone would stop banging on my head.”

With help from John he sat up and looked around. “They didn’t rob us. They could certainly fight, I will have to get more training.”

“Your stupid effort at trying to be the Lord of the Manor to everyone you meet, will be the death of us one day. Come on we must try and get cleaned up and get home before they send out search parties.” John looked around and spotted both swords, there was no mistaking which blade belonged to which man. Roger’s had a fine blade with spatulated quillions, leather over a wooden grip and a pommel with the family crest engraved, John’s blade however was dull and notched with a plain handle and a small pommel.

“I wonder where they came from, not from ‘round here or we would have recognised them,” mused John. “Where were they going?”

“Come on let’s get down to that brook and get cleaned up, your shoulder looks a bit of a mess,” said Roger as they staggered down to the small woodland stream and did the best they could to clean off the blood and mess. Roger's face had begun to puff up and John's shoulder was stiff and painful but not deeply cut. Gathering up their swords the two friends made their way home.

A distraught Matilda was cleaning and bandaging her son's wound while Jack questioned him as to how he got into the fight.

"That Roger will get you killed one of these days, its best if you break that friendship and concentrate on learning more of the business. I have several cart wheels to finish and there are plenty of scythes to prepare for the harvest."

"Perhaps he can learn to wield a scythe better than a sword." The comment came from a slender girl, two years younger than her brother John.

"We were caught off guard by those men but I must admit they were fast"

"I expect Sir Walter de Brehalle will want an explanation for his son's action." Jack's worried expression reflected the possible repercussions to his own son.

"Who were your visitors who went to the Castle?"

His father shrugged his shoulders and turned to go to the Smithy.

"Did they say who they were?" asked John.

Jack turned "No, they did not, and you would be wise not to be so inquisitive."

"Was Roger badly hurt?" asked his sister.

"No but I bet his father is going to have something to say."

"You had best stay away for a while lad," cautioned Matilda. "Let your wound heal and then help your father."

A month went past and John worked hard in his father's Smithy and his wound healed. There had been no sign of Roger and John made no move towards the Manor. He practiced with his sword under his fathers tuition, which surprised John to know his father was so accomplished. “In my youth,” explained Jack, “I served Sir Walter’s father and at that time he had a very good swordsman who spent many an hour teaching me to fight, not only with the sword, I think Sir Walter was expected to serve Thomas de Mowbray but it never came to pass.” John practiced hard, as he wanted to defend himself better than he had in the woods. One afternoon while he was resting on an upturned barrel, Joan appeared with a jug of cider and sat with him.

“Have you seen Roger, Joan?”

Joan blushed and turned away, saying, “Why should I want to see that boy, who got you into trouble. He needs to come and apologise to you.”

“Oh I know you have been seeing each other on the common, but has he said anything about what happened with his father and who were the visitors?” asked John.

Joan blushed and picking up her skirts and ran into the house leaving John smiling to himself. As evening fell John thoughts turned to Roger and what had happened to him. Should he go to the Castle and wait in their secret place by the walled garden or maybe staying here will give Roger time to come to him, another way would be to get a message to Roger through Joan? Tomorrow he would make up his mind.

“Don’t be frightened Joan, it’s only a woodland animal,” John tried to reassure her as they walked along the path towards the church.

“You don’t know what animal though, it could be a snake,” she said pulling up her long skirt.

“Just mind you don’t drop the basket, I’ve enough to carry with this barrel of cider,” exclaimed John.

They spotted the church through the trees and the rather round priest sitting by the door.

“ Hello my friends, come and sit with me.”

Joan handed over the basket but the priests eyes were on the barrel.

"You must be thirsty after your walk, let me fetch some jugs," he said as John put the barrel down.

"Not for me Father," replied Joan, who was not used to strong drink.

"All right Joan, but I am sure young John will join me." After chatting with the priest for a while John asked him if he knew who the visitors were at the Castle? "Yes, I know of them, they have gone now. They came to enlist Roger in the army they are putting together."

"Do you know their names?" asked John.

"One was Henri de Granville a close friend of Roger Bigod, he is forming a group to join an army." "Who are they going to fight?" asked John.

Father Aldred shook his head, he did not know or was not telling. "I have no knowledge of his companions, but they were obviously soldiers by their dress and bearing." Joan and John talked about the information they had as they walked home. Was war coming to England or was this army going to fight abroad.

II

Roger sat in the Castle's Hall waiting for his father. The large oak door was thrown open and two lurcher hunting dogs bounded in followed by a tall thickset man.

"Well, boy have you finished your work in the stables?" Roger stood up from greeting the dogs and gazed at his father. Since arriving home after their encounter in the woods, Roger told his father they had been set upon by brigands, but Sir Walter had already warned his son about his quick temper and willingness to fight so had banned Roger from the family and sent him to work in the stables and gardens. He had not seen his father's guests and only caught a glimpse of them when they left.

“Go down and get our horses ready, Ralf and I are riding over to Stoke.” Roger left the room. “I don’t know what I am to do with that boy,” said the Knight.

Ralf and his father strode out to the stables where Roger had prepared their hunting horses. The destriers were left munching on the hay, would they be needed soon? The destrier is a large horse capable of supporting a fully armoured knight into battle, de Brehalle had two in the stables. Roger watched them ride out and sat on a bale of hay with his thoughts, life at the castle was unbearable in his view, outcast in his own home. One of his duties was to exercise the destriers so putting a lead rein on one and a simple bridle on the other Roger led them out to the mounting block, jumped aboard the smallest and set off for the village. Riding across the common Roger glimpsed two figures the other side of some bushes. Carefully he approached, he did not want an encounter with strangers like the last time. Coming into full view were John and Joan picking blackberries.

“Ho, my good man, which way to the nearest Inn?”

John looked up in surprise and when recognising his friend let out a ‘Whoop’ and ran over to him. “Where have you been, what did your father say, who were the men who came to visit, why……?”

“Hold up John, let me get down and explain” said Roger, stopping John in full flow.

Joan meanwhile stood at a distance and smiled at Roger. “Are you recovered from your wounds Roger?”

“Yes, I am feeling better especially now I have seen you.”

“Don’t mind me,” laughed John. “I would like to know what your father said?”

Roger told them of his banishment to the stables and gardens and not being allowed to meet the visitors. “Were you recruited into their army, and do they know I was involved?”

“I don’t know, to both questions John, how did you know they were recruiting?” John explained what the priest had told them.

"I wouldn't mind a fight, That is what I've been trained for, but it is where and for how long." Roger had a glint in his eye as he said it.

"What about me?" came a sad voice from Joan.

"No, they don't allow women to fight," laughed John. "I will leave you two alone to sort it out." He went off back to the Smithy. John saw his father struggling with a large cart wheel and rushed over to help him. "Joan's talking to Roger on the common she will be here soon."

"What did Roger have to say for himself, did he say sorry for getting you into the fight?"

"No but he was punished by his father and is saying that he might join this army or whatever it is."

Jack stopped work and looked at his son "Do you feel the same?"

John thought for a moment and looked at his father "No father I am your son and mean to be the village Smith when you get too old, and in the meantime you had better teach me all you know."

"I am not too old to give up yet," Jack smiled as he spoke and grasped his son's arm. "Thank you for that John."

II

Several months went by and John worked hard in the Smithy. He saw Roger from time to time when he called to see Joan. One day Roger turned up dressed in new doublet and hose and his sword at his side.

"My father has enlisted me with Elric Fletcher, in Norwich. I am to report to the Castle by Friday so I am here to say good bye, is Joan here?"

John thought Roger looked nervous as he made this announcement. Elric Fletcher was known as a bully, as when he was younger he terrorised the young people in the surrounding countryside. His father had been killed in battle and his mother had died while giving birth so he had been brought up by the staff of Norwich Castle and been left a lot to his own devises. His ambition was to be one of Roger Bigod's lieutenants.

"I am sorry Roger, Joan has taken food over to the church and will no doubt stay a while with Father Aldred." John felt a pang of sorrow for his friend as he said this.

"No matter I will ride over to meet her. Farewell John, I hope to be home again after my training." So saying Roger cantered off in the direction of the church.

"I suppose we'll have a moody Joan about the house now," said Jack. "But it will give the other boys in the Village a chance."

"I don't think so father, she has strong feelings for Roger." John thought about the lack of a girl to walk and talk with but the village girls did not interest him. Was it his destiny to become a Smith like his father or was there an adventure waiting to alter his life.

"John, I want you to go to the Castle today and deliver these traps to the steward, I finished them a few days ago but have not had chance to go myself."

John slipped on his leather jerkin collected up the traps and walked off in the direction of the Castle. It was a bright autumn day and John whistled as he walked. His life at the moment was comfortable and the sun on his head made him feel more at peace with his lot. As he walked across the common he heard hoof beats behind him and he turned to find two ladies riding towards him, they were well dressed and rode fine horses. The older lady spoke commanding John to stand aside and not to frighten the horses. John stepped back and glanced at the younger woman who looked straight ahead and rode past.

John entered the Castle yard and saw the Steward striding towards the stables, catching up with him John gave him the traps.

"Come to my room and I will give you the money I agreed with your father."

John and the Steward entered the Keep and made their way to

the Steward's quarters. John marvelled at the fine furniture and drapes and picked up a silver ornament. "A gift from Sir Walter for serving him well," explained the Steward.

"A generous man?" said John. But not in his view. Sir Walter was hard on the villagers and demanded high taxes. A knock at the door announced a scruffy lad who brought a message that Sir Walter needed the Steward. Left to his own devices in the Keep John decided to look around. Most of the rooms on this floor were for staff and the kitchens. A delicious smell came from a door near him and at that moment a large woman appeared, she stopped short at the sight of John. "I know you, you're the son of the Smith aren't you?"

"Yes," said John quickly. "I'm just going, I had to deliver some traps to the Steward."

"Don't worry lad, come in and taste my soup, your father very kindly repaired one of my pots." She guided John into the warm kitchen where several girls were busy preparing food.

"Sit down by that table." The cook soon had one of the girls place a bowl of soup in front of John. He looked at two of them and thought that they were better looking than the village girls and wondered how he could get to know them better, probably difficult as they lived in the Castle. Returning to the village John's thoughts pondered on the difference between the homes in the village and the life in the Castle. The Smithy provided a good income and the family house was comfortable but many of the villagers were not so lucky and John had spent many hours with his father helping to put, what can only be described as hovels, back together before winter came.

He thought about the age old problem of the gulf between the poor and the rich, surely there could be improvement in the lives of the poor as it was them who worked the land and tended the animals. Without them there would be no rich.

Soon the Smithy came into view and John could see the smoke curling from the chimney. His mother would be preparing their evening meal after which Jack and the family would sit and talk. This was the time that John loved most, he did not envy Roger away from home, with strangers and in a strange city.

II

Mornings were colder now and as Roger awoke he was reluctant to leave the warmth of his bed, even though only a blanket covered him as he lay on a straw filled sack. Coughs and hawking filled the air as the trainee soldiers woke up.

"Get out of your sack Roger or you will miss what there is for breaking our fast." Roger's friend Roland aimed a kick at the recumbent lad. Sluicing water over their faces they hurried to the kitchens, food was laid out on a long table and it was first come first served. The two of them grabbed hunks of bread, cheese and a jug of cider.

"What is the first thing today? Not archery I hope as my shoulder has not recovered from the last time," groaned Roger as he rubbed the sore arm. "I would only reach two arrow lengths today."

After they had eaten the two of them walked down to the training ground and discovered that today Elric Fletcher had laid out wooden swords for battle practice and they were then to move on to practicing with their own swords against a large post, strengthening their wrists and arms.

"Nobody has said what we are preparing for," grumbled Roland. "Winter will soon be on us and I don't want to be out on a campaign in the snow."

Roger agreed and suggested. "Maybe we are going to join the Crusade," He wasn't aware that the sixth crusade had failed and the Muslims were in control of Jerusalem.

"At least it would be warmer," said Roland.

After a long morning of practice the two lads strolled out into the City. "I need a drink," stated Roland. "All that exercise makes you dry." They made their way to the nearest Inn, pushed their way to a table and ordered a flagon of ale.

"I would still like to know what we are preparing for, everything seems quiet in the City."

"Maybe the old Earl fancies Nottingham or we could be off to Wales, wherever that is," responded Roland. "But he will have a fine fighting force at the end of this training."

The two friends relaxed in the Inn and it was twilight before they returned to the dormitory, to find the place in a turmoil with all the young men collecting their belongings together. The hubbub of noise prevented Roger from hearing what was going on, he grabbed one of the men and asked what the commotion was about. "We are to go to our homes and return here to the Castle in three days with all our weapons and armour, if you have any," the man replied. Roger and Roland quickly gathered their belongings and went out into the courtyard where Elric Fletcher was organising them into groups.

"You there, de Brehalle, if you have armour bring it back and join this group, and ask your father if he would send one of his destriers for you to ride." Fletcher then dismissed them to go to their homes emphasising they must return in three days.

II

Jack called to his son, "John, I need you to go to the Castle and deliver these pieces of armour I have been repairing. They are for Sir Walter, but you had better see the Steward first."

John picked up the sack containing the parts and set off. The Steward was in the courtyard and John went to give him the sack of armour but the Steward said to him, "You had better see Sir Walter and see what he says about the repairs. Follow me." They climbed up the back stairs to Sir Walters quarters where they met a servant who informed them that Sir Walter was in the Great Hall. John's eyes opened wide when they entered the Hall, the room was the largest John had ever seen. Sir Walter was standing by one of the windows, he turned as they entered.

"The Smith has sent the repaired parts of armour to you my

Lord."

"Bring them over,lad," said Sir Walter, moving to a large table. John placed each part on the table and stood back. "Your father has done magnificent work on these besagues, they were really bent and damaged. I must send a suitable reward," exclaimed Sir Walter. A door at the far end of the room opened and two women entered. John recognised the women he had met on the common.

"Ah, Cecily, look what a fine repair the Smith has made on my armour. I must see if Roger's needs any work." "Why should you need to prepare our son's armour, he is not going into battle?" exclaimed Sir Walter's wife. "You never know what might happen in these unsettled times my dear," he retorted. "Avice, show the young man out and then call your brother Ralph to me." With his last comment Sir Walter strode out of the room. The young lady came to John and walked out of the room with him. John attempted conversation but it was clear the girl was shy. When they reached the courtyard John turned and said, "If ever I can be of service to you, my Lady, just send me a message and I will come." John hurried out of the Castle and did not see Avice's eyes following him and her cheeks glowing a bright pink. As yet there had been no suiters calling at the Castle. John had plenty of time to think of Avice on his way home and the differences in their situations. As beautiful as she was she was out of his reach, not like Roger and Joan were, Jack and Matilda were honoured by Rogers attention, the only worry was were his intentions honourable.

II

Roger eased the reins on his horse and let it come to a stop. He had ridden hard when he left Norwich Castle and the animal was blowing, he looked around and recognised the spot where he had first encountered the poachers. Roger dismounted and led his horse towards the village. He soon saw the Smithy and was tempted to stop to see Joan but he did not have much time to organise himself for the return trip, however it was not going to be so easy as the cottage door opened and John stepped out.

“Roger!” exclaimed John in surprise. “What are you doing here have they thrown you out already or have you escaped?”

“No, I am home to prepare myself for a campaign, or something,” and Roger explained what had happened in Norwich.

“It sounds as though they are after something, maybe more land. Will your father let you have the destrier?” “ I doubt it,” answered Roger. “I must go as I have lots to do before……”

“Not before you’ve spoken to me,” interrupted a small voice and Joan appeared through the doorway.

“I will meet you on the common at our usual place tomorrow morning,” said Roger. “I cannot linger now as I am dusty and tired from my travel.”

Joan, a little crestfallen, replied, “I shall be going to the church mid morning.”

Roger smiled and nodded to her, “I will walk with you.”

Roger moved off towards the Castle and the two siblings returned to the cottage. As was their custom they went to bed early and John lay awake listening to the sound of the night animals out hunting. A fox barked not far from the Smithy, then came the sound of the hens, but they had been shut securely in their coop. John’s thought turned to Rogers information about the forth coming campaign and wondered if it would affect their family. He knew he was now adequate with a sword but with his father they were too small a group to protect the Smithy. Perhaps Sir Walter would take them into the Castle and perhaps he would see the young lady again, she had heated his blood and caused feelings he had not known before.

Came the dawn and John was back to his old self and ready to work with his father, he told him of Roger’s information and Jack looked thoughtful.

“We will practice this morning and I want to show you something new,” Jack said as he went out to the Smithy and picked up a long bundle of cloth as well as his sword.

“Come now John we have a lot to do.” Father and son walked

off to the common where they had found a small glade to practice the sword play.

"Today, John, we will train to kill our enemy before he gets within the range of our sword." Jack unravelled the bundle and produced a beautiful longbow, over six feet in length it was taller than Jack. " The first thing to learn is to string the bow, I think your muscles are strong enough."

They practiced stringing the bow and Jack taught John how to hold the string and bend the bow by putting his weight forward into the bow. They shot a few arrows and Jack said they must return to the Smithy, but would come again tomorrow.

Roger caught up with Joan on her way to the church. They walked along together for a while and stopped just out of sight of the church.

Roger suddenly drew Joan to him, his embrace was intense and it was not long before his hands began to wander.

"Stop!" said Joan pushing him off. "I am not one of the girls from your City Inn, when I have a husband I shall go to his bed a virgin, and I think it will not be you. Your father will never allow you to marry a village girl."

Roger released her and stood back he looked at Joan and said. "Being friendly to a Knight's son is better than being married to a poor farmer." With that repost he mounted his horse and rode away.

Joan held back tears, she had been fond of Roger but her upbringing had made her strong willed. Father Aldred was waiting for her and seeing she was upset led her into the church where they sat quietly for a few moments. "I have taught you and John most of what I know, you can both read and write and there are only tales and my experiences to pass on now,if you wish."

"Yes, Father I would love to hear about your travels." Joan sat down and the Priest began a story of his time with the Knights on the Crusade.

II

John, walking across the common to meet Joan, saw Roger galloping back to the Castle and he kept looking ahead even when John called out. “I wonder what’s bitten him?” he thought.

Coming from out of the trees John could see a man approaching riding a huge destrier and leading two other horses one of which was loaded with baggage.

“Ho there, young man, is there a Smith in that village?”

“Yes, sir,” replied John. “He is my father, Jack Ivanson, so I can guide you there if you wish.”

“If you can ride, you may mount my spare horse,” said the man and dropped the lead reign of the saddled horse. John mounted and sat easily in the saddle. “You have ridden before young man,” observed the stranger.

“I ride horses to and from the Smithy when people want the Smith to look after them,” John explained. “Then tell me what ails the horse you are on?”

“ I think one of his shoes are loose,” answered John dismounting and lifting the leg of the horse. “Yes, this one will need attention now.”

“Well, done lad, let’s get him to the Smith. What is your name?” John told him and also about his family, how they had originated from Denmark, probably when the Viking farmers settled in the area. He found himself chatting easily to this stranger as they walked the horses to the village. The stranger dismounted as the village came into sight and they led the animals to the Smithy.

Jack inspected the horses and informed the stranger that all three of the animals needed work on their hooves.

“As my horses are to be with you for some time I must find

lodgings, is there an Inn nearby?" enquired the stranger.

Jack answered. "There is a small alehouse sir but no accommodation I would recommend, but I am sure you would be welcome at the Castle until the animals are ready."

"Who lives there now?" asked the man.

"It is Sir Walter de Brahalle's home," answered Jack.

"I would not be welcome at all," replied the stranger.

John looked at his father and said. "You would be welcome to my bed sir, as I have oft slept in the Smithy. There is plenty of hay and the Smithy is always warm." Jack agreed and Matilda went off to ready the room. "You are most generous, this is much better than some places I have slept in these past months. I must introduce myself, my name is Cedric of Wymondham and I have lately returned from lands across the sea. I ask that this is between your family and me."

"You have our word sir." Jack said raising his hand to his heart. The name was not new to him as Sir Cedric was the Earl of this part of the Shire and he also knew that he had been on a Crusade and had not been heard of for two years.

After the evening meal Sir Cedric and Jack sat talking with John eagerly listening to the tales that passed between them. He made his way to the Smithy and made sure all the horses were stabled, as he glanced at the bundles that had been taken from the pack horse he noticed they contained armour and spare weapons, obviously Sir Cedric was a fighting man. He wondered why their visitor did not want to stay at the Castle.

The following morning Jack was up early to start on the preparation of the horse shoes. As each horse was finished John led it back to the stable. Sir Cedric appeared, watched for a while then he noticed the bow in the corner and asked John if he could shoot. Jack said he had been schooling his son in archery and swordsmanship.

"You must show me how well you can use these weapons," said

Sir Cedric. Jack urged John to take Sir Cedric to the common while he finished with the horses. John strung the bow and fired three arrows at a nearby tree.

"Good shooting, a tight group, but now try that oak tree in the glade yonder."

John could see the tree stood over 500 yards away, he placed three arrows in the ground and fired, notching a fresh arrow as quick as he could. They strode over to the oak and there were two arrows together and one a small distance to one side.

" The first must have been off line," said a disappointed John.

"You will improve, and now let's see how good you are with your sword," with that Sir Cedric drew his sword and advanced on John the young man quickly drew his own sword and took up a defensive stance. They thrust and parried for several minutes until Sir Cedric stepped inside a late move by John and the young man found himself without his sword and the Knight's weapon at his throat.

"You have good potential lad, just need to know a few tricks and strengthen your arm. A new weapon would not go amiss." They walked back to the Smithy where Jack was nearing completion of his work. All three sat near the fire and ate the bread and cheese provided by Matilda. Sir Cedric complimented Jack on what he had taught his son. Jack recounted a battle he had been in when he had been on crusade, Sir Cedric was quiet and just listened. John looked at the Knight more closely he noticed the clothes were worn but of good quality and his boots had seen hard times, he wore a wedding ring on his left hand and on his right John noticed a heavy gold ring.

"I must ask if I may impose on your hospitality for one more night Jack?" the Knight announced.

"That is no problem, stay as long as you need," replied Jack. That night after supper, John again retired to the Smithy. Sir Cedric and Jack stayed talking for some time and eventually they stood, Sir Cedric handed a leather purse of coins to Jack, they shook hands and went to their beds.

Jack was in the Smithy early in the morning and sent John to the Charcoal Burners in the forest to ask them to send a load of charcoal to the Smithy and continue on to the Church to ask Father Aldred for a large bag that Jack had left with him many years ago.

"He will know what I want," said Jack. When John returned his father was working on the fire, he sent John into the house to talk to the Earl. Sir Cedric was sitting at the table with Matilda and Joan he signalled John to join them.

"I have to journey to Norwich tomorrow but I will return and when I do I wish you to join me as my Squire. I have spoken with your father and he is willing to release you if you wish to follow this path. You are ready for adventures and I need a man who can use the bow and sword. You will be trained and I will explain your duties. Give me your answer when I return and if it yes then be ready to depart the next day." With that announcement the tall Knight rose and went out to the Smithy. John strode after him.

"I shall leave the destrier here with my pack horse, see that they are exercised and ready for me."

"I thank you very much for your offer sir and I will give my answer on your return," said John.

Sir Cedric turned and saw the light in John's eyes and smiled to himself. Early next morning Sir Cedric left the Smithy and rode off towards Norwich. John watched him go, climbing the hill out of Dunston towards the City. Jack came and stood next to him. " Well son, do you now want your adventure, you did say you would stay here but I will not hold you to that."

"Thank you father, Sir Cedric seems an honest man but to serve him as a Squire will not be easy as I have no knowledge of what I will be required to do."

"Now don't worry son, Sir Cedric and I had a long talk about it and he questioned me a lot. He knows you can read and write and that you can fight," said his father. "He has the means to train you and the rest is up to you." He knew his wife and Joan would be sad to see John go but this was too good an opportunity to miss. Who knows where John could end up, dead on a battlefield or maybe a

Knight. Jack returned to the Smithy and carried on hammering and shaping his work, he stopped for a moment and wiped his brow looking at what he had made. "Needs a lot more work yet." That evening Jack was late coming in to supper and was very tired.

"You mustn't work so hard Jack, what is so important out there?" asked Matilda. There was no comment from Jack so the table became quiet. Joan thought about her last meeting with Roger and argued with herself that she had made the right decision. There was no future with the Knight's son who would never be the heir. Soon she would be on her own but while they lived she had loving parents who would protect her. With those thoughts she drifted off to sleep.

II

Roger rode into the Castle yard where Elric Fletcher stood issuing orders. "So you could not persuade your father to release his destrier to you, well that paltry animal you are riding will not last long in battle so you may as well stable it and join the foot soldiers." After saying this Elric strode off to the group of horsemen assembling at one end of the yard. Roger's heart dropped, if he was to be on foot his full suit of armour could not be worn and he was sure it would soon disappear. Well, he was not going to have that so he rode over to the wall, dismounted and tried to look as inconspicuous as possible. Soon Roland found him and the two friends talked about where they thought they would be going. The small army settled down with the foot soldiers camped in the castle grounds and the mounted men sleeping in the stables or what shelter they could find with their horses. Roger kept out of Elric's way and mingled with some men and horses in a small building near to the gate.

"It's a bit hot in here," complained Roland. "My mare is damp and smelly."

"Just be grateful we are not out in the field, and stop complaining Rolly, we'll need all the rest we can get I feel we have a long march tomorrow." At that moment there was a loud noise from the rear of Roland's horse and everyone put their heads under the blankets.

"When you said it was smelly, you weren't wrong," said Roger pulling his cloak tighter.

Early next morning before the sun had risen over the Castle walls, they were awakened by shouts, and the general activity of an army preparing for a march. Elric Fletcher was standing on the Keep steps shouting out orders and the Knights and mounted men filed out onto the field to join the foot soldiers. Roger squeezed himself into the middle of a mounted group and prayed he would not be spotted. When the army had assembled Henri de Granville rode out with his two friends, they were fully armoured as were their horses. John of Lancaster held de Granville's great helm while de Granville addressed the assembled men.

" Today we travel south to join forces with our friends in securing stability in this England. You will be fighting for your families, for justice and a rightful government. We will fight for the love of our country, we fight for ENGLAND!"

At this men shouted 'HURRAH' and banged their shields. de Granville signalled the mass of men to move off and their journey south began.

"That didn't tell us much," complained Roland.

Roger looked around to see who was listening and told Roland that he had overheard his father talking to Ralf that the Barons were fed up with the King and the way England was being governed.

"Who we are joining with, and where, I do not know," said Roger.

The army swung east to reach the river and there they saw many boats ready to take men, horses and equipment down river to Yarmouth. On reaching the coast the army camped in the old Roman fort between Yarmouth and Lowestoft. Roger, keen to keep out of sight of Elric, suggested that he and Roland should visit Yarmouth and sample the towns delights. The two friends arrived in the town which was full of men who had the same idea. Walking down by the docks they came upon several large ships anchored in the port. "I hope you're not sea sick Rolly, for it looks as though those are our next transport."

II

For three days there had been no sign of Sir Cedric and John was starting to think he would not see the Earl again. Jack tried to reassure him by saying with the country in a turmoil there could be many things to detain him. "I have a gift for you John, which should take your mind off Sir Cedric for a while."

John followed his father into the Smithy, from behind some old sacks Jack pulled out a bundle and gave it to John.

"I had to make sure my son was well equipped to serve a Knight properly," said Jack. John undid the bundle to reveal a magnificent broadsword. The blade glinted in the light from the forge and John felt no weight from the weapon as it was so finely balanced. The quillions gently curved away from the grip, which was leather bound. The pommel was finely carved with the figure of an eagle. John looked closely at the blade and saw engraving that spelt out on one side 'ALIS AQUILAE, (on eagles wings) and on the other 'DEO JUVANTE' (with God's help). John was speechless as he swung the blade.

"I have always wanted to make this blade from an old, large falchion that was given to me by a Knight I served in the Holy Lands," explained Jack.

"He told me it had magical powers but it did not save him from losing his life. It has been difficult to convert it to a broadsword, the metal looks and feels like steel to me but harder than I have ever come across. Now it is finished and I have given into the right hands. Fight with honour son."

John put down the weapon and clasped his father to him. "I will never forget this moment father."

"Here is the scabbard, not quite so new but serviceable. With your longbow and dagger you should be equipped enough for your first encounter, you will also find a small bag that was given to me by the same Knight, what is in there is only to be worn when you are invested as a knight, it has also come from a Holy Lands. I will tell you more of that when the time comes."

John's eyes glistened as he looked at this man who was more a friend than just a father. Joan came out to call them to the table, John called her over to show her his new sword.

"I am sure it is the best," said Joan. "I hate to think what it will be used for."

As they were finishing their meal they heard hoof beats in the yard. John went to the door and there was Sir Cedric on his horse leading another pack horse with many bundles on its back. The baggage was taken in to the cottage and the Earl produced gifts for everyone. Bed coverings, dresses and clothes for the women and men. "I have found true friendship here and I wish to show my appreciation." Sir Cedric told the family who were speechless as they surveyed the gifts.

"I have just the one daughter and no son and my wife died four years ago, so you have filled a gap in my life for a short while. My daughter is being looked after by my staff until I return."

They all sat down to the table together and Sir Cedric talked of the state of the country.

"There is going to be trouble for the King, Simon de Montfort is gathering barons around him. If the King does not meet their demands I see a fight looming. Henry is our lawful King and although he has made many mistakes I would hate to see someone like de Montfort or one of his friends, control the country."

On this gloomy note they all retired to their beds. John thought of Roger and wondered where he was and who with. Earl of Norfolk, was a powerful baron who had no love of the King and would be a supporter of de Montfort. Was Roger at Norwich Castle preparing for battle? Was Sir Cedric going to join the fight and which side would he support? Surely it would be the King.

John picked up the small leather bag his father had given him and found inside a large gold ring, he tried it on but it was too big. Looking closely at it he noticed a strange writings on it. With all the thoughts he had spinning around he dropped off to sleep.

Early next morning Sir Cedric was up early preparing his horses. "John, the second horse I brought yesterday is for you. He has seen battle so will not be frightened in a fight. You will also find a breastplate and helmet in that bag, it should fit you. The last item is a spear with our colours, you must also carry and care for my lance. We will take the destrier and I will ride my other horse and leave the pack animal here with your father." The Earl finished his instructions and went back into the cottage.

John packed what they would need and distributed the load among the horses. Sir Cedric appeared carrying his armour which he loaded onto the destrier, the last item he fetched from the Smithy, a large shield with his coat of arms, a red eagle on a field of gold. John thought of the inscription on his sword. After all the goodbyes the two of them rode out towards the South .

After a few miles Sir Cedric said to John. " hope we make Haywood Hall tonight where we will be given shelter and I hope to gain some news. We are on our way past London."

It was dark and the wind had increased as they approached Haywood, only a few flickering lights could be seen. They rode round to the rear and a groom came out to take their horses. John felt strange being treated as a guest, it was normally left to him to look after the horses, etc. The rear door opened and an old man approached them.

"Sir Richard is in the hall sir, if you will follow me." John hesitated but Sir Cedric signalled to follow him. The old man led them through darkened passages to the large hall where a tall man stood by a glowing fire, he greeted Sir Cedric and turned to John.

"My Squire, " said Sir Cedric.

"Welcome to my house young man," said Sir Richard then he ordered the old man to go to the kitchens and have the cook prepare a meal. John walked around the hall looking at the various weapons adorning the walls, Sir Cedric was in deep conversation with Sir Richard and John tried to keep a good distance from them although he would have liked to know what was being said. A large jolly lady came bustling in with a tray of various meats and a young girl followed bearing a second tray with breads and cheeses. The three men sat down and were soon enjoying the food. John began to feel the effects of his ride and the ale and his head dropped on his chest.

"Send the lad to bed Cedric, we have need of some important talk," announced Sir Richard.

John staggered up to his room and dropped exhausted onto his bed, it was the longest ride he had done and he was stiff, sore and tired, is it always to be like this he wondered?

The following morning they took their leave from Sir Richard, John had prepared their horses so they set off Southwards. They continued on their journey spending some nights with Cedric's friends and other nights saw them camping in the woods. John noticed the nearer they moved toward London there were more Knights and their men at arms moving in the same direction. As they neared the River Thames Sir Cedric explained that he had been summoned to join forces with Prince Edward's army which was gathering on the South Downs. The King wanted de Montfort beaten and the Baron's brought to heel. John was worried about Englishmen fighting Englishmen but he was Sir Cedric's Squire and would therefore follow him.

II

"Seen any fish Rolly?" queried Roger smiling as Roland leaned over the side of the ship and heaved.

"Go away can't you see I am dying?" said Roland.

"What, before the battle?" smiled Roger.

The two friends and the rest of the men from Norwich had been sailing for several days and had been told they were to land on the morrow. This was strange country to them both and they were excited to get ashore.

The men disembarked at Pevensey and moved inland to meet up with the rest of de Montfort's forces. The Baron's strength numbered some 5000 troops. Roger and Roland joined a cavalry unit and hoped Elric was too busy elsewhere to notice Roger was mounted. Meanwhile Sir Cedric and John had crossed the Thames at Windsor and rode to Windsor Castle to meet the King but learnt that the he had moved on to Lewes Castle.

"We will spend the night here John, we should make Horsham by tonight. We move towards Lewes tomorrow." Sir Cedric rode up to the Castle gates and spoke to a guard who opened them and directed the two of them to the stables.

They rose early the next morning and set off for Lewes, making good time they arrived in Horsham as night fell. There was an encampment there and Sir Cedric told John to make camp among the assembled men.

"I will search out the Prince for I feel he is with these men."

John found a place next to a group of men who were camped around a large tent where John assumed their Knight was resting. "Come and sit by our fire," said a cheerful man. "'tis a cold night. Have you eaten? Help yourself to what's in the pot."

"Thank you I am hungry and it smells good," said John and dished a ladle full of stew onto a platter. "What Knight do you serve?" John asked, this was met with a loud laugh from the men around him.

"This is no Knight lad, this is Prince Edward's tent and we are his guard."

"I meant no offence as we are looking for the Prince to join him."

"You are in good company then," smiled a man with broad shoulders.

At that moment the large tent's flap opened and a very tall man stepped out. The men stood up and looked toward the Prince, for it was he. "Easy men, save your strength and rest while you can for I see a hard fight before us." As the Prince finished speaking John could see Sir Cedric approaching. John looked at the men he would be sharing a battle with, they seemed a hardened bunch, and John relaxed and lay down in front of Sir Cedric's tent, he wanted to sleep but his mind kept thinking of what was coming, he clutched the leather purse that he had fastened round his neck containing the strange ring and felt better.

II

Roger and Roland found themselves in a cavalry unit under Nicholas Seagrave and a large contingent of soldiers from London. They moved nearer to Lewes and made camp on the Downs. Early next morning, while the mist was still hugging the ground, Roger and Roland were woken by the guards and told to mount up and join their unit.

"I've not seen a sign of the foe," complained Roland.

"I think we are going to see them soon enough," replied Roger.

At that moment the cavalry were told to move forward, some foragers from the King's army had been sighted near a stream. Suddenly Elric Fletcher appeared in front of them and called. "Forward lads, the enemy is by the stream. Keep as quiet as you can and we'll surprise them," and he moved off with the cavalry following. Suddenly they were upon the King's men and a fierce fight developed around the stream, the foragers retreated returning to their lines. Seagrave's Londoners came up behind the cavalry and the whole section moved towards the King's army. Out of the morning mist Roger could hear the thunder of charging horses and Prince Edward and his cavalry were upon them. The Londoners were outmatched and soon broke and it became a rout as the men ran before the charging cavalry. In the charge were Sir Cedric and John, Sir Cedric's destrier bowling men over as the Knight slashed left and right, John tried to keep up but in the melee he dropped behind. Coming across a group of stragglers John slowed his horse, the men turned, looked at him and raised their weapons, a mixture of swords and spears and one with an axe.

"We'll get this young cub, come on me lads have him off that horse," this came from the axe man who strode forward swinging the weapon. John spurred his horse, raised his sword and the arm with the axe was suddenly detached from the body and lay on the grass, the rest turned to run but John had the battle fever and rode after them swinging his sword. Another man went down, blood pouring from his shoulder, the rest scattered in all directions. John felt the exhilaration of the fight and hardly noticed the speed at which his sword attacked the foe. Eventually Prince Edward called a halt to the chase and turned his men to return to the main battle. When they came near to Lewes they saw that the King had retreated to the Castle, Edward launched a counterattack but the King's Marshall rode out and called them to cease fighting to allow negotiations to take place with de Montfort. John sought out Sir Cedric as they entered the Priory.

"I am glad to see you survived the fight, John. I lost sight of you after the initial charge."

"I was scared and excited, if you know what I mean, and now I'm glad to be back here. I am sorry I did not stay with you," said a breathless John.

The Earl looked at him and spoke to him, smiling. "We were going at a good gallop, but that's the Prince's way, charge in and sort it out later. I see you have blooded your sword."

John looked at the weapon and felt a certain sadness at what he had done. 'So this is war?' he thought. Kill or be killed. As John saw to the horses he talked to some of the other Squires and learnt that Prince Edward had surrendered to de Montfort as hostage, so they had failed in their endeavours he mused. What would happen to them now?

II

Roger and Roland had run with the rest, away from the charging

Prince. Roland suddenly veered left and shouted to Roger.

"Make for those trees, we can lose them in there." Riding swiftly into the wood the pair slowed to a stop and heard the charge go past.

"That was close," puffed Roger. "I thought we would be caught and this would be my first and last battle." Dismounting they crept to the edge of the wood. They could see a few stragglers being rounded up, and one small group appeared to turn to face the horseman chasing them.

"A bit of courage at last," whispered Roland. "Should we help?"

"No, we don't want to expose ourselves, or go up against him, look!" countered Roger. They witnessed John cutting off the man's arm and wounding the second. Little did they know they were watching Rogers friend. "You wouldn't want to meet him on a dark night, did you see the speed of those strokes?" Muttered Roland as they crept back to their horses. When they had waited long enough they mounted and rode off to find the rest of their group. Roger was disappointed he had not been part of the fighting but was pleased the outcome had been in de Montfort's favour. He was even more elated to find himself chosen as one of the Prince's guards. The prisoner's caravan wound it's way to Leicester where Edward was placed under guard. Roger found life as a guard tedious and looked forward to his visits to the town and it's taverns, he was soon known by all the bar wenches and many a night he did not make it back to his room. Guard duty did not please Roger or his friend Roland and they were constantly in trouble for being late on duty.

One dark night when the rain was soaking the ground and all were either in their beds or safe indoors, it happened that Roger had dallied longer with his current girl and was trying to get back for his tour of duty, when he met men coming towards him.

"Have you seen a tall man running this way?" questioned one man.

Roger pulled his hat further down and muttered, "No, I have

seen nothing on a night like this." With a cloud of doom hanging over him he reached the Castle to find Roland under guard and soldiers rushing everywhere.

"Where have you been?" whispered Roland. "I told them you had gone to the garderobe so get those wet things off quickly."

Roger threw the cloak and hat in the corner of their room and rejoined Roland.

"Prince Edward has escaped and all the guards on duty have got to go before Fletcher now." Elric Fletcher was not a happy man and he was not going to take the blame himself. He railed at the men and picked on the newest and smallest of the guards to vent his wrath. "I want to know how this has happened and you will find out who is responsible or you will wish you had died at Lewes." With that he stormed off to send more men out on the search.

II

In the king's camp the Knights and their men rested in the Priory for a day then started to return to their own lands. They had promised to return to the King should he call. John loaded their baggage onto the spare horse. Sir Cedric told him they were to make for his lands in Wymondham which would take several days. John hoped he would have time to visit Dunston and his family, would he see Roger, had he been in the Battle? These thoughts occupied his mind as they rode north. They arrived in Wymondham on a warm summer's day, before going into the town Sir Cedric stopped and dressed his destrier and donned a fine tunic.

"We must look our best as we are returning after a long absence. Put on your best tunic John and hold my lance up."

John looked round as they journeyed through the town. It was market day and the streets were busy, many people spoke to the Earl who was smiling and it was obvious that he was well liked by the inhabitants. There were many curious glances at John but he just smiled and sat straight in his saddle. A few of the young maidens giggled at him as they appraised this new young man who was to live among them. They rode out of the town and carried on towards the Castle, as they exited a small wood they saw a Castle standing on a small hill.

"Home," exclaimed Sir Cedric. "Too long have I been absent from my affairs. Come John this is now your home."

A horn sounded when the approached the draw bridge, which had been lowered. John could see men on the battlements and the Earl's standard was flying from one of the turrets. They rode through the main gateway and as they exited the second gate into the bailey a postern gate swung open a figure rushed out towards Sir Cedric who quickly dismounted and held out his arms. John saw that the Knight was clasping a young woman to him. John dismounted and stood holding the horses.

"Leave those John, the stable hands will take care of them. Come and be introduced to my daughter, Tania." John was confronted by an excited young woman, dark hair and slightly shorter than him. Introductions over they moved towards the Keep. The family rooms were furnished to a high standard for the period and it was apparent that Sir Cedric was not a poor nobleman like many at that time. His wealth came from wool, sheep from the land he owned provided the raw material and this was prepared by tradesmen in Wymondham then sent to Bruges to be woven into fine cloth, finally returned to Wymondham for the Earl to trade in London. "This is Rowan my Steward, he will show you your room and answer any questions. We will see you tonight at our meal." With that information imparted Sir Cedric put his arm round his daughter and walked over to the fireplace.

"Follow me sir." Rowan guided John to a very comfortable room. He looked around and could not believe that this large and well furnished room was to be his. Reflecting on the past few days John realised his life had changed from a peaceful existence as a Blacksmith to that of a fighting man, serving a powerful Earl, he would have to learn all the duties of a Squire as quickly as he could to repay the Earl.

II

Time passed quickly and John's days at Wymondham were very pleasant, he soon recovered from all the travels and the battle at Lewes. After looking after Sir Cedric's and his weapons and armour he would practice with his sword and bow joining the rest of the Castle's men at arms. Sir Cedric retained nearly 500 men at arms and cavalry, some quartered in the Castle and some scattered among the nearby villages, those that lived in the Castle drilled most mornings leaving the afternoon free which John made good use of by riding out to the town and the surrounding countryside. One cold but bright afternoon he was walking across the bailey to the stables when he met Tania going in the same direction. John had seen little of Sir Cedric's daughter except at meals and he hoped that she might be taking advantage of the pleasant afternoon.

"A fine afternoon, my lady, is it not?" started John. "One that will make riding that much more pleasurable."

"It is lovely and I am taking advantage of it to ride to Wymondham," replied Tania.

"If I am not imposing may I accompany you?" suggested John.

Tania nodded and they called for their horses. They chatted amicably on the way and John found Tania had had a good education as well as being well travelled. Sir Cedric had property in France, as did many of the Knights, the difference was that Sir Cedric was English, from Saxon stock, and had no French background. Tania was visiting a friends house whose father was the Mayor. John decided to walk around the town while the two women gossiped.

Wymondham was a small market town on the outer edge of the Shire. The inhabitants were mainly connected to farming and raising sheep for the wool trade. The rich soil allowed an abundance of crops which the farmers exported to London and other towns. John resisted the lure of a fine looking Inn and turned to walk back to the Mayor's house. He stopped suddenly as he glimpsed a tall man hurrying down a side alley, where had he seen him before? Entering the Mayor's house John was welcomed by a pleasantly plump man.

"I hope you found your walk interesting, the ladies are in the drawing room."

John thanked him and entered through the door indicated. He found the two friends accompanied by an older lady who introduced herself as the Mayor's wife. Tania, after goodbyes to the ladies, donned her cloak and joined John for the ride back to the Castle. As they rode John felt a sensation in his back as though someone was watching them.

"Why keep looking back John?" asked Tania. "It is not dark enough for robbers and no one is silly enough to attack us this near to the Castle."

"I have a funny feeling someone is watching us," explained John.

They reached the Castle without trouble and after handing the horses to the grooms John climbed up to the battlements and looked back the way they had come. No one was in sight, he paced around the walls and could see there was nowhere to hide near to the Castle moat as the land had been cleared for several hundred yards. John searched his mind for where he had seen the tall man before but with no success, he left the battlements and joined the rest of the family in the great hall for the evening meal.

II

Roger and Roland had spent an uncomfortable night in the dungeon, where Fletcher had banished them.

"I thought he would die with all that shouting, I have never seen a face so red."

"It is we who are likely to die," said Roger. "You shouldn't argue with him when he is in that mood."

At that moment the key rattled in the lock and a guard opened the door. They were escorted up to the hall and led before a man seated by the fire. Behind him stood Elric Fletcher.

"Although there seems to be no proof, you are accused of being partly to blame for the escape of our prisoner. Your record of lateness and tardiness make me believe you are not suited to the life of a soldier." Sir Henri deGranville looked at them with hooded eyes as he made this pronouncement. "I am sending both of you home and hope not to set eyes on you again."

The guards escorted them to the courtyard where their horses were standing complete with their baggage. They mounted and left the Castle and heading east. On the way back to Norfolk Roland turned to Roger. "Why should we go back to our families? We, no doubt, will be scorned and out of favour for some time. We should strike out on our own."

"What would we do, are you a Smith or a Carpenter, do you have any skills apart from soldiering, I don't think we would last very long?"

"That is what I mean," countered Roland. "We know how to fight, you are skilled with a blade. We could become mercenaries or robbers, but I don't suppose you would rob people."

"If there was a good reason, I could rob," said Roger. "There is a fellow up around Lincoln who is quite successful, it is said he robs the rich to give to the poor."

"We would be poor," reasoned Roland. The two friends rode on their way discussing the possibilities. After several days journey they came to the town of Stamford. They sat on their horses and viewed the high walls and the guarded gate.

"It might be possible to join their guard for a time, while we decide on what we are going to do," said Roger. Luck was at last on their side, they asked the guards at the gate where to enquire and made their way to the barracks to meet the Captain of the Guard.

" Yes, I am looking for men who have had some experience as most of the men from the town were recruited for Lewes. You can start tonight so don't disappear, find yourselves an empty bed and be back here at sunset."

"That was easy," said Roger. "It means we can't get out tonight."

"Do you good," replied Roland as he found a bed in a corner. "Let's get settled before we make ourselves known to the town wenches."

II

John strolled down to the stables after his meal and found his horse, he had become very fond of the animal and it was reciprocated. John had named him Anvil because he was strong and steady and it reminded him of his father. 'I wonder how they are?' thought John as Anvil nuzzled his neck ' I must ask if I can visit them now things are quiet.' Patting Anvil's black coat and stroking his nose John said goodnight to his horse and returned to the Keep. On his way to his room he saw a light under one of the smaller doors and stopped to listen. Suddenly the door opened and John was startled to see Tania standing there.

"Spying on me, John?" she said with a twinkle in her eye.

"I saw the light and there's not usually anyone along here," answered John.

" I'm only teasing, John, this is my work room, come in and see."

John entered the room which was well lit and warm. On a large table there lay bolts of cloth of all colours, silks and ribbons and several hides.

"I love making my own cloths, as well as for some of my friends, what do you think of this?" Tania picked up a gown of brilliant blue, held it against her and twirled around.

"It is beautiful." tammered John with his eyes on this bewitching woman.

“I may wear it tomorrow night as we are having a special dinner, but I expect you know all about it.” “Not really,” said John, a little bewildered. Tania put the gown back on the table and stood before John as though appraising him. John feeling uncomfortable, started for the door.

“Stay and keep me company for a while. I just have to finish this sleeve and it’s done.” Tania entreated. John sat down on a chair and watched while Tania’s hands busied themselves with needle and thread, it gave him a chance to study Tania. Not a great beauty but very comely and with her long black tresses she had a friendly and warm aura around her. Tania’s eyes looked up and she blushed at John’s gaze. John stood up. “It is time I went to my room so that I am fit for tomorrow.”

Tania went back to her sewing and bid John goodnight. John closed the door of the workroom quietly and walked to his room feeling his blood warm and a tingle through his body. ‘I must be careful not to become too friendly as she is Sir Cedric’s daughter and no doubt promised to a fellow Knight,’ thought John. ‘But she does affect me in a way I have not known.’

As the sky brightened on the next day John had just finished dressing when there was a knock on his door and Rowan entered to tell him that Sir Cedric wanted to see him as soon as he was ready. John descended the broad staircase and went to the Earl’s chambers. Entering his sitting room he was startled to see another man seated with Sir Cedric.

“Sit down John, you will know our guest.” said Sir Cedric

“I don’t think I …….Your Highness forgive me I had not seen you out of armour in daylight.”

Prince Edward smiled and gestured to John to carry on and sit. “I thought you had seen me in Wymondham.” declared the Prince.“In any case you have NOT seen me now,” he continued winking at John.

“The Prince has escaped and is on his way back to his father, he will stay here for a couple of days to rest,” explained Sir Cedric. “There will be other visitors today and I want you to check them off a list I will give you, and beware of any other persons who are not invited."

"I understand Sir, you can trust me,"

"I know that John, don't let anyone else in the Castle know what is taking place, or who is here."

With that Sir Cedric gave John a parchment containing the names of six Knights. John withdrew and after grabbing something to eat from the Kitchen he went down to the Bailey. John called the Captain of the Guard and informed him that Sir Cedric was expecting guests and they would need stabling for their horses. He casually strolled round the walls making sure all the guards were in position without alarming them. John stood looking out on the road from Wymondham and could just make out, in the gathering gloom, a small group of horsemen approaching, he hurried down to the Bailey to receive the first of the guests.

Henry of Almain and John de Warenne entered the Castle with a couple of retainers, John surreptitiously checked his list and welcomed the Knights who were then led into the Keep by Rowan. John started a conversation with the Squires but they were close mouthed and went off with their horses, so he wandered down to the main gate and stood looking out over the countryside. It was not long before most of the Knights had arrived, Gilbert de Clare, Alfred of Ely and Robert of Lincoln, the only one missing from John's list was Godfrey Maddison. John found the Captain and as night had now fallen suggested they raise the drawbridge, if anyone else arrived they would check carefully who it was before letting them enter.

As John returned to the Keep a soft voice called to him from the shadows. Tania's maid approached and gave a message that her mistress was waiting in the workroom and would like to see him. John's thoughts whirled around in his head, what did this woman want?

"Come in." Tania invited when John knocked on the workroom door. "Thank you for coming John, father has asked us to join them for dinner and I thought it would be nice for you to escort me." There was that merry twinkle in her eyes as she faced an awkward John, shifting from one foot to the other.

"I would be pleased to Tania, but I must go to Sir Cedric now as one guest has not arrived. I will meet you at the top of the stairs." He turned and hurried out down to the Earl's room.

John was standing by the stairs that evening when he heard footsteps approaching, turning he was confronted by a vision in gold.

Tania stood before him smiling. "I changed my mind from the blue," she explained. "It is the only one with our crest." John's eyes were drawn to the Red Spread Eagle across her left breast.

"You're beautiful," stammered John.

"You mean the dress, John?" she answered still smiling.

"I know what I mean," said "John.

Tania's maid arrived and they descended the stairs. Entering the hall they saw that all the Knights were there including Godfrey Maddison. As Tania moved into the room towards a seat by her father the Knights banged on the table to show their appreciation for their host's daughter. John found himself a seat lower down the table just as Sir Cedric stood and proposed a toast to the Prince.

The Knights relaxed and the evening became a jolly affair until the Knights began to feel the effect of good wine and mead. Tania excused herself and left accompanied by her maid.

On the following morning, as John roused himself from a heavy sleep, he remembered that they had arranged to meet in the hall, had Sir Cedric included him? He decided he would go anyway. As John entered Sir Cedric beckoned him and told him to assemble the other Squires and men in the Bailey ready to move off at noon. The Knights left early afternoon and John noticed that they placed Prince Edward in the middle of them.

"We shall see them again soon enough," said Sir Cedric. "Perhaps you would like to see your father before we join them.

Give him my greetings but make sure you are back in eight days."

Excitedly John ran to his room and started to pack his bag.

John heard a tapping at his door, when he opened it there stood Tania

"I've just heard you are going home," she said as she walked over to him.

"I am, but only for a few days and then I think we are going off to rejoin the Prince."

"So you were not going to say goodbye to me?" said Tania looking at John who moved towards her saying. "It all happened so fast and I will not have much time with my family, I am not sure you would miss me anyway." Tania lifted her head and looked at John who could see tears in her eyes, he reached for her and she clung to him as their lips met.

John pushed her away and said, "Oh forgive me, I should not be so presumptuous." Tania looked at him and walked into his arms again.

"Silly man," she said. "I have wanted you to kiss me ever since last night." They both stood back and John explained he was going to visit his father and when he returned he guessed that they would be off to fight again. Tania looked down and said. "Will you miss me?"

"I will be thinking of you every moment until I return," John replied. "I am not sure your father will be pleased as I am only a Squire."

"Then we will keep it to ourselves until the right moment," said Tania with a merry twinkle in her eyes.

John felt as though he was walking on air as he made for the stables, saddled his horse and rode out on to the Bailey, looking up he could see Tania waving from her window. He would have a lot to tell his family when he arrived home.

John approached Dunston savouring the sights and sounds of his home countryside. Arriving at the edge of the village he could see the smoke spiralling up from the Smithy fire, urging his horse on he heard the sound of hammering ring out and knew his father would be hard at work. Dismounting he hurried to the entrance and stopped short as he saw, not his father, but a young man swinging the hammer.

"Where is the Smith?" demanded John.

"He is in the house sir, William go and fetch the Master quickly." Said the young man as a small boy got up from where he had been sitting cleaning knives and daggers.

"Who are you?" queried John.

"Thomas, sir, I am Jack Ivanson's apprentice and he will be here as soon as William tells him he has a caller."

John turned as he heard the Cottage door and saw his father hurrying over. The two of them met halfway and embraced "I am so glad to see you John, we have heard so much about the fighting and there have been many visitors to the Castle, your mother will be relieved."

"I have a lot to tell you father but let's go in and see mother and Joan." Over the evening meal John related most of what had happened to him since leaving home, leaving out his part in the battle. Joan wanted to know if he had encountered Roger during this time.

"I haven't seen him or heard of him or his family."

Jack told him that Sir Walter had left to fight with the Barons leaving Ralf in charge, which had not gone well with the retainers. The Smithy was very busy that is why Jack had taken the two lads on. "We are getting work from all around," said Jack. "Even as far as Stoke and Newton."

"They know they can trust you and your work is second to none," said John. When the women had gone to bed John told his father of the battle at Lewes and how he felt afterwards.

"You are now a fighting man John and this will not be the last time you use your sword, keep up your practice so that when you strike it will be fast and sure." John also mentioned Tania and that he was not sure what to do, considering her position.

"Don't worry John, take your time and events will come to a natural conclusion, what will be will be." John thought to himself that that was no answer. They retired to their beds, Jack to think of the road his son was on, and John to dream of Tania.

II

Roger looked across at his friend Roland, they were sitting in their favourite Inn in Stamford. They had been enjoying the friendship of two of the local girls and had settled into a routine.

"Any truth in this rumour that there is to be another fight with the King?" asked Roland

"I don't know for sure, but they say that they are recruiting at Kenilworth. It will be changing one guard for another we might as well stay where we are," replied Roger.

"It is pretty dull here though, isn't it, apart from our evenings." Roland said as he squeezed the girl sitting on his lap After seeing the girls 'settled' upstairs they walked back to the barracks.

"I wonder how Joan is, and what that brother of hers is doing?" said Roger wistfully.

"You didn't get anywhere there you said, so I wouldn't bother with them."

"He was a good friend in spite of his haughty sister," countered Roger. The two men went to their bunks and started to clean their weapons as they had practice in the morning and they now had the reputation of being the two best swordsmen in Stamford.

More and more men started to pass through Stamford most saying they were on their way to Leicester.

Roland was becoming more restless each day.

"Something big happening and we ought to be part of it, when there is fighting you can 'find' lots of things, if you know what I mean."

“Yes, you can find your death,” replied Roger.

“Anyway I feel like another fight,” continued Roland.

Roger sat and thought whether another battle is what he wanted, he was enjoying the relative calm of being a guard at Stamford and there was a chance for promotion here especially if more men went to join de Montfort from the town. There was no prospects at home as Ralf would inherit the title and Castle when his father died, which could be any day.

Walking through the town one morning Roger met the Mayor who stopped him and suggested a glass of ale together. Sitting in the warmth of the Inn Roger relaxed and listened to the Mayor.

“Are you going to Leicester with your friend?” he asked. “He approached me this morning to say he felt a loyalty to de Montfort, so would go and join his army. I don’t think that was the only reason.”

“No, I shall not go with him, I am not eager to look for a fight, I hope soon that peace will come and we can lead a normal life.”

“Good, then I have an idea to improve the safety of the citizens and keep the ruffians out of Stamford. I want you to lead a roving group of guards to go to trouble spots and generally keep order, would you do that?”

“It certainly sounds a good idea,” replied Roger. “ I would like to do that it will be better than staying in one spot.”

“That’s settled then, we will meet in the morning and I will tell you what I want and pick the men for your group. There will be an increase in your money but now I must get back and sort out with the Captain how we are to organise these changes.” The Mayor shook Roger’s hand and left.

Roger smiled to himself as he thought about his new position, and the increase in his income, without Roland he might be able to keep more of it too. As Roger made his way back to the barracks he saw a group of horsemen riding through the town. He quickly ducked into an alleyway as he spotted his father and Henri de Granville in the group, no doubt off to join de Montfort. Roger thought about his new position and how it would fit with the

Captain, he liked Stamford and would like to stay here.

II

The sun was up when John raised his head from the pillow, he could hear people moving about and hammering coming from the forge. He quickly dressed and went down to the kitchen where his mother was busy baking.

"I thought you were going to sleep all day," said Matilda. John grabbed a hunk of bread and went out to the Forge. All three were working hard, sparks were flying and young William was busy with the bellows as Thomas heated up long pieces of iron while Jack beat them into shape.

"I'm off to see Father Aldred. " said John.

"You had better take some cider with you," called Jack.

"Will do," replied John as he went over to the stables and saddled Anvil. John whistled as he rode and took in the beauty of the countryside, there is nowhere like home, and then he thought of his other home in Wymondham and the woman who waited there. As the two men sat and enjoyed the cider John told Father Aldred about his adventures.

"What is the situation at the Castle now, is there any news of Roger?" asked John.

"Ralf is ruling the roost now and making a fine mess of it too. I hear Avice is to be married off to a Norman Knight. I have a brother priest in Stamford and he sent a message to me to say that young Roger is one of the guard there, but no news of Sir Walter." The priest continued with other village gossip until John took his leave and rode home. John spent the rest of the day helping his father and over dinner retold the information the priest had given him.

" Where is Stamford?" enquired Joan.

"West of here, I think," said Jack. John said nothing. He was not sure of Rogers intentions or what he was going to do as Ralf would not want him at the Castle. The following morning John loaded up the pack horse that had been left at the Smithy and saying farewell to his family set off for Wymondham. On the evening of the eighth day the Castle came into view and John blew on his hunting horn. The drawbridge was down and the outer gate open, as he came through the inner gate the postern door opened and Tania rushed out. Dismounting quickly John was just in time to catch Tania as she jumped into his arms. Holding her close John glanced over her shoulder and spotted Sir Cedric coming out of the main door and seeing the couple he spun round and went back inside.

John pushed the excited Tania away. "Your father is watching, behave, or I shall be told off."

Together they walked over to the stables where a groom helped John unload.

"I must see your father now." He said to Tania. "I will see you later if I am allowed."

"Of course you will be allowed," said Tania.

John looked at her with love in his eyes but a heavy heart, he knew his future lay with what Sir Cedric decided. He went to his room and cleaned himself up after the journey. With trepidation and weakness in his legs he made his way to Sir Cedric's rooms. John knocked on the large oak door and heard a stern voice bid him enter.

"I hope you found your family well, your father is a good man." Sir Cedric was standing by a window, with the light behind him John could not see his eyes to see if they would give an indication of his mood. "You appear to be very friendly with my daughter, John."

"Sir, it happened very quickly, I did not know she felt as strongly as she does."

"Do you feel strongly about her?" asked the Earl

"Sir, I do."

“Well, there’s a problem. You are going off to fight for your King, with me, and who knows whether you will survive. I have a mind to send her to her cousin in Lincoln to give you some space. Have you spoken to the Squires who came to the Castle recently?”

John shook his head and replied “They did not want to talk.”

“I have been remiss in explaining what happens to a Squire in his service to his Knight you had better look in the Library, there is a book there that will give some information, you may see then that given time you maybe in a better position than you are now to pursue my daughter. Until she departs for Lincoln I put you on your honour to control your emotions and be a true Squire.”

John could only nod his head and with a downcast look went back to his room. Later he walked into the Library and looked around, there were a few chairs and small tables, the rest of the room as expected was filled with shelves full of books, some very dusty and some that had obviously been used. He looked along the shelves not knowing what he was looking for when he suddenly found an open book on one of the tables. He sat and read the page that was open, it was a list of conditions for Squires attending their Knights at Jousts. Reading further John began to understand some of the tasks he would have to be accomplished in, to become an efficient Squire. There were pages describing the Code of Chivalry, Rules of Heraldry, Horsemanship, Weaponry and many more skills. Towards the end of the book it became clear that this was more of a guide for Knights to test their Squires and for what reason? To make him a Knight! John lay awake that night wondering if this was Sir Cedric’s plan, to take a lowly Blacksmith’s son and turn him into a Knight. With these thoughts racing through his brain John eventually slept. In the morning of the next day, while John was working out with the guards he was interrupted by the sight of Tania and her maid watching. John stopped his sword practice and walked over to Tania.

“Good morning John,” greeted Tania. “Will you walk with us I want to talk to you.”

Sheathing his sword John joined them and they made for the Castle gardens. The maid dropped back so that the couple could talk privately.

"My father is sending me to my cousin in Lincoln and I am only to see you with my maid present."

"He has already told me, I should have gone to him earlier but I went home instead, it made things worse. The question is how will this affect you?"

Tania looked at John, put her hand on his arm and stopped him speaking. "I love you John, I have done since that day in Wymondham, if I have to wait for you then that is what I shall do." John felt his heart surge and he longed to take Tania in his arms

"I love you too with all my heart but I have to follow your father as his Squire and abide by his decisions. I do know that if we are patient then we can be very happy." They looked into each others eyes and through the tears in Tania's John saw the love.

"I leave for Lincoln in three days time so we can walk and talk until then." They walked back to the Bailey and John resumed his practice. That evening he went back to the Library and looked for books to help him learn the duties of a Squire, he was determined to prove to Sir Cedric that he had made a wise choice when he offered him the position. During the next few days Tania and John met as often as they could under the watchful eye of Tania's maid. Sir Cedric was away but John kept his passion in check and was just pleased to walk with them in the gardens. Soon it was time for Tania to go, on that day John was away hunting with two other young men who had come back with Sir Cedric. Gavin was the son of a Knight that had been to the Crusades with the Earl. Carac, a younger man, was the son of a Norfolk nobleman. The three men soon became good friends, studying and relaxing together. John was the master of the sword even when the other two ganged up against him. Gavin was the better man with the lance and spear while Carac who was smaller, could outride them both and there was no one who could match him with the short bow on horseback. All in all they were a formidable trio. One morning while they were caring for their horses Sir Cedric appeared and called them to him.

"The King has sent word that I am to meet Prince Edward and

to prepare to crush the Barons once and for all. We are to meet him near Worcester and we leave early tomorrow morning. Carac, you are to stay here with enough men to defend the Castle and town if need be. John and Gavin prepare our weapons and horses, pack only what we need, we have a long journey ahead." With that Sir Cedric went back inside.

II

Roger was settling into his job as Bailiff, he patrolled the town with four guards and the level of theft and armed attacks had lessened. The Mayor was pleased and Roger now lived in a small house in the better part of town with his extra income he had also hired a maid who would come in daily to clean and prepare his meals. Life was good for Roger. Early one morning as the group patrolled the poorer part of town they heard carousing coming from an old Inn, the Fighting Cocks. Roger sent two of his men to investigate, the noise increased and the sound of swords being drawn prompted the rest of the group to rush in where they found the two guards facing a drunken crowd of ruffians.

"Landlord, show yourself," bellowed Roger. A fat man wearing a dirty apron appeared from behind a bar. "They were too many for me, your worship, and they wouldn't keep quiet," whined the man.

"Much more of this and I will close this Inn," said Roger. He spotted the most sober of the bunch and called him out. "What causes you to make merry at this time of the day, speak up or you will find yourself in gaol?" The man stood unsteadily before Roger and tried to explain that they had arrived late last night from Worcester and they were on their way home to the East, they had been fighting for a baron but had been routed by the King's men. Roger told them to gather their belongings and be outside the town walls in half an hour, there was a mad rush for the door and as everyone tried to get out at the same time. None got out as they were all stuck in the doorway. Roger sat down on one of the bar stools, laughing with his men. "I don't think we will see them again, but we must keep our eyes open as there will be more of them coming through," said Roger. He turned to the landlord and remonstrated with him. "Don't let this happen again. Have a couple of men to keep order or I will close you down." The landlord bowed and said he would do what Roger suggested. Roger wondered if Roland would be among the men passing through. During the next week more of the retreating army passed the town, Roger doubled the guards at the gates then suddenly the movement of men stopped and there were more going the other way.

"They have been persuaded to make a stand somewhere, and the Knights are rounding them up," said one of the guards as they walked the walls.

"We have not lost any more men," said Roger. "I think our boys know they are better off here."

A guard came hurrying up to Roger and reported that they had news of a large force of Knights and men spotted south of the town moving west.

"Did you see any banners?" asked Roger.

"We managed to talk to one of the pike men and they are part of Prince Edward's army going to Worcester," said the guard.

"No wonder the other troops turned round," commented Roger. A thought crossed his mind, should he report this news to one of the barons, but he decided against it and not get involved. Arriving home for his evening meal, Roger poured himself a jug of cider and settled himself in his favourite chair. The door from the kitchen opened and the maid walked in.

"You have beef tonight sir," she said. "I have also made a plum pudding."

"You will make me fat and lazy, Laila, would you join me tonight, I could do with some company?"

"Thank you sir there is enough, and my mother is visiting her sister so my time is my own."

Roger looked at her, a comely girl and she kept his little house clean and comfortable, I am beginning to feel that this is now my home he thought. Ralf could have his draughty Castle, this was better by far. They both sat down to enjoy the beef, Roger started a conversation by saying. “It is time you called me by my real name, you are more a friend than a servant.” Laila smiled and her face softened, she appreciated the fact that she had been very lucky that Roger had picked her out of all the girls that had tried to gain this position, however she also wondered what she might have to do to keep it. Roger and his group kept a vigilant eye on anyone entering the town, he posted extra guards on the gates to deter any fugitives, but everything quietened down,

II

On the morning of their departure John looked out over the valley and saw a huge encampment that must have arrived during the night. He and Gavin were ready in the Bailey when Sir Cedric with Gilbert de Clare, Alfred of Ely, Robert of Lincoln and Henry of Almain strode out of the Castle and mounted their horses. The group rode out with John and Gavin following leading the destrier and spare horses. A company of Sir Cedric’s men at arms joined them and the whole ensemble prepared to move off. John felt the excitement building in him.

“There must be over 1,500 men here. He “ he said to Gavin.

“At least that amount, but we had better keep close to Sir Cedric if we are to serve him,” answered Gavin.” hame Carac is missing this.”

John looked back at the Castle and could just pick out the young Squire on the battlements. The large company moved off with great noise and some confusion which soon settled down. A small number of townspeople had come out and stood waving at no one in particular, they had never seen this number of Knights and soldiers before. John looked to see if he could spot the Mayor’s daughter but there were too many men milling around. When they stopped for the first night’s camp John and Gavin picked a spot on high ground and pitched Sir Cedric’s tent and their own. They soon found a system where they could both work together quickly and efficiently. They sat round a camp fire and listened to the men tell stories of past battles which always ended with the teller winning. As they journeyed on many of the villages they passed were like ghost towns with people hiding behind locked doors. They fed off the countryside which did not go down very well with the inhabitants, imagine 1,500 hungry men being fed by the cooks who stripped the surrounding fields of animals and crops, payment was promised but the farmers hardly ever received any, most people wanted the fighting to stop so they could get on with a peaceful life. After several days march they at last came to the outskirts of Worcester where they found Prince Edward's army resting. Two days later the senior Knights were called to the Prince's tent and a plan of action was discussed, the Prince now had an army numbering over 10,000 men and he meant to finish de Montfort. Sir Cedric came back from the meeting and told his two Squires to prepare for battle. That night John lay awake thinking of home and Tania, would they be able to convince Sir Cedric of their love for each other. They were woken in the morning when it was still dark, the army was noisily getting ready. John and Gavin put on the white over tunic with a large red cross, at the battle of Lewes de Montfort's men wore a white cross and Prince Edward decided that he wanted his men recognisable. The army started to move, a section was despatched to the bridge over the Avon to stop any reinforcements reaching de Montfort, the rest climbed to the ridge overlooking Evesham. As they waited a thunderstorm swamped the armies, they could see through the driving rain the baron's forces aiming for their centre. The Prince gave the order to encircle the opposing force and the two armies met. The fighting was fierce, many remembered the defeat at Lewes and attacked with a bloody resolve. John and Gavin were in the thick of it beside Sir Cedric whose destrier was barging biting and kicking whilst his rider hacked left and right. John, on Anvil, thrust and swung his sword until he felt his arm would drop off but miraculously all three of them suffered no serious wounds. A lull in the battle allowed some small respite and Sir Cedric moved them foreword into where there was still fighting, it was not man against man but a slaughter as men took revenge on the army that beat them at Lewes. Sir Cedric pushed through the throng to where the Prince was trying to stop a group of men hacking at something on the ground, they found the mutilated body of de Montfort. The royalist forces gradually gathered on the outskirts of Evesham and Prince Edward called a council of his Knights to plan strategy to finish off any resistance. Sitting round their camp fire John fell into a dark mood.

"It wasn't a battle, it was a slaughter," he said to Gavin. "I hope our battles are not going to be like that." Gavin shook his head and lazily poked the fire. "Maybe we will return home tomorrow, I've had enough of mud and blood to last a lifetime."

Sir Cedric and his retinue returned to Wymondham where the men set up camp outside the Castle, Sir Cedric arranged a feast for them and the celebrations went on into the night. John and Gavin took care of the horses and stowed all the armaments away. Carac was waiting for them in the Castle and wanted a full report on all that happened.

"Let us get cleaned up first and go down to dinner, we haven't eaten a decent meal since we left," said Gavin. In the great hall they found the other Knights and Squires that had accompanied Sir Cedric, they sat down and the food began to appear chickens, joints of beef, a whole pig, geese and the centre piece, a swan. There was plenty of ale and mead and gradually everyone relaxed. Carac was still pressing for details of the battle but John really wanted to forget it for a while, the frenzy at the finish had upset him. The next day he finished his work in the Castle and Carac suggested they go into Wymondham as Gavin was on duty. The two arrived in the town to find it was market day, they wandered through the colourful stalls and chatted to the vendors. Many wanted to know what had happened at Evesham but John gave only a sketchy account.

"I am going to the Priory," said John and mounting Anvil rode off .

Sitting alone in the church he reflected on how he felt about fighting and living as a Squire. Sir Cedric was a kind man and John liked him, he was generous and supportive to his people, in the town and countryside. John felt he could learn much under his guidance. The life was certainly different to working in a forge. He returned to meet Carac and they journeyed back to the Castle together.

Over the next years life in the Castle settled down and apart from having to chase robbers and patrol the countryside around the Castle there was nothing exciting happening. John studied the books in the Library and listened to Gavin, he was determined to show Sir Cedric his gratitude for giving him the chance to better himself.

One evening Sir Cedric called John into his room. “I am going to arrange a Tournament in the valley. I will send invitations to my friends, I know Prince Edward has gone on a crusade, but I hope some of my friends are still here, send messages to those I tell you.”

“Are we not joining Prince Edward?” asked John

“No, one crusade was enough. Once we know how many Knights can accept my invitation we will get ready for the event, it will keep us sharp and ready, meanwhile you, Gavin and Carac had better train harder as I expect to win.”

John returned to the Bailey where his friends were already practicing and gave them the news.

For the next month the three Squires studied hard and honed their fighting skills, they did not want to let Sir Cedric down in the Tournament. John was rapidly becoming unbeatable with the sword and long bow while Gavin practiced new moves with his lance and spear, Carac could outride both of them and fire his short bow in rapid succession whilst guiding his mount with his knees. Watching from a window Sir Cedric felt a pride in their expertise, and thought about his daughter. He missed her company but he convinced himself he had been right in sending her away, perhaps he would bring her back for the Tournament.

The Castle was buzzing with excitement as the preparations for the Tournament got under way. Heralds were despatched to notify the Knights who had accepted Sir Cedric’s invitation. A Herald was also sent into Wymondham to tell the townspeople of the event. Traders will be setting up stalls and the population will no doubt turn out in force to see the fun. With people travelling in from the surrounding countryside the town's Inns will be filled and local houses will try to benefit by hiring out bedrooms.

John was sitting on the mounting block, resting after cleaning Anvil, when Carac ran up to him and said. "Guess where I am going John." John looked at him with a bemused smile, "I'm going to Lincoln to escort Lady Tania back for the Tournament. We shall be travelling with Lord Robert's party but I am to guard Lady Tania."

John leapt off the block and grabbed Carac. "You guard her well or you will have to answer to me," they both laughed and walked back inside the Castle.

II

Roger woke gradually, he was contented as he lay next to the warm body of Laila. He looked at her loose curls laying on the pillow, he was happy and at peace with the world. Suddenly there was a loud pounding on the door of the little cottage.

"All right, don't break the door down, I'm coming." Roger pulled on his trousers and walked from the bedroom to the front door, opening it he found one of the guards standing there.

"Sorry to wake you but we have a seriously injured man at the gate who says you can vouch for him. I was going to turn him away as it looks like battle wounds and he's not got long to go, but he insists he knows you."

"All right I will come with you."

They hurried off to the gate where they found two men with an old cart standing by the entrance. On the bed of the cart lay a man covered by a sack. Roger bent over the cart and looked at the face of the man who lay there, he immediately recognised him.

"Roland!" Roger exclaimed. The man made no movement, Roger could see he was still alive though badly wounded. "Take him to the Priory at once, I will come and raise the Prior."

The two men, pulling the cart, followed Roger, who rushed into the building shouting out for the Prior. Prior Clement was skilled in the art of healing and was soon at the side of the injured man. "He is very badly wounded and I am afraid my skills may not save him," he said, as he inspected Roland's cuts and a large hole below his ribs caused by a lance or spear. Roland was still unconscious at this stage and Roger could see that his breathing was shallow and irregular.

"I will be grateful for whatever you can do," said Roger. The Prior called one of the monks to him.

"This is Brother Joseph who is more experienced than I, he will do his best, and with God's help, try to save his life."

Roger stayed in the room while Brother Joseph went to work, the Benedictines were well known for their value as doctors. The monk worked on Roland for a considerable time and at last stood back, washed his hands and turned to Roger saying, "I have done all I can, but the stomach wound has damaged internal organs which I can do nothing for."

"I thank you for what you have done," said Roger

"He is still unconscious, and may not come round at all, time will tell. I am going to chapel now and we will pray for him."

Roger thanked the monk again and stood by the table where Roland had been placed, two monks appeared and without a word moved Roland to a small cell, placed him on the bed and left. Roger sat by the bed and looked at Roland, he remembered the good, and some bad, times they had had together. He was a good companion, thought Roger but too much fighting can only end like this. Later that evening Brother Joseph came to see how Roland was, he told Roger that the biggest danger was infection in the wounds, although he had removed several pieces of cloth from the hole in his stomach there could be some still there. The monk had only been gone for a few minutes when Roland opened his eyes. He was disoriented and asked where he was and who was Roger. Gradually his senses seemed to clear and he spoke to Roger.

“Is that you Roger? Am I hurt badly old friend, I can’t feel much.”

“ You have some bad wounds Rolly but you are in good hands, the Benedictines are looking after you. Were you at Evesham?”

“ Yes,” murmured Roland. “I fell foul of some of Sir Cedric of Wymondham’s men and they overpowered me. I thought I was going to die there then. There was a young Squire who could have finished me off but for some reason stopped before the fatal blow.”

Roland fell silent and his eyelids closed, Roger bent over his friend and he realised Roland was asleep. Roger visited Roland most evenings after his duties had finished. He had become friendly with some of the brothers and one evening as they sat talking a brother visiting from Lincoln told them of the Herald coming to Lincoln to announce the Tournament in Wymondham. He said that Robert of Lincoln was gathering a party to take part and would be travelling down in two weeks time. Walking home Roger pondered as to whether he would join the group, he was sure he could be given the time away as the town was reasonably quiet and his men well trained. It would not take long to improve his marksmanship and he had always been capable with the sword. The more he thought about it the more he became convinced he should make the journey. He brought the subject up with Laila that evening, she said that if he went she would go too. After lengthy discussion Roger gave way and agreed. He found out that the entourage would be stopping at Grimsthorpe Castle, he could join them easily there. He went to find the Captain but was told he had left and his servant did not know when he would be back. Roger went off to find the Mayor who informed him that the man had decided to return to his home in London and the town was without a Captain and he had planned to see Roger the next day to offer him the position. Roger was delighted and accepted with the proviso that he would go to the Tournament. The Mayor agreed and Roger returned home to tell Laila the good news.

II

The preparations for the Tournament were progressing well, the site had been chosen and the areas for the visiting Knight's tents and pavilions marked out. Sir Cedric, being the host, would be positioned on the Castle side as also would be the main stand where the dignitaries would sit. Opposite would be Robert of Lincoln's tents and at the other ends would be Gilbert de Clare and Alfred of Ely. The action would take place in the centre which was a long grassed area, long enough for two Knights to Joust. Smaller rings would be behind the tents for wrestling and cock fighting. John had been checking the stands and Sir Cedric's tents when Gavin rode up and asked if the centre was long enough?

"Come," said John. "I will get my horse and if you go to the far end we can see if it will do."

They faced each other at opposite ends, a labourer shouted 'go' and they both galloped towards one another. They passed each other opposite the stand and trotted round to meet at that point.

"Excellent," said John and Gavin agreed.

"Are you riding, John?"

"I hope to." John replied. "We may meet each other if we get that far up the competition."

Gavin laughed and shouted."Last one back to the stables cleans both horses." He galloped off with John in hot pursuit. John dug his heels into Anvil and the beast increased pace and overtook Gavin.

" Nothing can touch Anvil in a race, but you will not need speed in the lists," said Gavin as he led both animals away. John thought about the remark and as he helped Gavin. "Do you think we will be able to borrow a destrier for the Joust, you are right Anvil is not right for that activity."

" We will have to ask Sir Cedric." replied Gavin. That night as they sat at table John asked the question about the horses for the Tournament.

“Well, now that I have three destriers we will be able to show our friends we are kind towards our Squires,” said the Earl with a smile. “John shall ride the black and Gavin the mixture leaving me with my faithful grey, You will find saddles, barding and trappers in the side room at the stables. The trappers are in my colours.” (Trappers were large cloths that cover the horses, usually brightly coloured.)

John and Gavin grinned at each other. “Carac will need a lighter horse and he will find a black stallion there that will suit his purposes. Now practice your weapons and techniques to be ready for the bouts.”

The Squires could hardly contain their excitement and wanted to go out to the stables immediately. Sir Cedric managed to keep their interest in talking about jousting and the best way to win.

Only a week to go and the Tournament would be under way, already traders from Wymondham were coming out to claim the most favourable pitches. Soon the visiting Knight’s retainers started to arrive. Knights and their Squires moved up to the Castle and everywhere was buzzing. John was busy at the Tournament ground making sure people were directed to their correct camping grounds and did not see the arrival of Sir Robert of Lincoln. Late that evening he wearily rode back to the Castle and flopped onto his bed, he was not allowed to rest for long as Carac came beating on his door for him to go down for a meal.

“There is a surprise in the hall, remember I had to go to Lincoln to escort someone home?”

John leapt up and rushed down to the Great Hall, all the guests were seated and there beside her father was Tania. John’s heart skipped a beat and he bumped into Carac

“Steady John, don’t pass out in front of everyone. The Steward is beckoning us to take our seats.”

They sat down and John looked up trying to catch Tania’s eyes but she was engrossed in what Sir Gilbert was telling her. The wine, ale and mead flowed and the food vanished as soon as it was brought to table. The noise of men who had supped and fed well grew in intensity. Suddenly the Steward banged his staff on the floor and the babble ceased. Sir Cedric gave a welcoming speech and wished them all well in the competitions. The ladies who were present left with their maids and most of the men settled down to some serious drinking. John and Gavin slipped out.

"I'm not joining in that," said John. "If we're going to do well tomorrow we need a clear head."

Gavin nodded, "Carac has already gone to his bed and I'm off to join him." As they climbed the stairs. John bid him goodnight and walked along the passage, he saw a light shinning under a well known door and tapped on it.

"Come in," was the quiet response. He opened the door and entered the work room.

Tania was sitting by the fire with her maid. "Hello John, I hoped you would see the light."

John stood in the middle of the room not knowing what to do. He looked at Tania and then at the maid.

"I am so pleased to see you Tania, I have sorely missed you."

Tania looked at him. "My father knows I am here and as long as my maid is with me we can talk. I have missed you too, every day has been so hard to get through." John moved closer and sat next to her, glancing at the maid, he took Tania's hand and looked into her eyes, they were filled with tears.

"How long will you be here, is there some way your father will let you stay?"

"No, John, I am to return to Lincoln with Sir Robert."

"Then I will come to Lincoln."

"No John, to do that would spoil everything. Serve my father well and that is the best way for us to be together. I know it is hard, and I want us be together now but the wait will be worth it I know."

John looked crestfallen and Tania smiled at him saying,"you know I love you, be patient."

John looked at the maid and reached for Tania, gave her a kiss and said, " hear you and I will try, but not for too long."

John was in a black mood as he walked down the passage, he did not go to his room but climbed the stairs to the battlements. As he walked in the night air he gradually calmed down. Tania was right, Sir Cedric would never permit her to be with him without he gained some status and that meant gaining a Knighthood. John looked up at the stars and promised he would reach that goal or die in the attempt.

Rising early John was down at the stables preparing his new mount, the destrier. He had named him 'Hammer' he thought it went with Anvil and he intended that his mount would 'Hammer' the foe. Hammer's coat shone in the morning light, he was a very proud horse and stood tall as John adjusted the saddle and trapper, he did not armour the horse as the serious jousting did not start until tomorrow. Carac and Gavin came in and all three prepared Sir Cedric's mount as the rest of the Squires arrived and the stables became a hive of noisy activity. John, Gavin and Carac tied their mounts to rings set in the Castle wall and John led Snow, Sir Cedric's destrier, to the Castle door. The three men went back to their rooms and donned their armour, just padded jerkin covered with a chain mail vest, a breast and back plate, greaves for the legs and besagues for the upper arm and shoulder. They also had their own helms, John's had no visor but it covered most of his face. They all stomped down to the bailey where Sir Cedric was waiting, he stood by the mounting block dressed in complete armour, his helm had an eagle on the crown with gold and red feathers waving in the wind. John and his companions stood in awe and as the Earl lifted his visor they could see he was grinning from ear to ear.

"Does you good to dress up occasionally," he chuckled as he mounted Snow.

The entourage moved off Sir Cedric leading with John at his side holding his lance followed by Carac and Gavin. The visiting Knights had already gone down to their encampments and were preparing to join Sir Cedric in a grand parade.

II

Roger had arranged for the brothers to look after Roland who was still slipping in and out of consciousness.

The Prior assured him that all would be done to look after his friend. Roger had purchased a small cart and had trained his horse to pull it, not that the horse liked it much, he packed camping equipment and his bow and quiver. “Come on Laila, time to join Sir Robert’s group, they are camped on the edge of town.” Roger put his saddle in the cart and helped Laila to the seat. They trotted out to the campsite that was already being packed up.

“We’ll join that group over there,” said Roger. “There is a couple of women with them so you won't feel lonely.”

They introduced themselves and Roger talked to the leader of the little band a man named Robert Hud. Among his companions there was a tall and muscular man. Roger thought, if he is in the wrestling, I’m not. The caravan wound it’s way south at a gentle pace as they had allowed plenty of time to make Wymondham before the Tournament. Roger found his travelling companions very interesting. It seemed as though they had no particular trade, hiring out as mercenaries, or something like that. Robert and his female friend also spoke with a cultured accent and had obviously had some education. They were careful to keep out of Sir Robert’s sight, which intrigued Roger, their explanation was that they had not paid some taxes that were due. The party came in sight of the Tournament and as they came within hailing distance they were directed to camping sites. Sir Robert and his men went up to the Castle to join the other guests. After Roger had pitched their tent and unharnessed his horse he walk around the area to familiarise himself as to where the action would take place. He noticed a Squire directing men putting up the main stand where their host and dignitaries would be watching from, there was something familiar about him. Roger walked over to the place where he had last seen him but he was nowhere in sight. He asked one of the workmen who the man was.

“That is one of Sir Cedric’s Squires, his name is John,” replied the man. It can't be who I thought it was, considered Roger, he did not know any Knights only my father. Still puzzled Roger went back to Laila who had been cooking a meal for them. "Thanks Laila, that's just what I need. Have you spoken to our travelling companions any more?" asked Roger.

"I've spoken to one of the women and they say they have come to win some of the competitions, Robert, or Rob, as he likes to be called, is a very good archer and I guess the big one, called John, will win the wrestling. The rest of them are just ordinary men, one of them tried it on with me but I soon put him off." "He will have me to answer to if he tries that again," said Roger.

In the morning Roger and Leila stood by the edge of the main arena watching all the Knights, Squires and guards forming up for the Grand Parade.

"It used to be less organised when I saw my first Tournament," said Roger. "It used to start with a real free for all, but too many men got killed so now they have to play by the rules. Not so much fun to watch but safer."

The Parade was very colourful with all the Knights in their armour and the different trappers on their horses. The parade circled the arena, to great applause and shouting from the onlookers, and finished up with all the Knights in the centre, they then dispersed to their respective tents and next appeared at the main stand without their armour.

"See that young man behind Sir Cedric's chair?" said an excited Roger. "I am sure he is someone I know, but we are too far away to be sure."

"Well, I am not moving, here we can see just about all that is happening in the main arena. We can walk around later," stated Leila.

Roger strained his eyes but could not be sure, when he rode pass in the parade his helm hid most of his face. The first event was the Squires galloping the length of the tilt yard and trying to spear loops of coloured ribbon from crosstrees and on the return run hitting a shield which had a bag of sand swinging on the opposite side. If they were not quick enough the bag of sand swung round and knocked them off their horse. Roger did not see the man he sought, but a smaller Squire in Sir Cedric's colours raced up and down quicker than anyone and speared all the ribbons and struck all the shields, the crowd roared.

"Well done Carac," said John as Carac collapsed from his horse. "That must be the fastest time anyone has ever done." Carac sat on a box to get his breath back and grinned at John. The next event was something that Sir Cedric had brought back from the Middle East, sticking a spear into a disk on the ground at speed, the disk is soft enough that several disks can be speared at one charge. Gavin was in this one and was very fast but a Squire from Lincoln beat him into second place. There was a break in proceedings while the butts were brought out for the Archery competition. John had returned to the main stand.

"May I get you anything?" he asked Sir Cedric.

"No thank you," the Earl replied. "You may walk with Tania if would like, I think she needs to stretch her legs as she keeps wriggling in her seat to see where you are." Sir Cedric laughed and it was taken up by several who were sitting close. John and Tania blushed as they rose and left the stand.

Walking round the Tournament site they met many of the residents of Wymondham that Tania knew. John received many quizzical glances as he escorted her from stall to stall. Tania's maid hung back as much as she could to allow the couple to talk privately. They returned to the stand just in time for John to take his place in the first shoot of the archery competition. He lined up with seven other archers and they loosed at the first target, four were in the Gold so could shoot at the next distance, John took his stance and bent into the huge bow, the signal to loose was given and off flew the arrows, three were strait and true, one disqualified. The last distance again saw one disqualified which meant John was through to the next draw tomorrow. John went back to the stand but on the way a man stepped out in front of him.

" Hello John, that was good shooting but I know your strength as a blacksmith's son."

John was taken aback at first and then recognised his old friend Roger. They went over to an ale tent and sat down.

“We have a lot to tell each other and I am competing again soon, can you come up to the Castle tonight?” said John. Roger agreed and after a few moments they went on their way, John to prepare for the first joust, and Roger to meet Laila. John found Hammer being looked after by one of the young lads from the Castle “Thank you for walking my horse,” said John. “I have to get him ready for the first Squire’s Joust.”

“Can I help you, please sir, I have worked in the stables?” pleaded the lad.

“Of course you can, I shall be glad of the help.”

Between them Hammer was soon splendidly arrayed in his trapper and John fixed the barding (armour) to his nose, forelegs and chest.

“Oh he does look so wonderful,” said the lad. His eyes were shining and he asked, “Can I help you dress sir?” John laughed and nodded. Soon John was ready and as he mounted Hammer he felt that he was already a Knight.

“What is your name, lad?” asked John.

“Samuel sir but everyone calls me Titch, ‘cause I’m small,” replied the lad.

“Maybe in stature but not in courage,” smiled John and he rode out to the lists. Titch followed, he shouldered John’s lance and staggered after him. The Squires Joust was to see how the young men were able to charge with a lance and spear at another man on a horse, the lance tips were large leather ‘fists’ so they did not pierce armour. They could unseat the opponent if hit in the right spot. John fought three other Squires, unseated two but the third stayed in his saddle but fell when he reached the end of the list. Titch cheered and so did Tania and it even raised a smile from Sir Cedric. As evening closed in and the setting sun gave a rosy glow to the sky the Knights and Squires returned to the Castle, there was to be no formal dinner that night as most people were tired and wanted to be ready for the morrow. As John rode Hammer to the stables there was Titch waiting for him. “I will see to your horse sir while you serve Sir Cedric.”

John was pleased as he felt too tired to argue and Sir Cedric had just arrived back.

“I see you have stolen one of my Pages John,” remarked the Earl. “He’s a good lad, make sure he does as he’s told.”

John returned to his room and did not see Tania and thought it was just as well as evenings were the worst,knowing that she was not far away. There was a knock at his door and there was Titch.

“Your guests have arrived sir,” said the lad.

“Thank you Sam, that is what I shall call you because you have grown today, ask them to come up.” A few moments later Sam appeared with Roger and Laila. Roger looked around John’s room, taking in the spacious size, the glass window with a view of the Bailey and surrounding countryside.

“You are doing well here John,” he said as he stood by the large fire side.

“Sir Cedric has been very generous and I have a future here,” replied John. The two friends talked far into the night catching up with all their adventures, after a short while Laila’s head dropped and she drifted of to sleep. “Time we went back to our camp and let you get some sleep, are you competing tomorrow, or should I say today?” said Roger.

“Yes, but not ‘till later,” answered John. “Come again before you leave.” The next morning John was up early in spite of the late night, after a hasty breakfast he went down to the stables to prepare Hammer. He was astonished to see the horse already decked out in his finery and a smiling Sam standing by Hammer’s head, the big horse dwarfed him but somehow had a gentle demeanour as his head was almost resting on Sam’s. Gavin was laughing and said to John.

“We helped him with the armour but he wouldn’t let us do anything else, he managed to finish his coat and fit the trapper by standing on the mounting block!”

John thanked Sam and sent him off to the kitchens for breakfast as he and Gavin prepared Snow for Sir Cedric. On the way back to his room John went into the Hall and found the Knights busy breaking their fast. John approached Sir Cedric.

"Good morning Sir, Snow is ready and we will be assembled when you wish."

"Well done," replied the Earl. "We should have good sport today. You acquitted yourself well yesterday, John, shoot well today we need a good archer for what may come."

"Sir I ask a boon," said John.

"Go ahead, as long as it does not involve a certain Lady," said Sir Cedric with a stern face.

John continued. "There is a pony in the old stables that is not used, and I would like Sam, the Page, to have her to be able to keep up, as he is a little short and he spends energy getting to a place when he needs that energy to fulfil his duties."

There was silence as the Earl looked at John and then he laughed. "If he can ride her she is his as long as he is your Page."

John thanked the Knight and hurried to his room to get ready. As he neared his room he met Tania going to her workshop.

"Will you be at the Tournament today?" asked John.

"Yes, I am and I wish you good luck," he said. John looked around for the maid but she was nowhere in sight. Quickly he took Tania in his arms, she came willingly and they kissed.

"I don't know if I can stand being parted from you for very much longer, we should be together where we belong," murmured John.

"Time will pass quickly, my love,no one can part us now no matter how long we have to wait," said Tania.

She released herself as the maid approached and they went off to the workroom. John dressed himself ready for the contests and ran down to the stables. Sam was waiting for him standing by Hammer.

“Saddle the pony that is in the old stable and ride it to the Tournament so that you can keep up with us and it will stop your legs wearing out, we don’t want you to get any shorter.” Sam grinned and hurried off. John joined Gavin and Carac and the party moved off to the Tournament ground.

The sun had risen early on the second day of the Tournament, everyone was in good spirits and the colourful stalls were soon in business selling their wares. The first event of the day was a final of the wrestling match, a ring had been set up in the main arena. The perimeter was packed with people, the locals to cheer on the Wymondham champion who was up against the tall man from Lincoln. The bout was a close one but the man from Lincoln’s strength gradually overcame the local man and there were loud groans when at last the Wymondham champion could raise himself up from the ground no more.

The next event, archery, also included one of the Lincoln group, the man known as Robert Hud, as well as John who lined up with the seven other men who had won through. At the first butt only one man dropped out, John thought he had enjoyed the ale tent too much before stepping up to shoot. As the length to the butt increased the numbers of archers decreased as they lost, until only John and Robert Hud were left. Hud loosed first and scored a centre gold, John looked carefully at the distance, bent into his bow and loosed. The arrow flew true and sunk into the gold centre touching Hud’s arrow. The Marshall’s deliberated and eventually awarded the win to John, Hud shook John’s hand.

“You are the first man to beat me in competition, you must come to Nottingham where we shall be on my home ground.”

John returned to his place behind Sir Cedric and Tania to watch Carac flying down the centre of the arena firing arrows from horseback at various targets, there was nobody able to get near his score.

“Cedric, you have a fine group of Squires,” said Sir Robert. “Maybe they would like to come to me, as I will be heading for Scotland soon and there will be rich pickings for men like them.”

“What do you say John,” asked Sir Cedric, turning in his chair. “A chance to make your fortune?”

“Or lose my head,” answered John. “I owe you too much to desert you Sir. “

“ Well said lad,” continued Sir Robert. “I know there must be other reasons you wish to stay.”

Tania blushed and John looked at his feet and they all laughed. Now it was the turn of the Squire’s final Joust, Sam had Hammer ready and as John mounted, Sam stood back holding the next lance. John moved out to the lists and waited for the Marshall’s horn. His opponent was a man who had entered the Tournament on his own, with just a boy to assist him. He was older than the other Squires and was unlikely to achieve his Knighthood as he had no allegiance to any Lord. The signal was given and John urged Hammer into a gallop, at the last moment John moved in his saddle and lowered his lance as he had been taught, it caught the other rider in his side and catapulted him off his horse. There was loud cheering from the Wymondham crowd. John’s opponent caught his horse, remounted and rode back to his end of the List. A smiling Sam handed John his second lance and the opponents faced each other again. As they charged at each other John settled into his saddle but this time both their lances found their targets and both riders were unseated, the stranger was soon on his feet and crossing to John’s side drew his sword. There was immediate horn blowing from the Marshall as no ground fighting was allowed and a sword should not have been worn. John looked round at a shout from the side of the list from Roger who threw him his sword. John caught it and parried the first attack then stood to face the stranger, the man moved quickly to attack again but this time John was ready and all the hours of practice and his battle experience proved it’s worth as the man found his sword suddenly whipped out of his hands and John’s sword at his throat.

“Hold,” shouted the Stewards and stood between the two men.

The stranger was marched away as the crowed shouted and applauded at the incident. John walked, a little unsteadily back to where Hammer stood patiently and led him to his end of the list as the Marshal declared John the winner. After John had divested himself from his armour and taken his place in the stand Sir Cedric turned to him. "I remember teaching you that move some time ago, I am glad you had not forgotten." He turned to a steward."I want that man brought to me after the Tournament, he knew the rules and I want to know what grievance he bears."

An announcement was made that the Noblemen would not Joust this day, they did not want to be injured prior to their next commitment. This news brought loud mutterings from the crowd as there was speculation on what these commitments would be. There followed some spirited jousting between the young knights the victor being one of Sir Gilbert de Clare's men. The presentations of prizes for the victors of the various events then took place. John received a fine leather quiver full of well made arrows and a silver tankard. For winning at the lists he was presented with a fine Norman Shield emblazoned with Sir Cedric's crest and a mace. Sir Cedric rose and addressed the crowd thanking all for coming to see the Tournament and wishing them ' God's Speed ' for their homeward journeys. The Earl's guests returned to the Castle where there was to be a banquet to celebrate the event.

John, Gavin, Carac and Sam had finished all their chores and gone to their rooms to change, Sam was doing his best to clean himself up at the pump. There was a knock at John's door, when John opened it there was Tania's maid, she told him to go down to the workroom but she would be back when she had fetched some water. John hurried down the passage to the workroom, pushed the door open and immediately found himself in the arms of Tania. Their hungry kisses and embrace created its own heat and urgency, their inexperience and uncertainty of what to do next, however, delayed them long enough for the maid to return.

Flustered they broke the embrace and looked at one another.

"I go back to Lincoln tomorrow with Sir Robert, when shall I see you again?" said a sad Tania.

"I don't know," replied John. "We are waiting to see what Sir

Cedric is planning, I know Sir Robert is going to Scotland and I think Sir Alfred is joining him but nothing has been mentioned to me, except Sir Robert offered me a place to go to Scotland, it wouldn't mean I would be in Lincoln long and I would rather stay with your father."

They parted with many reassurances of their love for each other and John returned to his room to find Sam had laid out his best tunic and hose on the bed. After he had dressed he looked at Sam who had been hovering.

"Where will you eat, Sam?" The young lad explained that all the Pages went to the room next to the kitchen where there were long tables for all the staff of the Castle.

"Steward Rowan sits at the top table when he is not required upstairs, or the Senior Page takes his place. He makes fun of me, 'cause I'm small, but now I am a Page to you he may treat me better."

John smiled and made a mental note to speak to the Senior Page. The banquet was lavish, every one ate and drank their fill until the early hours. John tried to catch Tania's eye when she prepared to leave but she was intent on listening to her father. The morning found John and the other Squires heavy headed and loth to leave their beds. Sam had brought John bread and ale and said he was going to the stables. John arrived in the Bailey as most of the guests were leaving, Sir Cedric and Tania came down the steps but to John's surprise Tania was not dressed for travelling. A Guard came to John saying that someone wanted him at the Main Gate. Roger was there with a group consisting of the men who had competed in the Tournament, the big wrestler, a young troubadour and Robert Hud the archer, who reminded John he wanted him to come to Lincoln or Nottingham to compete again. They said their goodbyes and the group moved off to join Sir Robert. That evening Sir Cedric sent a message for John to join him at table and when he arrived the Earl signalled him to sit next to him, on his other side sat Tania, they smiled at each other as John took his seat. Sir Cedric congratulated all who taken part in the Tournament and the success that Wymondham had enjoyed, he was proud of his Squires and announced that there would be an extra financial reward for them.

No mention was made of why Tania was still at home.

John was practicing swordplay with Gavin in the Bailey, when Steward Rowan came to tell him that the Earl wanted to see him in his room, John followed him into the Castle, a little apprehensively. Sir Cedric was standing by the window, his favourite position, when John entered.

“Sit down John I have something to discuss with you and it is to go no further than this room.”

“ I understand sir and you can rely on me.”

Sir Cedric paced the room and then stopped and turned to John.

“The King is very ill, and Prince Edward is away on the crusade, it will be up to the Barons to hold the country together until he returns. I have to go to London to meet with them and I want you to accompany me. We shall leave early in the morning, you may take Sam to assist you, but put him on a better horse. We shall probably be gone for a few weeks or maybe longer. I have a small house not far from the palace where we shall be comfortable. Gavin shall make sure my wishes are carried out here and Carac has a task to complete and then join us in London.”

“May I see Tania before we go?” sked John.

Sir Cedric walked back to the window and stood in thought. “You may think I am being unfair by keeping you at a distance but I am the only parent she has to protect and guide her. You both have much to learn about life. You will see her when we leave in the morning. Now go and prepare yourself for the journey and remember what I said about Sam’s horse, I wish to reach London as quickly as possible.”

With that John was dismissed. On the way back to the stables he was filled with anger at the way the Earl had treated him over Tania, what did he think he was going to do to his precious daughter. Reaching the Bailey John called out for Sam and told him to select a suitable horse and also to prepare Anvil while he would deal with the Earl’s mount.

Early next morning all was made ready for the journey, John kept an eye on the main door to see if Tania appeared. He was occupied adjusting Anvil’s girth when a gentle voice said, “Don't squeeze him too much.” And a smiling Tania stood there. John looked at her.

“I shall not see you for a while, don’t forget me,” he said.

Tania smiled. “We will not be parted for long as I have asked father if I can come to London, I would like to meet some of the dressmakers.”

“But how will you travel, who will guard you?” said a worried John.

“We have plenty of men at arms and when Carac returns he can escort me,” explained Tania.

Although John was concerned he was also happy that he would see Tania in London, at that moment Gavin joined them.

“I will look after her while you are away,” grinned Gavin and John looked at him grimly.

“Don’t worry I am courting the Mayors daughter in Wymondham,” said Gavin.

“She never told me,” said Tania.

Gavin explained he had only just asked her father for permission to court her. John seemed satisfied and smiled as Sir Cedric joined them. The cavalcade was soon in motion with the Earl, John, and fifty mounted men. Tania went up onto the battlements to wave and John nearly fell off his horse by twisting round to wave back, Anvil snorted as though to say watch what you are doing. They stayed at various friends of Sir Cedric on the way to London, as they neared the great city the roads became busier and this slowed their large group. Sir Cedric decided to circle round London to reach his property on the banks of the River Thames west of the city centre. When they came to his ‘small’ house. John was confronted by a palatial building standing in extensive grounds that reached down to the river bank. The men at arms retired to a barracks in the grounds. John and Sam stabled their own, and Sir Cedric's mounts and walked to the main house. They were met at the door by the Steward, a tall well dressed man.

"Good day sir, may I show you to your room, if you should need anything during your stay please call me, my name is Merek." With that he turned and led them upstairs to a pleasant room looking out to the river. After John had changed from his travelling clothes and Sam had gone to find other Pages, he went down to the first floor. Looking in at each door John found a great hall, two well furnished drawing rooms, and coming to a closed door he knocked, was bid to enter and found Sir Cedric relaxing in a huge chair.

"Come in John, what do you think of my house?"

"It's very grand sir, I have never seen so many rooms in a house, it's more like the castle."

"Well, here in London we have to show we are important and powerful, it's all a game really but at the moment I must play it," replied the Earl. "Tomorrow I go to Westminster and see how the King fares and present myself to the Queen. You will accompany me."

John walked in the grounds down to the river and stood watching the fast flowing water rush down to the sea. He was nervous about tomorrow and could not see why, he felt there would be a happening that would not go well for him.

It was a chilly morning as John, dressed in his best doublet and hose with a new cloak. He walked with Sir Cedric and a tall man, dressed in sombre black, to the jetty at the end of the garden. They boarded a boat and were rowed down the river to Westminster. On the way the Earl introduced his friend as Henri Hausman from Bruges. They landed at Westminster and were escorted to the palace where they were led to an antechamber to the King's bedroom. The room was crowded with men whispering together in groups and casting their eyes around until they landed on someone, then they stopped and stared. John felt very uncomfortable in this company and longed to be out in the open air away from the obvious intrigue. A servant appeared at the door and called for Sir

Cedric.

"Come on John and stay close to me. Speak only if you are asked a question and answer truthfully."

The two of them followed the servant to another room where they were announced.

"Come Cedric, let me see you. A friendly and trustworthy face, I am glad you have made the journey to London."

Sir Cedric bowed low, with John also bending the knee. John looked up to see a regal lady beautifully clothed sitting in a large winged chair attended by several other women.

"Your Majesty, I came when I received the news of the King's failing health and am here to do your bidding, should you need me."

"This time I fear will be his last illness, his time draws near. Who is this young man with you, I only know of your daughter?" queried the Queen.

"May I present John of Dunston, my first Squire who has accompanied me to London so he may experience our capital city," answered the Earl. The Queen extended her arm and John stepped forward, knelt and kissed the ring that adorned the gloved hand. Queen Eleanor smiled briefly and continued talking to Sir Cedric. "Unfortunately Edward is still on his way back from the crusade so I am left to cope as best I can." The Queen asked Sir Cedric to sit near her and they were soon in deep conversation.

John gazed around the room taking in the rich tapestries and beautiful furniture, he also noticed the ladies who had also noticed him. Under their stares he felt his face beginning to redden so he stared into the large fireplace and tried to hear what was being said.

The Queen finished conversing with Sir Cedric and he and John took their leave and returned to the anteroom. Henri was waiting for them and after a few words with some of the men there they left and returned to the riverside. On the voyage back to the Earl's house he and Henri were deep in conversation, John picked up the occasional word,'cargo weight' 'interest rates' 'delivery difficulties' which he assumed related to the wool trade. They arrived back at the house and John found Sam exercising the horses, John watched him for a moment and recalled Sir Cedric calling him John of Dunston and his 'first' Squire, he wondered what 'first' meant. On the second day of their visit John and Sam rode into London to see the sights, they found the streets filthy and crowded compared with their home in the countryside. Anvil did not like the crowds, he snorted and shied, stamped his feet which resulted in him being pushed and shouted at, this did not improve matters and John guided him into a side alley to calm down. Pushing on through the smaller streets they came to a short hill atop which was a grand cathedral. John dismounted and told Sam to guard the horses while he visited the cathedral. The building, he found, was dedicated to St Paul and the inside was gloomy but at the altar end it was lavishly decorated, John knelt in prayer for a moment then returned to Sam. The two of them continued through the streets and joined a main thoroughfare heading south, soon they could see the tops of the Tower Palace. The Tower of London Palace was an imposing Castle, workmen were still busy carrying out improvements that the King had ordered. As well as being a Palace the Tower was also a prison and the gallows outside bore witness to this. John decided not to try and visit the Palace so they turned and rode off keeping to the shoreline. London was a major port and there were ships from all countries, moored and unloading, or vice versa. They could hear many different languages being spoken and the whole area was a hive of activity. Soon they left the port and approached Westminster, they heard the boom of a large bell being tolled.

"That sounds like it's coming from the Abbey," said John. Then they heard the cries coming from people who were hurrying towards the Palace.

"The King is dead!"

John spurred Anvil and followed by Sam they cantered off towards Sir Cedric's house. When they arrived they found the Earl had left for the Palace. Merek informed John that Henri Hauseman was waiting in a side room. While Sam looked after the horses John joined Henri and asked Merek to bring wine.

"I am sorry your King is dead," said Henri. "It will cause some difficulties with trade, I think."

"I am not sure what you mean," said John. "Prince Edward will soon be home when he gets the news."

Henri did not answer but carried on the conversation talking about the weather, the price of wool and the forthcoming visit of Tania. "How is the young lady, it is some time since I saw her?" queried Henri.

"She was well enough when we left and we, also, are looking forward to seeing her here soon," replied John. "A very attractive lady don't you think, I expect she has many suiters."

John was starting to get irritated by Henri's manner and was pleased of the interruption when Merek came with the wine.

"I see you wear a broadsword," continued Henri.

"I apologise for not disarming but I came here before going to my room so as not to delay you, if you were wanting just to leave a message for the Earl," explained John.

"That is not a problem," replied Henri. "It looks a fine weapon, may I see the blade?"

John hesitated and then drew the sword from its sheath.

"It is a fine weapon, crafted by an expert, is it from Toledo?" asked Henri.

John was not sure where Toledo was but answered the question by telling Henri that his father had made the sword for him.

"The weapon is beautiful, will you sell to me? I will offer you a very good price."

"No," asserted John "it would never be for sale."

When Henri said he would be leaving to visit contacts in the city John was relieved.

A few hours later Sir Cedric came back from the Palace, he called John to his room and told him that the King had died and was going to be buried in Westminster Abbey. After the funeral he and Sam were to return to Wymondham and wait for him. John sat in the Garden thinking of Tania, would she still come to London, he knew the Earl had sent messengers off to Wymondham but had said nothing to John. Sir Cedric went to Westminster early every day and Henri had disappeared so John and Sam amused themselves by boating further up river.

II

Roger journeyed most of the way back to Stamford in the company of Robert Hud and his friends, they proved to be excellent company and were in good spirits when the time came to leave them. Arriving back in the town Roger and Laila opened the door to their little house and Laila soon had a meal prepared and on the table. In the morning Roger reported to the Mayor and was informed there had been no major incidents whilst he had been away, and he had informed the guards that Roger was now their Captain. Roger met up with his men and life returned to normal. During the next months Roger began to think of Dunston and his home, he thought of Avice and the dream he used to have of he and Joan, John and Avice settled in the village, but it was just a dream as Ralf would be ruling the roost and John was leading a completely different life now. He felt a pang of jealousy when he thought of how their circumstances had changed. Laila tried to rouse him out of his black moods with not much success.

"Why don't you go back to Dunston and see your father, he must be wondering what has happened to you?" suggested Laila. Roger pondered the suggestion and then forgot it as there was an increase of outlaw activity in the area and he and his men were on full alert to spot any undesirables operating in the town. After the King's death Roger started to think of Dunston again, would the new King make changes to the nobles who had fought for de Montfort? Would he look for more devoted subjects in his Shires. Fighting for de Montfort had been a mistake, in hindsight. Roger asked the Mayor for time to visit his father where he would hope to find out the latest news. He planned to go at the beginning of the next month.

Roger and Laila's journey to Dunston was uneventful and as they came in sight of the village the sun was just beginning to set behind the trees. Roger could see there had been little change since he had left, but it did seem more deserted than he remembered. They passed throughout the centre of the village and moved on towards the Castle, the people that were out soon scuttled into their homes and slammed doors. Arriving at the Castle Roger was challenged by a man at arms who told him to wait while he fetched someone. Roger demanded immediate entrance but the guard said he did not know him and there were many robbers abroad. Eventually Boorman the Steward arrived, recognising Roger he bowed and led the way into the Castle. "Where is my father, I would visit him first?"

"Your father is not here, I will take you to your brother who will explain," said the Steward.

They entered the Great Hall and found Ralf sitting in front of the fireplace with the dogs laying before him. As soon as the dogs saw Roger they bounded over and made a fuss of him and Laila. Ralf stood up and stared at Roger.

"So you have come home at last, where have you been?"

"Where is father?" Roger asked.

"He was killed at Evesham, did you not know, were you not fighting there too, or did you turn tail like the rest of the cowards?" growled Ralf.

Roger stepped back and looked at his brother. "I fought the first time but I had enough of killing and I heard nothing from father to suggest he was raising troops again."

Ralf explained a messenger had come from Norwich to tell him of his father's death and that as next in line the title and lands passed to him and to go to Norwich to be officially instated.

"Who is this you've brought with you. I suppose you'll want bed and board 'till you leave," Ralf's tone implied he was not welcome.

“This is my wife, Laila, we shall only stay long enough to get my possessions and then we will be gone.” Ralf told Boorman to have a room prepared and bring food and wine to the small anteroom.

“I’m sure you will not mind if I don’t join you as I have estate matters to deal with which won't concern you as you have no claim on it. Take your personal possessions and you are gifted two horses, not destriers.” said Ralf. “I will not be here in the morning so I bid you and your wife farewell.” With that Ralf turned back to the fire and sat down.

Roger and Laila followed Boorman up to a small room at the back of the Castle.

“Boorman, what has happened to my brother, he was always a little aggressive but not down right rude to me?” sked Roger.

“My lord has had a hard time adjusting to being without your father. Taking over the estate has not been easy and he has upset many of the tenants. I expect it will settle down in time,” he said as he left them.

“So I am your wife am I” said Laila. “Is this a proposal?”

Roger took her in his arms and kissed her and said, “Yes it is a proposal, will you marry me, and I should have said it months ago.”

They smiled at each other, kissed again but a knock on the door interrupted their embrace. Laughing they opened the door to a woman bearing bed linen. As the woman made the bed Roger asked if his sister was at home, he was informed that she was in her room. Roger left Laila and walked to Avice’s room, he knocked and a small voice asked who was there. As soon as Avice heard her brothers voice she opened the door and flew into his arms before he had even entered the room. Once seated they both had lots of news to impart, Roger told of his adventures and Avice told a grim tale of the decline of the estate. Ralf did not know how to look after the estates and the rents were not coming in so there was little money. He put up the rents and sold some land but it was not enough. Some of the farmers had done reasonably well at the wool markets and the forge was very busy and she had heard Ralf discussing with one of his friends how they could force more money out of the successful businesses. Roger knew this was a problem countrywide and with the death of the King there was a kind of limbo. Roger fetched Laila and introduced her to Avice and together they discussed their future. Avice would go to her uncle in Norwich with her mother, who was in poor health, they would ride there with her maid and two men at arms who were close to her father. Roger decided to collect his personal effects ready to load in the morning, he also wanted to visit the forge on the way home and see what Jack had to say, he knew he could rely on his knowledge and find out what they would do if Ralf made a move against them. He could also give Jack news of John and see Joan, if she would see him. The next morning Roger went down to the stables to claim his horses, the stable hand was the same as when he left and was pleased to see him.

"We miss you sir, it's not been the same as when you and the lord were here. Are you coming back?"

"No, I am not returning. I have just come down to collect two horses that have been left to me by my father, do you know which they are?"

"Aye sir they be these," said the man and led out a fine stallion and a mare.

"Are you sure these are the ones?" asked Roger.

"Oh yes sir, I saddled them with your own tack and it fitted like a glove, so they must be yours," said the stable lad, with a wink. "The two horses you arrived with I've turned into pack horses ready for your journey."

Roger quickly brought down his baggages and he and Laila were ready to depart before Ralf had risen. Avice came to a window and waved as they rode away heading towards the village.

They could see the forge was busy as they approached, the glow from the fire lit up the entrance and the sound of hammering drowned the chorus of the birds. They dismounted and went to the cottage meeting Matilda as she came out bearing bread and ale which she almost dropped.

"Mercy, it's young Roger," she cried in amazement. "Go into the house, I'll be back directly after I've given this to Jack and the boys."

Roger stepped across the threshold and there was Joan sitting at the table writing in a big book.

"Hello Joan," said Roger. Joan looked at him in amazement and was even more stuck for words as Laila came in and stood next to Roger. Joan rose from her chair and came to the couple.

"Hello Roger," she said and turned to Laila.

"This is my wife, Laila, we came down to see what has been happening at the Castle," explained Roger.

Joan looked at them both and her eyes flicked down to Laila's left hand, no ring she thought, has Roger been up to his old tricks. They sat down at the table just as Jack came hurrying in wiping his hands on a piece of rag.

"This is certainly a surprise," said Jack. "Have you seen John, is he coming this way soon?"

Roger gave them as much news as he could about John and told them how good he was at the Tournament. He told them that John had gone to London with Sir Cedric and he hoped to see him when he returned. Roger questioned Jack on what was happening to the village under Ralf's time as lord of the Castle. Jack's reply was what Roger feared.

"He has no idea of what the farmers do to maintain their business, whether it is arable or the sheep, he put's 'taxes', as he calls them, up so high the farmers can't pay. Then he is trying to take their land. He has tried it on with me and I wont have it, he needs a Smith for his own work so he has held off from pushing me, but I fear it will come to a fight when he tries to get more money from me. His father was tough but fair where Ralf has no idea how to get the best from people. If it carries on like this there will be trouble as we hear the men at arms are also beginning to leave."

Roger listened to this with a sinking feeling, all his father had worked for was being thrown away. Roger thought to himself that it would have been better to have left the estate to him, but he had no experience either, their father had never trained them in how to manage the land. After sharing the midday meal with Jack and his family, Roger and Laila started their journey back to Stamford.

Jack had not been back to the forge for very long when Ralf and half a dozen men at arms reined in at the front of the cottage.

"Jack Smith come out!" called Ralf.

Jack came and stood in front of Ralf.

"Politeness dictates that you dismount before any conversation, sir," said Jack looking at Ralf who backed up and still sat on his horse. "I cannot see to your horse if you are still sitting on him," continued Jack.

This statement got through to Ralf and he realised that there was no other blacksmith in the area. Ralf dismounted and approached Jack. "Under the present economic climate I have to increase the rent on the Smithy, the unrest in England has forced this upon me," he said.

Jack looked him in the eye and replied. "You increased our rent only one month ago and that made it higher than in Norwich, what is this new figure you propose?"

Ralf quoted a figure and Jack said that was unfair and did he want the Smithy to close.

"I have to pay my lads and have enough to feed my family and to buy wood and charcoal, I might as well pack up and become a soldier again." Jack said.

Ralf mounted his horse and shouted to Jack that he wanted the increase by quarter day, which was in four days time. Jack called the two lads in from the forge and they sat round the cottage table with Matilda and Joan to discuss what had just happened.

"I must get word to John, he might be able to get Sir Cedric to help," said Jack.

"I could go," volunteered William.

“Or me,” joined in Thomas.

“I think William should go, Thomas and I can manage most of the work at the moment. Go at first light it should not take you long.” said Jack.

II

Sir Cedric called John to his room and told him that the funeral of the King was the next day and immediately it was over he wanted him, with Sam, to ride as quickly as possible back to Wymondham taking four men at arms with them. There were crowds at the funeral and as soon as the service was over John and Sam slipped away and joined the men at arms at the house. An hour later they were away making good speed to home.

Arriving at Wymondham John spoke to Gavin and told him of the events in London, he said Sir Cedric would be returning in the next few days. At the evening meal Tania joined them and it was obvious that she was pleased to see John back, after the meal John sat by her and related the trip to her.

“It was a shame we could not have seen London together, Sam was no substitute, and I think he is trying to grow a beard which would put anyone off.”

There was a general feeling of goodwill that they were all together, apart from the Earl. When the hour was late John suggested that they all retired to bed, as he said it he wished it was him retiring to Tania’s. John woke in the early hours and paced the room, what would he have to do to prove he was worthy of a knighthood and able to claim Tania. As daylight pushed night away and birds began their chorus John decided to assume the position Sir Cedric had given him. If he was senior Squire here he would make sure the Castle was in tip top condition for Sir Cedric’s return. He called Gavin and Carac and put the proposal to them, they did not seem surprised.

“You know more than us because you study longer and you fight better than us, in most things, and you were here before us so

I have no problem, as long as you don't start shouting at us," said Gavin and Carac agreed. So the three of them set about improving the Castle. Cleaning up was an easy task but John wanted to repair walls and improve security and this required persuading the Castle mason to fall in with their plans. Eventually the Castle was a hive of activity and one day when Tania was returning from Wymondham she had difficulty in getting in through the second gate.

"Sorry about that," said John. "We wanted to make the arrow slits like a cross so the archers can fire sideways easier."

Tania laughed and she and her maid went on to the Keep. Everyone was in their respective homes, eating their evening meal when a Page entered the great hall where John and the others were dining, and approached the top table where Tania was occupying the chair next to the Earl's empty one.

"My Lady there is a man without who wishes to see the Earl, I told that he was not available, as I did not wish to say he was not here," said the Page.

John rose and said, "I will go to see what is so urgent, if you so wish." Tania nodded her head and John followed the Page to the Bailey where he saw William standing by his horse. John felt a feeling of foreboding as he hurried over and asked.

"What is the problem William, is my family all right?"

"Yes sir, everyone was well when I left but your father asked me to bring some news."

John led William into the Castle and into an anteroom where William explained the threat that had been issued by Ralf. John felt his anger rising and questioned William on whether other farms had been dealt with the same way. William said that it was normally the Steward from the Castle that went out to the other tenants, Ralf did not stir himself only to hunt, he had come to the Smithy himself expecting that Boorman would get nowhere with Jack. John sent William into the Hall to join in the meal while he thought about the news he had brought. There was no way to discuss it with Sir Cedric as he was probably on route home, so he must make decisions himself. He was pacing the room when the door opened and Tania, with her ever present maid, walked in.

"What is it John, is there trouble?"

John explained what William had told him and Tania was horrified.

"Why can't landlords run their affairs the same as we do, we have no major troubles with our tenants."

John said he would think about the problem for an hour or so and then if he came up with a plan he would call her to discuss it. It was only half an hour Later when John knocked on Tania's door.

"I must go and protect my father but I must also try and protect the village too so the best way is to go to Ralf and show him that my father is not alone and this is not the way to behave. I intend to depose him and take the Castle. I am sure Sir Cedric will understand but I must take action now. I will go and rest in the forest near Dunston so that we are in position at first light, I will take Carac and 100 men at arms. I know Ralf has only a few fighting men as they went with his father and not many came back. If I meet resistance from Ralf to my proposal that he should surrender the Castle to me I shall take it by force."

"This is a bold move," said a shocked Tania. "What will my father say, you are his Squire so whatever you do will reflect on him?"

"I also know he would not want to see villages treated this way, it is the route to another rebellion. Dunston is near enough for us to administer and I am sure once we hold it the men in Westminster will grant it to us, and maybe more. If anyone at Norwich tries to argue against it they will remember where they stood in the last conflict!" replied John.

He kissed her, in spite of the squeal from her maid and strode out to find Carac.

The force assembled outside the Castle and John explained what he intended and received a supportive cheer when he finished. They rode off with John riding Anvil with Carac at his side, just behind came Sam with Hammer. They skirted

Wymondham so as not to arouse the town and reached the forest and quietly camped with no fires. John lay down feeling nervous, he was sure of his plan but not so sure of Sir Cedric's attitude. In the morning as the group began to ready themselves, John dressed in ordinary doublet and hose as his plan was to first call on Ralf to establish what had taken place. He mounted Anvil and with Sam in attendance rode out to the Castle. His force was well hidden and as John approached the main gate everywhere looked calm and serene. A loan sentry challenged him at the gate and when John said he wanted to see Ralf he was told the master had gone to Saxlingham the day before on a rent collection tour and was not expected back until later that day. John turned back to the forest somewhat deflated, he told the men and sent them further into the forest so they could light fires and make a meal. John called Carac to him and told him he would visit his father to tell him what was happening. Within half an hour John was in front of his family explaining that he had come to reason with Ralf, he neglected to include that he had an armed escort. Jack listened carefully.

"I think you have reacted a bit too soon John, you should have waited for the Earl to come back."

"Who knows when that will be, they are too busy ruling the country between them, now the King is dead and the Prince still away, Ralf could be here with his men any day," responded John.

"Well, don't go too far, I would like to come with you but I must think of your mother and sister as well as keeping the forge going," said Jack.

John went back to his men in the forest and found them roasting a couple of pigs.

"I hope they were paid for," said John. Carac told him that a smallholder with several animals had offered them, Carac had found out he used to be farmer but had been turned off his land by Ralf for not paying the new rent. As they were cleaning up the remains of their lunch a lookout came hurrying to John to tell him that Ralf and his men had returned. John mounted Anvil and with Carac set out for the Castle. The guard saw them coming and sent someone in to warn Ralf who had not yet dismounted. Ralf appeared at the gate and waited for John to reach him.

“Ah, the blacksmith’s son returns then, are you not happy cleaning a Knights boots?”

“More happier than you will ever know,” replied John. “I come today to tell you not to intimidate my family or try to extort money from them.”

“Oh and by what authority do you say such to me?”

“I need no more authority than to protect my family, and to offer it to anyone else who wants it, from your tyrannical yoke.” By this time several people had gathered nearby and several shouted out in agreement. Ralf went red in the face and glared at John, some of Ralf’s men had begun to come through the gate and see what all the fuss was about, emboldened by this Ralf called them to arrest John but no one moved as at the forest edge they had spotted John’s men slowly advancing. He gave a signal for them to stand just behind him. Ralf again shouted for his men to arrest John and one or two began to move forward. John warned Ralf to call them back as he would not be arrested. Ralf was now consumed with anger and started to go with his men towards John who gave a signal and his men charged in a compact group towards Ralph. The men at the gate tried to go back but were met by men trying to come out to see what was happening in the melee that ensued Ralf’s horse reared and unseated him. As he struggled with the animal and tried to get up into his saddle, unsuccessfully, John rode up to him and looked down.

“Will you yield to me and surrender your Castle or shall I take it, and you, by force?”

As he said this John unsheathed his sword and had it at Ralf’s throat, Carac’s force drove at the gateway and stopped any chance of the gates being closed. Most of Ralf’s men had run back into the Bailey with just a few standing by him with swords lowered. Ralf dropped the reins of his horse and stood looking up at John, still with the sword inches from his throat.

“You will never get away with this, I will have your life for this outrage.” Ralf spat out the words.

Calmly John spoke to him again. “I ask you again,do you yield?”

Ralf looked at John then at his sword and the men around him and being the coward he was, offered his sword to John.

“In the face of these odds I yield.”

John lifted his sword from Ralf's throat and raised it aloft. “I take this Castle and all its entitlements in the name of Sir Cedric of Wymondham, as surrendered to me by Ralf de Brehalle.”

There broke out loud cheering not only from John's men but also many villagers and farmers who had suddenly appeared. John told Carac to see there was no looting and to put guards on the gate also to see any of Ralf's men were rounded up and put in the dungeons, Boorman suggested Ralf and the officers be sent to the West tower where there was only one entrance. John agreed and then rode into the Bailey and dismounted. Boorman stood in front of him and bowed.

“I would like to remain in service here sir, I am willing to pledge allegiance to whoever takes control of the Castle.”

“Thank you Boorman, I will need you as you know the Castle and I do not. Sam stable my horses, find Carac and meet me in the main hall.”

John's adrenalin was still flowing high as he stomped into the Main Hall and sat himself down at the large table there. Sam and Carac came in and John issued orders that the Castle should be made secure, guards posted, battlements manned and a courier brought to him.

“A lot to do for our small force,” said Carac.

“We must send for reinforcements from Wymondham,” responded John. “We can clear out the Castle of Ralf's men, that will help.”

After John had sent the courier off to Wymondham they started to close the Castle down for the night.

John found an empty bed and tried to get some sleep but the thought of what he had done kept churning around in his mind keeping away that pleasant blankness that sleep can bring. The morning brought no relief and he entered the Hall with some trepidation. A place had been set for him and Carac and food was on the table.

"Have the prisoners been fed?"

" Yes," said Carac. "Ralf has asked to see you."

"Any sign of reinforcements? I had hoped they might march at night," said John.

Carac told him that everywhere was quiet and the Castle staff were going about their duties as though nothing had happened.

"Everything went so quickly, I still can't believe what we have done," said Carac as he finished eating and prepared to check the guards and bring Ralf down to John.

"Wait," said John. "I will see him later, when I have thought a little more on our position. Send out scouts to see what the atmosphere is like in the villages, two men should do, Fredric and Steven would be the best, they are level headed and will bring back a true report. We need to know if I have poked a stick into a hornet's nest."

As they sat at the table a guard came in and reported that there was a large crowd of people at the South gate. John followed him to the gate and on arriving called out to the crowd.

"Do you have a spokesman, or someone who can speak for you?"

" Yes, we do," said a voice that John knew well and his father stepped forward.

"Open the postern and let him in."

John greeted his father and asked what the crowd wanted.

"They have heard that Ralf has been defeated and want to know what is going to happen, as do I. How did all this happen son, are you now ruling this village?" asked Jack.

"As I am here then yes I will be in command until I hear from Sir Cedric. How did they know so quickly and what do they expect?"

Jack explained that the quarter day was tomorrow so they were all coming to the Castle, they were worried what was going to happen as most of them would not be able to pay the new rents.

"Go and tell them that no rents will be collected until I have seen the records and then I will look at each tenancy and we will reach an agreement on what they should pay, until then they are to carry on with their work as we need the crops and the animals to survive."

Jack smiled at John's words, he could see his son had grown up. Jack went out and spoke to the crowd who cheered and most turned away to go back to their farms, all but a number of rough looking men who gathered round Jack. John prepared to open the gate and assist his father but Jack re-entered the Bailey

"Those men are ex men at arms that Ralf threw out when times got tough they want to know if they can be of use?"

John thought for a moment. "Let them through the postern one at a time and I will speak to them."

After he had spoken to them all only two were told to leave, it transpired that most had been living in the forest and were on the edge of becoming outlaws. John sent them to the battlements and told all but four of his own men to come down and be ready in the Bailey. A shout came from the battlements that a rider was coming, it was one of the scouts and he came to report to John that he had seen nothing out of the ordinary to the North. John sent him to the kitchens for food and despatched another rider to watch the road from Norwich. John told a guard to bring Ralf to the hall. John and Carac sat at the table when Ralf was brought in.

" You cannot keep me as a prisoner, I demand to be released, and when I am you can be assured that I shall be on my way to see the King." Ralf demanded.

" You will have a long way to go as the King is still abroad. I don't want you here either but I must wait for Sir Cedric to decide on your future and until then you will reside in the West tower, take him back."

The guard escorted Ralf back to his room. John decided to get some fresh air and went up onto the battlements, he could see the smoke curling upwards from the Smithy in the still air and thought of his peaceful life there, such a lot had happened since leaving his home, he knew he had changed, but was it for the better? He suddenly had the urge to go home to see his family but he could not leave the Castle yet. After their evening meal John and Carac walked through the Castle talking to the staff who had remained, they appeared to have accepted the situation and responded to John. That night he slept easier and drifted off to sleep thinking of Tania. He rose early and went back to the battlements, the night guards had seen nothing to report. The morning was crisp and the mist lay close to the ground, it was very still. His reverie was broken by the sound of a galloping horse as the courier returned from Wymondham. John ran down the steps to meet him as he dismounted.

"What news from Wymondham, will Gavin send reinforcements, is Tania there?" asked John.

The courier held up his hand. "The Earl has returned and he says to hold the Castle 'till he arrives and keep any prisoners you have especially, Ralf de Brehalle."

John's nerves did a somersault and he thought this is it, now I shall know if what I have done is right, he went to the kitchens and grabbed bread and cheese. Going into the Hall he met Carac.

"Will you get some of the prisoners up and get them cleaning the Castle please. Sam saddle Anvil and your own horse I want to have a look round the outside of the walls."

When they were outside the walls John could see that the de Brehalle's had neglected the upkeep of the Castle. Several places needed repair and the ground had slipped back into the moat, there was no water in it at all. A shout came from the battlements and they quickly rode back into the Castle. A sentry was waiting for them with news that there was movement at the forest edge. John called Carac and a dozen men at arms to him and told them to close the gates and prepare to defend them, while he bounded up the steps to the battlements. Coming out of the forest he could see a force of mounted men, as they came closer he suddenly recognised the lead rider and horse.

“It’s the Earl on Snow, and he is in full armour.” said John. “Open the gate and form an honour guard and hope he has not come to throw us out.”

John went down mounted Anvil and rode to meet Sir Cedric.

The column of armed men with the Earl at its head look very impressive, with the Earl’s banner flying in the breeze and the sun reflecting off the spear tips of the men. John turned and rode in at the side of Sir Cedric who’s helm was being carried by a page. They dismounted and Sir Cedric faced John.

“I have come with the reinforcements you requested but who are we fighting, I see no army outside laying siege. Let me get out of this tin can and you can explain yourself.”

John led Sir Cedric into the Castle where Boorman was waiting.

“Take Sir Cedric up to the master room and ask Sam to attend him,” said John.

“Come with me John, you can talk whilst I change, I am eager to know what has happened.” He followed Boorman. Sam appeared, out of breath, and helped the Earl divest himself of his armour. John related what had happened with Sam nodding his head in agreement.

“So, you took the Castle in my name did you, and Ralf surrendered without bloodshed. You have been very lucky, there is no leader in Norwich since Bigod has gone and the monks are now running things there so we can claim all the villages that are tenants to this Castle and include a few others that will link with Wymondham, and I don’t believe there is anyone strong enough to oppose that. Your family feud has increased our lands very nicely.”

A smiling Sir Cedric sat back in his chair and laughed. After being away at the crusade for so long Sir Cedric had lost some villages and this windfall, created by John, would fill some gaps until he could take back what he had lost around Wymondham. John nearly collapsed with relief.

“After we had taken the Castle, I was concerned but the villagers are not opposed to what has happened.” John told him of the meeting and what he had arranged.

“We will talk of this tomorrow, let’s eat, all this excitement has made me hungry,” said Sir Cedric.

Ralf was called to Sir Cedric the following morning and he again protested at the way the Castle had been taken from him, Sir Cedric stood and looked at him in the eyes.

“I’ll not wast my time with you sir, I shall send a message to your family in Normandy and they must meet you at Calais as that is where you will be delivered by my escort, think yourself lucky you were not killed and I have not asked a ransom for your release. Take him away!”

The next few days were a whirlwind as they visited all the farms and other tenancies between the Dunston estate and Wymondham.

“When the King returns I must go to London and get these lands agreed, you must accompany me. The time might be right to make a play for Norwich.” mused Sir Cedric “in the meantime I leave you here to take charge and sort out these rents fairly as I must return to Wymondham.”

After Sir Cedric had left John found some records of the villages. John and Sam visited all the tenants and in the majority of cases came to an agreeable settlement. John was getting impatient to finish so that he could report back to Sir Cedric and more importantly see Tania, he had been too long away from the love of his life who might start to forget him.

At last the time came when one morning John and Sam left Dunston Castle in Carac’s hands and set off for Wymondham, they reached the town late afternoon and could see the Castle glinting at them as the sun lowered itself toward night. Sam blew his hunting horn as they approached and the gates were open when they arrived. As they came into the Bailey a figure was there waiting and as soon as John dismounted Tania was in his arms, looking over her shoulder he could see Sir Cedric watching from a few yards away. "Welcome home John, when you have finished devouring my daughter come and join me in my room," said the Earl as he turned back to the doorway.

"I have missed you so much, John," cried Tania. "Don't ever leave me for so long again. I have been bad tempered with my maids (a young girl standing near nodded her head) and have had days when I have not spoken to anyone."

The two of them linked arms and went inside, with the maid close behind.

John knocked on Sir Cedric's door and was told to enter. He gave his report and informed the Earl that the Tenants were now paying their rents also the shearing had gone well, his father had more work than he could cope with and was contemplating opening up the old forge in the Castle. He was also having a stone house built to replace the old cottage. Sir Cedric was pleased with the progress and told John that another trip to London would be made soon as the King was returning in a few weeks time.

"In the meantime you are still to meet Tania only when her maid is present, I assume from the display when you arrived, that your feelings for each other are the same." Sir Cedric smiled as he said the last few words.

II

Roger and Laila settled back into their routine, Laila did not broach the subject of their marriage and Roger threw himself into his work in sharpening up his men and cutting the crime in Stamford. One morning after breakfast, Roger asked Laila if she would like to visit the church near their house. Laila was surprised as they did not go to church very often, only when Roger thought it would be a good idea to show himself as an upright citizen. When they arrived the priest was waiting for them and as they sat in the church he talked to them about what the church expected from them if they were to wed. Laila was so excited and Roger agreed to everything while the priest smiled, having heard all this before and knowing few kept to what they agreed to that day. They arranged to be married on a Saturday in four weeks time. Laila and Roger walked home together with Laila feeling as if she was ten feet off the ground Before they reached their cottage Roger stopped at a house nearer to the centre of the town which had a small alleyway at the side, he produced a set of keys and opened the front door.

"This is ours as from next week," he said to an open mouthed Laila. "The Mayor owns it and we will rent it while I am Marshall, my new title, of the town. There is a stable at the rear and a room which I can use as a place to talk to the men and write my reports."

Tears were rolling down Laila's face and she threw herself at Roger and hugged him. "I have never been in such a grand house and will we share it with others?" she asked.

"No, my love, this is just for us, but dry your tears and I will show you the rooms, we will have to get some more furniture as well, I will see about moving ours as soon as I can."

After a tour of the house the two of them walked back to their cottage hand in hand. There was a softness to their love making that night, a true joining of two people who had at last found happiness in each other. Little by little Roger learned of what had happened to his brother and he felt sad that his family home was lost, perhaps he could have taken over the Castle himself but with no troops and an uncertainty of who would support him it would have failed. He decided to send a message to John inviting him to the wedding and then he would gain the full story of what happened. Roger worked hard to protect the citizens of the town, he organised more patrols outside the walls to find out what was going on in the nearby villages and the name of Robert Hud was spoken of more and more.

Laila went to the market one day and was surprised to see a group of men that she recognised, it was Robert Hud and his friends that they had met at the Tournament, they did not see her and for some reason, she couldn't explain, she did not make herself known.

When Roger came home that evening Laila told him of what she had seen.

"As long as they behave themselves I don't see they will cause any trouble, the gate guards will have made sure that they are not carrying bows or swords, as is the rule for visitors to the town," said Roger. "I am going out again so I will see if they are still around."

There was no sign of the group and the night guards had not noticed them so Roger forgot about them. A loud banging on his front door woke Roger the next morning.

"All right I'm coming," he shouted. "Anyone would think the town is on fire."

When he opened the door there were two men there who both tried to speak at once. Roger calmed them down as he led them in to the parlour. One man was a jeweller and the other his next door neighbour a cobbler. It transpired they were early risers and when they went to open their shops they found they had been robbed. The value of the thefts differed greatly, the jeweller had lost many hundreds of pounds, he claimed, but the cobbler found only four pairs of boots had gone. Roger sent messages to close all the gates and to check people leaving with new boots, he rode round to the West gate where there was a crowd of people trying to get in and out, Roger told the guards to open the gate but keep a careful eye on those entering and exiting. The extra security drew a blank and Roger increased his patrols and posted a reward for the capture of the thieves. Roger's thoughts turned to what was happening in the town and the surrounding countryside, with more and more men wandering about either deserters or the flotsam from the recent battles. The town was well policed but outside travelling was extremely dangerous, robberies and killings by marauding gangs was common place.

News had come to Roger that a stranger had been seen entering an Inn well known for being the haunt of thieves and troublemakers. Roger and two of his men entered the Inn and walked up to the bar, the landlord hurriedly closed the door that led into his private room.

"Who is staying here?" sked Roger. "I am looking for three visitors who were seen entering this Inn." "They've gone sir, they only came in for a drink then left.”

Roger quickly went round the bar, pushed the landlord aside and opened the door into the private room just in time to find three men being thrust back into the room from a side door where Roger’s men had been waiting.

“Take them to the Gaol and this poor specimen of an Innkeeper,” said Roger to his men who had come in through the front door. Roger looked on the table in the rear room and there were several items of jewellery laid out. After he had questioned the three he found that they were regular thieves and were the culprits that had stolen from the Jeweller, they were also wearing almost new boots. They had a deal with the landlord who sold the jewellery over the counter at lower prices. Roger felt very satisfied as he made his way home that evening, he was looking forward to his meal and a quiet night in with Laila, who had been a little distant the last few days. Roger sat in his chair after his meal and rested his feet on a stool. Laila came into the room and stood looking at him. “Sit down, my love, you are looking a little tired,” said Roger.

“I am tired and that is why I want to talk to you. We are about to have a new member of the family.”

There was silence for a few minutes as Roger realised what she was saying and then he jumped out of the chair, knocking over the stool and hugged his wife.

“This is the best day of my life, our own family.” Roger gently lowered Laila into the chair he had just vacated and started fussing over her.

“ top, Roger, I am fine and nothing will happen for six months yet.”

Roger, however, went on making plans for a nursemaid and altering a room for a nursery. Laila laughed and told him to calm down while she explained what she wanted. Roger dashed out soon after his breakfast to tell the Mayor their good news, and anyone else he came across. It was not all good news at this time as there had been more robberies outside town. The outlaws were growing in numbers and the Mayor was eager to call the Earl of Cornwall at Rockingham Castle to provide troops to guard the roads. Roger agreed but did not want any outside interference in the town, he assured the Mayor that he and his men could cope. The Abbey became very busy at this time caring for travellers who had been attacked.

Some days later Roger received a message from one of the de Mowbray's asking him to come to the Castle and discuss the rising outlaw problem in the area. Roger set off early with two escorts so that he need not travel at night. de Mowbray was in his hall with three other men when Roger arrived and they needed no introductions.

"Hello Robert," said Roger, and he nodded to Robert's companions, a tall man whom Roger had seen wrestle at the Tournament and his friend the troubadour.

"You know Robert?" asked de Mowbray.

Roger explained their meeting at the Tournament and how well they had done.

"Robert has news of the movement of outlaws in this area and has offered his services to me. I asked you here because the movement is in your direction," said de Mowbray. Roger told them that he had sent messages to Rockingham asking for support but had no reply before he left.

"They do not appear to be organised, just thieving and causing mayhem as they go, but why south? Where are they aiming for?" queried Robert.

"Ultimately London I suppose," said de Mowbray.

" I don't think so, I have a feeling it is somewhere closer," replied Roger. Roger was nearer the truth than he knew. After a night of discussion they decided that Robert and his men would shadow the outlaws and find out, if they could, where they were heading and why. Roger awoke early the next morning and was on his way home by first light. This was the best time of day to ride, with the sun beginning to chase the darkness away, birds singing to welcome the golden globe, and a freshness that cleared the head from the fog of sleep. He kept his horse going at a mile eating trot and was soon in sight of Stamford. Laila welcomed him home, she had been worried about all the reports of violence on the roads.

Roger's guards had seen men passing the town and some trying to gain entrance but they had kept them out.

Roger kept watch on the movement and noticed the majority were turning east and he thought of John.

II

"We leave for London in three days, so if you are intending to go back to Dunston now is the time to ride," announced Sir Cedric one morning. John agreed and called Sam to make ready. Within the hour they were on their way, keeping at a brisk trot they soon glimpsed the Castle through the trees and Sam blew his horn.

Carac welcomed them and wanted to know all the news from Wymondham. Carac told them that there had been an increase in groups of outlaws preying on travellers passing through the forest, so far Dunston was quiet and a programme of building better housing was taking place. John and Carac discussed how they could increase the number of men at arms without allowing any outlaws into the Castle.

"I am going to be away for a few days in London with Sir Cedric," said John. "I am sure you will be careful and check up the past history of any one you decide to take on."

They enjoyed a dinner together with the men who were responsible for various duties in the Castle and as John surveyed the group round the table he felt a glow of pride. They had found a home and were determined to build on what they had, even the moat was taking shape. He approached the Smithy the next day and over lunch discussed with his father the possibility of his mother and Joan moving into the Castle while the country was still in a turmoil. Jack was insistent that the Smithy continue working as he had so many orders to fulfil.

“William could move into the house for a while with Thomas, I would be here every day and Matilda and Joan would be safe,” said Jack.

“That’s fine,” said John. “I will make sure you have a couple of armed men to escort you.”

John and Carac toured the farms, mills and other properties within the ownership of the Castle, it was a large area to try and protect but with a strong response force they felt everywhere was in reach of the Castle in an hour.

John and Sam set off midmorning the following day to ride back to Wymondham, aiming to reach Wymondham by noon. They were riding through the forest when two men appeared in the middle of the track and signalled them to stop, John looked left and right and said to Sam.

“Ride like hell Sam, don’t stop for anything!”

Anvil responded and took off scattering the two in the track John could hear Sam close behind him, he felt the wind of an arrow that came close but they were soon out of range. They slowed to a walk after a good distance had been put between the robbers and themselves.

“I saw the branches moving on the side of the path,” said John. “We must make sure anyone who is travelling goes with a party of armed men.”

They carried on to Wymondham where they found armed patrols in the streets. When they arrived at the Castle there were many more armed men inside than when they left. Gavin came out to meet them and told them that there were groups of deserters in the woods, Sam related their adventure on the way home. “Something will have to be done soon to find these men work or clear them out,” said John.

Sir Cedric and John met to discuss the situation and decided that John should go to his friend’s wedding with Tania, her maids, Sam and a strong escort. The journey to Stamford was uneventful due to the size of their party and when they arrived and met the Mayor he was only too pleased to find accommodation in the town for them. The day of the wedding arrived and the house was in a turmoil, after Roger had dressed he was banished to an Inn until after the ceremony. Laila, helped by friends, dressed and prepared to walk to the church, she would have preferred a simple ceremony with the villagers in the woods like her parents but Roger's position demanded a proper occasion.

They left the house, Laila dressed in white and pink with a floral headdress. Roger was already in the church with John.

"Thank you for standing for me John," whispered Roger.

The ceremony concluded and they withdrew to the town hall where a feast had been prepared. The wedding was a joyful occasion and the meal, speeches and copious amounts of beer and wine that was drunk raised the spirits of the whole town. John could see that Roger had found a place to be happy and with his new wife and looked forward to good future. John kept close to Tania and during the service clasping her hand. He hoped and prayed that it would be their wedding bells that were rung out from the church soon. Tania retired to the Mayor's house, with her maids, after the festivities in the evening, so John did not get the chance for a goodnight kiss, perhaps just as well. On their way back to Wymondham the next day there were even more morose groups of men loitering along the route, one knot of men tried to stop the cavalcade but there were enough men at arms with John's party to stop any aggression before it developed into an attack. John breathed a sigh of relief when they were safe within the walls of the Castle, once they were all settled and he had been to see the Earl he walked up to the workroom hoping that Tania had gone there before retiring, as he walked along the passage he could see alight under the door. He knocked softly and a small voice bid him enter. Tania sat by the fire and her maid opposite her.

"I was coming to say goodnight," said John. "Will we never be alone?" He looked at the maid as he said this who stared at the embroidery in her lap.

"You know my father's order John, I cannot go against him."

"Then I must shorten the time to our wedding as being near you and not able to touch you is making me so frustrated. Goodnight to you,dearest heart, you have my love as always," said John as he stole a kiss and went to his room.

Sir Cedric gathered his entourage together outside the main gate, he and John were up on their destriers clothed in their armour, Sam was attending John and there were two other pages with the Earl. A force of 150 armed men also sat ready on their horses.

"I do not think we shall have any trouble from outlaws," said Sir Cedric as they moved of at the start of their trip to London. He was right and after an uneventful journey they entered the grounds of the London house. John made sure everyone was settled in and the horses were stabled when a servant came to say Sir Cedric wanted him.

"My tailor is coming here tomorrow and I want him to make you some new clothes for your presentation to the King after the Coronation. We shall be in the Abbey for the ceremony and then in the palace after which I have a special task for you, I will explain later."

John walked out into the gardens in the evening sunshine, life was almost perfect, if only he could see someway to speed his progress to Knighthood and claim the prize of Tania as his wife, life would be idyllic.

He was deep in thought, as he gazed out over the water that was turning a deep red from the setting sun's reflection, when he felt a small hand slip into his.

" ello John," said Tania. "You are deep in thought, was it about me?"

"Yes, as a matter of fact it was, you are always in my thoughts," said John turning and catching her in his arms. A discreet cough signalled that the maid servant was still in attendance. John threw caution to the wind and kissed Tania long and lingering. Tania pushed him off.

"Calm yourself my sweet, we will be together soon."

"Not soon enough," retorted John. "I will burst if it goes on much longer."

They walked arm in arm round the garden until the chill of the night drove them inside. John lay in bed that night thinking of the slender body of Tania pressed against him, he was determined he would find a way to have time with her alone. He was woken by Sam and told that the tailor was here and he had slept in, Sam brought breakfast for him and helped him dress. John entered Sir Cedric's chambers to find a fussy little man measuring the Earl.

"Come John remove your doublet and let the Taylor measure you for new clothes. I want my man to look his best, Pilchard, or I will pop you in the sea to join your brothers."

The little man busied himself with his tape and notebook muttering and clucking, John could make out that he was named Pelcharde and not a 'leetle feesh'. Sir Cedric was in a good mood and chatted to John about the forthcoming coronation.

"Let's see your bow, John," and John obliged with his best bent knee.

"Yes, that will do, remember you will only have your ceremonial dagger so there is no sword to get in the way. I want you to come to me this afternoon so that I can discuss an important occasion with you."

As Sir Cedric told him this John felt a nervousness and wondered what he had, or had not done. He wandered to the stables after the midday meal and found Sam brushing Hammer so that his black coat shone.

"He is a beautiful animal sir, I have polished his harness too."

"You are very accomplished at what you do Sam, I could not be without you now."

John patted Hammer's neck and rubbed his nose and the great horse lowered his head and nuzzled at him. Walking back to the house to meet Sir Cedric John thought about the time that had passed since he met the Earl in the wood near the Smithy, he had certainly grown up in mind and body, he was now at a crossroads and was not sure what roads were available or which one to take. Whichever road it was he was determined Tania would be there with him, imagining life without her made his heart sink. Pulling his shoulders back he strode into the house and up to Sir Cedric's room.

"Come in and sit down John," invited the Earl. "How have your studies in the library been going?"

"My time has been a little limited sir, over the past months, but I have managed to study most of the important parts, and carry out some of the practical tasks."

"I have been watching your achievements over the time we have ben together and you have shown to me that you have the skills I have been looking for in leadership, fighting ability, managing the running of a Castle, sobriety and controlling your feelings, especially where my daughter is concerned. Overall I am saying that it is time that you won your spurs." Sir Cedric finished and John felt his heart leap and a tingling enveloped his body. "I would, naturally, carry out the investiture myself but an opportunity has presented itself that could not be missed."

The Earl smiled as he finished this last comment. "The day after the coronation the King will perform the ceremony to four young men who have come through a trying ordeal. You will spend the night, after the coronation, at prayer in the Abbey to prepare yourself for the investiture the next day, how say you John?"

"I am overwhelmed sir, and I thank you." John sat there speechless for a moment with the Earl smiling at him.

"I will see you in the morning when we shall take the boat to the Palace to be ready for the grand procession to the Abbey, until then I charge you not to meet with Tania until after your investiture, do you understand?" John rose from his chair and for some reason bowed low to the Earl and left the room. He walked out to the garden in a daze. Everything seemed suddenly to be going so fast. A mist was settling over the river and gave it a surreal atmosphere, a boat appeared and the white cloud swirled around the boatman partially hiding him, like a ghost he drifted past. The temperature dropped and darkness fell and John pulled his cloak around him and went back into the house.

When John awoke the next morning the house was buzzing with

excitement as everyone prepared for the coronation, whether they were taking part or just spectating. Sam came to John with his new clothes and helped him get dressed and then went down to the hall where Sir Cedric was gathering his friends and the staff that would accompany them. The company boarded their barge which joined the flotilla of river craft that was making it's way down the Thames to the Palace. As they alighted at Westminster quay they were met by large crowds that had come to see the spectacle, they lined the path all the way up to the Abbey, cheering at all the dignitaries as they passed by. Sir Cedric led his group to the great door of the Abbey where Marshals were ready to show them where to go. Sir Cedric with Tania at his side, looking magnificent in her court robes (so John thought) were placed near the coronation chair, while John found a place with other Squires and lesser nobles. John could see or hear, very little of the ceremony from where he was and was pleased when the King finally stood and the cry went up, "God Save the King" and the procession moved down towards the great door where the King appeared with his Queen Eleanor at his side, the crowds cheered and the procession proceeded to the Palace. When John arrived at the Palace he searched for Tania and found her with the Earl talking to a group of Nobles near the King. Sir Cedric called him over and presented him to Edward, the King.

John did his best bow as the King spoke. "So this is the young man you have been telling me of, Cedric. What have you to say for yourself for invading one of my Castles and then giving it to this rogue here?"

The stern face of the King turned to Sir Cedric as he said this. John was trembling inside but found his voice.

"There was an injustice sire, which had to be redressed so that your people could live and work in peace." The King smiled and then laughed. "I think we shall be hearing more of this young man in the future, twill be best for him to support us and not be against us I warrant."

Edward stretched out his hand for John to bow and kiss his ring.

" shall look forward to seeing him again tomorrow." Then he

turned to speak to others who were waiting to gain his attention. John thought of what the King had just said and thought of the ceremony that would take place tomorrow. Sir Cedric signalled to John to follow him to the side of the room. Tania stood by her father smiling at John and the Earl spoke to him.

"You may pay attention to my daughter later but now listen to me. There are many here who do not like my friendship with Edward so keep close council while you are here. Tonight you are to go with two young men, who I will introduce you to, and spend the night in the Abbey at prayer, they will guard you until morning when you will be brought to me, do you understand?" John nodded. "I will tell you what is going to happen next when I see you in the morning. Find Sam now and after the banquet tonight he will take you to a room where you can change."

John looked at Tania and received a smile in return, what a day this is, so much happening in such a short time! His mind went back to the books he had studied and he knew his Vigil was imminent.

The banquet was a sumptuous event, course after course washed down with wine or mead. John tried not to overindulge but still felt bloated when the servants began to clear the tables and the nobles began toasting the King and Queen. John slipped out and found Sam who led him to the Abbey and thence to a small side room where he changed into a simple white tunic and joined three other young men dressed the same. Accompanied by several other men, some John recognised as young knights they moved into a side chapel for Vespers followed by Mass.

After the service the three young Squires knelt at the altar rail and their Vigil began. John found it hard to focus his mind at first, then gradually he started to think of the road he had already travelled and the actions he had taken and the help he was going to need as a Knight. His prayers centred on his future life and the guidance he would need.

At dawn three very tired young men went back to the side room to dress, Sam was there to assist John and together they returned to the house. John went up to his room and collapsed on the bed for a couple of hours when Sam roused him to dress and go down to Sir Cedric. The Earl was standing by the front door resplendent in his court clothes, the sun reflected from the gold chain that hung round his chest.

"Ah, good morning John, though tis nearly afternoon, come we must not keep His Majesty waiting."

He strode off to the boat waiting to take them down river. John followed with Sam close behind. When they reached the barge they found Tania, her maid and another lady who was introduced as Lady Elizabeth, a friend. When they reached the Palace and entered the Great Hall John was surprised to see so many people and then he began to recognise people he knew, his father and mother with Joan, Carac and Gavin, Roger and Laila and even Father Aldred. A Marshall called everyone to order, trumpets sounded and the King and Queen entered and moved to the thrones. A Herald announced the four young men's achievements and that they had fulfilled their obligations toward Knighthood. John was called forward first and knelt in front of the King who raised his sword and touching him lightly on each shoulder.

"I dub thee Knight, rise Sir John Ivanson of Dunston, Knight of my realm." Giving the sword to an equerry the King received John's hands in his. "Do you, John of Dunston, swear to serve me faithfully and support me when I ask?"

"I do Sire," answered John.

Edward signalled him to rise and smiling sat back on the throne, the onlookers applauded and John moved to stand beside Sir Cedric. When the other squires had been invested everyone gathered around tables that had been laid out with food. John found his family and was congratulated by his father, mother and Joan. Jack asked.

"Where will you live, will you remain at Wymondham or will you settle at Dunston?"

John replied that he was not sure what would happen next until he had spoken to Sir Cedric. John tried to find Tania to introduce her to his family but he could not see her in the crowd, it was not until the evening that people began to disperse and John was able to take Jack and his family over to Sir Cedric and Tania. "Good to see you again Jack, I often think of that day when I came upon John by the woods and you and your wife looked after me so well, a great deal has happened since then. How is Dunston getting along now that de Brehalle has gone?"

"Very well sir, we need someone in the Castle to govern us though as people soon slip back into bad habits," answered Jack. Sir Cedric looked at John. "Perhaps we can rectify that soon, meanwhile Carac had better return to Dunston and make sure everything is as it should be."

Roger had been hovering on the edge of the group and John called him over.

"This is a very good friend of mine sir," he said to the Earl.

"I know you, do I not. A de Brehalle, brother of the one John sent back to Calais and an enemy of the King." "Not any more sir, now the Marshal of Stamford and a King's man should I be needed."

Roger drew himself up as he said this.

"And who is this young lady?" queried Sir Cedric.

"My wife Laila," answered Roger and there was a look from Joan. The Earl invited Jack and his family to return to the house with them and they left the Palace. That night John sat on his bed trying to remember all that had happened that day, his hand went to the little leather purse at his breast and took out the ring. Placing it on his finger he was surprised to find it fitted, he looked at the strange letters engraved on it.

The next few days were like a holiday to John, with his family around him and Tania accompanying him, life was good.

Roger and Laila were the first to leave after only a day as Roger's position meant he was needed back in Stamford. John promised to visit when he could, this would be sooner than both of them thought.

Jack left for Dunston soon after to tend to his business at the

Smithy, John would be visiting Dunston Castle soon he thought, Carac and Gavin decided to accompany Jack which would offer them protection should they need it. John and Tania were then left alone, apart from her maid, while Sir Cedric went to and fro from the Palace. They were all seated at dinner one evening when Sir Cedric announced that they would leave for Wymondham the next day, it was time to get back to the normal running of his estates. As they left the London house the sky was filled with black forbidding clouds, they had not journeyed far when the rain began to fall and they were forced to shelter under trees in a small wood, the men at arms were used to roughing it but the ladies in the party grumbled as they tried to pull their cloaks tighter around themselves. The horses too had a hangdog look as they stamped on the earth and started to turn it into thick mud, a break in the clouds came and the party moved on. Several days journeying brought them in sight of Wymondham and as they entered the town it was noticeably quieter than usual, a few people were out going about their business but they hardly looked at the travellers as they rode through even though it was their lord.

Sir Cedric told Gavin to go to the Mayor and ask for a report. The Castle came in sight and as they drew nearer they could see the drawbridge was raised.

"Sound a horn," said Sir Cedric. "I fear there is something wrong."

Carac sent a clear call on his horn and they saw the drawbridge lower and a rider came out of the Castle towards them, he rode up to Sir Cedric and spoke to him. The Earl turned towards them and ordered everyone to make haste to the Castle. When they had dismounted in the bailey Sir Cedric called John.

"There are large bands of armed men roaming the countryside and the scouts report that there is a man trying to get them organised and form a small army and take the town. You must ride to Dunston with all speed and find out what is happening there. I can only spare you one hundred more men and take Carac as well, report the position there as soon as you can."

There was feverish activity as John organised his party while the rest were being gathered to protect the town, he only had a few moments to speak to Tania and then they were off.

John approached Dunston with a little apprehension and was glad when he came out of the forest and could see the Castle, Carac sounded his horn again and John was surprised to see a drawbridge lowered.

"Someone has been hard at work in our absence," said John. "Do you know anything about this Carac?"

"I left instructions when I left for London, it was to be a surprise for you," replied the young Squire. John was even more amazed to find water in the moat.

"We found the original spring that keeps it full," explained Carac. They rode in over the bridge and halted in the Bailey, a troop of men at arms were lined up and as John dismounted the captain called out.

"Three cheers for Sir John." An embarrassed John smiled and acknowledged the welcome. Boorman was waiting by the main door and said to John.

" Welcome home sir, your rooms are ready," and he led John to the rooms de Brehalle's had occupied. They were large and well furnished and had double aspect windows looking out over the Bailey and the countryside. John sat in a chair and thought of the day, Boorman had said, 'welcome home' but was this home? The Castle had been taken in Sir Cedric's name and was part of his lands, what was the future going to bring to John, he did not want to be an adventuring knight, that would mean no Tania, in fact little had really changed in his situation. During the following weeks John and Carac toured the tenant farms, mills and all the businesses that came under the jurisdiction of the Castle. Sir Cedric had confirmed the boundary marks of all the estates when he was in London and overall the Earl had gained considerable land. Everywhere they went they were told of the fear people had that they would be attacked by marauding groups of outlaws. John promised regular patrols and he sent out scouts to search for these groups but had no success to date. They had been back in the Castle for only two days when one of the scouts came in to report that a large body of men were gathering south of Saxlingham and there was definitely a leader who was organising them. John sent a courier to Sir Cedric with this news and asked for more men to protect the Castle and villages, he also started training the men for war.

At the evening meal John spoke to Carac and his captains. “We must be ready to repel any attack on the Castle and organise skirmish parties to reduce the size of the rebel band. Strike and disappear, will be the order until we are ready to take them on in battle.”

Carac nodded. “The Castle is ready and I know we can hold it with the minimum number of men, the moat is full and the walls repaired, we also have improved the archer slits as you suggested.”

“From the reports I have,” said John, “they do not appear to be well organised and they have no heavy weapons, but I intend to have a look at them myself tonight.”

Carac was not happy about that, however he agreed that if John was well protected it would be useful for him to see the opposition and judge their strength. That evening a group of men came from the town to volunteer as soldiers, several had weapons from past campaigns. As the darkness spread over the countryside, John and seven men rode out of the Castle towards Saxlingham. They stopped at a farm near to where the outlaws had been seen last. The farmer, one of John’s tenants, hid their horses in the barn, he told them where the outlaws were camped and John and his men started off in that direction. The camp fires were the first sign of the enemy and John crept stealthily forward. The outlaws were enjoying a supper of roast pig, stolen from the farms, and were relaxed and taking their ease. In the light from the fires John could see a man talking earnestly to half a dozen better dressed men, he was gesturing towards Saxlingham and sweeping his hand across his body. John suddenly started, he knew the man, it was Ralf de Brehalle. How had he returned to England and then here? John crept back to a safe distance and signalled his men to go back to the farm. Once mounted they rode quickly back to the Castle. John found Carac and told him what they had found.

“It’s obvious he wants to try and take the Castle back,” said John. “I did not see enough men for him to be able to do that but I am wondering who was he talking to.”

Sir Cedric’s scouts came back to tell him that there was an increase in the outlaws and deserters congregating to the South west of the Castle and town. They told the Earl that there were approximately 200 in the main group. Sir Cedric called his captains together and decided to use his cavalry to disperse them and drive them south west if they could, the Kings army was mustering in that direction in preparation to march on Wales.

With his normal garrison and the addition of volunteers from his tenants Sir Cedric mustered over 1000 men, a good 400 were cavalry. Leaving sufficient numbers to protect the Castle and town he decided to send 300 of his men at arms to Dunston. After several successful sorties against the outlaws they did break them up with most making for the South. The Earl kept patrols out around the town and countryside to keep the outlaws on the move, they did not appear to want to stand and fight.

John was pacing the battlements when he noticed movement at the edge of the forest. Approaching towards the Castle he could see a column of men.

“They are ours, I can see a standard and that is Sir Cedric at the head,” said an excited guard.

John descended to the Bailey to welcome the troops who were crossing the drawbridge with the Earl riding Snow.

“Thought I would come and see for myself how you are coping,” said Sir Cedric. They went inside to the hall and John explained his strategy. Sir Cedric listened and made comment.

“I agree that it will the right thing to do to attack first while they are still organising themselves. I am surprised that Ralph is involved, I wonder who is behind him.”

That night John moved out with 100 skirmishers and crept near to the outlaws camp.

"Carac, take 50 men to the left and on my signal attack, kill as many as you can and withdraw quickly."

John waited, the clouds hid the light from the moon and all was still. The horn rang out and the night exploded into yelling and shouting. As John drew his sword he felt his ring hot on his finger, as he went forward his sword felt light in his hand and it seemed to have a life of its own as it lunged and sliced at the outlaws. As quickly as it had started the fighting finished and the skirmishers came together. As the group hurried back to the Castle Carac reported he had lost three men and John had two missing, their bodies were carried back. Once they were behind the Castle walls John called them all together and congratulated them on a job well done. They had succeeded in killing and injuring a good number of the outlaws.

"Get some sleep now as I expect some action in the morning."

Joining Sir Cedric in the Hall John discussed the night's activities.

"They will not get caught like that again," said the Earl. "It will keep them awake tomorrow night, if they are still here."

John retired to his bed and soon fell into a sound sleep.

As the sun rose the following morning the troops were ready and John gave his orders. They were to march out towards the outlaws camp and form a three prong attack to sweep the enemy out of the woods. John made it clear that they must take prisoners especially any high ranking persons. The signal was given to move off with John at the Centre, Carac on the left flank and the guard captain taking the right. As they approached the woods a ragged line of men stumbled clear of the trees, some leaders trying to get them into some sort of order. John halted and called the archers to draw bows, the first flight decimated the front line of the outlaws, this caused more confusion. Five mounted men tried to gain control and John guessed one of these would be Ralph, he put his mounted men to the charge and tried to head off the five, who attempted to retreat into the trees. John's charge brought them into contact quickly and he soon found himself facing Ralph yet again. The two men circled their horses and suddenly Hammer decided it was time to attack and jumped forward slamming into Ralph's mount and unseating him. John, on Hammer, towered over the fallen man and shouted to him to yield. Ralph got up onto his feet and in a fit of anger rushed at John, Hammer neatly sidestepped and John slid from his back and drew his sword. The two men faced each other, Ralph full of anger carelessly rushed at John who parried the thrust and dealt a heavy blow to Ralph's leg. He stood over the fallen man and again asked him to yield. Ralph dragged himself up onto his good leg and made a swipe at John but it missed and the momentum made him stagger into another man who quickly turned and drove his sword through Ralph's side, piecing his heart. Before the man could withdraw his weapon John had his sword at his throat and the man yielded.

"I thought he was one of your lot," the outlaw exclaimed. John knelt by Ralph but as he removed his helm he breathed his last. John remounted Hammer and looked around to find that most of the fighting had ceased and his men were rounding up the outlaws. Carac had four men closely guarded and John rode over to find they were Frenchmen.

"Take them back to the Castle and put them in the tower until we find out what they are doing here."

With the death of Ralph the conflict ceased, some outlaws faded away into the woods but most of those who had not been killed were rounded up and marched back to the Castle.

The prisoners were crowded into the Bailey and John tried to pick out the leaders, those he sent to the dungeons. In fact John knew he could not feed more than about 100 more men so he decided to march them off to Norwich where they could be put to the ships. Sir Cedric joined John when he questioned the Frenchmen they found that Ralph had convinced them that there was a rich reward if they helped him to regain Dunston. They were becoming suspicious the night of John's attack and had been arguing with Ralph and were talking of returning home with the men they had brought with them.

"Well, your men will be home before you if they are some of the ones sent to Norwich." said John. The men were sent back to the tower and John and the Earl discussed sending a message to their families for a ransom to release them.

Eating a breakfast together John and the Earl talked over the previous days happenings.

"This rabble could have been larger and more aggressive had they been led by better men," commented Sir Cedric. "You adopted the right strategy of surprise and your men are well trained. I leave this Castle and the surrounding lands to your care, we will sort out the details with the clerks when you are next in Wymondham and agree the boundaries and the annual tax that I shall expect. How say you John?"

John sat silently for a moment, everything was happening so quickly.

"I am honoured sir and I will do all I can to justify the faith you have put in me."

"Good," said Sir Cedric as he rose from the table. "I will go back to Wymondham now and no doubt I will be see you again very soon." He smiled as he said this and clasped John's arm.

After the Earl had left John called Carac to him and they arranged to meet at Dunston Smithy by midday to visit the larger Tenants. John rode out to visit his father and found him and his lads very busy, the forge was burning brightly and there was a sound of hammers at work on the iron. Jack saw John approaching and stopped his work to greet his son.

"It is good to see you son, we heard of the trouble at Wymondham and that you had beaten the outlaws. We were worried that some may come this way but we have seen no one."

"That eases my mind, father," he said, as they walked back home. "I see the house is finished, you have made good time in completing it."

"There are still some finishing touches to make but I wanted to make sure it was complete before winter. The builder is now working in the village helping with the stronger houses. We have started a village fund so that eventually all will have better houses."

"A very good idea and when we know more about the Castle finances I will make a contribution, we need to support our villagers so that the work on the farms does not suffer," replied John. "Sir Cedric is looking at ideas over at Wymondham to do the same."

These ideas were new in the countryside and John understood not all land owners agreed with him and the Earl, they said it would make the serfs idle if you made them too comfortable. Some Lords were indeed too harsh and the land suffered. Carac arrived and he and John, with Sam and a small escort, rode off to visit the rest of the farmers.

II

Roger was getting restless, the town was quiet and his guards kept control mostly without the need for him to be there. The baby was due very soon and he was a little nervous that he would become too domesticated and he wasn't ready for that. He decided to visit John and find out what was happening in Dunston, he would be back for the birth, he insisted to Laila, who was not pleased with his decision.

"You have a maid now and many lady friends and I shall not be long, but I must find out if there is anything left for me at Dunston," explained Roger to an unreceptive Laila.

Roger set off for Dunston early, he enjoyed riding at this time, there were less travellers on the road and air was crisp and invigorating. His horse sensed his mood and broke into a trot that soon ate up the miles. He was looking forward to meeting John and seeing the Castle again, it had been his home for many years. His thoughts turned to the future and what he should do when he went back to Laila, if God was kind he would be a father and that brought extra responsibilities. The life he now led was comfortable enough but it no longer held a challenge, he thought about his soldiering days but they were gone unless there was another war. In this thoughtful frame of mind he found himself riding through

Dunston common. Coming out of the trees he could see smoke curling up from the houses in the Village as the inhabitants prepared their evening meal. He was ready to eat too as the bread and cheese he had consumed for his midday meal was long forgotten. He was hoping that he would be in time for supper at the Castle, that is if he was welcome. Past the Village he saw the welcoming lights from the Castle windows, he also noticed the new drawbridge and moat. The drawbridge was up and he could see a guard on the battlements so whoever was in the Castle was prepared to keep out unwelcome visitors. Roger cried out to the guard that he was a friend of John's and wished to visit him. After a short wait the drawbridge rumbled down and Roger crossed into the Castle. John was there to meet him and the two of them went to the great hall. Roger's eyes were opened to the improvements that had been made and he could see that John had definitely taken charge of the Castle. He noticed one or two of the old servants and felt pleased John had retained them. Then a familiar voice offered him a glass of wine.

" oorman, how are you, a joy to see you here and looking well," exclaimed Roger.

"Thank you sir I am very well and happy serving Sir John," eplied the Steward.

John explained that Boorman had been invaluable when he first took the Castle and in a sadder vein he told Roger how his brother had met his death. Roger was quiet for a moment and then said to John.

"My brother always thought he was bigger than he really was and I knew he would never be able to govern the land like our father, I am sad that he died but I am glad you did not kill him. As you have been granted the Castle and lands our family has no claim and I accept the situation and wish you every success."

John clasped Roger's hand and smiled at him and said. "Come let's eat, the cook is still the same and a very good one too." After they had finished their meal the two of them walked the battlements, a full moon lit their path and they could see its reflection in the surrounding moat.

"So you are soon to be a father. That will be quite a commitment to bring up a child."

Roger replied that he was looking forward to the challenge but he knew in his heart that he was not sure that he wanted the responsibility now. The next day as Roger looked round the Castle he could see the improvements that John had already made and he suddenly felt sad, for his father and Ralph. He pondered on what had happened to Avice and his mother as he had heard nothing since they went to Norwich. The following day he found John in the stables told him he was leaving. John wished him well and said to let him know when the baby was born and he would come to the Christening.

II

Over the years activity increased on the land that John governed, sheering was in progress in preparation for the Charter Fair at Wymondham. John was discussing the finances of the Castle with Boorman and commented that they should have their own Fair if it meant better revenue to the Castle.

"Yes," replied the Steward. "That certainly would help in many ways. We would attract more traders and we would be able to deal direct with the cloth merchants from France or Bruges." John instructed him to find out the way to obtain the Charter.

"It is time we employed a Reeve to look after our lands, see if you can find someone suitable and I will talk to them on my return. I am going to Wymondham with Carac to talk to the Earl."

On arriving at Wymondham Castle, John asked a Page the whereabouts of the Lady Tania and he was told she had gone to her workroom. He bounded up the stairs and knocking on the door he heard a voice bid him enter and there was Tania. John gathered her in his arms and kissed her passionately, the maid squealed. "Sir, Sir, that is not allowed, the Earl will be cross."

John released Tania who stood gazing up at him with a smile on her flushed face, he dropped to one knee and said, "Tania, will you be my wife and share the rest of our lives together?"

" Oh yes please," Tania replied and pulled John to his feet so she could kiss him again.

The maid squealed again but this time she clapped her hands in delight.

"I am going to your father now so pray that he will agree to our betrothal." He left and went to Sir Cedric's room.

"Come in," called the Earl, responding to John's loud knock.

"Excuse me sir, I have something important to ask you," John said a little breathlessly.

"Your wool is not ready for the Fair?" interrupted Sir Cedric.

"No sir that is fine it's…"

"You want to give me your ideas for your shield," said the Earl cutting in again.

"No sir, I want…"

"I know, you want to return my men to me, well that's good news" said Sir Cedric, interrupting for the third time.

"It's not that at all sir, I.."

"You want to marry my daughter." This time the Earl's voice was softer and John was not expecting this. "No sir ….I mean yes sir that is what I have been trying to ask you," said a confused John. The Earl stood smiling at John and clasped his arms .

"I am delighted this day has come at last, John. You have waited very patiently and I give my blessing willingly." John stood looking at the Earl and heard himself saying, 'thank you' but seemed rooted to the spot. Sir Cedric laughed and said. "You had better go and tell her, don't you think, and then both of you come down to see me."

John hurried back to Tania who hugged and kissed him and they both went down to the Earl. Sir Cedric held his daughter and stretched out his hand to John.

"You have my blessing and I am very happy to see that your

love has endured the test of time. If you are agreeable I would like the wedding to be soon and I hope you will choose the Abbey for the ceremony." The Earl looked at Tania as he spoke.

"I am sure we agree to both points," she said. They sat down together to discuss the plans and when they had finished John and Tania left to go to the Abbey and meet with the Abbot. Abbot Filbert was in his garden when they arrived, he stood and stretched his back.

"This is a job for a younger man, my old bones don't take kindly to this bending. What can I do for you young people?"

"We have come to ask you to marry us," replied John.

The Abbot smiled and asked them to accompany him to his office where they discussed the service.

"The Earl will want the best for his daughter," said the Abbot. "We will not disappoint him, or you."

The day was fixed for three weeks hence and they returned to the Castle with the news.

"It hardly gives me time to get everything done," said Tania. "There's the dress and all the arrangements, it's too soon."

Sir Cedric calmed her and asked if she would mind being married in her mother's dress which he had kept all these years. Tania had seen the dress and said at once that she would love to wear it. The dress was beautiful and had been made for the Earl's wife in Flanders. They discussed their plans as they sat down to dinner and the events of the day began to become clear to the young couple, they kept smiling at each other and then at Sir Cedric, who smiled back. Tania excused herself and went to bed leaving the Earl and John still talking.

"I want Carac to come back here so I can carry on with his training." aid the Earl.

"That fits in with my plans as now Sam is older, and bigger, I would make him my Squire and start his training," said John.

"Good," continued Sir Cedric. " ou must manage your own affairs now, especially as you will have a wife, and next a family.

The lands you have produce a good return and your vassals and peasants do not give you much trouble do they?"

"Not yet," said John. "I intend to improve our relationship with them so that everyone benefits."

They both became tired and decided to leave further details until later. John wanted to get back to Dunston as quickly as possible to make sure all was well and to see his family and tell them his news. He wanted to go tomorrow and take Tania with him if the Earl would agree.

John left early in the morning without Tania, she said she could not ride at the moment and did not feel very well. John put Anvil to a fast trot as he was eager to get back to Dunston. John arrived at Dunston Castle just as the light was failing. He summoned Boorman to bring him up to date with what had been happening. "I have a man to see you regarding the position of Reeve," said Boorman. "He has held that position in Leicestershire but wants to come nearer to his home in Norwich."

John asked when the man could be seen and Boorman said he would arrange it for tomorrow.

The next morning Boorman brought the new man to John who was sitting in the great hall.

"What is your name?" Asked John. "I have been told you have had the position of Reeve elsewhere."

"My name is Roderick, my father was a shepherd west of Norwich, he and my mother died of dropsy and my brother now has the flock. I worked as an apprentice to the Reeve at Leicester but when the Earl was killed we were dismissed. I wish to return to Norfolk sir."

John looked at him intently and perceived a tall well built man of about 25 years who returned his gaze, but not insolently. John offered him the position on a trial basis for six months and Roderick accepted. "Tomorrow you will accompany me when I visit the Tenants and we will discuss what I want you to do after the trip."

Roderick bowed and left. John called Boorman to stay, and told him of the forthcoming marriage. “Congratulations, my Lord, I will hire some new maids to serve her Ladyship when she arrives.” “Good” aid John. “She will bring her two personal maids with her, they will need accommodation.”

“It shall be done sir.”

John called for Sam to come to the Hall, when he arrived he looked nervous.

“I have groomed your horses sir and they are comfortable in the stables.”

“Thank you Sam but that is not what I want you for. You have served me well as a Page but it is time you moved on.”

Sam looked even more nervous.

“Would you serve me as a Squire?”

Sam grinned and suddenly knelt on one knee and said he would, and faithfully. John stood and grasped Sam’s hand to raise him up.

“Tomorrow I want you to come to me and we will discuss what you need and what the training will entail.” Sam,still grinning, said he would be there and walked out of the Hall even taller than he had entered. John turned to Boorman.

“That’s cheered him up, now I need a new Page for my personal needs.”

“I have a lad who is the son of one of the cook’s and would be very suitable,” answered Boorman. John agreed he could start as soon as Boorman had instructed him in his duties.

The next morning John went out to the stable to have Anvil saddled for him to ride to his parents.

Jack and Matilda were delighted to see their son and receive the news of the impending wedding. He spent some time discussing with his father some work he required carrying out at the Castle, he asked where the Mason was and had he finished in the Village.

“I want to make some alterations to the Castle and also some additions, if he wants the work it will take him over the winter period.”

Jack asked John when would he be at the Castle, as he had a delivery to make. John said he would have time on his return from Wymondham but was puzzled as he wondered what the delivery could be, perhaps it was something Carac had arranged.

Joan returned from her trip to the church and was excited to hear the news of the wedding. John passed on a message from Tania.

"Tania would like you to be one of her Ladies, if you are willing. If you are, she asks you to come back with me to have the dress made by her seamstress. Tania likes to design and make her own dresses so I expect she will be involved. What do you say Joan?"

Joan was speechless for a moment and then threw her arms round John and said she would be delighted and honoured.

"You can stay at the Castle, if mother doesn't mind being on her own. We have plenty of room."

John arrived back at Dunston Castle to find Roderick with Boorman going over the lists of Tenants and their rents.

"I see there are not too many who are in arrears," said the Reeve. "Not like in Leicester where the Earl was too lax in collecting what was owed."

"I find that firm persuasion without actual force brings the best results." aid John. "I explain how it is in their own interest to get the best from their land, or flocks, and if they are fair with me I will do all I can to help them. After all it ends up helping me."

Roderick agreed and thought to himself that it was unusual for such a wise head to be these young shoulders. Sam entered and said Anvil was ready to ride again so the three of them set off to visit the tenants.

Joan arrived the next day with her horse loaded with all her baggage.

"Come to the hall and we will have a meal before we depart," said John. "I will have your baggage loaded on to our pack horse. This is Sam my Squire."

Sam bowed and thought to himself that the young lady would make a very agreeable companion on their ride to Wymondham. After their meal John set off with his party of Joan, Sam and six men-at-arms. The afternoon was warm and John thought how he loved this part of the country, he still found it hard to take in all that had happened to him over the past years. The sun had set and night had closed in as they neared Wymondham Castle, Sam blew his horn and the gates were open for them as they arrived.

Tania met them at the door and greeted John with a hug and a kiss, she grasped Joan's arm and they went off chatting together. They passed Gavin on the way who turned and stared after Joan.

"Will your sister be staying long?" he asked John.

"At least until the wedding," replied John, as he went to see Sir Cedric in his room. After reporting to the Earl what he had been doing at Dunston they fell to discussing the wedding.

Tania and Joan hurried to Tania's rooms and there Tania brought out her mother's wedding dress.

"Oh it's beautiful," said Joan, "you will look so pretty in it."

Tania then held Joan's arm and they went to the sewing room to look at material for the bridesmaids.

John called Sam to him in the morning. "Sam, you need a name that more befits a Squire, what was your father's name?"

"My real name is Stephen sir, and we are Fletchers."

"Good then, Stephen Fletcher, follow me." John led the new Stephen to the library to show him the books but Stephen could not read.

"I will ask Carac to school you in your duties while we are here and I must see the Priest about teaching you to read and write when we return."

They found some books with pictures and Stephen was enthralled and John could see a light in his eyes that foretold of someone who would learn quickly.

II

Roger arrived back in Stamford in the late evening and after stabling his horse went into the house. He surprised Laila, who was resting. They embraced and Roger could feel the large mound of her stomach where the baby lay.

"How are you?" queried Roger. "Are you looking after yourself?"

Laila replied that with the maid and her friends she was fine although very tired. Roger told her about his visit to Dunston and how there was nothing there for him and that John was now the Knight controlling the lands that had belonged to his father. Laila sensed the disappointment that Roger felt.

" hy don't you go down to the Inn and the barracks, to see your men and friends, I am going to bed to rest?" Roger decided that he would do that and set off for the Inn. Except for those men on duty, most of his men were relaxing over a jug of ale. They were pleased to see him and the sergeant told him that the town had been relatively quiet whilst he had been away. After several jugs and ribald chatter the men began to drift away leaving Roger slumped over a table.

"Have you no home to go to?" said a soft voice and Roger opened his eyes to find a girl leaning over him showing an ample bosom. "You'd best come with me and rest your head."

Roger staggered to his feet and followed her. When Roger awoke his head throbbed and his mouth was like a dried parchment, it was a few moments before he realised where he was. A movement by his side reminded him he was not alone in the bed as the girl who had taken him to her room sat up.

"Time you was gone and leave money on my dresser."

Roger levered himself upright and when the room had stopped spinning, managed to dress himself and find his purse. He left with the girl giving him a parting word that she would be happy to see him again.

In the morning air Roger gradually began to take stock of the situation. He walked back to his house and thought what he would say to Laila. Arriving at the house he was surprised to find the front door open and several women rushing about. Laila's maid came to him. "Oh sir, your wife is in labour and there is a problem!" Roger quickly went to the bedroom where he found the midwife trying to calm Laila who was moaning and screaming alternately.

"Come Roger, you should not be in here," said one of the women, whom Roger knew. "We will tell you when she has delivered."

Roger moved as though in a dream, and went down to the stables. He could still hear Laila's screams as he stroked his horse. "Why punish her when it was me who sinned," he said. Then all went quiet and he went back into the house just as one of the women came down the stairs.

"Come into the parlour Roger," she said and Roger followed her into the room.

"How is Laila, can I see her and what of the baby?" The woman turned to him.

"The midwife did all she could but the baby was born too soon and did not survive."

Roger stood in shocked silence for a moment and then made for the door. He ran upstairs to the bedroom and stopped at the open door. The midwife turned to him and stood back so he could see Laila laying stiff and white faced, the strain and anguish still showing what she had gone through. Roger dropped to his knees beside the bed and tears streamed down his face.

" 'm sorry my love, so sorry. I shall never forgive myself for what I have done."

He turned to the midwife who shook her head and said the strain had been too much for Laila. Roger asked where was the child and she pointed to a wrapped bundle on the dresser. Roger stood up and walked over to the dresser, the midwife stood in front of him. "You don't want to see sir, I shall take it away."

"What was it?" cried Roger.

"A little boy sir, it never drew breath."

Roger flung himself out of the room and went out of the house. He walked round the town, not seeing anyone or anything, gradually his mind became clearer and he knew he must go back to that house where his love lay shattered, a love he had broken and now was lost for ever.

On the day of the funeral there were only mourners from Laila's family and friends and they kept their distance from Roger. Word had spread about what had happened and even his own men were distant to him.

After Laila's affairs had been settled, such as they were, Roger went to see the Mayor and resigned his position saying that he could not continue.

"What will you do now?" asked the Mayor.

"Go and visit my sister and mother in Norwich, after that, who knows."

Roger left Stamford the following morning, riding his stallion and leading a laden packhorse. He passed through the guard house in silence and headed out into the country, he did not look back, it was a period in his life that he would try to forget.

Roger arrived at the house where his mother and sister were staying to find his mother had also died and Avis was about to get married to a young, but successful, butcher. He stayed with his sister for the wedding but became listless and decided to travel to Nottingham where he had heard the Sheriff there was looking for good men. Several days later Roger arrived in Nottingham and made his way to the Castle where he was hoping he could find a position. His funds were now very low and he needed to find gainful employment, it was not however, to be with the Sheriff. Without sufficient funds to spend long in the city Roger headed out to the forest. The first night he camped by a stream, caught himself a rabbit and was cooking it over a fire when two armed men walked into his campsite and demanded to know what he was doing there? Roger stood up.

"I am just a traveller and I have stopped for the night, who are you?"

As he spoke he moved slowly into a position that he could see both men. He suddenly drew his sword and threatened both men.

"Now leave me alone or I might have more than rabbit lying here before me." The men laughed and several archers appeared through the bushes led by a man Roger recognised.

"Robert, is this how you greet a friend?"

Robert greeted him and asked what he was doing here in the forest. Roger told him of the events that had led him here. Robert was sympathetic and led the way to their camp, which surprised Roger. The camp was like a small woodland village with a small forge and several cooking fires.

"Where did all these people come from?" asked Roger.

"They are villagers who have been turned out of their homes or are being persecuted by the Normans," explained Robert. "We are classed as outlaws and the Sheriff often sends men into the forest to try and capture us, but we know the forest and it's paths and the soldiers do not."

Robert also disclosed that they obtained money by holding up travellers who looked rich enough to have heavy purses, they would then pass some of this to the poorer villagers.

"We are a happy community and we even have a Priest who looks after our souls and performs weddings and funerals," said Robert. He asked Roger to join them and as Roger sat down to a meal he thought maybe this would help to alleviate his black moods. The next day Roger realised that there was quite a sizeable fighting force gathering in the forest. One morning as the camp was rising and preparing for the day, a lookout came in and went up to Robert to report a small caravan of people were going through the forest. It was a bishop on his way to Nottingham and his purse would be fat, full of indulgence payments and offerings to the Saint in his church.

"I can see he is ready to do good works for the parish," said Robert with a grin.

The men grouped around him as he outlined how they would ambush the travellers.

"No unnecessary violence now, if they surrender peacefully we will let them go. Come with us Roger and see how we treat these fat leeches."

The 'hold up' went peacefully enough as the soldiers with the bishop realised there were too many outlaws for them to fight. With loud protestations the group were walked to the edge of the forest and sent on their way.

"That should get some of the fat off him," laughed Robert. "By the time he gets to Nottingham he will have lost some of his lard and all of his money."

When they arrived back in camp everyone crowded round to look at the horses and the weapons they had captured, the cash, Roger noted, went into a chest that Robert had where he slept. Roger stayed with Robert for several months and he witnessed many travellers being relieved of their valuables. However he decided this life was not what he wanted, it had filled a gap and increased his funds but it was time to move on. One day a group of men came into the forest on their way to join King Edwards army in Wales and Roger decided to join them and said farewell to Robert and his band of outlaws. With his new companions Roger travelled to Wales to join the King's army.

II

John stayed another day discussing plans with the Earl and enjoying the evening with Tania and Joan who were planning the wedding. He thought that when it was all over and they were settled in Dunston he would have the time to organise his tenants and land to provide the maximum profit for all to enjoy. His plan was that all his Tenants should work to a common goal with a fund that could be accessed by all, under his watchful eye. By sharing the wealth that they created there would be more purpose to their lives and an incentive to increase living standards.

John and Stephen with their men arrived back in Dunston to find John's father waiting for them.

"Did you have a good journey?" said Jack.

"Yes, thank you," replied John as he handed his horse to Stephen. "Is there some trouble?"

"Not at all John, I wanted you to have this gift I made. It was really for your investiture but I did not finish it in time." Jack paused and led John into the Castle and into the Hall. Supported on a stand was a beautiful, complete, suit of armour, it had been tempered so that it glistened in the candle light, a blue black colour. John was overcome and clasped his father to his breast.

"Thank you father a truly magnificent gift, I must try it on." John stripped to his undershirt, he asked Stephen, who had just come in, to fetch his protective suit that he wore under armour. Stephen assisted John to don the armour and it fitted perfectly. John stomped around the hall stretching his arms and making jabs in the air.

" It is so light, can it be strong enough to deflect a blow?"

His father laughed and answered him, "I have worked with metal all my life and you will find this withstands any blows aimed at it."

John tried the Helm and again it fitted well to his head with a beaked visor and a ridge across the crown, there was a fitting for his crest when he chose what it would be.

"I have also a shield but I do not know your crest."

John told him he was still undecided but would tell him as soon as he had made a choice. When John had divested himself, with Stephen's help, they sat down to a meal together and John told his father that Joan would stay with Tania until after the wedding.

John, Stephen and Roderick rode out to visit the Tenants and see what was happening on the land, he was still waiting for news of his application to hold a market in Dunston. The wool buyers would be visiting Wymondham soon and he wanted to make sure there was a good amount from Dunston. They rode out to their furthest farm in the East, near to the fens, and found a cluster of cottages where the men were gathering reeds in bundles. They stopped and chatted with the people who said, as far as they were concerned they had no landlord and paid no taxes to anyone. Their main concern was the occasional raider who missed Yarmouth and Lowestoft and ended up pillaging their settlement. John said that if they sent a message to him he would come to their aid for the price of a few bundles of reeds. This was acceptable to them but they would talk to their leader before agreeing. As they rode away John turned to the other two.

"It is wise to have a lookout in this area, especially if there are raiders maybe from France. We need to be ready to protect our lands. We must meet this leader of theirs."

When they had completed their tour they returned to the Castle where John settled down to study the finances. Father Aldred had taught him well and he had a good grasp of mathematics, he needed it as the Castle accounts had been poorly kept by de Brehalle, as long as the sale of their wool reached expectation then there would be money to spare. The arable land and the cattle also needed to produce a profit so that the farms could be updated both in equipment and their buildings. With these thoughts spinning around in his head John retired to bed. As he lay waiting for the welcome sleep to overcome him he thought of Tania and of his approaching wedding, he was a lucky man, he prayed there were no evil happenings waiting to disrupt his plans.

The day of the wedding drew near and a messenger arrived to ask John to journey to Wymondham Abbey for a rehearsal. John, Stephan, a page and six men-at-arms set off for Wymondham. They stayed at the Earl's Castle overnight and John sat with Tania for the evening meal, which was the closest he was allowed. Tania and Joan kept glancing at each other and smiling throughout the meal. Sir Cedric was in a good mood and when all the ladies had departed he joined the remaining men to enjoy drinking with them. The following morning John's head was feeling a little sore as he walked the battlements to get fresh air, but by the afternoon it had cleared and the rehearsal went well. On the morning of the wedding many of the guests that Sir Cedric had invited had travelled some distance and started arriving early and the Castle was filled with talk and laughter. The weather was bright with the sun shinning and everyone in an excited mood. When John arrived at the Abbey there were many people outside wishing him well and when he stepped through the great door he was astounded at the number of people who had come. As he walked to the front he noticed many Lords and Ladies that he had met at the London house, they were smiling and nodding to him as he passed. Gavin stood at the foot of the altar steps waiting for him, as John had asked him to stand for him. Just behind were Carac and Stephen looking very knightly in their new clothes. John took his place and at that moment trumpeters sounded the arrival of the bride. As the bride and her father entered the Abbey choir sang accompanied by several instruments, John stole a glance down the aisle and gasped as his eyes beheld a vision floating down the aisle towards him. When at last Tania was by his side he thought his mouth would split from the smile he'd had upon it. Joan arranged Tania's dress and John noticed that her own dress was a beautiful golden one. John hardly heard the words of the service and had to be prompted occasionally to say the replies. The service seemed extraordinary long to him, not that he had any recollection to go by. At last the Abbot pronounced the blessing and with Tania on his arm John started the walk down the aisle a married man.

There were crowds outside the Abbey, everyone from Wymondham had turned out to see the couple and they shouted and cheered as he and Tania walked to the carriage that the Earl had arranged. They drove slowly back to the Castle waving to bystanders, the carriage was not the most comfortable of vehicles but in their euphoric state this did not interfere with their embrace although it did cause one or two giggles. The Castle staff who were not at the Abbey, were lined up to welcome them home and guide them to the Great Hall where a wedding feast had been prepared, it crossed John's mind that he would like to have gone straight to their room! The guests soon started arriving and Tania and John's arms were soon aching from all the well wishing handshakes. The food was sumptuous and the wine and ale flowed, Sir Cedric was on good form and welcomed John into his family and not to be outdone Jack did the same for Tania following up with the fact that she could call on Matilda at any time, specially when baby sitting was eventually needed which brought laughter from the guests and blushes from Tania. The celebrations were reaching a raucous state when John looked at Tania and whispered that it was time leave them to it. Amongst some very suggestive comments they tried to slip away to their room, but it was not to be as a merry crowd carried the pair saying it was a local tradition, John was worried that they would stay. When at last everyone had gone and they were alone they stood facing each other in the large bedroom and slowly began to undress. John beheld a beautiful woman before him and he enveloped her in his arms, their mouths met and still clasped together they finally reached the large bed that lay behind its curtains, these will hide their first night as a married couple.

Dawn filtered through the windows and lit the embroidered curtains that surrounded the bed, John awoke and sensed the warm body laying next to him, he thought of the previous night and his body began to react, turning he reached for Tania and thought, there is plenty of time before we need to rise. Later that morning the two newlyweds entered the hall to find it completely deserted, a maid entered, giggled and ran out. Merek appeared and asked if they required any food but there would be the usual midday meal in a short while, John and Tania smiled at each other and said they would wait. Merek said that the Earl had gone hunting and would be back towards sunset. The happy couple walked out into the gardens, it was a clear day, if a little cold, as autumn approached.

"We must go to Dunston soon," said John. "I must find out what is going on there and we shall be shearing before long."

Tania nestled closer to him as they walked arm in arm. "I will have to sort out the household too, I am taking some of my ladies, including Joan, so I hope there is room for us."

John laughed and said there was ample room and she could bring whoever she liked as long as she was happy. When they came back to the Castle Sir Cedric had returned with a large deer, he was smiling as he saw them approach.

"You decided to awake then. I thought I might have to batter the door down to see if you were still alive." Tania blushed and

John stammered. “No one woke us.”

The Earl laughed and walked with them back inside the Keep. Two days later John, Tania, Joan, Stephen, John’s men at arms and two ladies with four pack horses rode off to Dunston. The day was bright and clear and as they rode through the forest they could smell the wood smoke from the charcoal burner’s fires, it was almost idyllic. They came to Dunston as the sun was setting and a gentle mist was forming over the grass. They crossed the drawbridge and entered the bailey where the whole Castle had assembled to greet them. Boorman, resplendent in a new coat, assisted Tania to dismount and welcomed her. A banquet had been prepared in the Great Hall for all the staff and as John and Tania took their seats at the top of the table everyone rose and Boorman proposed a toast to the couple. John looked down the tables and felt proud of the people who were now their people, almost like a big family he thought. Many of the Tenants had been invited and the atmosphere was merry and light hearted. Some wandering minstrels had been hired and one of their number was an amateur Juggler who kept them entertained. At a suitable time Tania and the Ladies withdrew and the men fell to drinking and telling stories, some of which were quite unbelievable. John remained for a while and then made off to his rooms. Tania was in their bedroom and Joan had just finished putting away her clothes when John arrived.

“How are you liking looking after my wife?” queried John.

“I like it fine sir,” answered Joan.

“You don’t have to address me as sir, and certainly not in private.”

“You are a Knight and I was brought up to be polite.” All this was said with a twinkle in her eye and Tania laughed.

“I am fortunate to have such a lady to attend me, and doubly fortunate that she has a handsome brother.” John realised they were joking with him and he was glad that they had made good friends in only a short time. Joan left and John began to strip off his cloths, Tania turned to him and let the nightgown she was wearing, fall to the floor. John stood looking at her for a moment, admiring her beauty. Tania looked down at him. “I think you are ready for bed by the look of it.” John reached for her and they moved to the bed to enjoy each other once again.

“Today I will ride east again to visit the Fens and the small hamlets there,” announced John to Stephen at breakfast.

“We will take 20 men with us, go and round them up and bring bows and spears, we may see some game in the rushes.”

The party set off and as they passed through the villages people stared at the number of armed men moving through their lands. They reached the edge of the Fens and could see the tall reeds stretching out before them. A small group of men stood by the side of the Fen.

“Good morrow sirs,” said John.

The men explained they had heard them coming from scouts along the way and remembering John’s promise to help, should they need it, they had decided to meet him. The leader spoke.

“There is movement on the seaward side of our land. Two ships have come into Yarmouth and a large armed party of Flemish men have come ashore and are moving towards our main settlement.”

John offered his men to strengthen the garrison at their settlement. Aelfraed, their leader accepted readily explaining they were not fighting men as the Fens were a peaceful area. John sent out his best scouts to find out more about the intruders. Aelfraed led them through the rushes on paths they could not see and John thought they could soon be lost without a guide, so who was guiding the Flemish men?

Suddenly their guide stopped and signalled them to be quiet, out of the rushes appeared one of the scouts. “They are camped in a small clearing just beyond those trees you can see, there are about fifty of them,” explained the scout.

“They are between us and our settlement,” said Aelfraed.

John dismounted and signalled his men to do likewise quietly.

“We need to get either side of them, then we can surprise them on three sides. I will go forward first and try to find out what they are doing here, I will call you forward if I am not satisfied."

Aelfraed pointed out paths they could use to get into position, the men split into three groups and started off. John, Stephen, Aelfraed and five men remounted and moved towards the Flemish men. As they rode into the camp the intruders sprang to their feet and picked up their weapons. A tall man shouted in French to stop and he turned towards John who was shocked to find himself looking at Henri Hausman, the man he had met in London.

"Ah my friend" said Hausman stepping forward. "How good to see you again, welcome to our camp, please join us in a mug of ale."

His men began to move forward with their hands on their weapons.

"Please get down from your horse, we are here peacefully but you are outnumbered and …." Hausman was interrupted by John. "No you are wrong, it is you who are outnumbered and surrounded." At a given signal John's men rose up out of the reeds. Archers with bows drawn and men with spears ready.

"Lay down your weapons, all of you, and then we will discuss what you are doing here," commanded John. As his men collected their weapons John noticed two men trying to hide themselves in the throng of soldiers. "Bring those two to me, " John told Stephen.

A tall Flemish man approached John and presenting his sword to him said that he was in charge of the soldiers and in view of the circumstances, he formally surrendered to John, who smiled and thought, 'you had no alternative'. He said they had been paid by Hausman to accompany him on a private venture and he needed guards to protect the money he was carrying. When the two Englishmen arrived John recognised them as his farmers from the southern tip of his lands, they both had large flocks of sheep.

"What are you doing here with these men?" asked John. The two men looked at each other and did not reply. John faced Hausman.

"Now sir, what are you here for, creeping around the Fens with a foreign armed band and bags full of money? I am sure King

Edward will be interested in your answer."

John thrust his face towards Hausman's as he said this, and glared at him. John instructed Stephen to take the prisoners back to their ships while he put Hausman and the two Tenants under guard. They were getting very nervous and had been talking to each other, John told the guards to split them up and he would question them one at a time. When Stephen and the prisoners had left John called the guards to bring one of the farmers to him and to cut a switch from one of the trees. John looked hard at his Tenant, a man called Henry Thatcher.

"Why would you get involved with that man?" asked John.

While the guard stood by practicing swipes in the air with the switch. The man stood stubbornly silent. John grabbed him by his shirt and ripped it from his back, he was about to tell the guard to lay it on when the other man cried out.

"We was offered money sir, to sell our sheep to him so that he owned them and could have all the wool." "Shut up you fool," said Thatcher.

"It was you who talked me into it," said the other Tenant. "You said at the meeting we would all be rich." Thatcher stood defiant.

"Are you going to tell me what is going on or will you feel the strength of my guard's arm?" warned John.

The guard stepped closer and was raising his arm when Thatcher broke and said that Hausman had bought the sheep, they were to look after them and at shearing the wool would be collected by Hausman's men and taken to Brugge without Hausman having to pay the market price. John realised that this would seriously diminish his income if Hausman roped many more into his scheme. Thatcher said that Hausman was talking to all the shepherds in the area. John decided to take the three men back to Dunston while he pondered on what he would do. Aelfraed thanked John for his response but as there was no danger to his people immediately, he invited John and his party, including the prisoners, to his village to wait for the men to return from taking the Flemish men back to their ships. The village was very basic and John could see that most were poorly housed. They welcomed the men and the prisoners were secured in the only wooden hut with stout doors. Although poor, the village was clean and generally the people appeared happy. A meal was prepared which they all enjoyed after the excitement of the day. It was late evening when Stephen returned and they set up camp at the edge of the village. Stephen reported they had no trouble persuading the Flemish men to board their ships, in fact they were pleased to do so as they had insisted they were paid before leaving Brugge. The officer who had surrendered his sword had told Stephen the whole story of the subterfuge Hausman had employed to get the men to accompany him. Stephen had returned his sword, as John had suggested, and he soon had all the men on board. John and Aelfraed talked long into the evening and the result was that Aelfraed and his villagers would report to John any movement towards his lands and in return John would purchase reeds from the village and supply arms to Aelfraed's men, he still felt vulnerable from these Eastern shores but to overcome that he, or Sir Cedric, would have to control the whole Shire.

Riding back to Dunston John and his party detoured to the farms where the two traitors had held Tenancy. He called the farm hands together at each and asked them to put forward a man who they could work for and who would be able to take over the Tenancy. After some deliberation each farm agreed on a man and John said to them both he would confirm their position at the first quarter day when rent was due, if they proved themselves worthy. The day was nearing its close when they reached Dunston, they could see the welcoming lights of the Castle and Stephen blew his horn for the night watch to lower the drawbridge. John was met at the door by Tania who greeted him demurely, whispering in his ear that he would be greeted properly later. The evening meal was full of the talk of what had happened on their trip, John called Boorman and told him to see the prisoners were fed and Hausman was to be imprisoned in the tower. Sleep came to John immediately after their love making and Tania looked at him and smiled. Her man was a strong man but a fair one, and she loved him for it.

John spent the next few days making sure his fighting force were being trained and kept up to scratch, he promoted a selected number to assist Stephen who had taken overall responsibility. The time had come for him to look for at least two more Squires but where from was the question. John decided to visit Sir Cedric and with Tania, Stephen and a small detachment they rode over to Wymondham. On arrival they were greeted warmly and after some refreshment John and the Earl went to his room to discuss what had happened in the Fens.

"My first concern is what to do with Hausman?" started John. "Should he go to London or can it be dealt with here?"

"We can hold a trial here as it concerns our farmers and our security," said Sir Cedric. "I can preside as Judge, I have the King's and Parliament's authority, unless you would prefer to take him to London."

"No, I believe that it would be in our interests to show our farmers and tenants that we can be deal with situations like this," said John.

They decided to transport the prisoners to Wymondham the following week with the trial set for two days later.

"As far as your Squires are concerned I have a young man here who you might find suitable. He is the son of a friend of mine and is visiting me at the moment," said the Earl. "We will see him at our meal tonight and you can talk to him then."

They talked further on the plans for John's lands and how he saw the farms co-operating more together so that there was less duplication in their efforts, He also wanted to set up his own contacts with the Flemish merchants. Sir Cedric was interested in how John had enrolled the Fen men to help him. Their talking finished John went to find Tania and the two of them walked the battlements arm in arm. The sun was setting and the surrounding countywide was bathed in it's golden glow, they could hear the sounds of the kitchens preparing the evening meal, and the stamping of the horses in the stables.

"Do you miss living here?" asked John.

“I am very happy at Dunston and I am enjoying making it our home.”

John bent and kissed her neck and she turned so that their lips met and their hearts were intwined in that golden light.

John was introduced to a young man when they went down to the Hall for their meal. His name was Tristan and he bowed to Tania and John who clasped his arm in a firm grip which the young man returned.

“Sit with me and tell me about yourself,” said John. Tristan had been brought up in Nottinghamshire, his father was a minor Knight and had taught his son most of the skills a knight would need, by the end of the meal John thought him suitable to take on as a Squire but decided to leave the decision to later. It was a convivial evening and they were entertained by a wandering band of minstrels who kept them amused with song and rhymes. Sir Cedric was in good voice but John thought he must be a lonely man now with no wife or daughter in the Castle. He remembered the lady in the London house but could not recall her name and he had never seen her at Wymondham. Eventually the festivities of the evening drew to a close and they all retired to bed. They stayed at Wymondham for a further three days giving John and the Earl time to discuss plans that Sir Cedric had for the future. The journey back to Dunston was uneventful and John had the opportunity to speak more with Tristan, whom he had asked to accompany them, the lad sat a horse easily and had a confident air about him. John’s only concern was how he would get on with Stephen. They were welcomed back to the Castle and Stephen reported on the work he had been doing with the men-at-arms, John was impressed and congratulated him and introduced him to Tristan. Later that evening John talked to Stephen and said he was thinking of asking Tristan to be a Squire, Stephen’s reaction was to say that he liked Tristan and welcomed the plan. John asked Tristan to sit with him and invited him to be one of his Squires to which Tristan readily agreed. He brought the two Squires together and explained that he would expect them to discharge their duties as Squires equally between them and he would leave them to arrange that themselves. The two lads smiled and shook hands and walked off together and suddenly stopped and returned to ask John his plans for the next day.

John laughed. "I think you had better take turns in looking after me, and the other one look after the duties in the Castle. Tomorrow I want Stephen to go to Aelfraed and ask him to come to Dunston and then with us to Wymondham for Hausman's trial. He can bring companions with him if he likes. So Tristan can accompany me when I have decided on what I am doing."

John walked up to the room that Tania had turned into a sewing room and found her and Joan busy chatting and laughing.

"Not much work going on here then," said John. "I am to my bed now as I have a busy day tomorrow."

Tania smiled and with Joan, walked off to their rooms.

"I will be but ten minutes," said John and went down to the room he used for a place to be able to think and plan, it was comfortable there and Boorman had placed weaponry around the walls and some drapes, he relaxed in a chair and thought of the coming trial. His head began to nod and he jerked himself awake, he stretched himself and went to their bedroom. Tania was sitting up in the big bed, John thought she never looked more beautiful. He quickly stripped off and climbed into bed, Tania opened her arms and John sank into their warm embrace. They fitted together as though they had come from the same mould and even their movements were in unison. John's feelings soared to the most dizzy heights and afterwards they lay together inside a cocoon of love.

Stephen returned with Aelfraed who had brought his wife and two large well built sons with him as well as four pack horses loaded with reeds. John greeted them and thanked Aelfraed who said it was a small price for the weapons John had sent. He also told him he now had spies established along the coast and in Yarmouth where he could receive advance knowledge of shipping activity. When his guests had settled in, John and Aelfraed walked the battlements talking of the coming trial and the possibility of other people trying the same scheme as Hausman. Aelfraed said he was nervous at standing before a court but John assured him the case was already proven against Hausman and it was just a formality to prove his guilt. That night the evening meal was a jolly affair as Aelfraed had an unending repertoire of tales from the Fens, most of them not repeatable to children! During the meal an unexpected guest arrived, it was Gavin, with a message from Sir Cedric. Joan was obviously well pleased and made room for him to sit at her side as John broke the seal and unrolled the message, but made no comment as to it's contents. Later, in the privacy of their room, Tania asked what was in the message.

"It is just information about the trial, there will be two other noblemen present from court, and he sent Gavin because he could not stand his lovesick face around the Castle. The puzzling part is that he wants me to travel in full armour as a show of strength."

Tania said she would tease Joan tomorrow about Gavin but she was pleased that Joan had an admirer.

Early the next morning Jack arrived at the Castle with the last part of John's armour, the shield. When John saw it he smiled broadly and thanked his father for it was a shield to be proud of, the design on the front was as they had discussed, a mailed fist holding a broadsword with a background of green. The Castle came to life with everyone preparing for the journey to Wymondham. John went back to his room where Tristan helped him dress for John was wearing his new armour and all the men with him were dressed in chain mail and helmets, it was to be a show of force. Tania and her ladies left first with Stephen and an escort, an hour later the prisoners were brought to the Bailey and secured on their horses. Tristan brought out Hammer and assisted John to mount, he did not find it easy in his armour and hoped he would get used to it. Tristan had John's lance and helm the latter now proudly displaying green and golden plumes from the crest. They made a fine show as they left the Castle and there were a few villagers at the roadside who cheered them on, not really knowing what it was all about. Riding through Wymondham was a different story, there were crowds lining the streets and everyone was wanting to know what was going on at the Castle. There were all the Lords up from London and now John's entourage arriving with prisoners, rumours were rife.

John and his retinue rode into the Castle Bailey and were met by Sir Cedric and a group of men, most of whom were richly dressed apart from one man in black and a cleric. The Earl stepped forward and greeted John who dismounted from Hammer, with Tristan's assistance.

"You make a fine sight, John, no one would think of attacking you." And Sir Cedric winked at John. "Come in and change then come to the hall and meet our guests."

Later when John entered the hall he the group of men he had seen on arrival fell silent. Sir Cedric stood next to him. "I would like you all to meet Sir John of Dunston who captured Hausman and uncovered this plot." The first to greet him was Alfred of Ely who introduced him to two Barons from London. A short plump man, richly dressed, just nodded to him and the man in black stood back and said nothing, but then turned and spoke to the cleric. Sir Cedric moved to the edge of the room and said to John.

"The man who did not speak to you is Philip of Southwark, he has interests in Flanders and I am not sure why he came. The man dressed in black is a Judge from London as I have a vested interest in the proceedings and could influence the outcome. The cleric is Father Boniface who is always with him."

The Earl suggested they all sat down and they could discuss the coming day's programme.

The evening meal was more convivial although John could feel the sharp looks that came from Southwark and wondered why, he had never seen the man before so could not understand the ill feeling. When John eventually retired he was glad of the fact that Tania was there to make him forget the day.

John was up and dressed when Tristan came for him to attend Sir Cedric in the hall. The great room had been turned into a courtroom with a raised platform for the Judge and a section for a jury. People from Wymondham were filling up the seats at the sides and John saw Tania and the ladies coming in to sit at the rear of the room. Sir Cedric called him into a side room where he found Aelfraed already seated. Stephen and Aelfraed's sons were there too looking a little nervous.

It was their first time in a Castle and they looked as though they were on trial not just witnesses. John could see through the half open door that the hall had filled up and the Judge was taking his place.

John was called to state what had happened in the fens, then it was the turn of Stephen. Aelfraed and his sons to corroborate the facts. The two farmers were called one at a time to give account of what happened and there were discrepancies and differing facts of what happened. They also blamed each other and Hausman for getting them into this mess. When Hausman took the stand he complained that as a foreign subject he could not be tried by an English court. The judge pointed out he had committed a crime on English soil and he would be tried by this court. Philip of Southwark spoke for Hausman saying it must be a huge mistake and John capturing them had frightened them into saying things that were not true. The last part of the drama was when Sir Cedric produced a letter that John had given him, it had been written by the Flemish officer and given to Stephen before he left with his men. The letter explained how they had been employed by Hausman and had not known the true nature of the expedition until John had captured them. The letter also stated that this officer had been approached by other men to carry out similar raids.

The Judge instructed the Jury to go to the side room and consider their verdict and return to their seats when ready. They had only been gone for twenty minutes when they returned.

"Who speaks for you?" asked the Judge and a man stood up and touched his forelock.

"It's me sir," he said.

"Have you reached an unanimous decision from what you have heard here today?" sked the Judge.

"We have sir," answered the man.

"Do you find the prisoner, Hausman, guilty of the charges or not?" said the Judge, looking down at him.

"Guilty, sir!"

There was an outburst of cheering which was quickly suppressed and the Judge then asked for a decision on the two farmers and the verdict was again 'Guilty'. The Judge proclaimed that he would set the sentence after a break for half an hour. Half an hour later the Judge returned and called for the prisoners to stand before him, he spoke to them.

"Henri Hausman. You are found guilty of a crime against our King and Country which is Treason, therefor you are sentenced to be taken from here and hanged by the neck until you are dead, and may God have mercy on your soul."

The Judge then pronounced the sentence on the two farmers that they were to be flogged and banished from the King's lands for ever, the younger of the two fell to the floor. The guards marched the prisoners back to their cells and people began to disperse.

John sat on a bench with his head down, it was different when you are in battle and you killed a man but this was too clinical and he regretted not ending it in the Fens. Sir Cedric found him and asked him to come to his room. When they were seated the Earl said that the verdict and the sentence was right and would send a signal to anyone else that tried that they would get harsh treatment if caught. Hausman would be dealt with at dawn tomorrow but the two farmers he felt should be punished at Dunston to also send a signal. John was silent for a moment while Sir Cedric spoke to him.

"This will strengthen your position at the Castle and the surrounding lands and show the Tenants that you are willing to punish wrong doing severely."

John nodded in agreement but felt a little apprehensive inside. When he awoke in the morning Tania tried to lift his mood, all night he had twisted and turned and only slept in short periods. He met Stephen on his way to the Bailey where they joined Tristan and Sir Cedric. Night had not receded yet and a black gloom hung over the Castle as Hausman was led out to gallows that had been erected overnight. The priest accompanied him and read prayers as the noose was placed over his head. Hausman remained silent even when asked if he had anything to say. As the weak sun rose the trap was sprung and Hausman dropped, there was complete silence with all the faces turned towards the swinging body.

Gradually everyone walked back into the Castle and made their way to the Hall to break their fast, it was a sombre meal even though they all knew it had been a just decision.

“He will be buried outside the Castle,” said Sir Cedric to John. “Have you made plans for your journey back to Dunston?”

John replied that he had arranged to leave at noon and arrive at Dunston in the evening, he could then carry out his part of the sentence at dawn the following day. Tania and Joan came into the Hall and said they were not hungry, they had watched the execution from a window.

“We shall be leaving at noon,” said John. “I must inform Tristan and Stephen to be ready.”

After saying his farewells to Sir Cedric, John and his party departed for Dunston. This time Tania and her ladies rode with him, they made good time and arrived just as night began to darken the skies. When John had changed from his armour Boorman informed him that Roderick wished to see him.

“Well, Roderick, what news?” asked John. “Have you found new Tenants for the vacant land.”

“Aye sir,” answered the Reeve. “Two of Thatcher’s shepherds will do nicely and we will have no further trouble, they can work together to make both farms profitable and share some of the costs. What is going to happen to Thatcher and Carpenter?”

John explained the Judge’s verdict, the flogging would be in the morning and they would be taken to Yarmouth, put aboard a ship to take them to the farthest land away from England.

“I’ll move Thatcher’s wife and child back to her folks in Stowmarket. Carpenter had no family but his cottage will need a good clean as he lived like a pig,” aid Roderick.

“ See that Thatcher’s wife has this money,” said John, passing him a small pouch. “It is part of what he would have been paid for the fleece.”

John joined Tania for their meal and began to feel calmer knowing that after tomorrow he could get back to running his lands as he wanted to.

As the sun rose on the next day Stephen and Tristan stood either side of the two prisoners who were tied to fence rails in the Bailey. At John’s signal the flogging started, 100 lashes each. Carpenter soon lost conscience and Thatcher was barely alive when they had finished, they were dragged off and cold water sluiced over them.

John spoke to the Squires. “Let them have the rest of the day to recover then tomorrow I want you, Stephen, to take them to Yarmouth and book passage to Italy, an edict has gone out to all ports to bar them from entering this land again.”

With that John turned on his heel and strode back into the Castle and calling Roderick to him told him he would ride with him to visit all the Tenants within the next few days. In fact it took longer that anticipated as John wanted to spend time with the men who tended his land and raised his sheep and cattle. They discussed the coming fair, the market and collection of wool, many asked when they would have their own wool fair and John said he had already written to London asking that they could obtain a charter which would bring foreign traders to Dunston. Staying the night as a guest in some of the houses John realised he must improve the economy of his land so that Tenants could improve their living standards. Overall the trip was a success and John felt revitalised and started to make plans to improve the Castle.

Tania had settled to married life at the Castle and on the next visit from Sir Cedric she was the perfect hostess. After the evening meal during that visit the Earl sat in front of the fire in John’s room and said he was worried at the murmuring he was hearing from Norwich, the Barons were unhappy that the King had neglected the City, but still demanded high taxes. Sir Cedric knew that if there was an uprising the King would expect him to put it down as he was still in Wales. It crossed John’s mind, as they talked, that if that happened he would be involved too. That night he needed the love of his wife to take his mind off the thought that he might be fighting again. Sir Cedric departed the next morning and after a few weeks life became calm again and John remarked to Stephen that no news must mean good news, but keep the men practicing and in readiness.

John, Tania and Joan were visiting Jack and Matilda and John noticed the women, when they were talking together, often cast glances at him, when he asked Tania what it was about she blushed and it was nothing. However nothing became something one night when Tania was laying in John's arms and he said as he was stroking her belly. "You are eating too well wife you are getting quite plump." Tania smiled at him. " I have to eat well as there are two of us to feed now."

John thought for minute then sat up and looked at her. " You mean….?"

" Yes," she said, "we are going to have a baby."

II

Water dripped down on his helmet as he tried to find shelter against the stone wall.

"Dam this Welsh weather, does the sun never shine, I've been soaked to the skin for the last month." A disgruntled Roger exclaimed to his companion.

"It's all right building the bloody castles but why can't we live in them. We get sent out to chase these invisible men who shout at us in a language you can't understand, I tell you I'm sick of it."

"What you gonna do then?" asked his friend.

"I don't know, get drowned I expect," answered Roger as he walked along the wall to a gap, he peered around the edge and immediately withdrew his head as an arrow just missed it. They moved back and sought a more protected space.

“We should try and get round them,” said Roger.

The attackers were pressing hard to clear the King’s forces from the area. Roger stopped and listened, he could hear horses and he knew that this band of Welshmen did not have cavalry.

“I think we are going to be helped at any moment.”

Sure enough the Welshmen started to withdraw as the cavalry charged in. The chase passed Roger and he stood up to see what the outcome would be.

“That was very timely and welcome, perhaps I can go and get dry somewhere. I.. aaaaaaah!”

Roger’s voice was cut off as an arrow entered his throat, fired from one of the last Welshmen to leave.

His fellow soldier knelt by his side but Roger’s wound was fatal and all he could do was to stay until Roger’s life expired. It was not the end the son of de Brehalle had expected but that was the story of his life.

Eventually when the news reached John he thought for a while of their earlier friendship but then dismissed it as an event of war, he had not seen or heard from Roger for some time. He wondered if Avice had received the news. He decided to send one of his men to Norwich and see if she could be found.

Tania’s news caused a great stir in the Castle and everyone congratulated them. John walked about feeling ten feet tall as though no one else had fathered a child. Matilda became a frequent visitor as she helped Tania prepare for the coming birth. John had sent a messenger to Sir Cedric and it was not long before he arrived at the Castle, he was as pleased as everyone else. Whilst the Earl was there he also warned John that trouble was brewing in Norwich between the citizens and the Priory. Riots had broken out and law and order must be restored. John told him his men would be ready if needed. It was only three weeks later that the message came for him to join Sir Cedric outside Norwich. He was to take his troops to the river crossing at the south of the town and wait for the message to advance on the Castle. As soon as the courier arrived John moved forward. They met groups of rioters as they progressed and these they broke up and told them to return home or face the consequences. When they reached the Castle they found the citizens openly fighting the Priory guards. John's force pushed through the melee and split a few skulls in the process, they positioned themselves between the two groups and blocked further conflict in the main square. John reached the gates of the Castle and forced their way in where he ordered his men to clear everyone out. He marched to the Great Hall and instructed his men to search the Castle for any who might be hiding in the building. "Stephen, post guards on the gates and let nobody in. Tristan, take a detachment down to the Priory and tell the Prior I wish to see him here now, and if he wont come quietly, bring him anyway."

John issued these instructions as he walked to a window and saw a group of mounted men approaching, he recognised Sir Cedric's standard and went to the main door to greet him. The two men walked back to the Hall where the Earl said to John.

"Well done for seizing the Castle without too much trouble, my men are positioned at the main entrances to the City while you made your way to the Castle. There are some of the local Baron's on their way to see if they can get something for themselves out of this. I will stay and talk with them as I have the King's seal to back up what ever I decree."

At that moment Tristan entered with an elderly monk and four companions.

"I have brought the Prior, but we had to fight our way into the Priory and several citizens were slain I am afraid, they have destroyed some of the monastery."

"Bring the Mayor and Bailiffs here as soon as you can round them up," said John.

Sir Cedric turned to the Prior and asked him what had started the riots. The Prior drew himself up and accused the citizens of trespassing on his land and he had a right to protect the Priory and Cathedral. Tristan came back with a rather rotund man and five men with stout staves.

"You have incited rioting in this City and caused death and

destruction," said the Earl to the fat man who said he was Mayor. "What ever your grievance no force should be raised against the house of God."

The Mayor tried to justify his actions but his words fell on deaf ears. Sir Cedric then spoke again.

"I am appointing a Sheriff here in Norwich who will have overall control of the City in the King's name. You will obey the laws that are set and if there is more trouble I will make sure the ringleaders are punished most severely. Do you understand?"

"Yes, my lord" replied the Mayor.

The Prior was not happy at being ordered about by Sir Cedric and said he would return to the Abbey and Sir Cedric would find him there, as he was responsible to the Archbishop and not a common man. The Earl nearly went purple and told the Prior in most graphic terms what would happen to him if he did not do as he was told. He told them both that they should return the following day at noon. When they had departed Sir Cedric and John discussed what steps they would take to keep law and order until the Sheriff was appointed, they had just concluded when four of the Barons arrived. Sir Cedric was acquainted with all of them and they soon relaxed when he told them of the his decisions, they then all fell to sampling the Castles cellars. The following morning as the Baron's, and their sore heads left, Sir Cedric said to John.

"Until I have found the right man to be Sheriff I need you to take the position, if you will? It should not take me long to find the person who will meet the requirements to take hold of the City. What is your answer?" John thought for a few moments remembering what he owed the Earl.

"I will do it while you select your man."

Sir Cedric clapped him on the back and told him he would not regret it and it would be good experience for him. John sent Tristan back to Dunston to tell Tania and ask her to come to Norwich to stay for a while if she would. John and Stephen started a programme of patrols by his men and the men Sir Cedric had left with him when he returned to Wymondham. The City settled down and the normal life of a busy community gradually returned. The augments regarding the Fair and how it was run became the sheriff's decision which pleased the citizens and they began preparing for their Wool Fair. John was concerned about his wool and decided to use the Norwich Fair to sell his and any other land owner's who wished to participate. The fair was one of the biggest the City had seen.

The day Tania was to arrive John could not stand still, he marched about the Castle giving orders that were not necessary and interfering in all that was being prepared. Stephen tried to calm him down but gave up when he started to shout at him. Tania and her ladies, with Tristan and an armed escort arrived in the afternoon and after John had embraced her she asked him if he had missed her. When John said he had been very busy and he hadn't been away long to miss her, Stephen nearly bent double with laughter and had to quickly disappear. Peace came to Norwich and the citizens came back to their Cathedral although every time they went to a service they had to pass the ruin of the gate they destroyed. John set frequent armed patrols in the City and the surrounding area to ensure there was no chance of a second uprising. One morning, as he walked his dogs in the grounds of the Castle a courier arrived. John noticed he was in Royal livery and hurried in to find out what message had been brought.

'Greetings to Sir John of Dunston' started the message. 'His Royal Majesty sends his thanks for rescuing his favoured City, Norwich, from the hands of the rebels and informs you that he will visit his City as soon as possible. A member of his household will arrive to ensure the correct arrangements are made. His Majesty also wished for a Tournament to be arranged whilst he visited the City.' The courier asked if there were any questions and John said if he would rest and sup with them he would write a reply to the King that the courier could return with in the morning. John and Tania sat up late that night discussing plans for the Royal visit, fortunately Tania had brought her cook with her not knowing the situation of staff at the Castle.

The courier was up and ready to depart when John came down to the Great Hall.

"I have penned a reply to His Majesty, for you to take." He passed a sealed parchment to him. The young man left on his journey and John sat down and wrote a message to Sir Cedric which he dispatched immediately and then went to eat.

John quickly sent invitations to the Barons to participate in the Tournament and tasked Stephen and Tristan to prepare the field adjacent to the Castle. They discussed the forthcoming visit with John and then left to make sure their troops were patrolling the City and that there was no more trouble. John called as many of the builders in the City he could find and started them on repairing the gateway of the Priory that had been damaged in the riots. Once all was underway John sent messages to the Barons, the Mayor and the Prior informing them of the visit of the King and inviting them to call the next day to discuss details. At the end of the busy day John and Tania retired to their rooms and could at last catch up with their personal lives and how Tania was progressing with her pregnancy. For several days the City excitedly, for the most part, prepared for the Royal visit, with the route the procession would take being cleaned and made free from the usual dross that medieval streets had. Tania was busy with Joan and Matilda making new dresses for the visit when John entered and told them that a courtier had arrived and he would be busy with him checking over what had been arranged. A messenger arrived to inform John that the Royal Progress had reached Wymondham and were staying there for the King to hunt.

The day King Edward and Queen Eleanor arrived was warm and sunny and the people of Norwich turned out in crowds to line the streets to see the colourful procession pass. The royal couple were popular although his taxes were not. After the King and Queen had been settled in the Castle Sir Cedric, who was in the royal party, spoke to John.

"This is a wonderful opportunity for you, make the best use of it. I will assist where I can."

At the banquet that evening everyone was in high spirits with music being supplied by minstrels from the City. The royal couple retired early, the guests left and Sir Cedric and John were alone.

"His Majesty was in good humour tonight," said John.

"Let us hope he remains so."

They continued discussing the Tournament until sleep beckoned them and John made his way to bed.

John was up early and down to the Tournament Field in the morning. Stephen and Tristan, with the help of Castle staff and citizens, had built an exceptional Tournament Field. There were Jousting Lists, tented area for the contestants, stands for the crowds and a covered platform for the King and Queen. John found his Squires and congratulated them on what they had achieved. Midmorning sunshine greeted the crowds as they began to fill the stadia, their first call was to the various food vender stalls and ale tents. The combatants began to arrive at noon and there was a buzz of excitement as Squires prepared their master's horses and weapons, all lances had to have padded points and swords to be blunted. A small crowd of men were congregating at the archery butts, eager to try their hand at competing against experienced archers. John left the Grand Hall, where the royal couple had been receiving the Barons and City dignitaries, finding Tristan he was told that everything was ready.

John approached the King and informed him that everything was in place for him to open the Tournament, Edward nodded and rose to leave the hall.

When Edward and Eleanor came out of the Castle and into the sunlight the crowds cheered and the King smiled and raised his hand.

"A moving sight Sir John," aid the King. "The field has a fine look about it, I hope the ground is not too firm at the lists, my opponents will want something soft to fall on when I unseat them.eh?"

John was a little taken aback as he had forgotten that Edward enjoyed competing at the Joust and was usually very successful. They made their way down to the Royal Stand and there the King stood and looked over the crowd and pronounced.

"*Je declarer que le tourney commence.*"

This was received with more cheering. Down by the archery butts John could see a figure he recognised as he lined up for the first shoot, it was Carac. The King called John to his side.

"You have a tent for me to don my armour?"

John crossed his fingers behind his back and said he would make sure the King's Squire was ready. Quickly leaving the stand he found Tristan and asked if he had thought about a pavilion for the King and breathed a sigh of relief as Tristan led him to the largest pavilion, the Knights and Barons were preparing themselves. "You and Stephen have excelled yourselves this day," said John.

"There is even one for you Sir, and Hammer is ready and waiting," replied Tristan.

John laughed and thanked them again and made the point that they were becoming indispensable, he walked over to the archery butts just as Carac was about to shoot. The young Squire had lost none of his expertise and his arrows flew straight into the gold. Looking round John noticed Gavin with Joan on his arm, walking towards him.

"Are you entering, Gavin?" asked John.

"No not in archery, if Carac is competing I wouldn't stand a chance," Gavin replied. "But I will be at the Lists later."

John went back to the Royal Stand and said to the King that his Squire had everything ready for him at the pavilion flying the Royal Standard.

"Thank you John, will you be taking part?"

John said that he would and that he had been drawn in the later jousts against the Barons. The jousting started with the young Knights and older Squires competing, Gavin did well and had not been unseated when the turn of the Barons and older Knights took to the Lists. One of the Barons, Arthur Griffold, unseated Gavin, dismounted and attacked him with his dagger, a Marshall quickly intervened and dismissed Griffold from the Joust (no swords were permitted in a friendly Joust, and no fighting after being dismounted). His brother Henry Griffold, shouted at the Marshall and was obviously angry at the decision. The King called one of his Courtiers to him and whispered in his ear whereupon the man left the stand. The Joust continued and John left the stand to ready himself for his encounter, he noticed the King was not far behind him accompanied by Sir Cedric. As John rode to his designated end he was aware of the murmuring as the crowd appreciated his armour and he felt proud for his father's work. He donned his helm and received his lance from Stephen, as he did so he looked at the opposing Knight and was surprised to see Henry Griffold. John had expected a Baron from Holt but he thought to himself I have more reason to unseat this loudmouth. The Marshall gave the signal and the two Knights thundered towards each other, lowering their lances they each looked for the best place to hit their opponent. John swayed slightly as they came together and also dropped his lance slightly. The move unsettled Griffold who missed but John's lance struck home and it took all Griffold's skill as a rider to stay on his horse. They both stopped at the end of the List and selected another lance and faced each other for the second charge. This time John swayed in the opposite direction and lifted his lance, it struck home and Henry Griffold was dumped from his horse to the ground where he lay winded. John reached the end of the List and dismounted to see if he had hurt Griffold but the man was up and striding towards John swinging a mace. The Marshall was running to them, shouting at Griffold to stop but the Knight was in a fit of rage and swung at John who had by this time retreated to the end of the field. Suddenly John felt the handle of a sword in his hand. He could feel the ring throbbing, it was his own sword that Tristan had given him. With two quick parries and a thrust, John sent Griffold's mace spinning away, he had to restrain his sword arm or Griffold would have been sent to the beyond without his head. The crowd roared as the Marshall arrived and tried to arrest Griffold, John stopped him.

"Let the buffoon go and let us get on with the Tournament."

Griffold turned away and walked to his horse amid derisory chants from the crowd and much laughter. John reached his pavilion and sat down while Tristan fussed about.

"Who is my next opponent?" sked John.

“ Whoever wins the next bout between Sir Cedric and one of the Barons,” answered the Squire.

John got up and went out to mount Hammer as Stephen told him that the Earl had won at the first charge. John mounted and reached out for his lance.

“Good luck sir,” said Stephen. “Tristan has gone to the far end.”

John closed his helm, the signal was given and the two men began the charge. John tried his usual feint and managed a glancing blow to Sir Cedric, who had also jolted John. They turned and gripped their second lances as the charge began again. John tried for his alternative feint but Sir Cedric was expecting it and suddenly John felt a powerful blow to his chest and found himself flying from the back of Hammer to land with a thud on the ground. When he had regained his breath he stood and bowed to Sir Cedric who waved an acknowledgement. He walked Hammer back to his pavilion. Divesting himself of his amour John went up to the stand to see who would face Sir Cedric, the crowd were cheering and John looked over to the lists and there was the King mounted and ready to face Sir Cedric. Their first charge resulted in neither scoring a hit as they thundered past each other. At the second attempt each scored a hit but no one was unseated. The King altered his tactics at the third charge and was rewarded with a perfect hit on the Earl who swayed in the saddle and eventually slid off. The cheering from the crowd brought a smile from the King, raising his lance in salutation as he rode back to his pavilion. When they had all changed and were seated in the stand the King presented the trophies and gifts to the winners of the various events. John applauded Carac as he came to receive his reward for winning the archery.

A fine banquet had been prepared for that evening and they were all nursing aches and pains as they sat for the repast. The King thanked everyone for making it a successful Tournament and announced he would be staying for a further three days. The next day the King attended Mass at the Cathedral, celebrated by the Bishop of Lincoln who was travelling with the King’s party. On returning to the Castle, King Edward summoned John to him.

“I have been hearing about your exploits, from Sir Cedric, and it would appear that you have a genuine interest in the success of your lands. I am therefore granting you the lands that you already hold for Sir Cedric plus the ports of Yarmouth and Lowestoft. Sir Cedric agrees with this decision and will support you when needed. You will also receive your charter for the market and wool fair at Dunston.”

John thanked the King and promised his fealty. The King looked at him and said that he might call on him in the near future. That evening only the King’s party, and John with Tania, sat down to a meal. Queen Eleanor was deep in conversation with Tania no doubt talking babies, thought John, when Sir Cedric asked the King what was happening in Wales.

“The situation is such that it will need my intervention before long,” muttered Edward.

The King arose the next morning and decided that as the weather was fine he would hunt. John quickly sent Tristan and Stephen off to arrange beaters. It was nearly mid morning before the hunters left the Castle and entered the forest, so a halt was called to take food and wine before the business of killing animals began. The hunt proved to be successful the King bringing down a Stag with a fine shot from his bow, the hawks brought in a bag of birds and rabbits too. They were all in good humour on the way back to the Castle when dark clouds began to build in the sky. The King and his party put spurs to their horses and galloped off to the shelter of the Castle. John and his Squires, stayed back to oversee the delivery of the game and made slow progress. They were nearing the edge of the Forest when out of the trees rode Henry Griffold and four men at arms.

“Lost your protector have you?” snarled Griffold. “Now you can face me with proper weapons and no stupid Marshall to interfere.”

As he finished this outburst he drew his sword and spurred his horse towards John. Tristan and Stephen drew their swords and moved to cut off the men at arms while John calmed Anvil and drew his own sword. John and Griffold met with a clash of steel, Griffold's mount reared and threw him to the ground. John quickly dismounted and waited for Griffold to stand. They circled each other until Griffold attacked slashing and lunging, John danced around him parrying the attack. Griffold in desperation and rage pressed hard and John knew he would have to end the fight so with a consummate display of swordsmanship he disarmed his attacker and with his sword at Griffold's throat said.

"Yield, or I run you through."

Griffold stood and let his arms drop, as John lowered his sword he suddenly stabbed at John with a knife that he had hidden in his sleeve. John's sword leapt in his hand and with extraordinary speed ran Griffold through the heart. As John withdrew his sword he could feel the ring pulsating on his finger, looking around he could see that the men at arms had been reduced to two and the others had surrendered. John stood and cleaning his sword as he approached the two men at arms.

"You will come with me and report this action truthfully to his brother," he said. The men nodded and John told them to put Griffold's body on his horse ready to move off to the Castle. When they arrived Sir Cedric was in the Bailey.

"What's this, extra game?"

John explained what had happened and said he would take the body to the Griffold's estate. The Earl held up his hand.

"No, I will send a messenger to tell them to come here as I would like to speak to that family myself."

John went to his room where Tania made a fuss of him, she was getting quite large as the birth approached. John tried to assure her he had been in no great danger as Tristan and Stephen were there, omitting to tell her that they were also fighting at the time.

They lay together in bed as John pondered on what would happen when the Griffold's came. It had been a natural reaction in a fight to finish off your opponent, would the King get to hear of it or would Sir Cedric handle it himself, he was also still mystified by the way his sword seem to be connected to his ring. Perhaps he should take the ring off. All these thought were racing around in his head as he turned towards Tania and found she had fallen asleep.

John came down to the Hall early and found Sir Cedric already there.

"Good morning John," said the Earl. "You slept well I trust. I talked with the King last night of your escapade and he will talk to the Griffold family when they arrive, there is history between them and the King wishes to settle it."

John looked puzzled and hoped this was not a bad omen. The midday meal had just finished when the Griffold's were announced. The hall was cleared except for John, Stephen, Tristan, Sir Cedric and the King there was also a clerk in attendance. Arthur Griffold entered the Hall accompanied by an elderly couple and two men at arms, four of the Castle guards stood behind them.

The King, sitting on a raised platform, spoke.

"Remove those armed men at once, what is this a rebellion?"

The two men at arms withdrew immediately and Arthur Griffold said. "They were here for our protection Sire as from past events we were not sure what to expect."

The King's face turned red and he stood up, with the raised platform and his own great height his anger permeated the whole room.

"Kneel before your King you insolent dog!" he roared.

The Griffold's before him sank to their knees and bowed their heads.

"You seem to cause me to lose my temper every time we meet Sir Roland."

The King addressed this to the old man.

"Fetch a chair for the lady and then tell me why your son was in the forest. Was he poaching my deer again?"

The old man, Sir Roland Griffold, looked up at the King.

“I am sure my son meant no harm, your Majesty, he was returning home after the Tournament and called to see a charcoal burner in the forest to arrange a delivery for us.”

The King looked down on him.

“This was in the opposite direction of your home and you have your own charcoal burners near to your manor. Do not protest sir, your son died as a result of his stupidity in attacking one of my valued subjects. You will return to your home and see to the burial of your son and Arthur will come to London immediately after and join my guards where my captain can keep him under watch. I would not want him to follow in his father footsteps and be disloyal to his King.”

Arthur looked at his father with questions in his eyes and Sir Roland bowed his head.

“Leave now before I remember too much.”

After saying this the King sat down and beckoned Sir Cedric to him.

“Have one of your men journey with them to make sure I am obeyed.”

The Griffold’s departed and King Edward said he was going to rest and would see them at the evening meal. “What was all that about? queried John. “How was he involved with the King before?”

Sir Cedric said that if the King wanted him to know he would tell him.

That evening as they ate the King was in a jovial mood, he had rested well and he spoke of the campaign in Wales and that he would have to deal with Llewellyn again, this was the second time he had mentioned it and John wondered if he was trying to tell him something and then dismissed the thought. If the King wanted his services he would soon tell him.

When the Edward and his entourage left the next day crowds lined the streets and cheered the Royal Couple until they were out of sight. The visit had been what the citizens had needed and now they could get on with their lives, even though they had to pay the fine for the damaged caused by the rioting.

Sir Cedric promised John he would be back as soon as possible with a Sheriff and John could then get back to his own lands.

For the next months John worked hard at getting Norwich back to a thriving and peaceful City, as well as making sure Dunston did not suffer too much by his absence, he was helped in this by Tristan and Stephen as well as Roderick who looked after his Tenants. One night Tania was very restless and the next day she began her labour, Matilda and Joan were there to look after her while John walked up and down in the Hall. Several of the older men who had families tried to calm him but with no success. At last the Castle echoed with the sound of a baby's cry and John rushed up to their room. Throwing open the door he was confronted with a smiling Matilda and Joan and there in the bed was Tania with a little bundle in her arms.

"How are you and what is it?" said John, standing by her side.

"I am fine, and IT is your son, here hold him and see how beautiful he is," laughed Tania as she held up the child to him. John held the little bundle gently and pulled the cover away from the baby's face, his heart nearly burst with pride and joy even though he would not have called the screwed up face beautiful.

"Well done Tania," he said as he laid the baby back in her arms and kissed her. "You must rest now, I will send a messenger to your father."

A proud John came out of the room and seeing his two Squires embraced them and told them the news. Stephen said a celebration was called for and John agreed but said they were to wait until Tania was strong enough to enjoy whatever they decided. Sir Cedric arrived and grasped John's hand.

"Congratulations my boy, how are they?"

John told him everything was fine and accompanied him to see his daughter and grandson. Later that day another grandfather came as Stephen had been to fetch Jack. In the Hall that evening they all gathered and toasted the new arrival.

"Have you named him yet? " asked the Earl.

"No," answered John. "Tania and I will discuss it and try to decide on a name that will not embarrass him in later life."

Sir Cedric then announced that the new Sheriff for Norwich would arrive the next day. John went back to Tania to tell her the good news that they would be going home soon.

As John and Sir Cedric were walking in the Castle grounds the next day Tristan came to tell them that a stranger had arrived to see the Earl, his name was Edgar. Sir Cedric introduced John to Edgar and said he was the man he had selected as Sheriff of Norwich. John said he would give him every assistance while he settled in. Edgar was well built man in his thirties who then brought forward a shy young woman.

"This is my wife Edith."

Joan stepped forward and taking her hand said she would show her the Castle. Sir Cedric and John discussed with Edgar, what had been happening in Norwich and the trouble with the Griffold's. Sir Cedric departed saying the King had asked him to return to Court. John suggested to Edgar that they made a tour of the Castle and meet some of the senior members of the staff.

They came to Tania's room and they could hear the chatter of women's voices with the occasional baby's cry. John knocked and was bid to enter, when they entered the room there was Tania, lying in bed, Joan and Matilda talking to a flushed Edith who was holding the baby. Her eyes sparkled as she greeted her husband and showed him the baby. Edgar looked embarrassed and said that they should move on and he would see his wife later.

John said. "You will have to excuse the ladies, a baby seems to make them all excited. I must say I am proud too."

Edgar said that Edith was his second wife and his first wife had died in childbirth along with the baby, but he was hopeful that he and Edith would have a family. That evening as they sat down to their meal Edgar commented on the excellent food, John told him that the cook was from Dunston and would be returning with them so he would have to find a new one. That evening John climbed into bed and snuggled up close to Tania. “I’m sorry dearest but I am still recovering from the birth so please have a little patience with me,” she said. John moved slightly away but Tania pulled him close and entwined in each others arms they fell asleep.

It was a beautiful autumn day as John, Tania, the still unnamed baby and their entourage set off to return to Dunston, as they progressed through the City several citizens waved and wished them well. The Mayor had come to the Castle that morning to say goodbye but John reminded him he would be back.

John and Tania had settled on naming their son ‘Harold’ and contrary to the Bishop and Prior’s wishes the christening would be in their own church. Soon they saw the towers of home and John felt excited to be back and to involve himself in the affairs of his estate, especially as they were now his alone. As they came out of the woods and made their way to the Castle, Dunston villagers began to appear going in the direction of the drawbridge, they waived and called greetings to the couple who replied in kind. When the returning family entered the Castle they stopped and stared at the decorations everywhere and the crowd of locals as well as all John’s staff, men at arms and Boorman standing on the steps of the main door wearing his best cloak.

“Welcome home Sir and my Lady, and a very special welcome to your son.”

The crowd cheered and people crowded round as they dismounted, all wanting to see the baby. John said to Boorman.

“We would like to refresh ourselves first, is there anything organised that we should be aware of?”

“Yes, sir, we have arranged some entertainment for the villagers and there is an ox roasting. As it is a warm day I have erected a stand in the grounds so you may sit with your son for all to see.”

John thought it a lot of fuss but realised this tiny infant would one day rule these people’s lives so it was natural for them to have an interest. The rest of the day was a whirl with people bringing gifts for the baby and many of John’s Tenants wanting to speak to him. He called Roderick and said he would like him to join a meeting of all the staff in the morning.

The next day when John appeared at the meeting he had the baby in his arms and smiling said.

“Meet the next Duke of Dunston.”

All the people there crowded round and wished him well, John passed the baby over to Joan who was standing by and sat down. John started the gathering by thanking everyone for looking after his interests while he was away. He asked what was needed urgently and asked Stephen and Tristan to make notes, he also told the assembled company that his area now included Yarmouth and Lowestoft which would give him control, when he had established his authority, of two ports and a route to export of their wool. After the meeting he called Roderick to him and said he needed him to find any weakness in the perimeters of his area where they would need extra patrols. He said to Tristan to organise a strong, well armed party of men and they would be visiting the two ports very soon. That evening as he sat discussing events with Tania he asked her if she had met the Priest yet.

“No, I am waiting until we can go together, you know him better that I.”

“We must make it soon,” replied John. “People will want to know what to call the little fella.”

John, Tania and the baby made the journey to the church in the woods a few days later and found Father Aldred busy pruning some of the bushes that surrounded the church. The old priest stopped his work and came over to them. “Welcome especially to your new family member, come and sit and tell me what you have been doing, it seems a long time since we have been able to talk.”

John explained how busy they had been and then asked him if he would undertake the Christening of the infant at which Father Aldred beamed and said he would be delighted. John told him he would send some men over to help make the church ready for the number of people who would attend. The priest asked why they did not have the service in Wymondham Abbey but John replied that Dunston was their home so here was the right place. On the way back to the Castle, John and Tania discussed who they would ask to the ceremony in view of the church's size.

"Let us keep it to just the family and close friends," said Tania and John agreed.

"I must also speak with the Bishop. Father Aldred is getting very frail and we must find somewhere that he could retire to."

The day of the Christening went off well and the party afterwards, for all of Dunston's staff, Tenants, soldiers and villagers proved to be a happy, if somewhat noisy, affair, young Harold was certainly welcomed to Dunston on a day to remember. Sir Cedric with his Squires was relaxed and in good humour and Joan was pleased to be with Gavin for the day.

John and Tania settled into the routine of family life and John set off with Roderick to make sure all the Tenants were gathering their wool. One evening as they sat at their meal John announced that he would take both his Squires and visit his new towns of Yarmouth and Lowestoft, it was time to let them know they were part of his fiefdom. On their way to Yarmouth they diverted to the fenlands to meet Aelfraed and learn any news that his spies had gleaned when in the two ports. They stayed and slept at Aelfraed's village moving off early the next morning. Many heads turned as the people of Yarmouth saw the large group of armed men riding into the town making their way to the house of the Mayor.

Tristan knocked on the door which was opened by a servant.

"Tell your master Sir John Ivanson of Dunston is here."

The servant scurried away and immediately a portly man appeared, bowed and bid them enter. John accompanied by his Squires entered and followed the man into a large well appointed room.

"Please be seated sir. I am Martin Flower the Mayor and have been appraised that you might visit us very soon."

"Good," said John. "You will be aware then, that Yarmouth is now in my fiefdom, I have the document here should you need confirmation."

"A messenger came from London, Sir John, with the information so although we did not know when you would come, you are expected," continued the Mayor. "We have a house that is available to you on the edge of town should you wish to stay."

John was impressed that there seemed to be no rancour in the man and said he would be grateful if he could be directed to the house. The Mayor called a servant and they all departed to edge of town where John was surprised at the large house that had been prepared for them and the land that could accommodate his men. He said he would meet with the Mayor and his council in the morning so the Mayor and his servant departed. This is going too well, thought John, is the Mayor covering up something? When everyone was settled he called Tristan and Stephen to him and suggested that they take a few men each and stroll round the town, very casually. When they reported back they described some late night activity down at the docks that stopped as they approached.

"We must have a closer look at that tomorrow night," said John.

The Mayor called the next morning and offered to take John to see the leading citizens and business men. After meeting the town council and other people John had the distinct impression there was a tight 'club' controlling Yarmouth. He decided he would hold an 'Open House' the next morning and sent Stephen out to pin some hurriedly prepared posters in prominent positions. Later that night John and his men quietly made their way to the docks area. There were two large vessels tied up and several men loading what looked like large boxes, John spoke to Stephen.

"See if you can find out where they are coming from, and be careful."

Stephen moved off and disappeared into the darkness. John tried to move a little closer signalling his men to stay where they were. He recognised one or two of the 'business men' he had been introduced to earlier. On board one of the ships there was a loud bang as something was dropped and the raised voices, to John's surprise, spoke in French. He worked his way back to his men just as Stephen returned.

"They are bringing the packages from a large building four streets away, there are guards but they are very relaxed and not very alert."

John spoke to them saying. "We will make our way back to our house as there are not enough of us to challenge them. Tomorrow we will raid their store house and find out what they are being so secretive about."

There were several visitors to see John the next day, some were just inquisitive and some just wanted a moan against the taxes but there were just two men who came and were obviously very nervous. John gradually put them at ease and managed to find out that the Mayor controlled the town through fear, his thugs soon visited anyone who did not comply with his rules or extra taxes. Jobs at the docks were only given to men who could perform a favour for the Mayor or be in one of the 'gangs'. He also learnt that groups of men arrived on some ships but as soon as they landed they disappeared. Conferring with Stephen and Tristan did not suggest any answers as to where the men might be going.

Later, John with Stephen and Tristan, led all their men to the storehouse, the guards ran when they saw how many armed men they would have to face. John entered the building and found bails of wool neatly stacked ready to go aboard one of the ships. They also found bundles of weapons and a few barrels of wine.

"Now we can see what the game is," aid John. "They are exporting wool without paying the tax and foreigners are coming in for some reason we do not know. Where are they getting the wool from? The Mayor must know what is going on, that is why we are put on the outskirts of the town. Stephen, I will leave you to guard this building while Tristan and I will pay the Mayor a visit."

John and his men moved off to the Mayor's home. He hammered on the door while Tristan went to the rear, an old man opened the door and nervously told John that the Mayor was not at home. They searched the house but found no one. John grouped his men together and made for the docks where on arrival they found one ship in mid channel with sails filled and heading away. The second ship was still at the quayside and John quickly took his men aboard and captured the crew who surrendered immediately. The Captain came to John first of all indignant but under John's questions told him that they were French, trading with Flanders for wool and he had brought some men, twenty in all, whom he understood were to guard some sheep some miles inland. Henri Hausman immediately sprang into John's mind, was this still some remnant of his scheme and who was running it now? John said to the Captain that any wool on board belonged to England until the tax was paid, faced with John's men the Captain agreed to unload what was there and return it to the storehouse and then leave.

John went to the church where he told the Priest to ring the bells to summon people to the church. The church soon filled with the townspeople who sat waiting to see what this man and his armed band wanted. "My name is Sir John Ivanson of Dunston, and Yarmouth has been granted, by the King, as part of my fiefdom. This is my first visit to you and I find corruption and smuggling here. I shall be arranging for you to elect a new Mayor and council but until then I shall leave my Lieutenant and a detachment of men to keep the town in order. I shall be at the Mayors house tomorrow to hear any petitions you wish to bring to me. Anyone harbouring the Mayor or his friends I shall deal with harshly."

There was a quiet moment while what he had said sunk in and then a swell of murmuring as people began to talk together. A man stood up and called out and the church quietened.

"I am William Fisher," the man said. "We are not all thieves and villains here. We are grateful that we now have a lord and we hope the town will become prosperous again. I and several of the town's tradesmen would like to meet with you tomorrow sir."

" I welcome it," answered John.

The following day they came and agreement was reached with them to form a town council, also selecting their own Mayor. John left Tristan in Yarmouth to see that the new council was accepted and the Port was secure. He made one order that the Mayor's house be cleared and left empty. Leaving Yarmouth behind John and Stephen journeyed south to Lowestoft.

When they arrived in the town John was surprised to find a

welcoming committee consisting of the Mayor and the local council. John dismounted and the Mayor stepped forward.

"Welcome to Lowestoft Sir, we were advised of your visit and are at your service. Please accompany us to my house."

John stopped him with a gesture. "Wait a moment, I wish to go to the harbour first."

The Mayor bowed and led the way to the docks. There were three ships tied up at the key side and John went to the first and called for the Captain. A tall man came down the gang plank with a fussy little man holding bundles of papers, the Captain introduced himself and said the other man was checking his cargo.

"I hope there is no contraband on board," said John.

The little man insisted that all was in order for all three ships. John went aboard and looked in the hold which was full of bails of wool, he checked them off against the paper the custom's man had and was satisfied all was in order. The party then moved off to the Mayor's house. Looking for any signs of deceitfulness John question the men and carefully and he was pleased when all the stories tallied. Talking to the Mayor later he found that the man was suspicious of what was happening in Yarmouth and knew that it could not go undetected for long.

"I tightened our security and made certain no smuggling was going on here. We had heard of the events in Norwich and we also knew of your run in with Monsieur Hausman. I am a friend of Aelfraed so we learn what is taking place."

John smiled, this information could be important and maybe form the basis of an information network. He went on to tell John that the Flemish Traders in wool were offering all sorts of inducements to obtain their wool cheaper or to take over flocks here in England.

"I thank you for your information," said John. "You must keep your bailiffs alert."

John spent two more days in Lowestoft and then left to return home.

II

It was a gloomy and windswept afternoon when they arrived back in Dunston. John was glad when he was able to stretch his legs out in front of the fire and talk to Tania. Young Harold was now able to sit on a rug and John could see he had grown since he had been away. Hopefully he would now have time to spend with his family. Tania told him that her father had been called to Court and had left on this day, John yawned and stretched himself.

"I am hungry, let's eat."

Sitting in his room later he was looking through letters that had come whilst he had been away when he spotted one from his father. Jack had written to him to tell him what was needed to put the Castle Smithy back into production. John thought that it made sense for his father to move into the Castle, Matilda and Joan would be on hand as companion forTania and help with Harold.

John decided to walk to the Smithy the following morning, the weather had cleared and being on his feet made a welcome change from sitting on a horse. His father was busy at the forge when he arrived so John sat on a box, his thoughts were accompanied by the noise of the hammer and the smell of metal being cooled in a tub. It took him back to the days of his youth when life was easier and he was not having to think of how to govern a Shire. Jack joined him and listened to his proposal and agreed that it would be agreeable and sensible to move to the Castle, he would put William in charge here and he could use the house as he was now married to a village girl. That settled John set out back to the Castle. This move proved to be a good decision as future events unfolded.

Looking at the Castle John walked the perimeter of the moat and noted some areas that needed repair, he would get the men onto it before winter set in. He met Tania at the gates waiting for him.

"There is a messenger inside with, he says, letters from my father. He won't let me see them."

John hurried in and the messenger handed him a leather satchel which he took to a table and sat down. The satchel contained two parchments, one was from the Earl and one had King Edward's seal. John opened the one from the King and read that he was summoned to court, the Earl's letter explained that the summons was to discuss the problem in Wales and he should make haste. Tania was not pleased.

"You have only just come home and you are off again," she grumbled.

"You know I have to obey this summons, if Matilda can manage Harold there is no reason that you should not accompany me. You can take Joan and there are plenty of ladies in waiting at the Palace if you need more."

They asked the messenger to stay the night, to which he agreed.

After their evening meal John sat thinking about the summons and the subject of Wales, did this mean the King was going to attack Llywelyn again. Going to bed Tania was still chattering about having to arrange everything at short notice but she smiled and John could see she was also excited.

The journey to London was uneventful, with overnight stays with friends. John was accompanied by his two Squires and an escort of men-at-arms. They arrived at Sir Cedric's London house and were welcomed by the Earl himself and a very pleasant woman introduced as Lady Ann Falmouth. After they had settled in John and the Earl met in his private room.

"Bad news I am afraid John," said the Earl. "The Welsh have revolted and it has escalated to be a threat to the King's rule. He is intending to organise an all out attack against the rebels. I shall be returning to Wymondham to raise troops and I am sure the King is going to confirm that you will join me."

John was quiet for a moment, he had hoped for a time at home after his journey to the ports but if called he knew his duty was to the King and the Earl.

"You are to come with me to court tomorrow and we will

receive the final decision then," continued Sir Cedric. "I feel the answer will be to go after Dafydd and it will be off to Wales whatever."

When they arrived at the court the next day, the place was buzzing with the preparations for the march to Wales. Various Dukes, Earls and Barons were departing to their homes to assemble their forces and meet again. Sir Cedric appeared with the King and John bowed, he was rewarded with a nod of the head from the King and a signal from the Earl to follow him. They walked to a small garden where the King stopped and said he expected John to provide additional men for Sir Cedric and he looked to him to support his efforts in subduing the uprising in Wales. When they left the palace Sir Cedric said he had been right and that they were bound for Wales. He told John to collect his men together and meet him at Wymondham as soon as he could.

"I am leaving now so I hope to see you within the week," he said.

John hurried back to the London house to tell Tania the news.

"I must make all haste home but you and Joan may stay awhile with the Lady Ann, I will leave you a guard." John found Tristan and Stephen, told them to rouse the men and prepare to leave within the hour. Tania was not pleased that he was leaving so soon.

"It is not fair that you are going away immediately after coming home."

John had no defence other than the King had ordered it, he kissed her and went to meet his men. They rode at a fast pace and only rested when the horses could go no further. People in the villages they passed through kept out of the way of these grim fighting men. They sighted the towers of Dunston and quickened their pace as in their minds they could taste the fresh cooked food and the soft beds of home.

Boorman welcomed John home and said that everything was in order also Roderick would speak to him after he had eaten and rested. John spoke to Tristan and Stephen and told them to tell the men-at-arms based at the Castle to be in the Bailey in the morning and to go and bring in the men who were bound to fight for him, in from the farms. Later that night John calculated he should be able to raise over 500 armed men to take to Wymondham and join with the Earl's troops and still leave enough men to defend the Castle. When Roderick came he assured John that all would be well whilst he was away he was now respected by the farmers in his position.

It was not the best of days as they set out for Wymondham, an east wind was blowing and the persistent drizzle made everything soaking wet.

"It is good practice for Wales I'm thinking," remarked John to Tristan. "They say it's permanently wet in that country."

They made a large convoy as they moved out with horses, carts and men. John rode Hammer and Anvil was led, all his amour and weapons were in a cart. The column bypassed the town of Wymondham so as not to destroy their streets and finally camped outside the Castle.

They joined a large camp already there and John recognised some of the colours of Barons from north of Norwich, plus the Earl's troops. He joined Sir Cedric in the Great Hall which was filled with the leaders of the troops camped outside. The Earl called and they all turned towards him.

"I am pleased to see such numbers," he began. "I know there are some disputes between a few of you and I do not want that to escalate so Sir John Ivanson's troops will serve as camp bailiffs as I know he will deal fairly with any disputes. We will depart at first light tomorrow and I will give the order of march later. I remind you that we are to go and fight for our King and Country so let us make the time on the march to join together as an unbeatable army."

There were a number of cheers and banging of tables but John could see he would have his work cut out to keep order with such a large number. Sir Cedric waved him over.

"I know that was a surprise but I also know you have a well trained force who are loyal to you and I hope, to me."

John said he would do his utmost to keep order and left with Tristan and Stephan to organise patrols. It was still raining which did not improve the mood of the men, but most of them were tired from the day's marching and soon settled down trying to find shelter and get a night's sleep. There were a small number who were drinking hard, but these gradually fell into drunken stupors. John returned to the Castle to sleep and left Tristan and Stephen to organise their patrols. He was lucky to have a dry bed in a room to himself, most of the other 'guests' were laid out in the Hall or wherever they could find a comfortable corner.

John woke early and went down to the camp to find his Squires, Stephen met him and told him Tristan was out with a patrol but they had had a quiet night, a few with too much ale but nothing they could not handle.

John thanked him and said he and Tristan were to rejoin their men and prepare to move. Most of the camp were awake and loading wagons, the rain had stopped and there a mood of anticipation of what was to come.

Soon the whole cavalcade was on the move, they were making for Bishop's Lynn where another Baron was joining them bring their strength up to a rough count of 3000 fighting men. Pressing on they reached Chester and there joined with the rest of the army. John's men formed part of Sir Cedric's force, with two-thirds of his men being bowmen his was a valuable force. The camp outside Chester was very large and the provenders were having to go far afield to find food for all the men.

John was summoned to a meeting in Sir Cedric's pavilion. The Earl said to him.

"We need good intelligence John, I want you to take a group of your men and go out and find out as much as you can as to what the enemy are up to, where they are camped and what their strength is. Keep me informed by messenger and take care of yourself."

John went to find Tristan and Stephen, they were competing

with a group of archers as to who could shoot as many arrows in the shortest time as they could, into a hat nailed to a tree. John stood and watched for a moment when he suddenly realised it was his hat. After much laughter Tristan explained that John was the only one with two hats, so he wouldn't miss one!

The three of them sat and discussed the Earl's plan and Stephen thought they should form three groups, then they would cover more ground, this met with approval from the other two so they fell to discussing who they would select. They agreed that the men should be proficient bowmen who could handle a sword if needed. They must wear strong jerkins and light chain mail, if they could find enough, and dark cloaks with no insignia. They would need to be mounted so that they could move quickly, and to send messages back to Sir Cedric.

They fell to selecting the men and ended up with thirty, more would be too conspicuous. With this decided they went back to their men and began to set the plan in motion, the trouble came when they had more men who wanted to join them than they needed. Eventually the groups were formed and they began to get everything ready as they had discussed. Before the camp was awake the next morning John's group moved quietly out, they planned to move a group each morning so as not to be too obvious. They disappeared into the morning mist like wraiths, their cloaks and hoods making them as the ghosts of the dead soldiers of battles fought before. John made for the coast and the fishing villages hoping to find news, he knew that as the boats moved from port to port freely they picked up information. Nearing the first village John sent out a scout to find out if there were enemy soldiers about. The man returned saying the village was quiet and there were no groups of armed men in the vicinity. They moved around the village and made for the coast. As the day brightened they tried to keep to the trees so as not to be obvious. At the next village there was more activity as people went about their daily lives, so John and four men rode in. Fortunately one of the men in the group was Welsh and still spoke the language and could reply to the greetings they received as they ventured up the main street. He told John that some of them asked if they were going to join David against the English, if they were they should go further south as he was gathering a force at Hawarden. John sent a courier back to Sir Cedric with this news and gathered the rest of his men to go south and find the Welsh.

They were riding through the forest when the scent of camp fires came drifting towards them. One of them crept forward to see who and how many were cooking their breakfast. He returned and reported to John that there were a large group of Welshmen waking up, they didn't seem to be in any hurry. John signalled to his men to spread out and circle the camp, when they were in position he raised his horn and gave a quick blast.

The Welshmen were thrown into confusion as John's bowmen loosed a cloud of arrows into their midst from their hidden positions, many died in that first attack. John blew a second time and his men drew swords and swept into the encampment shouting as loud as they could while cutting down the enemy who were trying to defend themselves. John faced a great brute of a fellow who was wielding an enormous axe, John lent back as the weapon scythed towards him and he ducked under the swing and stabbed at the man's middle feeling the point enter the soft flesh, but the man steadied himself and brought the axe back to strike again, John bent double as he managed to avoid the swing and he struck at the man's unprotected legs. The big man fell with a roar of pain and John raised his sword and plunged it through the neck of his opponent. He swung round to find that most of the Welshmen were down and the remainder had surrendered. They gathered all the weapons together and bound the prisoners that could walk, two of John's men had died and there were no others with serious wounds.

"Bury our friends and take their personal possessions to give to their families, four of you take these prisoners back to Chester," said John. "Hurry, as the noise may bring others and we need to be away."

They disappeared back into the trees and after they had distanced themselves from the battle ground they rested and John thought about his next move. They had won that encounter easily, it would not be that way next time, thought John. The enemy were now warned and his party would be depleted if he had to take prisoners every time. Continuing through the woods they moved ever closer to Hawarden, suddenly his scouts came running back to tell him that an enemy patrol was heading towards them.

“Dismount,” called John and the horses were collected and moved into the trees. The Welsh were close behind and John’s bowmen only loosed a couple of flights before the enemy were on them. Fierce fighting started and John found himself facing two men who were determined to end his life, as he fought them off he shouted “BOX!” as loud as he could, a move they had practiced with all his men backed together with bowmen in the centre. The move was successful and the Welsh found them selves facing a solid square of swords with arrows flying out from the middle, many of them went down and John shouted “Charge!” the Box broke with his men falling on the enemy. With their battle blood up it was not long before the Welshmen were defeated but before John sounded his horn to stop, a frenzy took hold of his men and when he at last put the horn to his lips there was not an enemy standing. One of his men brought him a pouch full of papers, John looked through them and realised there was important information of support going to David’s army, he had lost another six dead and two seriously wounded, it was time to return to Chester.

Riding into the English camp John went to find Sir Cedric.

“Glad to see you made it back in one piece,” said the Earl. “What news do you have?”

John reported on what they had found out and Sir Cedric told him that it tied in with what the other patrols had reported. He suggested the next move would be to find a boat to take a force up the coast and come ashore as near as possible to Rhuddlan Castle. John left to find his Squires and arrange how to split his forces.

“Stephen, I want you to come with me on the next patrol and Tristan, you provide a guard for the Earl with the men we leave. Stephen, select bowmen and good sword’s men we shall not need the horses when we board the boat so there will have to be some to return our mounts.”

John gave these instructions and walked to his own tent to prepare. That night they left the camp and proceeded to the coast, looking for a village that could provide two or three boats to take them up the coast. The first village they came to had only small boats pulled up on the beach so they rode on in the darkness. The next fishing village had a small harbour and John could see several boats that could carry them, tied up at the quays. The men dismounted on the outskirts of the village and John with Stephen and the man who could speak Welsh, walked down to a building showing lights. They entered and found themselves in what could loosely be called an Inn. The men who were drinking there turned and some stood up.

"Good evening," said John. "You will know by my voice I am English, I am not here to fight you even though my men surround your village. I wish to offer some employment to those who wish to take it."

He held up a purse and shook it, the coins jingled and he let one fall out. The gold glistened in the lamp light and he could see most of the eyes in the room became fixed on the winking coin. He was gambling that these men were fishermen and were not too interested in the fight with the English as they must have been selling their catch to Chester and surrounding towns. One of the men walked forward.

"What is it you want?"

John explained he wanted transportation for his men up to the headland at the mouth of the estuary. The spokesman turned and a discussion ensued and eventually four men stood before John.

"We will take you, if we can agree a price. How many men are there?"

John said he wanted to see the boats before he gave any further information. They all walked down to the harbour and were shown four large fishing boats, capable of carrying all of the patrol. John and the man who had become the fisherman's leader agreed a price. The tide would be right for them to leave at dawn and John said he would bring his men down to camp at the harbour which would also guard the boats.

"I shall leave enough men around the village to discourage any attempt to warn the forces of David."

At which the leader laughed and said that would not happen as they did not support the rebellion as it interfered with their livelihood. John wondered if he had paid too much but he smiled and shook the man's hand to seal their bargain. As dawn approached several of the fishermen arrived to prepare the boats and John's force packed up and stood ready to board. Several of the soldiers looked very nervous as they walked up the gangplank as it was their first trip on the sea. John spoke to the men who were to return with the horses and told them to wait until they were embarked and on their way. Soon all the boats were underway and with the sails hoisted they started to make good speed out of the river and into the estuary. John had not been to sea either, only a trip on a lake, but he found the sensation of the boats movement exhilarating and he smiled to himself. Soon they hit the swell of the tide and the boat's movement became more exaggerated, many of the men made for the boat's side and some released their breakfast to the fishes. The headland came into view and the Captain of John's boat asked him where he wanted to be put ashore.

John sprung a surprise by asking him to round the headland and take them further along the coast, he said this while holding up another purse and smiling at the Captain.

"Or would you prefer that we take command ourselves?" he said.

The Captain called to the other boats and they sailed round the headland and along the coast of North Wales. "Take us into the mouth of the River Clwyd and we will go ashore there" said John.

The Captain signalled the other boats to follow him and it was not long before they were in the mouth of the river.

"This is far as we can go without grounding," said the Captain and steered his boat to the bank. The men disembarked and a few fell to the ground giving thanks while some just lay trying to recover from the seasickness. Stephen soon had them up and in some sort of order.

“We will make for Rhuddlan Castle,” said John. “ end out forward patrols and lets move off.”

He paid the fishermen who thanked him and said he could hire their boats anytime at these rates. The column marched away and John hoped their intelligence was correct that Davids forces were not in this area, but there was alway chance there were sympathisers looking to make a name for themselves. Nearing the Castle they could hear the sound of voices and John called a halt as one of the scouts came back to report that the Castle was under siege from David’s men. The column moved into the woods and John went forward to see what was going on. The Welshmen were congregated at the main entrance and a small gate at the rear of the Castle, there was little organisation as they fired the odd arrow at the walls and shouted at the soldiers inside to come out and fight. Some had started to tunnel under the walls with the intent to start a fire but had not gone far and were sitting on the side of the trench drinking ale, another group were cutting branches off a large tree trunk which was obviously going to be a battering ram. The whole atmosphere lacked any urgency or organisation. John went back to his men and deployed the bowmen to cover the main gate and the two trenches, he then sent Stephen with the rest to be prepared to storm the gate on his signal. When all were in place John gave the signal for the bowmen to fire and suddenly the air was filled with arrows arching their way to their targets. Pandemonium broke out in the Welsh lines as men fell wounded or dying, they ran to find shelter but John’s well trained bowmen found them as they ran. John blew his horn and out of the trees swept Stephen and his band making for the main gate of the Castle, cutting down all before them. The defenders in the Castle opened the gate and rushed out to join the fight. The battle did not last long and out of the melee stepped the leader of the Welsh signalling his surrender, John walked to him and received his sword. The remaining Welshmen were herded into the Castle and sent down to the dungeons. John called Stephen to him.

“When they have cooled down take some out as a burial party and clear up outside, make sure they are guarded as we don’t want them running off to join David.”

Since Llewelyn's death John had hoped that the fighting would finish but David still continued, so John fortified the Castle and waited for news from the King. They had time to care for the wounded and look after their weapons while the Castle builders carried on with the work that had been interrupted by the Welsh. John found the Captain of the Castle guard a likeable fellow and they talked at length on the best design for Castles. John filed these away in his mind with the prospect of using some of them for Dunston, if he ever got home. He was walking the battlements one afternoon when men appeared moving towards the Castle, they were part of the retreating army of the Welsh. John sounded the alarm and instructed Stephen to prepare for an attack. The Welshmen tried to storm the gates but were soon discouraged by John's bowmen, and a familiar sight of dead bodies littering the field made them withdraw. When night fell John could make out the glow of campfires in the distance but no more attacks came. They were all awakened by the sounds of battle as King Edward's army caught the rebels. As John looked out from the battlements he saw riders galloping towards the Castle, one unfurled a standard and John recognised the crest of the Earl. A courier from the Sir Cedric brought the news that the King's army was approaching, they had success in the field and commanded John to meet him at Wrexham as soon as he was able. There was also a letter from Tania that had found it's way to him. The letter contained the good news that everything was well at the Castle though she missed him dearly. He read the letter several times and longed to go home, fighting for your King was a duty but he yearned to be at Dunston with Tania, especially as his son was growing daily.

The following day another larger group of riders were spotted and as John could see more clearly he noticed that there were more horses than riders.

"It's our men," e shouted excitedly. "We shall ride to Wrexham thank God."

The next day they set off in high spirits with the knowledge they would be at least nearer their homes.

The stopped several miles short of Wrexham to make camp while John and his Squires with four men-at-arms rode towards the town. The town appeared quiet and when Tristan entered a nearby Inn he did not arouse suspicion, there had been no sign of the King or his troops. Tristan returned with this news and John was puzzled as he would have thought that some activity would have been seen around the town. They returned to where they had left the rest of the men and decided to spend the night there, but John forbade any entry into the town. In the morning John and Tristan rode back into the town stopping at the Inn they had previously visited, as they walked in a man approached them an asked if they knew of Sir John Ivanson.

"Who wants to know?" queried John.

Several heads turned and John said that he had seen a group of men on the outskirts of town and if he stepped outside he would direct him. Outside the Inn John revealed himself and the messenger delivered a package to him saying he came from Sir Cedric. The letter inside explained that David had been given up by his army and captured, he was to be taken to Shrewsbury and be judged by parliament. The Earl said that there was no need to come to Shrewsbury and John could take his men home, he asked that John visit Wymondham to inform Rowan what was happening. John thanked the messenger and rode back to their camp. The men could not wait to start their journey home so John ordered them to break camp and start for Wymondham.

The journey home was mainly uneventful, who would want to tackle this group of heavily armed men eager to get home. They stopped and made camp at night but were soon up in the morning and back on the march.

John had time to think as they made their way home, why did the King not want him to stay and fight or was it Sir Cedric's decision? Whoever it was John was glad that he did not have to run the risk of losing more men. They had been pushing on in their desire to reach home and were becoming very tired and irritable, some times tempers rose and blood was spilt so John declared that they would rest up in Nottingham forest for a few days. Once the camp had been set the men began to relax and enjoy the break.

John was resting in his tent when a guard called to say they had caught a man who said he knew him. John recognised him as one of the men who was at the Tournament in Wymondham.

"What brings you to our camp, Robert?" he asked.

"I like to know who is camped in the forest, you might have been from the Sheriff, though I don't think he would have this many men," Robert replied.

"We are on our way home and needed a rest, I am surprised to find you still a free man after what I have heard," said John.

Robert laughed and said the forest was the best hiding place in the whole of England. They sat and talked for a while and then Robert left and disappeared into the night.

'A strange man' thought John 'still an outlaw after all this time'.

As they approached Wymondham the mood of the men lightened as they knew it would not be long before they were home. John ordered that they camp in the valley outside the Castle while he went forward to find out who was there. The guards who had been left opened the gate as soon as they saw him, and John dismounted in the Bailey and made for the main door which was opened by Rowan.

"Greetings my lord, I am pleased to see you. How is the Earl?"

John replied that he was well the last time he had seen him. He listened as he thought he could hear a child's cry. Rowan smiled.

"The lady Tania is here sir and waiting in the Hall."

John bounded up the stairs and into the Hall, Tania came running into his arms and he held her tight, full of love for her.

"Pooh, you need a wash!" said Tania as she pulled away and looked at him.

"Come here, wench, and hug your man, smelly or not. You can come up and wash me yourself."

Tania blushed crimson and turning showed John that they were not alone. There stood a smiling and laughing group consisting of Joan, with Harold, Matilda and a lady that John had seen before in

London.

"I am sorry to embarrass you, especially Lady Falmouth, you must think we are very uncouth here in the country."

"Not at all," replied Lady Falmouth. "I come from the country myself, not far from here."

John picked up Harold and with Tania walked over to the window.

"We are staying here until tomorrow as I am trying to arrange a Mass in thanksgiving at the Abbey so I will stay here with you tonight, if you'll have me?"

"What do you think, just try and stay anywhere else," Tania's reply was said with a sparkle in her eyes?

Tristan entered at that moment and told John the Abbot had agreed to the Mass and would be able to celebrate at one hour from dawn. John thanked him and asked him to tell the troops.

The evening meal was finished and it had been convivial, John found Lady Falmouth (Ann) a good conversationalist. Joan had put Harold to bed and every one started to yawn. Tristan and Stephen returned to the camp to make sure everything was quiet and no one had had tried to leave for home. John stretched and signalled he was ready for bed, with hand clasping Tania's they retired to their room. As they undressed quickly and lay together in the bed Tania whispered to John words of love and he responded with his caresses which brought them to a passionate joining of their bodies. After the first rushed coupling they lay quietly and then after gentle caresses their love making became deep and passionate that brought mind and body to a peak which left them breathless and they went to sleep as one united.

The journey to the Abbey was quite a spectacle, mounted men, bowmen and men-at-arms forming a column with John riding at the head. When they had entered the Abbey, John joined Tania and the Mass began. The Abbot was in his element with so many in attendance, as most of the town had turned up as well, even the cloisters were packed with people. John felt it was fitting as it gave a finality to their adventures in Wales and prepared them to return to a normal life with their families. After the service they formed up again and went back to their camp where they packed up and started their final part of their journey home.

Riding out of the trees John could see Dunston Castle in the evening sun, he always liked this view and he turned to Tania.

"Home at last, I have longed for this day. I cannot imagine how anyone can go on a Crusade and be away from home for so long."

"Perhaps they feel it is their duty to claim back the Holy Places for Christianity," replied Tania.

"Maybe," said John. "It is going to take Saint Peter himself to shift me from here now I am back."

They stopped in the meadow outside the walls and John spoke to the men and thanked them for all they had done.

"Don't spend all the money the King has given you on beer, just enough to keep the landlord happy. I will be seeing you all when you have rested and are back tending your farms. Good luck to you and now return to your homes with God's blessing."

There was a general milling about as they parted from friends they had made during the march into Wales, the soldiers who were left went off to their barracks with Stephen and Tristan. John and his party made for the Castle and were met in the Bailey by Boorman and Roderick. At the evening meal that night John looked around at his family, three generations were there and he felt a certain amount of pride as he watched them talking together and catching up with the latest news. King Edward was now building his Castles to contain the Welsh and John was hoping that he could be busy with his own estates and progress with some ideas he had for improvement. He was looking forward to being with Tania and living a family life, he hoped he could add to the family too, he intended to try.

The next months were spent in catching up with what had happened while he had been away. Roderick had been helping to keep the farms going and they had managed to start some shearing, this would now increase as the men returned. John still wanted their own wool trade with the Flemish traders and he thought about ways this could be achieved. Winter was approaching and John toured the farms to make sure farmers and animals were prepared, he granted extra payments so that roofs could be repaired and to make sure there was enough food for all. A constant visitor, now that Sir Cedric had returned to Wymondham, was Gavin. Tania said to John that there would be a wedding soon as Gavin and Joan were together as much as his duties allowed.

II

Preparations for winter and Christmas were well under way. Jack had improved the forge in the Castle and was producing new hinges for doors as well as locks, keeping all the horses well shod, repairing weapons and generally helping to improve the Castle.

One autumn evening as the sun was setting John walked the battlements, he liked this time of day as he said his head was clearer. He noticed two riders making their way to the Castle, he could not recognise them but could see they rode with some urgency. He descended to the Hall and waited to see who would arrive. Boorman entered and announced that the men were from Norwich with a message from the Sheriff. John read it with a sinking feeling, his peace was about to disturbed. Two of the North Norfolk Barons were unhappy that John was controlling Yarmouth and checking every ship for contraband. They had decided to take matters into their hands and take Yarmouth by force, they were already on route with a force of 200 men-at-arms. John called Stephen and Tristan to the Hall.

"We have to take to a force of arms again, I had hoped for a quiet life until next year at least."

Stephen said, "I will prepare the men, 250 should be enough and they are now well seasoned warriors so it should not take long to send this lot packing."

"I admire your confidence but I would like to stop them before Yarmouth, I don't want fighting in the streets," said John.

Stephen left to send out scouts to find the route the Barons were taking. They decided to make for Burgh Castle at first light and hope to stop the Barons there. There was a chill in the air and the autumn mists still lay close to the ground when the force left Dunston and headed east. John had used nearly all the horses as he wanted to move quickly and arrive at the Castle in time. They were just leaving when one of the scouts returned with the information that the Barons were moving to the coast and had camped for the night near the village of Ludham. John decided to push on with all speed to the coast north of Yarmouth, he told the scout to go back and follow the Barons. The Barons were not expecting any opposition so they delayed their departure from their camp allowing John to arrive outside of town in good time to deploy his men. He positioned bowmen in sand dunes either side of the main access to Yarmouth, he then waited with 50 of his mounted men-at-arms. After the fast ride from Dunston he was feeling very hot in his armour and Hammer was breathing heavily with steam rising from his coat, which did not help John to cool down, he gave the signal to dismount and sent a lookout further up the tracks. The lookout was soon back to say the Baron's force was in sight. With Tristan's help John mounted Hammer and positioned himself in the middle of the track with Tristan and Stephen either side.

"Hold your positions and remember we are better than them, we are here to protect our friends, and our interests."

As he finished the Baron's appeared. They pulled up when they saw John blocking their path. One of the Barons rode forward with two men as escort.

"What is this?" he asked. "I am William Fitzherbert and I am going to Yarmouth, move out of our way!"

"I am Sir John Ivanson, what reason do you have to ride to Yarmouth with so many armed men? This is my town and you are welcome but your men will stay here."

"So you are the young pup who has risen on the support of Cedric," the Baron replied.

"**Sir** Cedric, you mean. I am here in my own right as Yarmouth has been included in my fiefdom by the King. Now return to wherever you came from and keep off my lands."

“You will not stop us with that bunch behind you so look to yourselves as we shall go where we please!” exclaimed Fitzherbert. He turned and rode back to his men and had them form an advancing line, they moved forward slowly as the majority were on foot. When they were about 100 yards away John gave the signal for the bowmen to rise this caused the advancing troops to charge and the first flight of arrows were loosed with devastating results, many of the Baron’s men were felled. A second flight caused even more chaos but by now Fitzherbert was charging and the mounted men reached John’s group. Some of the bowmen were picking of the stragglers at the rear while the rest drew their swords and moved to join the fight that was taking place in the centre. John’s men met the charge and swung into action with their swords, John made for Fitzherbert and drove Hammer into his horse. Hammer had trained for this and used his size and weight to knock the Baron’s horse sideways while John brought his sword down heavily on the man’s shoulder, it sliced through his chain mail and suddenly the arm was gone. Fitzherbert screamed and fell from his horse, John only glimpsed this as a mounted man was coming at him with a spear. He swung his sword sideways and the head of the spear was deflected and almost cut from the shaft, again Hammer went forward and John ran the man through. Men were grunting, shouting and dying, in the killing frenzy it was a miracle that friend did not kill friend. John came through the main fight and turned to see the second Baron raise his sword and cry.

“Stop, we surrender, throw down your weapons.”

John rode through the melee to the Baron who offered his sword to John, he accepted it and the fighting stopped. The two sides withdrew and started to care for the wounded. Fitzherbert lay where he had fallen, still conscious but bleeding to death. The other Baron knelt by him and closed his eyes as life left him. John addressed him.

“What is your name sir?”

The Baron stood. “I am Cuthbert of Aylesham, I know of you and did not expect to meet you in these circumstances. I will gather what is left of our men and return home.”

"You are not Norman," said John. "Why are you with this dog, a man who stamps on the neck of the people in Anglia, I know of him."

"It is true I am Saxon but have accepted Norman rule to save my position and do what I can for my people. How did you know we were coming?" queried Cuthbert?

John looked at him. "That is for me to know, there are more people than you think who despise the Normans."

John looked for Tristan and Stephen and spotted them tending to wounded, he called to them and asked how many they had lost. Tristan said that three had died in the melee and two bowmen who had joined the fight, they also had four seriously wounded, the rest were fit to travel. John spoke again to Cuthbert.

"Bury your dead and take the rest home and stay out of my land. Pass the message to the rest of the Barons that they will suffer the same should they wish to invade."

Cuthbert inclined his head and gave the orders to his remaining men. John looked over the battlefield and was saddened to see so many corpses, the most being killed from the accuracy of his bowmen. He gave orders to Stephen to tie our dead to horses and take them and the bowmen back to Dunston while he went with the wounded and the rest to Yarmouth. Entering the town he found William Fisher, the elected Mayor and some armed men waiting. William stepped forward and addressed John.

"Thank God you are all right Sir, we could hear the fighting from here. Bring your wounded to our apothecary and he will do his best to heal them."

John thanked him and the wounded were taken off. The Mayor invited John and Tristan to his house where they met his wife and son. After getting out of his armour and supping a glass of ale John asked if they had experienced any more smuggling.

"Not recently, they know we are searching the ships and sometimes the crews, but we have heard the contraband is finding it's way ashore on the North coast."

John congratulated him and said if he needed help to call on him, he would pay a visit to the two ports in the New Year. The Mayor invited John and Tristan to stay the night he said they had room for his men in the building next door which they were converting into a barracks. John was dead beat and accepted the offer, his head hit the pillow and he was fast asleep.

He rose in the morning to the smell of fish cooking, not his favourite breakfast dish, and going down was offered a plate of some smoked fish, he struggled to eat it and was sure he had bones stuck in his throat but he smiled and thanked the Mayor's wife. Going out side he found Tristan with the men ready to depart. They had found a cart for the wounded and were all eager to get home.

When they arrived back they found that Stephen had arranged burial for the dead at the church tomorrow.

Tania was overjoyed that he had returned unhurt and Harold came running to him. John realised he was missing his son's advancement. That night Tania was eager for her man and John found it hard to keep pace with her after all the riding he had been doing.

"Just give me a minute to recover," he pleaded. Tania laughed and called him a weakling at which John responded with renewed vigour.

In the morning as they gathered to go to the church John tried to comfort those who had lost husbands and assured the wives they would not be turned out of their dwellings immediately. It was a sad procession as they made their way through the wood to the little church. After the service John invited them back to the Castle to show his gratitude for what they had done. He pondered on the plight of the widows and thought about a solution. If the farms really did well would it be possible to build a small village of single houses to look after widowed and older women and men, who could no longer work? Each farm could support those that lived in the village, it would release workers cottages.

When everyone had gone John said to Tania that he would make a visit to Wymondham to bring Sir Cedric up to date with what had been going on.

“Yes, we can all go and father will see how Harold is progressing. Joan will be pleased to see Gavin too,” remarked Tania.

After several days, when John and Roderick had finished visiting all the farms, the family set off for Wymondham. Sir Cedric was pleased to see them and formally introduced Lady Ann Falmouth, John noticed the sparkle in the Earl’s eyes as he walked with them to the Hall. When they had all settled and Harold had been the centre of attention, Sir Cedric asked John to join him in his room. The Earl asked him to relate what had happened at Yarmouth, he said he had heard reports on the confrontation and that Fitzherbert’s son was trying to raise an army to attack Dunston, but he was only a boy and no one had joined him yet.

“I have let it be known I agree with your actions and would support you if there were any trouble.”

John thanked him and said that his men were now a formidable force anyway. The Earl replied he needed to talk to the Barons and calm down any ill feeling they had. Sir Cedric was obviously very happy to have a grandson and he and Lady Falmouth spent the rest of the day spoiling him. Gavin disappeared with Joan until they all met for the evening meal, where they announced they were to marry. All in all it had been a very happy day and something that was needed after all the recent troubles.

On their journey home John spoke to Tania.

“Your father is very friendly with Lady Falmouth, has he known her long?”

Tania replied that she had been a friend of her mother’s and after her death had continued that friendship with her father.

“It is good that he has a female friend in his life,” said Tania. “Whether it will develop into anything more, time will tell.”

One evening after John had been training with the men he drew his sword and read what his father had inscribed on the blade. The weapon was certainly the best he had ever handled, light yet very strong, the edge was always keen and so well balanced in his hand. The men thought him a master swordsman but John knew that a lot of his success was down to the sword, it was if it had a life of its own. He discussed it with his father and Jack told him that when he was fighting in France a man had given him the falchion that the sword was made from, and had told him it had come from an Island off the coast of Italy where there was a great volcano, and it had been made from material thrown out of the depths of the earth. His father said he didn't believe that there was anything magical about the metal that made the sword, he had just made the best sword he was capable of.

"Make sure when you fight with it, you fight for good," said Jack.

"Where did the ring come from father," asked John. "Don't tell me that it too came out of the fiery depths?"

Jack looked at his son and said. "No, it did not come by fire but by death. I nursed an Arab man for a few days, who had been wounded and before he died he gave me the ring and said to guard it well and only release it to a man blessed by Allah, that is their God. I thought it would complete the gift, and you are blessed by God I am sure, my son."

John said he would try to always fight on the side of good, and went away deep in thought. Make one hundred of the same sword and he would be unstoppable, but why would he want to do that, life was good and he had all he wanted. He sheathed the sword and put it where he could reach it if required. He also thought about his armour, after the fight at Yarmouth there were no scratches or dents, was it the genius of his father in his work, and not some mystical metal. As Christmas approached and the weather turned colder, John and Jack discussed ideas on how to make the Castle warmer. The Barracks certainly could do with more heat and if the men were made more comfortable they are more likely to stay and not drift away.

"I know how the Romans did it, they made tunnels under the floor and heated the air before it went through." Jack said.

"Could not do that in the Castle," said John. "You would not get under those stone floors."

They reached no conclusion and decided to talk about it again.

II

Harold was growing fast, he ran about the Castle with everyone spoiling him and often Tania would have to go looking for the imp who could often be found in the kitchen being given treats by the cook.

John introduced him to riding by placing in front of him as he exercised Hammer, this produced lots of giggles from Harold. Just before Christmas the snow fell and lay heavy and deep around the Castle. Snowmen sprung up around the Bailey much to Harold's delight, boughs of Spruce were brought in, Holly and Mistletoe began to adorn the Castle rooms. The snow was now quite thick on the ground so John invited Father Aldred to stay and say Christmas Mass in the Castle Chapel. A new Priest resided at the church as Father Aldred's infirmities had forced him to retire. It was easier for the villagers to get to the Castle than to the Church in the woods. Gavin had somehow managed to negotiate the deep snow to arrive and spend Christmas with Joan.

Christmas Day was certainly one to be remembered thought John as he sat at head of the table with Tania, all the family together. This is what happiness is. When the snow had cleared and the country life was back to normal John decided to make the trip to Flanders and try to negotiate with the wool merchants to come to his fair. He was telling Tania one evening about his plan and said if she wanted she could come with him. Tania looked at him.

"I can't come with you, I would love to but the sea crossing may not be good for a pregnant woman."

John leapt out of his chair and rushed to embrace her.

"What good news, I didn't guess, perhaps I will postpone the trip. I can make arrangements to go later." Tania said to still go as it would be some months before the birth and they need the best deals for their wool. "I will take Tristan with me and leave Stephen here, he knows the men better and he will be able to go the next time." John decided.

That night John was particularly tender towards Tania, he was very happy and told her she must take special care of herself. Tania smiled and told him not to worry as it was a function of a woman, to give birth.

John set about organising his trip, he sent a courier to Yarmouth to find out when ships would be leaving for Flanders, he told Tristan to prepare for the trip at which Tristan asked was it a big ship they would go on as he was not comfortable when they were on a ship before. John went out to the stables where he found Stephen talking to the grooms.

"Stephen I am going to Flanders to try and convince some of the wool traders to use our fair. I want you to look after my wife and the Castle while I am gone."

Stephen replied that he need have no fears for his family or the Castle while he was away. They had just finished speaking when a courier arrived from Sir Cedric, in the pouch was a letter which said that the Earl had been thinking of John's idea to have his own Wool Fair and with the letter was an introduction to a Jaap van de Groon, a wool trader of Brugge. John smiled and thought Sir Cedric must be reading his mind.

The party consisting of John, Tristan, two of the senior men-at-arm and two pack horses with samples of wool, departed in the early hours one morning. John wanted to reach Aelfraed's camp by late afternoon giving him time to go into Yarmouth and arrange passage for them all. Aelfraed was pleased to see him and welcomed them all, John and Tristan went on into Yarmouth and met the Mayor who accompanied them down to the harbour and introduced them to the Captain of the ship that would take them to Flanders. John was relieved to find there was accommodation for their horses. Tristan gingerly went up the gang plank but agreed this was a much bigger vessel than the one he had been on before but would have preferred to ride to Flanders which caused a laugh from the Captain. They were asked to be on board before noon the next day.

As they sailed across the channel they gazed intently at the dark line on the horizon that gradually formed into the coastline of Flanders. Tristan, despite his fears, had enjoyed the journey once he had got used to the rolling motion of the vessel. They docked in Brugge and were quickly unloaded onto the dockside. John set off to an Inn that the Earl had recommended that would be able to stable the horses. They found the building on the edge of the City and John went in to talk to the innkeeper. Fortunately his French was understandable, he had kept in practice talking to the Earl and Tania. At the evening meal that night they were regarded with some suspicion and John tried to engage some of the locals in conversation but did not get further than the usual greetings. As they departed for bed John wondered if his language skills were up to negotiating with the Flemish cloth merchants.

Next morning the landlord of the Inn directed John to Van de Groon's house which was situated by one of the many canals in the City, he gave the two men-at-arms the address and directions and told them to stay in the Inn and guard the horses and packs. The weather was cold and there was biting wind as they set off for the house, Tristan grumbled and said he would have preferred to stay at the Inn. They arrived at the house and rang the bell, a man servant opened the door and John explained they would like to speak to Van de Groon. They were conducted into a fine room to see an elderly man sitting in a large armchair in front of a roaring fire, he looked up at the two men.

"Good morning young man, you have come to see my son Jaap?"

John was impressed with the old man's precise English.

"Yes, that is correct sir, we bring greetings from Sir Cedric and he wishes you good health."

"Sit down, sit down," continued the senior de Groon. "Jaap should not be long. I have known Cedric a long time, he served with me on the Crusade, of course I was younger and fitter then. Now I am comfortable in my advancing years with a good son to look after me. Ah, here he is." The door opened a young man of about the same age as John, came in.

He extended his hand and said.

"You must be John, the friend of Sir Cedric, hello I am Jaap. I see you have met my father."

Jaap walked over to a table and the three of them sat down leaving the old man by the fire.

"I have made a good contact for you with one of the Traders, he will be here in a moment. His name is Henri de Bleese. His English is not so good but you speak French, yah?" John nodded. "One thing you must know," continued Jaap, "there is much unrest here at the moment, so be careful when you walk out. There is a problem in who we trade with so be watchful and speak English not French, where you can."

The man servant opened the door and announced Henri de Bleese. A young man entered and introduced himself to John and Tristan then joined them at the table.

"My father and I are willing to discuss with you a trade agreement but we would need to see some of your fleece and test the quality," said Henri.

"We expected this," said John. "We have brought some fleece with us, it is at the Inn, under guard."

They sat discussing what would be needed in a Wool Fair, and how many fleece would be there. The meeting broke up with John arranging to visit the de Bleese house with the sample wool tomorrow. Jaap invited them to stay and eat with them and over the meal a general discussion centred around the trouble brewing in Bruges. On their way back to the Inn Tristan remarked on the groups of men standing around, some of them gave John an enquiring look.

"Let's get back to the Inn and see if there has been any interest in our visit, somebody must have seen us arrive with the pack horses" said John.

The two men-at-arms were with the horses when they arrived, Alban told them no one had been and the wool was out of sight. John explained that they would all go together in the morning to the house of Henri de Bleese, which was situated by one of the canals on the outskirts of the City. That night John slept fitfully, he was thinking of Tania and he could also hear people moving about outside the Inn. The morning brought grey skies and a drizzling rain as they made their way to the house of de Bleese. The wool was still wrapped well and came to no harm, but the four men and horses had to bear the unpleasant weather as they rode on. Reaching their destination Jaap was waiting for them and they were guided into a large barn where the wool was unloaded and they could shake the water from their cloaks. Leaving Alban and Chad with the wool they followed Henri into the house. He turned to John.

"My father will be here later and we can look at your wool. I hope he can get here without trouble, there was some rioting last night, did you hear it?"

John said he had been disturbed but had not heard actual rioting. They sat in Henri's comfortable house and waited as the rain still came down outside. There was a noise at the door and a tall man appeared who Henri greeted as his father and introduced John and Tristan.

"I am very pleased to meet you, I am Philip de Bleese, head of the House of de Bleese and we are one of the best cloth makers in Bruges. Let us go and look at your fleece, the quicker you return to England the better in these circumstances."

They went out to the barn and unwrapped the wool, de Bleese inspected it thoroughly and after a while stood and said to John.

"This is a very good grade of wool, fine for turning into cloth. If the rest of your flocks can produce this quality then we shall both be very pleased. Come back to the house and we can discuss how we proceed from here."

John was feeling pleased that the journey looked like being successful but kept a straight face and hoped he could cope with the business side. Philip was obviously used to dealing with the English Wool Fairs and set out his usual terms. John queried several points and gained better terms for Dunston with a date to be set after shearing. Henri wrote up the terms and gave John the parchment and then produced a bottle and glasses from which they toasted their venture.

The evening sun was hiding behind some dark clouds as they rode back to the Inn. Groups of men were standing about and John could sense a mood of unrest like a dark blanket covering the City. They were grateful to arrive at the Inn with no trouble.

John and Tristan went down to the Harbour to find a ship for their return journey. Among the several that were moored there was and English ship bound for Lowestoft on the early tide tomorrow. John arranged passage for them all and they could board tonight. As the rain had now stopped they decided to stretch their legs and walk the horses back to the Inn. Halfway there they were confronted by a group of men demanding that they give them their horses. When John refused and stood in front horses. The men rushed forward with swords drawn. John and Tristan quickly drew their own weapons and stood ready. John stepped forward and met the first man, his sword became a blur as his adversary fell to the ground with his throat cut.

John sensed the second coming at him and with a quick reverse thrust ran him through. Tristan had overpowered another and was holding him at sword point against a wall, he was begging for mercy as he had a wife and children. The last attacker was standing in shadow and made a move to run but John reached him before he started and after a quick parry and thrust a third body was laying in the street. Tristan looked at John.

"What shall I do with this fellow?" he said.

"We will take him back to the stables and tie him up, if we take him to the authorities we shall be delayed," answered John. "With all that is happening around the City tonight let's hope they won't worry about this until later."

As they finished tying the man up and asking Alban to watch him while Chad collected their belongings, Tristan looked hard at John.

"Why do you look at me like that?" asked John. "Help me to move these into the canal?"

"I have never seen swordplay like that, it was so fast!" said

Tristan.

"It is a well balanced weapon," said John as he, himself, could not remember clearly what had happened. This sword certainly had a mind of its own.

Collecting up all their belongings they made their way down to the harbour. The Captain was waiting for them, they were soon aboard and easing their way down the estuary.

"I will be glad to get back to England," said Tristan.

They all agreed as they found places on deck to try and sleep while the ship silently slipped away from Flanders.

When they docked at Lowestoft all of them were eager to get off the ship and be on their way home. Once moving towards Dunston their mood lightened and John thought about what had transpired during their visit. He was sorry he had to kill those men but the situation at that moment meant kill or be killed. They stopped for a meal and rest by the village of Loddon, villagers had seen them and brought food and drink, it was the first time they had met their Knight from the Castle. John thought about this and wondered if there was some way he could meet more of the people in his fiefdom.

As soon as they saw the towers of the Castle their mood lightened even further and they started singing, or a noise that could be construed as such.

Tania was waiting in the Bailey and rushed to him as he dismounted, Joan was there with Harold who was excited as much as they all were. Later, sitting by the fire John relaxed and recounted what had taken place in Flanders but left out details of the fight, he had also commanded the others to keep quiet regarding this episode.

"I must see the Earl as soon as possible," he said to Tania. "He will need to know details of what we have agreed about the Wool Fair."

"Think about that tomorrow," replied Tania. "Now it is time to go to our bed."

John yawned and agreed. John looked at Tania laying beside him, he touched her tummy and noticed there was just a little thickness there.

“I wonder if Harold will have a brother or sister?”

“I would like him to have a sister,” said Tania. “I expect you want another boy.”

“No, not really, I just hope you are all healthy and all goes well.”

Tania snuggled closer to him.

The next morning John went down to the forge and found his father. He told him of the fight in Bruges and what had happened when he used the sword.

“There is some power that guides this weapon. I am not sure that I like it.”

“I think the power comes from you, not the sword. You fit together and your skill is enhanced,” said Jack. John did not reply but thought to himself that there was something strange about the sword.

John worked hard making sure his garrison were well trained and able to protect his fiefdom, he made the rounds with Roderick and informed the shepherds of his visit to Flanders. They were very pleased and asked if it meant more for them and when told that it would, they shook John’s hand and said he would have the best fleece in Norfolk. Tania continued to grow and as the summer came let Joan take more charge of Harold so she could rest. John found his conjugal rights restricted but understood and remembered that it did not go on for ever. Sir Cedric visited often accompanied by Lady Ann, she seemed to like the family atmosphere at Dunston.

II

One sunny afternoon Stephen came to John to tell him that a young man was outside the Castle at the end of the drawbridge, demanding to see him. John thought it odd that he would not come into the Bailey, so he followed Stephen to the where the young man sat his horse. John noticed the man had a companion with him and they were both wearing swords. Stephen went onto the drawbridge and called to the young man. "Who are you and what do you want? Will you come forward into the Bailey where we can talk?"

"I will not step into your trap, I wish to speak to John Ivanson, is he here?"

John kept himself hidden while Stephen was talking but he had a clear view of the man and did not recognise him. The young man called back.

"My name is Nicholas Hausman and I claim revenge on John Ivanson for my father's murder. Tell him to arm himself and meet me here in one hour and I will have the revenge I seek."

Stephen replied. "This is the home of Sir John Ivanson, a Knight of King Edward's and you would do well to go back to your home and remember your father was tried by a judge and jury and found guilty of his crimes. I will inform Sir John and he will decide whether to come out to you or not."

Hausman inclined his head and the two of them rode away. Stephen came into the Bailey and John told him he had heard it all.

"Prepare Hammer in all his regalia and bring a tournament lance."

Stephen went to prepare Hammer and John went into the Castle calling for Tristan.

"Fetch my armour and help me into it."

John, with Tristan's assistance donned his armour, strapped on his sword and stomped off back to the Bailey where Stephen stood holding Hammer's reins. Hammer was resplendent in his trapper and armour as John was helped to mount he was hoping his strategy would work. Placing his helm on his head he was ready, he rode out of the Castle with the sound of a horn and Stephen at his side bearing his lance. Housman and his companion were facing him a few yards from the drawbridge.

"Who challenges me?" roared John.

Houseman raised his lance.

"I, Nicholas Hausman, for the wrong you did my father."

"When you fall, where will you be buried?" enquired John. Taking the lance from Stephen he rode towards Housman who grasped his lance and kicked his horse into a charge. Hammer need no urging as this was what he was bred for. They sped towards each other and John used his same technique as in the Jousts and his lance struck home and lifted Nicholas clean out of his saddle. John quickly reined in and turned towards the man on the ground, who was not moving. His companion was holding up his hands shouting.

"He yields, have mercy," as he rushed to the fallen man. John pulled Hammer to a halt and called to Stephen. "Take him in to the Castle, if he is alive, and fetch the Priest."

He dropped his lance and let Hammer have his head, galloping off to calm both of them down. Nicholas was carried back to the Castle and put in the tower, he was certainly alive but in pain, The Priest announced he had suffered broken ribs and a broken leg. Stephen said that if John had not used a tournament lance the man would be dead. John returned and went up to see Nicholas, the man was conscious and in pain. John said he would talk to him later. He went back to the hall where he met Tania.

"His father was a villain how do I make him understand that?"

"You can't, my love," said Tania. "My father might and he should visit us again soon."

John shrugged and wandered off. He had felt a certain exhilaration when he rode out in his armour, he needed a few more fights, but where? The King was still occupied in Wales and he'd had enough of that wet place. Maybe he should go on a Crusade, in the meantime there was plenty to keep him occupied at home.

After three days John asked Nicholas's companion if he was fit to talk to and the man said he was. John went to the tower and found Nicholas sitting in bed with bandages round his chest and his leg bound up between two pieces of wood.

"You should have killed me when you had the chance," said the injured man.

"You may be right but it would have been for the wrong reasons," replied John. "Your father committed crimes here in England and he paid the price. The Earl of Wymondham will be here soon and will explain to you what happened."

"Will you not tell me," implored the young man. "All I have heard is that you captured him and hung him."

"The first part is right, I did capture him, but he was tried by a court in Wymondham and sentence was carried out there. A Judge came from London and he had someone to speak for him. What am I going to do with you, you can't travel yet so I guess you will have to be my guest until you are fit."

He then told him the details of what had caused the demise of Henri Hausman. At the end Nicholas told John that he did not know his father very well as he was always away, mainly in France. He had been told by some of Henri's friends that he should take revenge and kill John.

John left him to think about what he had told him and went to meet Tania. She was sitting the garden talking to Harold while Joan walked with Gavin, John saw her and said.

"When are those two getting wed, we need to know so we can arrange another companion for you?"

"There are plans afoot in that direction but you must be patient until they tell us. You are unsettled, my love, come tell me what ails you?" she replied.

"I suppose it's this business with Hausman, I will have to make up my mind what to do with him soon."

After Sir Cedric had visited them and spoken to Hausman there was a definite change over the young man, he pushed himself to be active and get his strength back. John found it easier to talk to him and he learnt more of life in Flanders and the cloth making industry. The time came when he was fit enough to travel and they agreed, with his companion's help, he would leave the next day.

As life returned to normal John's thoughts turned to the two Squires and he resolved to push them on, it was time they accepted the responsibilities of knighthood, he would ask the Earl on his next visit, if he would conduct their investiture. One afternoon a young knight called at the Castle, John's first thought was that another Hausman family member had come after him, but when the man dismounted in the Bailey and removed his helm it revealed Gavin. He asked where he could find Jack and John accompanied him down to the Forge. He left Gavin with Jack and guessed the reason for his visit. On his way back into the Castle he met Joan and asked her to come with him to the Hall. Jack and Gavin came into the Hall and Jack announced that he had agreed to Gavin's request to marry Joan, Joan leapt up and went to Gavin and stood by his side, it was difficult to embrace him in his armour. Gavin asked to be excused so that he could divest himself of his 'tin suit' and Joan was left hugging her father and John together. That evening he sat in his room thinking about the future and he decided to ask Gavin if he would like to live in Dunston, if so he would talk to Sir Cedric. Gavin was older than his two Squires and his experience would be an asset to the Castle, John's plans could now start to take shape.

Talking together in Sir Cedric's room John was able to outline some of his plans and the Earl agreed for Gavin to move over to Dunston and also for Stephen and Tristan to finish their quest for knighthood at Wymondham culminating in the investiture at the Abbey. During their discussion's John learned that the Earl still had property in France and suggested that John might like to visit there and assess the situation. This would be the adventure that John was looking for, a journey into another country.

Spring turned to summer and the year rolled on. Tania gave birth to another son, that pleased John and Harold who was delighted that he had a brother.

John was walking in the Castle gardens when he received a

message that Stephen's and Tristan's investitures were to take place and arrangements were made for all of them to travel to Wymondham. The occasion went well and after the two young men's night vigil the ceremony took place in the Abbey. John was proud of the two men and what they had achieved while in his service. They were both to return to Dunston and take up positions there under John. The next big event was Gavin and Joan's wedding which had been arranged to take place just before Lent, it was a joyous occasion and many of the Tenants came to wish them well.

Tristan walked up the stairs to John's room, this was the first time he was to meet him since he had returned from Wymondham, he knocked on the door.

"Come in," called John. "I am glad to see you Tristan, I want to tell you of a trip I am taking and I want you to accompany me."

He then explained that he would be going to France and taking Alban and Chad as Squires.

"I want you to accompany me, I need a man with experience."

"I would be pleased to accompany you Sir, after our last trip to Flanders it has given me a taste to see more of the world," replied Tristan.

John continued by telling him he had arranged with Stephen to support Gavin here at the Castle while they were away. The next days were spent preparing for the trip, and making sure horses and weapons were in good condition. Tania was quiet during this time and John knew that she was not happy that he was going away, after speaking with her father she had accepted that John needed the excitement of new horizons and would be more settled on his return.

One evening as John walked the battlements of the Castle he looked down and saw Tristan still training his new destrier, John had acquired it from Sir Cedric and Tristan was getting used to being up on such a large animal. They were twisting and turning and Tristan put the horse to an old sack laying on the ground, the horse obediently stamped on it and snorted. All war horses were trained to shove, bite and kick opposing horses and also stamp on fallen bodies, Hammer excelled in all of these. John wondered if they would need these skills on their travels, France was an unsettled country these days.

The day of their departure came and as they rode away from the Castle John turned and saw Tania standing with Harold and the baby and felt a pang of regret.

They rode on towards Yarmouth where they would spend the night and find a ship that would take them across the Channel. William Fisher was pleased to see John again and offered hospitality to John and Tristan with their Squires accommodated above the stables. Early in the morning John, accompanied by Fisher, went down to the harbour. The Mayor said that a ship had come in the previous day and would be returning to Caen in two days time. They found the vessel and called for the Captain, he came on deck and invited them aboard, in his cabin John explained that he needed passage for his group and they agreed a price for the voyage. In the interval before they departed John decided to ride over to Lowestoft and meet the Mayor whom he found in good health and the town thriving. As soon as he returned to Yarmouth they boarded the ship and prepared to sail. The voyage was uneventful and standing on the harbour of Caen John realised they had no friendly place to call on.

"We will set off south into Normandy," he said. "We can make camp at the day's end and discuss our plans." As they made camp that evening John looked at the information that Sir Cedric had given him, the first place to make for was the town of Villedieu les Poeles where they would find a guide to take them on. When they arrived at the town they found it was a centre for making copper articles and it was full of the sounds of the coppersmiths at work. They stopped in the town square under the inquisitive stares of several towns people, John asked if anyone knew Monsieur Garrond, the name that Sir Cedric had given him. This was answered with stoney silence and cold stares.

"There's an Inn," said Tristan. "I will go and ask there."

"Take Chad with you," said John. "He does not speak French

but two are better than one in a strange place." Tristan returned with the news Monsieur Garrond had been arrested by the King's men. He was asked if they were going to visit their English friends. John was puzzled as the Earl had said the Chateau was looked after by a French family, who also tended the vineyards. They moved on and headed towards Brittany and the town of Rennes where John hoped to find out more. As they travelled on they became aware of a distinct antagonism towards them and heard that Brittany was under attack from the King of France, this made them avoid the main towns and move on as fast as they could. They eventually came to the region north of Rennes and looked for the small town of Guipel where they hoped to find the Chateau. The place was more of a village than town and as strangers they were initially viewed with suspicion. John visited the church and met the resident Priest. He asked if he knew where the Chateau Vent was.

"Yes, my son, it is but two leagues north from this church. Have you come to visit your English friends?" John looked at him.

"I have come at the request of the owner Sir Cedric of Wymondham and he told me the estate is being looked after by Monsieur Trouville, I know there are many English families here but not on this estate."

"We have not seen the Earl for a long time and then two men came with instructions to take over the Chateau. They say they are his men but they do not act like the Earl. He was always generous and kind and a good employer as most of the villagers rely on the Chateau for work. We have not seen Monsieur Trouville since these men arrived."

John explained to the Priest that Sir Cedric did not send these men, whoever they are, and he was here to find out what was gong on. That evening as they sat in their camp John discussed the situation with the others. "In the morning we will go to the Chateau in full apparel and give off as much authority as we can even though we are only four."

Out of the evening gloom a voice hailed the camp and two men appeared. John stood to greet them.

"Good evening sirs, welcome to our camp, how can we be of

service?”

“We have spoken to our Priest and he has told us of your mission. There are several of us who used to work for Monsieur Trouville at the Chateau and in his vineyards and we would want to help the Earl recover his property, if you needed us,” said one of the men. “My name is Gerard Vigneron and there are about fifty of us.”

John asked him and his friend to sit and join them. He said his intention was to call at the Chateau in the morning and if he, and his friends would like to gather at the gates he could use their help, if needed. Gerard said.

“They have about twenty men they have recruited from the local riffraff and are not looking after the vines, this has been worrying us as it is our livelihood.”

After a few glasses of wine and conversation the men left.

“Who the hell are these men,” said Tristan. “I know Sir Cedric has not been here for a while but as far as we are concerned it is his property.”

They halted about five hundred yards from the gates in the morning and could see there was a gate guard. The group of villagers met them with an assortment of weapons, swords, scythes, axes and a few with bows. John and Tristan were in armour and so were their horses, they told the villagers to wait while they approached the gate. They rode up to the gate and said to the guard to open it as they had the authority of the owner. The man looked confused and said he would have to speak to his master.

John put Hammer at the gate and the great horse pushed the gate down with ease.

“Tell him Sir John Ivanson is here to take over this property.”

The man ran up to the Chateau and very soon John saw two figures running towards the stables. John and Tristan charged over to where they had disappeared and found the two men frantically trying to mount horses. They charged into them and the two men fell to the ground, some of the villagers had caught up with them and pinned the men to the ground. John and Tristan dismounted and looked at the prisoners. John exclaimed.

"We know these two!"

The villagers forced the two men to their feet and John removed his helm.

"Thatcher and Carpenter, what are you doing here? Find somewhere they can be locked up securely while we go to the Chateau."

John and Alban moved off as the villagers rounded up more of the trespassers. Entering the Chateau they searched the first floor and found, locked in a room, Monsieur Trouville his wife, son and daughter. They were weak and in poor health, the room had two straw matrices, a table, four chairs and a bucket. When John entered they cowered in a corner, afraid of this man clad in armour. John spoke calmly to them and told them who he was and Madam Trouville broke down in tears, her husband stood in front of John and held out his hand.

"When you have had something to eat and drink I want to know what has happened here," said John.

He went out to where he had left Tristan.

"Where are they?" said John.

"We have locked them in one of the store houses," replied Tristan.

"They can stay there until we find out what has been taking place here. Where is Gerard?" said John. Gerard was with the villagers who had rounded up the rest of the intruders.

"There were some who resisted," Gerard explained. "They will not bother anyone any more. There are no casualties from our men. Two of these prisoners came with the men you know."

"Thank you for all your help," said John. "Let's find out what has been going on here."

They questioned the prisoners and it transpired that the ship had put in at Brest and Thatcher and Carpenter had made good their escape. They were making their way to Caen when they reached Rennes they heard of the English Lord and his vineyard. They had recruited the riffraff and taken over the Chateau. John went back to the Chateau and found the Trouville family much recovered and full of gratitude for their release. Some of the villagers were workers who had been thrown off the estate and immediately began to clean and tidy up the house. John and Tristan change into more comfortable clothing and discussed what their next steps would be. That evening the house had been transformed as servants began to return and most importantly the cook was back in the kitchen. Over a late meal Monsieur Trouville told John that the money from the last grape harvest was hidden and the two villains had not found it. All in all it had been a successful day but John was tired and it was soon obvious as his head kept dropping so excusing himself he went to bed.

He was rudely awakened by Tristan shaking him.

"They've escaped. One guard killed and another injured!"

John quickly put on some clothes, grabbed his sword and dagger and followed Tristan to the scene of the escape. There had been a man who had escaped detection when they were rounding up the other men employed by Thatcher. He had returned and killed one jailor and severely injuring the second then helping Thatcher and Carpenter to escape. Chad and Alban had saddled two horses which Tristan and John quickly mounted and set off towards the coast which was the direction the two prisoners had been seen heading. The sun was just coming up when they could see three men making for a wood some distance away. John and Tristan spurred their mounts in that direction hoping to cut off the escapees before they reached the trees.

They only just made it and the three men on foot slashed at the horses as John and Tristan drew their swords and told the prisoners to give themselves up. John jumped from his horse and before the startled men could do anything his sword had parted Thatcher's head from his body and was going after Carpenter who tried to run but was pierced through before he had even turned the third man fell to his knees begging to be spared. Tristan had also dismounted and grabbed John's arm.

“Stop he is unarmed John,” he shouted.

John, breathing heavily lowered his weapon. Tristan could feel John’s arm trembling as he fought for control.

“It has a mind of its own,” said a shaking John. “ I must get rid of it before it lands me in real trouble.”

He wiped the sword clean and told the third man to bury the bodies, he sat down with his back to a tree. Tristan looked at him and said that he only used the sword in defence or attacking enemy so maybe he should keep it and learn how to control it better. When the burial was done they went back to the Chateau and agreed with the villagers that the prisoners should be taken to the nearest town and handed over to the authorities.

John spent a fitful night, the actions of the previous day weighing on his mind, did the sword have some fearful power. He rose early and went down to the stables, saddled his horse and rode to Rennes arriving at the Benedictine monastery of Saint-Metaine just as the office of *prime* was finishing. John found the Abbott and asked if he would hear his confession, after which the Abbott suggested that John place the sword at the foot of the High Altar and pray. As John knelt there he heard someone enter and turning his head he saw Tristan walking up the aisle. The young man knelt beside John and the two of them joined together in prayer. A sudden intake of breath from Tristan made John open his eyes and he saw the sword had a gentle glow around it. Tristan stood and stepped back but John could not move, he was transfixed by the swords glow, he could read what his father had inscribed on the blade clearly ‘DEO JUVANTE’.

John stood and picked up the sword, sheathed it as the suns rays continued to pour through the upper window like a spot light directly onto the altar where the sword had lain. John smiled and turned to follow Tristan.

John and Tristan rode slowly back to the Chateau, both deep in thought. It was an experience they would both remember for a long, long time. When John arrived he went straight to his room and considered what had happened, when the sword had been made his father had worked normally, there had been no unusual occurrences. He vowed to learn to control the weapon to his way of fighting. The next morning, after a meeting with the Trouville's, John walked out to the gardens and found Tristan and Alban practicing with their swords.

"Come and join us," called Tristan.

John thought for a moment and then walked over to them and drew his sword. They practiced for a while, thrusting and cutting and comparing various moves. John relaxed and his expertise began to show without any danger to opponents, especially when he fought both of them and disarmed them both. As Tristan picked up his weapon he called to John.

"I said it was you and not the sword."

They walked back to the Chateau together and after meeting Chad they shared a meal and began discussing when they should return home. Brittany was not the most comfortable place for Englishmen as there was a movement to take it back to France. John called Monsieur Trouville and when the man arrived he said.

"I have the necessary papers here to permanently lease the Chateau and lands to you. Sir Cedric wishes a Frenchman to legally operate this property, how say you? Is this acceptable to you?"

Monsieur Trouville said it was most acceptable and this would allow him to expand the vineyard. Having concluded the business John told him they would be leaving in the morning.

II

The four adventurers left early to find their way to St Malo hoping to find a ship bound for England. When they arrived at the port they found it very crowded mainly with English people trying to get back to their homeland. Alban found a reasonable Inn that could accommodate them all, including horses, and John with Tristan went to the harbour in search of passage on a ship. No Captain wanted to take the horses and John decided to send them back to the Chateau with Alban, he also included his suit of armour, just keeping a chain mail vest and helmet. Alban agreed that he would stay with the horses and when everything had settled down make his way home. The three of them went from ship to ship but without success, it appeared that everyone was trying to get to England. Eventually they returned to the Inn and ordered a meal, the Innkeeper came to them and said as it was so busy he wanted payment in advance as he didn't know who they were. Tristan was quite offended and stood up.

"Do you know who you are talking to?" he said. "This is Sir John Ivanson, a personal friend of Sir Cedric of Wymondham and owner of the Chateaux Vent, so mind your manners."

The Innkeeper said how was he to know and now he did know they were most welcome as he purchased wine from the Chateaux. After a good meal and a few glasses of wine they were ready for their beds, John was soon soundly asleep. Suddenly he was woken by movement outside his door but before he could reach his sword several men burst in and held him down on the bed. A tall thin man looked down on him. "Dress yourself, you are now a prisoner of King Phillip of France."

John's hands were tied and he was led downstairs. At the bottom of the stairs he saw at the body of Chad who had obviously tried to stop the French but had paid with his life. Outside in the yard he was bundled into a cart where Tristan sat also bound hand and foot.

"Did you see Chad?" aid Tristan.

"Yes," answered John, "a brave man murdered by these villains."

"Quiet," said the leader of the group, "we had no choice."

The cart trundled and bumped out of the yard and in the dim morning light made its way along the coastal road on their route to who knows where.

As they passed through the towns the cart and its occupants drew many an inquisitive glance.

John wondered what had happened to his weapons and was not

until the third day that he saw his scabbard, sword and bow strapped to the tall man's horse, if only he could free his hands. They untied him to eat but he was watched closely and when finished immediately tied up again. He managed to talk to Tristan but when he used English they were told to keep to French. John had been trying to find out the leaders name but the other soldiers, for that is what they were, would not tell him. At one stop, at an old Inn near the outskirts of Paris, the landlord spoke to one of the guards and called the leader *' Monsieur le Corbeau'* or in English *' The Raven'*. They trundled through the streets of Paris to an old Castle where John and Tristan were taken to a tower that had two rooms and off the smaller room a garderobe. The larger room had table and chairs and in the smaller a large bed. The window was barred but also high up in the tower. Their guards left and locked the large solid oak door. They were both dog tired after the journey and were soon sharing the large bed sound asleep.

In the morning they were brought bread and cheese, water and their clothes. They washed and ate and John remarked.

"They had this planned, they have collected our clothes and weapons from the Inn. It must have been the information we gave to the Captains of the ships we were trying to buy passage from."

"But why bring us all the way to Paris?" asked Tristan.

"I have my suspicions from what Sir Cedric told me," said John. "The French King needs money so he captures what he thinks are wealthy men or from wealthy families and holds them for ransom." Tristan moaned, "I shall be here for ever as my family has no money."

They sat discussing this when the door was unlocked and *le Corbeau* entered the room with two guards.

"Ah my friends I hope you are comfortable and you have everything you need?"

John replied, "How long do you intend to keep us here. I was not aware that we were at war?"

"We are always at war with the English," said *le Corbeau.* "Until you are driven from all our lands we shall be at war.

However that is not why I came. We have sent a message to Sir Cedric stating that we want a certain amount of money for your release, as is customary. Until that reaches us we ask that you assure us you will not try to escape and for that you will be moved to more comfortable surroundings and allowed to walk in the gardens. Do I have that assurance?"

John looked at him and said, "It is our duty to try and escape to our country and our families, you would do the same. What we will say is that we will not kill any guards or your staff when we do escape."

The Frenchman laughed. "Then you will never escape because you would have to kill all of them to leave this Castle. I think I will take the challenge and you will be moved tomorrow."

He looked straight into John's eyes and then swept out of the room.

They were roused early the next day and escorted to a different tower where they were led to a suite of rooms that were better furnished. They now had a large room to sit and eat with two smaller bedrooms and the usual garderobe. An old woman appeared and brought water to wash and a jug of wine.

"Not a very appetising bed companion," said Tristan.

"That's the idea," said John. "You would not be able to get round her to assist you in escaping."

That night John lay in his bed thinking of Tania and wondering if she was missing him and if she knew of his plight.

Several months went by as John and Tristan waited for news. They walked every inch of the garden looking for places to get out without being noticed. The Castle was very near the river and they could hear boats going up and down. There was just one window that looked out over the gardens but it was heavily barred, and the other wall had the guarderobe. All other windows faced inwards to the garden and bailey. John kept thinking and planning but with no success. They did not see much of their captor, the old woman said he had gone north to war. The days began to get shorter and nights longer as winter arrived, fortunately they were kept supplied with wood and there was always a large fire burning. One evening as Tristan was returning from the guarderobe he commented.

"It's freezing in there, the wind blows right up your arse. It's a good job we are up this high over the river or you would get a wash at the same time."

John spent a good deal of his time trying to find a way that they could break out of the prison. He noticed that the guards had become more relaxed around them and there seemed to be less in number. Given time an opportunity was sure to arise. To try and break out of the garden was impossible, there were too many guards and it only led to the Bailey. John had looked at the guarderobe as a means of reaching the river but the holes were too small and landing in the filth below was not very appetising. A guarderobe was a small bay built out on the wall of the Castle where the normal functions of emptying your body's waste went through a hole and straight down the wall. That night he looked at the project again, would it be possible to widen the hole? There were two holes and if they restricted use to just one then they could work on the remaining hole to try and widen it. No one other than themselves ever went in there. The problem was how could they cut through the stone that the Castle was built from, then Lady Luck shined upon them. Some repairs where being done to the battlements near their tower and the builders had to come into their part of the garden. A plan began to take form in John's mind.

"Don't drink all your wine tonight," said John over their evening meal. "Put it in this bottle."

"What's the idea?" asked Tristan.

"We need at least three bottles for an idea I have," answered John.

When the old woman came with their meal John complained that he was not sleeping well and would she bring an extra bottle of wine to help him. After some grumbling the woman said she could do better than that and went out. When she came back she handed John a little leather purse and told him there was a powder inside that her mother had taught her to make from mushrooms and that a small amount in a glass of wine would make him sleep, but not to overdo the amount or he might sleep forever. John thanked her and pocketed the purse. The next day was one of those early autumn days that was still warm and sunny, they prepared themselves for their usual trip to the gardens but this time taking two bottles of wine, one dosed with a small amount of the powder. They sat on the grass and listened to the builders working on the battlements, The work finished for the day and the builders came down through the garden.

"Hot work on a day like today," said John.

"It certainly is and working up there in the sun makes it hotter," replied one of the two builders.

"Sit awhile and join us in a drink," said Tristan.

"Now that's an offer we can't refuse," said the second man and they both sat down. Tristan offered the dosed bottle of wine to them and John drank from the other. It did not take long for the drug to work and the two men were soon fast asleep. John opened their bags and found there were several hammers and chisels, taking one hammer and two chisels he closed the bags. Dusk was falling and John tried to waken the men. One of them gradually came round.

"That must have been strong wine or we were very tired, we will miss our meal if we don't hurry. Help me rouse my mate we must go quickly."

"We were also asleep I think it was bad wine," replied John.

They gathered up their bags and staggered off. Mid morning the next day the builders returned, they were still groggy from the drink the previous evening and blamed the castle servants for sending poor wine. John went back to the guarderobe while Tristan kept an eye on the builders, when they started hammering, so did John hoping nobody would notice any difference in the direction of the noise. His luck was in as a large slab of stone fell almost immediately and there was soon quite a large hole in one side of the guarderobe. As more stone fell so the stench rose from the piles of excrement at the bottom and John had to stop and go outside the room to breath. At last he thought the hole was big enough and went down to the garden to join Tristan.

"I will drop the hammer and chisels in the grass and they will think they left them there," said John.

Sure enough the builders came into the garden and one of them tripped on the hammer and said.

"I told you I hadn't dropped it over the side, it's here, and the chisels. Must have left them last night. Don't offer us a drink tonight, we're still suffering from the last one."

With that they left and said they would see them tomorrow. John and Tristan went back to the guarderobe and looked down the widened hole.

"Do you think we can get through there?" sked John.

"Looks all right, but I don't fancy it much. It's where we land worries me, in all that muck, and it's quite a drop," replied Tristan.

"We can dive into the river and get cleaned up, my main concern is that we have no weapons, except our daggers. I wonder what he has done with my sword, I must get it back," said John. "Let's have our meal and think it over."

After the old woman had left them John told Tristan of his idea.

" f we tie the covers together from both beds it will lower us enough to drop without hurting ourselves." "That's if we can get through the hole," said Tristan.

"I am sure we can, but we will need some food so don't eat all the next two meals and then we will go," said John as he put some bread in a bag.

When the old women brought their food in the morning John asked for more bread as they were hungry midday, after a lot of muttering under her breath she came back with the bread and some cheese. They were about to go down to the garden when two guards arrived and looked around their rooms, fortunately Tristan had just made use of the guarderobe and the smell prevented them looking in there. They stood by the door as an officer of the guards came in and told them there had been no reply from Sir Cedric so they were to be transferred to a larger prison in two days time.

When they had all gone John said to Tristan.

“We go tonight.”

Tristan nodded and wished he had not used the guarderobe.

As the sun set that evening the two men prepared to make their escape, they tied the bed covers together and with their possessions in their bags they moved into the guarderobe. They had changed into their oldest clothes, and put their only change of clothes into the bag. Tying the bed covers to the table they jammed it in the doorway and lowered them through the enlarged hole.

“Not far to the ground as far as I can see,” said John.

“You go first, then if you break your neck I’ll stay here,” said Tristan, with a grin.

John lowered himself into the hole, it was a tight fit but with a little wriggling he was soon hanging on the makeshift rope and descending hand over hand. Reaching the end of the covers he looked down, he pushed himself off from the wall, took a breath and let go. He landed on the edge of the soft muck that lay at the foot of the wall and gave a tug on the covers for Tristan to follow. As expected they were messy but not as bad as they could have been. They stood at the waters edge and removed their clothes and washed themselves as best as they could, putting on their fresh clothes they ran along the base of the wall for a few yards and John said.

“From what I could gather from the occasional talks with the old woman, we need to cross the river.”

Tristan asked, “How far across is it?”

“This is one of the narrow parts but it is quite deep near the Castle. Tie your boots to your bag and let’s get on with it,” aid John.

“Wait, what is that up ahead?” asked Tristan.

They crept along the wall until they came to the end of the Castle and found a garden fence with a gate and tied to a stake was a small boat.

“There are no oars,” said John. “We will have to use our hands.”

Untying the boat they clambered in. Pushing away from the bank and moving into midstream the current took them and they were soon out of sight of the Castle. Going round a bend in the river they drifted to the side and paddling with their hands they made it to the shore. They had landed near a small wood so made their way into the wood to find a place to rest until daybreak. Sitting round a small fire, trying to keep warm, they discussed what they should do next. There would be a hue and cry in the morning when it is discovered they had escaped and the river would be searched so they needed to get away as far as they could.

“I think we should split up,” said John. “You go north and try to find a boat for England, I will go back to the Chateaux and recover our belongings and make my way back with Alban. This should confuse them for a while as it is not what they will expect.”

“What about your Sword?” said Tristan. “It is too precious to leave in their hands!”

“I know,” replied John, smiling inwardly.

Tristan firmly believed that the sword had magical powers. There were many objects that purported to have mystical powers and many Knights spent years searching for them but John came from a family that had a strong faith and their feet on the ground, however John wanted to recover the sword, his father had made it and he was a better swordsman with that particular blade in his hand. As the early light filtered through the trees John and Tristan parted, Tristan heading north and John west towards Brittany.

John cut himself a stout staff and made good progress the first few days. He was approaching Alencon when he remembered the English had been driven out of this region, he wondered if his French would arouse suspicion. John’s beard had grown and he was dishevelled in appearance so he hoped that if he mumbled he would be able to impersonate a tramp. That night he found a stable and covered himself with straw to keep warm, he was awakened with the sound of hammering. He had spent the night in a stable attached to a Smithy and the Smith was preparing some horse shoes. John cleaned himself up as best as he could and walked into the Smithy.

"Good morning sir," he said to the Smith. "Is there anything I can do to earn a breakfast?"

The startled Smith turned and looked at him. "Where did you come from, sleeping in my barn were you? You can feed the horses and clean them out, and bring me some water from that well."

John fetched the water and then went to the horses, the Smith called to him to bring the black one to the forge. John brought the horse in and stood stroking his muzzle and talking quietly to it.

"You like horses?" asked the Smith.

"You'll want him quiet if you are going to shoe him," answered John.

"Know about shoeing horses do you?" aid the Smith.

"A little," said John.

"Get the old shoe off while I bring the new one over."

John lifted the horses leg between his knees and pulled out the old nails and the shoe dropped to the floor, he picked up a file and prepared the hoof to receive the new shoe. The Smith brought the new shoe over and placed it on the hoof. There was a pungent smell as the shoe marked the hoof.

"Good fit," said John as the Smith hammered the shoe to a more perfect fit and then cooled it in the bucket and handed it to John who nailed it on.

"You have done this many times before," accused the Smith. "How is it you are not working?"

"I am making my way to see my family and have been robbed," answered John. "They took my horse and all my belongings so I am making my way on foot."

"Where are you making for?" asked the Smith.

"Near to Rennes," said John.

“You might be in luck, finish these horses and we’ll talk over breakfast. My name is William,” and the Smith offered his hand.

“Henri,” said John extending his.

They finished the work and went inside the Smith’s cottage where his wife cooked up a plentiful meal. The Smith said to John, as he sat back.

“I have a relative in Fougeres and I look after his horses and his carts. The bay mare is his and I have been repairing his cart. If you would deliver these to his farm you would not be far from Rennes. My lad will go with you as there is another cart to bring back, and it will be company for you.”

Someone to keep an eye on me too thought John. He was relieved to think that he would not have to walk all the way and this would be a good disguise. Three days later John said his farewells to William and set off for Fougeres and William’s cousin. He was only a few miles from Alencon when they were stopped by a contingent of French soldiers who told him they were looking for two escaped prisoners, they questioned them and then rode on. It took him several days to reach William’s cousin in Fougeres, camping overnight in the cart. William’s cousin was a large hearty farmer who welcomed John and said he must stay the night and his son would take him to Chateaux Vent in the morning. John was woken at first light and they were quickly on their way, the horse greeted him with a whiney as an old friend. William’s son talked about the farm, the land, the problems in the region and the fact there might be a fight, John did not have to say much at all. When they reached the gates of the Chateaux John thanked the lad and said he would walk up to the house. He went round to the back and found Alban coming out of the stables leading Hammer. Alban started back in surprise and said, “What do you want, we have no work at the moment so be off with you?”

Hammer snorted and made straight for John, Alban tried to hold him but the big horse was too strong for him. When he reached John his large head came down to nuzzled John.

“Hello big boy,” said John. “Have you missed me, I am very glad to see you.”

Alban realised who it was and stopped trying to pull Hammer away.

After they had greeted each other John said he wanted to go to speak to Monsieur Trouville and he would tell Alban the full story later. Sitting down after a meal John told them what had befallen Tristan and himself. Alban could not believe it but Monsieur Trouville said he was not surprised as many of the French knights had become poor due to funding their armies and then loosing their battles and not gaining any spoils.

After John had rested and had his beard cut shorter he looked through the weapons they had and picked a sword that felt reasonable but not like his own. He practiced with Alban and was still a good fighter but he missed the balance and speed he had with his own blade. They prepared to leave the Chateaux and John decided to go back to the Castle where he had been imprisoned, Alban was not keen on the idea but John wanted to find out if *Monsieur le Corbeau* had returned.

"They will not recognise you when you go to enquire, and I doubt that they will recognise me with my new beard, but I will wait out of sight."

Alban was still not convinced. Monsieur Trouville's eldest son, Jacque, persuaded his father to let him go with them to give them credibility as French travellers should they need it, a decision that would prove invaluable later. They set out with John riding Hammer, Alban on his own horse leading a pack horse with John's armour and the rest of their baggage, Jacque on a stallion with another packhorse. They were in high spirits as the little convoy headed off towards Paris. As they neared Alencon John said he would call on the Smith and pay his respects for the way he was treated. William came out into the yard as they clattered in on the cobbles, he looked up at John sitting on the great horse

"What can I do for you sir?" he asked.

John dismounted and replied. "You can accept my grateful thanks for helping me, and we have brought your cousin's son to meet you."

William stood back in amazement and then clasped John by the arm and said.

"After you had gone we had soldiers here looking for an escaped prisoner but I knew nothing. I did wonder if that tramp I hired was not what he seemed."

They all laughed and William invited them in to partake of a jug of wine where John told him the story of what had happened. That night they camped in a field behind the Smithy, moving on in the morning towards Paris. It was a gloomy and rain filled day as they approached the Castle and John could see a pennant flying from the battlements, did it mean that *Le Corbeau* was at home? John asked Jacque to go to the Castle talk to the guards and see what he could pick up. When Jacque returned he said that the Count was away fighting in Flanders.

They packed up and moved towards Flanders and as they neared the borders they met many wounded retreating from the battle front. John spoke to a nobleman who was lying on a stretcher and attended by servants. The man was quite angry at what he perceived as poor command of the battles, he told John that they had been fighting for land south of Ghent when they were attacked from the rear by a different Flemish Duke's men. He was determined to see the King and bring the French army together and attack Flanders in a full scale war. John thought to himself that he must find *le Corbeau* before that happened or he would be trapped here for a long campaign. Soon after they crossed the border they came across a small town that had grown up near a monastery, there were several men at arms walking up the slope to the monastery some wounded and most looking tired. John found an Inn that suddenly had room for them when they heard John was English. After settling their horses they enjoyed their first home cooked meal since they had left Brittany. John asked the landlord where the wounded men had come from.

"They are the defeated French from a battle just a few leagues from here."

John immediately wondered if *Le Corbeau* would be there. He suggested he and Alban take a stroll round the town before turning in.

"We might pick up some information," he said.

There were not many lights in the street and as they came out of the Inn they nearly fell over two soldiers supporting a third who had been wounded. Speaking in French John asked them who was their commander and was told the Duke de Salpetriere, he recognised the name as being near the Castle they had been imprisoned in.

"I am sure that is *Le Corbeau."*

Alban looked mystified as John had spoken in French but one of the soldiers said.

"That's him, it's a name he got as a young man, he collected sparkling and pretty things."

"Yes, and he did't pay for them either," said the other man.

John wished them good night and continued his walk.

Dawn was just breaking as John woke his two companions, there was a white frost outside and they shivered as they dressed. Alban went down to prepare the horses, Jacque packed their belongings and John paid a sleepy landlord. They moved off in the direction the wounded men had come from, there was no one else about at this hour and their journey was undisturbed until the sun began to rise and they came across a village that appeared to be full of Frenchmen. They made their way through a wood, keeping away from sentries until they had left the village behind. All was quiet, even the birds had forgotten to sing, they slowed their pace and kept a careful lookout. Suddenly a voice called out to them to halt and out of the trees came a group of Flemish Guards. John noticed they were also being covered by well placed crossbow men. They were escorted to a man clad in armour with a flowing cape. John explained their purpose and asked the nobleman if he had heard of the Frenchman.

"Oh yes, we know him," he answered. "He likes to creep up on you and hit you from behind. He is probably skulking around here now. We came across him and his men last night but lost him in the darkness."

John asked if he might join their detachment and was told he would be most welcome. The Flemish men soon made them welcome and wanted to know what part of England they were from, John explained that Jacque was a personal friend and not a spy. The nobleman introduced himself as Peter the Count of Kortrijt and said he knew Sir Cedric and had imported his wool. The men were preparing to advance towards the village that John had seen on his way and Peter suggested that they ride with him. John donned his armour and prepared Hammer, with Alban's help. They moved off and John felt a thrill go through his body as he prepared for battle. They found the French had fortified the village, blocking the street with overturned carts and placing archers in the houses. Soon arrows were flying from both sides, John kept a look out for *Le Corbeau* but could not see him. The Count directed men to spread out and surround the Village the horsemen then formed together ready for a charge. A horn sounded and the charging horsemen made for the lowest end of the barricade, John felt Hammer's muscles tense as he gathered himself and flew over the obstruction. They were soon into the cut and thrust of the melee, John kept looking for his quarry as Hammer bit, pushed and trampled his way through the throng. John sat high slashing with his sword and feeling it bite into flesh as he came through the first line. Still no sign of the Count and John spurred Hammer through the fighting men and into a clear space then he caught a glimpse of a man disappearing into a side street. John spurred Hammer after him and caught him as he tried to negotiate a cart that had been turned on its side.

"Fouchine, I have you, turn and fight me!" alled John.

The Frenchman stopped and turn to face John, he kicked his horse and rode at John with his sword raised. They clashed and John parried the stroke but felt a shudder up his arm, they whirled and slashed their horses kicking up the dust when suddenly Hammer bit into the neck of the smaller mount of Fouchine. This gave John the chance to drop low and thrust his sword into his opponents thigh, Fouchine gasped and dropped his guard giving John the opportunity to deliver a killing blow. The Baron tried to lift his sword to protect himself but the blade suddenly seemed to be too heavy and John's blow struck home into *Le Corbeau's* neck and he fell from his horse. John went to him and removed his helm but he could see the man was dying.

“The sword would not hurt you,” murmured Fouchine. “I could not lift it, it served me well until today but it knows to whom it really belongs…” and life passed from him.

John picked up the sword and felt the familiar balance in his hand, he almost thought the blade glowed but dismissed it as a natural pleasure in retrieving what was his. He mounted Hammer and rode back to the centre of the village where Peter was rounding up prisoners and ordering his men to search the village for stragglers.

“Count Fouchine is dead,” said John. “One less French Lord to worry about.”

Peter smiled and raised his hand in salute.

John found Alban and Jacque, who were unscathed, mainly because they had kept out of the way. They went back to the Flemish camp where celebrations were getting under way with plenty of ale and wine.

The following morning John and his friends said goodbye to Peter and departed, Jacque back home and John and Alban to the coast. John offered Jacque a position in his household but he said he would stay with his father so returned to Brittany. Alban and John made their way to Bruges where they found a ship going to Yarmouth and with some negotiation they managed to buy a berth for themselves and their horses. The sea crossing was uneventful save that Alban was not a good sailor and spent most of the crossing flat on his back. Reaching Yarmouth John made contact with the Mayor who was pleased to see him and offered rooms at his house. After a generous meal that evening he was eager to learn of events since he had been away, the mayor said that Gavin had visited him and that he sensed no problems at the Castle. The good news was the Shire was coming together and the farmers were beginning to see the results of the cooperation. John was eager to get home to his family but he owed the Mayor the courtesy of hearing him out. The sheering must have been successful as there had been more bales of wool passing through on their way to

Flanders, the Mayor reported, but he also said that taxes had been increased. He did not know much of what was happening in London except there had been more warships than usual putting into Yarmouth for supplies and telling of several battles at sea against the French. John retired with his mind full of what the Mayor had told him and eager to get home and find out from Sir Cedric what was going on. His final thoughts before sleep took over was of Tania, French and Flemish girls could warm your bed for a night but there was no comparison to a wife's love and affection.

As they sat at breakfast an urgent knocking came at the door and a servant announced that Tristan was asking to see John who rose and welcomed him. Tristan recounted his uneventful journey through Flanders and across the Channel. They had passed a naval flotilla heading down the Channel towards the French coast and Lowestoft was full of stories relating to battles against the French. John was concerned that the ships carrying his wool would get through but Tristan said the action was further south. He said to Tristan that he was leaving for Dunston within the hour, Tristan replied that he was ready to go now.

They rode hard and reached the village just as light was failing, John could see the lights from the Smithy as they pushed on to the Castle. Approaching home John could see that the drawbridge was up and the Castle secured for the night. Alban blew his horn and heads appeared on the battlements. John cupped his hands around his mouth and called.

"Open the gate to Sir John Ivanson, your Lord."

One of the heads disappeared and the drawbridge began to lower, when the gates opened a detachment of men arms appeared led by Gavin. John dismounted and waited for them to reach him.

"Welcome home Sir" said Gavin.

"I am glad to see you guard the place well Gavin."

John smiled and grasped his arm. They walked back into the Castle and reaching the Bailey they saw the main door open and a figure came rushing through, the next moment Tania was in John's arms. They walked back inside clinging to each other and reached the main Hall where Jack, Matilda, Joan and Stephen were standing with large smiles on their faces. After the welcomes were over John explained briefly the events that had kept him away from home so long. He learnt from Gavin that Sir Cedric had waited before replying to the demands for ransom. He said that if he knew John at all he would be trying to escape so he had sent word to France that he needed proof of John's capture. Eventually John went to his room to change his travel stained clothes, Tania followed and stood and watched while he divested himself of his dirty clothes and washed himself, she moved towards him and undid her dress and let her clothes fall to the floor. John held her in his arms and felt the desire he had for her pound through his blood. They moved to the bed where their love for each other was expressed in the passionate movements of their bodies and the cries of ecstasy, after which they lay breathless in each others arms.

"Did you really miss me?"

"I did, every night. I missed you and Harold and… what are we naming our second son?" asked John. "Edmond" said Tania, looking up at him. "It means protector."

"Good, we will need a good protector. Let's go and see him."

They dressed and crept into the next room where the two boys lay sleeping. John felt a swelling of pride rise up through his body and he held on to Tania. They joined the others and he continued telling of his adventures while a meal was brought.

"Tomorrow I shall go to Wymondham to see the Earl," said John.

"Gavin will accompany me while Stephen and Tristan bring our men at arms up to fighting fit. From what I learnt in Yarmouth we may be needed."

They all went to their quarters and the Castle was quiet apart from the occasional calls of the Guards.

John made an early start to meet Sir Cedric, he noticed that his Tenants along the route were already in the fields and some of them waved a hand. I must visit them soon myself he thought, to keep morale high.

Arriving at Wymondham John was shown up to the Earl's chambers who greeted him warmly.

"Welcome home John, it is good to see you fit and well. I expect Gavin explained why I delayed the payment of a ransom, and here you are as I hoped."

"It was a right decision Sir, as the man is now dead."

He sat and told the Earl all that had happened on his visit to France. Monsieur Trouville had written to Sir Cedric thanking him for giving him the control of the Chateaux and the way that John had rescued him from Thatcher and his crew. Sir Cedric discussed the recent decisions the King had made regarding the increase in taxes and that he was taking control of the wool industry, which did not sit well with the Earl but he now had a voice as he had been chosen to sit on the new Model Parliament. They discussed how they could raise the money for the increase taxes without causing too much distress to their finances. John said that he now had good connections in Flanders for their wool, but if the King was taking control they would have to be very careful if this was to continue. The Earl also warned John that Scotland was now a hotbed of unrest and there would be fighting there before long. John asked if Gavin would stay at Dunston, now that he was married? Sir Cedric said he had been thinking of that and his decision was that he should come back to Wymondham where he needed him. John thought it would be a wrench for Joan to leave the children but it might be good for her to be away from her mother and father. They finished their discussion and the Earl said to John.

"Be prepared to receive a call from the King to join him in a march against Scotland."

John rode home with many thoughts on his mind, he now wanted a peaceful life with his wife and sons, but the country always seemed to be in turmoil. Maybe he would not be called to go to Scotland, he had heard it was a barbaric place, worse than Wales, he had enough problems at home with the new taxes and the King's attempt to control the wool trade. He paused at the edge of the woods and looked at his Castle in the afternoon light. So much had happened over the years since he had met Sir Cedric and had become a Knight with the responsibilities that went with that title. He had a duty to his King but he felt a stronger duty to his family, his land and his Tenants. He urged his horse on and continued towards his home, Gavin and his escort had also fallen silent sensing that their Lord was troubled. Tania was waiting for him in the Bailey and Harold stood looking at his father, John could see he was growing up and he would have to spend more time with him to mould him into an heir to the Castle. The evening meal that night was quieter than usual as Gavin and Joan were leaving the next day and John was still concerned about what he had learnt in Wymondham.

Rising early John felt clearer in his mind on the course he should take. Rousing Stephen and Tristan he told them to assemble all of the Castle troops and then proceed with intensive training after he had inspected them. There were at least three hundred armed men in the Castle, with the family and servants this grew to a further fifty, all supported by the income from the land and the wool. When required John could call in extra men from his fiefdom and field an army of at least one thousand men, all these needed training and if they were to be effective they needed weapons and armour. John called Roderick to meet him in his room. "How did the shearing go, were we up on last year?"

"Yes, Sir, very much so and the quality was improved, our Flemish buyers were impressed and we have new enquiries from Flanders," answered Roderick.

"Well done there will be extra money for the best Tenants and an increase for yourself. I think the time is right to employ someone to take charge of our finances, I believe Sir Cedric has a spare abacus," said John thoughtfully.

"I know of a man Sir, he is the son of our biggest farmer and he has been at the learned school in Cambridge," said Roderick.

"Send him to me and we will discuss this again."

With that parting shot John went hunting for Tania, he found her in the kitchens talking to the cook with a young girl holding Edmond's hand. Harold saw John and immediately walked to him, John put his arm round his shoulders and Harold lent into him and John felt his heart swell.

"I am going to the fens and I shall be away overnight," said John.

Tania pouted and twinkled her eyes at him saying.

"I shall have to have a stable lad come to me then."

John slapped her rear end and laughing went of to prepare for his journey with Harold walking beside him.

John, Stephen and their guard arrived at Aelfraed's village just as the sun was setting. They were greeted warmly and were soon seated in front of a roaring fire in Aelfraed's cottage supping from large pots of ale.

John was brought up to date with what was happening in the Fens and also a report from Aelfraed's men in Yarmouth and Lowestoft. The main topic was the state of the wool trade now that the King was interfering, Aelfraed suggested it might be a good idea for John to visit Flanders and set up his own contacts. John agreed and asked if Aelfraed would be willing to allow the wool to travel through his fens to the coast. If there was a suitable agreement he said he would protect the shipments until they were on board.

Arriving home John called Tristan and Stephen to him and explained to them what he was intending and he wanted their support, they both agreed they would follow him whatever he decided.

A young man arrived at the Castle and Roderick introduced him as Edgar of Loddon, son of one of the largest free farmers that owed loyalty to John. He told John he had finished his studies at Cambridge and would like to work for him as a bookkeeper and secretary. John welcomed him into the Castle family and Boorman accompanied him to his room. As Boorman left John could see age beginning to tell on the man but he still valued his service. Stephen reported that the men at arms were now well drilled and he had increased the number of patrols through the fiefdom, they would have plenty of warning if unwanted strangers came into their area. John realised it was time to go to Flanders and put in place the next part of his plan. Stephen would accompany him and two other men, he said his goodbyes to Tania and the boys, Harold wanted to go with him and John had to reason with him to stay and guard his mother, they then departed for Yarmouth. They spent the night with Aelfraed and in the morning Aelfraed took them down to a small quay outside Yarmouth where a sailing barge was moored. The Captain was a jolly man named Robin Fisher and he welcomed them aboard. There was a small cabin where they were to take cover if the weather turned inclement. They set sail and the Captain said he was making for a secret cove on the Flanders shore, when they arrived they were to meet their contact in a tavern. On entering the establishment they were greeted like long lost friends by Peter the Count of Kortrijt. When introductions were over John and Peter got down to business, Peter was the agent for several cloth makers who wanted to buy John's wool direct at obviously advantageous prices, he had large buildings near this village to store the wool and it would become the distribution point. John thought there could be a reciprocal trade in cloth eventually, both men mentally rubbed their hands.

"The biggest problem will be the French ships if they know what we are doing so secrecy is important," said John. "The fact is that we are going against the King."

"That gives the venture the spice I like," answered Peter.

John thought to himself that he was taking the most risk. They spent the night at one of Peter's chateaux not far from the coast and after a very good meal they fell into bed. The next morning John said that they would journey to Nieuwpoort to find berths for their passage home as the Barge had returned after dropping them off. Peter gave them a note for a friend of his who would be able to help Arriving in Nieuwpoort they made for the house of Peter's friend who went with them to the docks and spoke to a ship's Captain. He said he had room on his ship and he would be leaving within the hour. They thanked Peter's friend and went on board. The ship took them back into Yarmouth and they had to walk back to where they had left their horses with one of Aelfraed's men on guard. John remarked that his feet were sore and he hadn't walked so much since he had left France. Spending that night with Aelfraed they finalised their plans for shipping the wool to Flanders.

It was a fine morning as they set off for home, John was pleased that everything had gone well and then thought perhaps it had gone too well, was trouble coming! He was deep in thought as they neared a small wood when suddenly an arrow thudded into the ground in front of him. He kicked his horse into a run and made for the trees. More arrows were coming at them and one struck one of their guards. As they reached the wood John stopped and quickly dismounted.

"Quickly, get into some cover," he said as he caught the guard who was about to fall from his horse.

John lowered him to the ground as he could hear movement of men through the trees. Stephen and the remaining guard stood in front of John but the man was dead with the arrow in his heart. John stood and drew his sword, the three of them faced the outlaws as they came out of the trees.

"I am Sir John Ivanson, and this is my land," shouted John. "Yield now or face death."

The leader of the outlaws stopped and laughed. "Perhaps he has a purse as big as his mouth lads," he said. As the rest came together John counted eight men but not all had swords and only two held bows. John stepped up to the leader and said.

"I have work for men who want it and cold steel for those who rob."

The man laughed again and lunged at John who side stepped and thrust his sword straight through the man's chest. It was though time stood still, everyone froze as John withdrew his sword and looked at the remaining outlaws.

"Who is next?"

One of the bowmen lifted his bow and was immediately felled by a dagger thrown by Stephen. The remainder turned and fled back into the trees.

“Good throw, Stephen,” said John. “We must clean out these woods and send word we will not tolerate outlaws here.”

They hoisted the dead guard onto his horse and set off for Dunston. With the higher taxes and pressure being put on land owners, John could see more of this type of incident appearing. He was fortunate that his fief yielded good profit so he must use it to protect all his tenants and friends. Arriving home Tristan informed John that several groups of men had been seen making their way to the coast, possibly to escape the call to arms from the King. John met the two young Knights together with Roderick and worked out a plan to take a reasonable sized force around the farms and see that the farmers and shepherds realised the dangers and were prepared. That evening John sat in the hall in front of a blazing fire and looked at the growing family, Jack was now slowing down and relied more on the lad who had been taken on in the Smithy, Matilda still helped Tania and was a good companion. Harold and Edmond were growing fast and Tania had employed two girls from the Village to help her. The two young Knights would need rooms of their own at sometime, but where? With the moat surrounding the Castle the only way to expand was up, he would have to talk to the builder and see what could be done.

Coming in from a morning ride John found he had visitors, Sir Cedric was sitting in the Hall with Tania and the children. The Earl suggested that they talk in John’s chamber and when they were seated he said.

“I am here to tell you that I have to raise a force to assist the King in his ventures in Scotland and this is to include you and as many men as you have.”

John sat in thought for a moment and then replied to his friend and mentor.

“I will not lie to you and I will tell you I am not in agreement with this Scottish venture. I know we must protect our boarders but I think there is more to this than we know.”

“You are right,” said Sir Cedric. “The King wants to subdue the

Scots once and for all They have come too far south and his intention is to vanquish them and drive them back behind the border. To do this he will need a good sized army."

John sat and deliberated and decided to tell the Earl of his plans to export to Flanders himself, and to do this he would need all his men to protect the farms and the shipments. Sir Cedric smiled and said.

"If you support him now you will find that the taxes will be ended and you will have control over your own wool trade without going behind our backs."

John said he would give his answer in a few days. After Sir Cedric had gone back to Wymondham John thought hard about the implications of taking his men to Scotland. He would loose some to death and some to desertion and he could not afford to have that happen. However if what Sir Cedric had said about the taxes and wool trade were true then he must support the King. A compromise would be to take a smaller force using the excuse of lambing and the increase of outlaws. With these thoughts in mind he went to find Tania and talk to her. His two sons were growing fast and the years were slipping by and any time away meant time lost with his family but as Tania pointed out supporting the King would be better than going against him. John sent a messenger to the Earl asking when would he depart for the North and saying his force would join him.

II

The departure day came and John and Tristan with five hundred men set off for Wymondham to meet Sir Cedric and his contingent. The combined force with baggage train and support staff numbered close to one thousand five hundred men. They joined the Kings army and marched towards the Scottish boarders, chasing the remnants of the last Scottish invasion back to their homeland. They were approaching Berwick on Tweed when the scouts reported they had seen a number of armed men in the woods on the South side of the River Tweed. The Scots were going to try to delay them reaching the bridge into the town. John rode up to Sir Cedric.

"I'll take my men and circle behind them."

The Earl agreed and as the main army moved on to the town, John's force set off to the right of the wood. They circled behind where they thought the Scots would be and started to move into the trees. It was not long before they were spotted and a blood curdling yell warned the rest that they were being attacked from the rear. John's bowmen quickly took a stand and loosed arrow after arrow into the yelling horde, Tristan blew his horn and John led the charge of horsemen into the melee. The bowmen drew their swords and followed them, John drove his new destrier forward and the horse barged his way into the fighting men, stamping and biting while John laid about him with his sword. A huge brute of a man came at them screaming and shouting, Mace, his new horse, responded to John's knee pressure and side-stepped, the man was swinging an axe and as he missed, John took off his head. The fighting was ferocious and the wood seemed full of yelling Scots, then John caught sight of Sir Cedric's foot soldiers coming in from the other side, suddenly the yelling subsided and men could be seen trying to make their escape back to the town, with their bits of cloth skirts flying in the wind. There is always an eerie silence when a battle finishes and the dead are counted, those near death are helped along their way and wounded put on carts. John had lost eleven of his men, six dead and five who would not fight again. He met the Earl who was also dismounted and talking to the wounded.

"What a crazy, frightening bunch," said John.

"Hatred of the English spurs them on," said Sir Cedric. "We haven't seen the last of them, so be prepared." They rejoined the main army and moved on towards Berwick. The Kings forces had taken the bridge and had joined with a force that had entered the town from the West. John accompanied the Earl to a Council called by the King who had taken up residence in the Castle. Edward outlined a plan to march on Edinburgh and establish a governing body there to control the Scots. John would have preferred to be marching home, he had had enough of this wild land and wanted to be back in the relative peace of his own home. When he returned to the house they had commandeered he called Tristan and told him of the plan. On the march north they encountered small groups of Scots who disappeared before the army, John wondered if they were gathering for a final battle. They left the land they marched over scorched and bare, feeding off the villages they passed through and killing those who opposed them and some who didn't. Edward was bent on showing them he was King and rebellion would be severely dealt with. John did not like this kind of warfare even when Sir Cedric tried to convince him that it was the only way the Scots understood. He went out on a scouting party to see some more of this inhospitable land. He saw that the standard of living was far below that in the South, people scratched an existence from the rocky soil and it was only in the larger towns and cities that their wool trade allowed some citizens to become rich. Returning back to Edinburgh John was given instructions to go back to Berwick on Tweed and start collecting men who would be needed to build the walls around the town that Edward had planned. They were pleased to leave the mountains behind and were soon marching along the shoreline to Berwick.

Arriving in the town John commandeered the town hall for his base and started to send out for the men he needed. A man approached him who said he was the King's Mason and had already designed the walls so John put some of his men to supervising the labourers.

Edward returned to Berwick on Tweed to make sure the walls were going up according to plan and John was given leave to go back home. Tristan and the men were in high spirits to be on their way back to Norfolk but John warned them to stay alert as there were still roving bands of Scots below the border.

They camped outside York of a few nights and John journeyed into the city to see if the new cathedral had been finished. There were still workmen busy around the building which John could see would be very large when finished. Tristan found him looking at the new altar and called to him.

"We should move out of this place as there is sickness here, it is fortunate we are camped out of the city." John joined him and they went back to their camp warning everyone to stay out of the city and they would move on in the morning.

They marched on getting ever nearer to Norfolk, they lived off the land and stayed away from the main roads. As they neared Norwich the mens spirits rose, they even broke into song as their feet took them nearer to Dunston.

As they approached Dunston Woods the scouts came back to report that there were several armed men on the track and some were cutting down a large oak. John halted the column and sent Tristan to investigate, he sent the men to the edge of the wood and to keep out of sight. When Tristan returned he brought disturbing news, he had ventured to the other side of the wood and had seen a large force of men attacking the Castle. There were ranks of archers shooting fire arrows high into the Castle and a small catapult firing rocks at the walls. He had crept as near as he dare to the men cutting the oak and it was clear this was for a battering ram should they succeed in lowering the drawbridge. Tristan said he thought there were about two hundred men that he could see.

“Did you see a standard,” asked John.

Tristan answered he could see nothing clearly. John called his captains together and organised his attack, take out the men in the wood first quietly if possible then bowmen to fire at the catapult and any other foe. This would be followed by his horsemen charging the archers while the rest, under Tristan, followed to destroy who ever it was attacking his home, but John told him to leave a group of horsemen in the woods to defend their rear.

“I do not understand who would do this,” said John. “We are not at war with our neighbours.”

“Remember you fought two Barons in Yarmouth,” remarked Tristan.

“You think this might be a reprisal, if it is then they will go the same way as last time.”

John’s temper was rising and he strode over to the baggage and donned his armour while the rest of his men prepared for the coming battle.

He called out, “Tristan, clear these interlopers out of the woods and the rest of you prepare to chase these beggars from our lands.”

Tristan sent a runner back to tell John the woods were now clear and he could bring the rest of the men up. The bowmen stepped out of the trees and walked to within range, there was no alarm from the attackers, perhaps they thought they were their own men returning. They soon thought differently as arrows were finding their marks and men were falling. The crew of the catapult were the first to go down and then it was anyone who turned to face them. There was pandemonium for a few minutes as someone tried to organise the attackers to face this new challenge. John’s Squire sounded a horn and John led his horsemen in a charge down the slope to the Castle. They met the attackers head on and a fierce fight began, John and Mace were in the thick of it until the rest of his men reached them then pushed through the melee to see if he could find their leader. He came through the main fighting to see four riders making off and by their armour he could see they were nobility. He set off after them with Tristan in pursuit. Mace, even though he was a big horse, had a good turn of speed and with John urging him they began to gain on the four when out of the wood rode the horsemen that had been left there. The four riders in front of them turned and tried to outflank them but it was too late and John was amongst them. As Mace barged into the first rider John swung his sword and just missed the gap between his helmet and shoulder, the rider spurred his horse but Mace hit him again and threw him off balance. John parried a thrust from his opponent and then thrust his sword into the unprotected part under his shoulder this made him drop his sword and he called out.

“I yield.”

John turned from him to find one other man slumped in his saddle from a blow that Tristan had inflicted and the other two surrounded by the group from the wood. One of the men called to John.

“I am Robert Fitzherbert, son of the man you murdered in Yarmouth, I demand the right of single combat with you to avenge my father.”

John removed his helm and asked Fitzherbert to do the same. The remaining man also bared his head and John was surprised to find himself looking at Cuthbert of Aylesham who was also at the event in Yarmouth. John looked at him and said.

"You know very well it was not murder and you were trespassing on my land. I told you not to cross my path again or I would have your head, it appears I now have two opponents, well so be it. I have the choice of weapons and ground, for you young man," he said looking at Fitzherbert, "sword, and on foot here."

With that John dismounted and replaced his helm. Fitzherbert dismounted and drew his sword and immediately rushed at John who parried the blow and stepped back. Fitzherbert sensing he had the upper hand pushed forward with a flurry of swings, John parried them and sized the man up. He noticed the young mans swings were misdirected on a back swing so after the next forward slice he made, John stepped in drove his sword up under his breast plate. Fitzherbert staggered back as John withdrew his blade, he tried to gather himself to continue and John said.

"Enough, you are severely wounded."

The young man drew himself up and swung his sword again saying.

"To the death!"

John's sword felt alive in his hand as he stepped inside the swing and the blade entered Fitzherbert's unprotected throat. He fell and John went to him and removed his helmet, as the young man's eyes fluttered to a close John said to him.

"It was not murder."

John stood and looked for Cuthbert who had dismounted and was looking fearfully at John.

"I am not a skilled swordsman so I yield to you now and you may do to me what you will."

John thought for a moment.

"I charge you to return home and not to come south ever again. I will ask the Earl to increase your tax to recompense the damage you have inflicted here."

Cuthbert bowed and said he agreed.

"I wonder how the rest of the Barons in North Norfolk will look on this," said Tristan.

"No doubt Sir Cedric will have an opinion when he gets back," said John.

The remaining attackers had been rounded up and John told them of the Baron's deaths.

"You are free to return home, after you have buried all the dead. Remember we are all Englishmen and should not fight among ourselves. Save your strength for when we fight off invaders."

With that he rode towards the Castle which had now lowered the drawbridge and was opening the gate. He entered his home and found his family waiting for him, Tania ran to him as he dismounted and he took her in his arms. Looking over her shoulder he espied a young man standing holding his brother's hand and a nurse with a toddler.

"Have I been away that long?" asked John.

"You have my love," responded Tania. "You left me with something to remember you by, a beautiful baby girl, come and see her."

John said he wanted to get out of his armour first so as not to frighten her, but before he could move the younger boy ran over to him and said.

"You have been a long time away father, will you stay with us now so we can learn to fight like you?"

"I will I promise, my son. These old bones are getting tired," answered John.

The older boy had moved closer.

"We know how to fight and we would not have let them in."

"I am sure you would not have, and I thank you, Harold, for protecting your mother, brother and sister," said John as he put out his hand to Harold.

The young man was hesitant but shook the proffered hand and suddenly put his arms around John.

"Let me get out of this tin can and we will talk together," said John, a little taken aback.

After he had refreshed himself and they were sitting in his room, with his new daughter on his knee, John turned to Tania.

"Perhaps the country will settle down now and the other Barons will leave me in peace. Come Ceolwen, I love the name you chose, we will all dine together tonight. That is if you can keep awake," he said to the little girl who giggled and jumped down.

It was a joyful occasion in the hall that night a they all relaxed and related what had happened since they had last sat down together. Jack and Matilda were now looking frail and John was glad his father had handed the Smithy over to William and had employed a new lad in the Castle forge. John, Tristan and Stephen had inspected the Castle and found no serious damage, the fire arrows had burnt a couple of roofs which could repaired easily. Sadly there had been two deaths in the Castle guards and ten had died in the battle outside. In the following days John visited all his Tenants making sure they were up to strength and that the wool was making it's way to Flanders. He sent Stephen over to meet with Philip de Bleese to make a second outlet as wool was piling up in the warehouse.

II

The years had dealt kindly with John and he still had good health and vigour and his energy was felt by all who had dealings with him. He decided to make a journey to Wymondham to see Sir Cedric, he had heard that he was returned from the North, he planned to take all the family and this pleased Tania. They set off one bright morning with a strong escort, though there had been no reports of trouble. Alban sounded his horn as they approached the castle and they found the gates open and Sir Cedric standing in the

Bailey to welcome them. John looked at him and noticed how much he had aged, still fit but slower and heavier. The Lady Ann was still at the Castle but not as a wife, which did not please Tania. Later, as John and the Earl sat talking it became clear why he had not wed the Lady. She had two sons and if she had tied the knot with the Earl they would have inherited Wymondham. Sir Cedric spoke to John.

"You have always been like a son to me as you know, so I am making it official and legal that you shall be my heir when I die. There has to be continuity to run the estate and the area I am responsible for as Earl. I want you to come to London with me to make this official and we will see the King at the same time."

John was stunned at this announcement and it was a few moments before he responded.

"You do me a great honour Sir, it will take me a while to get used to this."

"You have two sons John, so the line of succession will be stable for a few years unless war intervenes."

The Earl grasped John's arm and the emotion could be felt in the air. They made arrangements for their trip to London and John went to tell Tania of the news. Tania was full of questions about where would they live, would they move to Wymondham, what would happen to Dunston, would he be an Earl and what would that mean. John fended her off as best he could but some of the questions he knew he would have to find answers for to satisfy himself.

They returned home and John accompanied Roderick on his next tour of the tenants, he found most of them in good humour owing to the increase in their income due to the new arrangements with Flanders. John considered increasing his business with Philip de Bleese to give Peter of Kortrijt some competition. Settling back in Dunston John spent more time with his sons making sure they attended their lessons he also devoted time with Harold to school him in archery and sword play, The lad was developing into a strong young man and he had to have his wits about him to keep ahead of the boy. Ceolwen was growing too and Tania was schooling her how to be a young lady. She was a quiet girl, not like her mother.

They had not been home long when word came that Sir Cedric had arranged the trip to London, he requested that the whole family went and also to bring Tristan. The whole cavalcade moved off and with his protective men at arms they caused quite a stir as the processed through the villages. Harold and Edmond were fascinated with the London house and the River Thames, they soon found a spot in the garden where they could watch the boats going up and down. Ceolwen was fascinated and it took all the boys time stopping her falling in the river. One morning they spotted the Royal Barge, Edmond was disappointed that the King was not on board.

Sir Cedric returned from a meeting with the King to inform them that he had decided to stand down as the Earl of Norfolk. He was finding it difficult as his age increased and as he now had a successor the King had agreed that John should take the position now. The ceremony would take place the next day to which they were all invited. Dressed in all their finery they set off for the palace.

Most of the Nobles were assembled and King Edward stood and stated that as an Earl John must support his King at all times. John stepped forward and knelt before his sovereign who placed the belt and sword around John and congratulated him saying he was looking forward to having him join him on his next venture. John's heart dropped as he knew this would be another march to Scotland. The necessary parchments were signed and they went to an anteroom where a meal had been prepared. The King was in a jovial mood and teased Tania and told Harold he must study hard and become a Knight.

Returning to the London House John was in a thoughtful mood and later in bed he was rather perfunctory in his love making which did not please Tania who said she might as well go to a nunnery. The next day a servant reported that a sickness had struck many people in the City and John decided they would not venture out, Harold and Edmond were disappointed as they wanted to see the sights so John arranged a River Barge so they could at least view the Westminster Palace and other buildings from the water. When they returned Sir Cedric and John decided that it would be better to move back to Wymondham as the Earl wished to make sure that John took up his position with the least amount of trouble. They knew the North Norfolk Barons would not be happy with the new situation as John had already crossed swords (literally) with two families. That night they celebrated John's new position and Sir Cedric's retirement, many of his London friends said they were pleased that he would be joining them and adding to their strength in running the country.

When they eventually arrived back in Wymondham John and Cedric spent many hours in Cedric's room discussing the best way to approach the changes that they had to make. John's thoughts were who should reside at Dunston, should he make that his base. He rode to Dunston with just his escort, leaving Tania and the family at Wymondham, by the time he reached the Castle he had made his decision. On entering the Castle he found everyone in a sombre mood, Boorman came to him and told him his father was seriously ill.

When John reached his fathers room Matilda told him that the doctor had said it was a malfunction in his heart. Jack could only manage a whisper to greet his son and John could see he was very weak, he looked at the leeches the doctor had recommended and wondered if this was the right treatment. John found Stephen, who was sympathetic, but like most people believed Jack's fate was in the hand of God.

"I need to speak with you as soon as my father improves, there are many challenges facing us and we need to be prepared."

At that moment Boorman came to him and said, "Your father is calling for you."

John went with him and found that the old man was near death. John grasped his hand and Jack opened his eyes, looked directly at John and with a final expulsion of breath life departed from him. John looked down at his father and thought of all that the man had given him, life, tuition and help as he grew, he left the room and walked up to the battlements, a favourite place when he wanted to be alone with his thoughts. Sir Cedric brought Tania and the family home for the funeral and John told him he had decided to put Gavin into Dunston and he would take residence in Wymondham. The Earl was pleased and said he agreed to John's decision regarding Gavin.

When John had moved into Wymondham and Sir Cedric had moved to London John thought about how he would approach the Barons. He sent a messenger to the Sheriff of Norwich telling him he would visit him and to assemble all the Barons at the Castle. In the message he also asked him to suggest to the Abbot it would be a kind gesture to celebrate High Mass whilst he was there. John wanted Tania to accompany him to which she agreed and the whole family set off with their retainers and two hundred mounted men.

John sent riders ahead who announced what was happening and as the column progressed through the villages crowds came out to see. The streets of Norwich were crowded with onlookers as the information that the new Earl was coming to the City. Arriving at the Castle the Sheriff welcomed them and conducted them to the Great Hall, there he had arranged a chair on a raised platform almost like a throne. John changed his cloak and placed his Earl's coronet on his head then climbed onto the platform. The Barons and city dignitaries had gathered in front of the platform some had found chairs but most just stood. John walked to the edge of the platform and spoke to them.

"Some of you I know but most of you I do not," he started. "We are all of the same Shire and have all pledged allegiance to our King. I am now your representative to that King. Sir Cedric has moved to London and will work for us in Parliament and as the King's advisor, for our part we must live together in harmony and work towards making this a great Shire."

There was some murmuring from the assembly.

"If you have something to say, say it now," said John.

A rather overdressed young man stood and said. "We are quite happy looking after our own business, we have no need to be involved with anyone else."

"It is polite to tell me your name before speaking, young man," said John.

"William of Holt," he replied.

"Well, William of Holt, when you are besieged by the French please do not call on us, as we will not know you," said John.

There was more murmuring and several of the men moved away from Baron Holt and his friends.

"This is all very well," said a thick set man. "How do you see us benefitting from all this cooperation, I am Hugo of Fakenham."

"We have the example in the south of the Shire," replied John. "My Tenants enjoy a standard of living not seen elsewhere, because we work together. I intend to show you how this is achievable. Today I want your allegiance to the King and your Earl, those who freely give it, step forward."

The Sheriff was the first to move and knelt in front of John, placed his hands between those of the new Earl and swore his allegiance. Gradually more came forward and the Sheriff noted their names. There were some who left and John asked the Sheriff to send their names to him. When the ceremony finished John removed his coronet and he brought Tania and the children into the Hall, they moved about talking to groups. A banquet had been prepared and as they sat down the general mood lightened and there were many laughs at the bawdy jokes that were told. After the festivities the Sheriff told John that the Abbot had arranged a High Mass in the morning. Later in their rooms John asked Tania what she had found out in talking to the people who were there.

"They are ready for a change," she said. "They think that Cedric was away too much, which I suppose he was, fighting for his King and going on a Crusade. There is a lot of interest in what you said about improving the economy of the Shire."

The following day they attended the High Mass in the Cathedral and the place was full. Most of the Barons and some families were there. After the Mass several of the Barons returned to the Castle and asked to speak to John. Gathered together in the Great Hall they discussed arrangements to visit Wymondham much to John's delight as they appeared positive. John spent time with the Sheriff the next day and suggesting ways that the Castle could improve it's defences and also be a central point for the Shire. After spending a week at the Castle and meeting the City dignitaries and other senior citizens John and his column moved off towards Wymondham. Passing back through the villages John began to realise more fully the responsibility he was undertaking, many Earls and nobility used their position to gain wealth and make the peasants even poorer so they could indulge themselves. He would make every effort not to fall into this trap and he knew Tania would help.

They arrived back in Wymondham and John talked with Gavin at some length, he wanted him to continue the way John had organised it. Gavin pondered on that for a while, but he agreed, there was nothing wrong with what had gone before so why 'rock the boat'. John was pleased he could leave Dunston in hands he knew were safe. Joan would be a help for her mother who wanted to stay in Dunston. He felt more relaxed now that the future was taking shape, his next challenge would be a journey to Bishops Lynn and talk to the Barons and nobility in the west of the land he had to govern.

Laying beside Tania that night John felt a familiar urge and turned towards her.

"Are you sure you can manage, old man," she said with a twinkle in her eye.

"I could take on three of you, wench," he replied as they shed their night shirts and he crushed her in his arms. Snuggled up together afterwards John wondered if there would be more children, he was very happy with the family size at it is. Finally they drifted off to sleep.

II

The next few days John made sure he got to know all the Wymondham staff, Rowan had always been friendly but now seemed to have a new lease of life and made sure that everything that John wanted was produced in double quick time. John smiled as young Edmond began to follow Rowan about, the Steward did not seem to mind as he answered all Edmonds numerous questions. Harold spent most of his time in the stables or at the practice field, honing his skills with the sword and bow. John coached him when he could but did not let him use his sword although he wondered what would happen when his son eventually had it in his hands. There had been no word from Sir Cedric or the King's Marshall regarding what was happening in Scotland, John secretly hoped he would not be called upon. He decided to circle south and visit many of the small villages that were in this area which was mostly left to itself. They departed with a large force of men and carts that were laden with cloths and seeds. The earth around the edge of the fens was rich and John calculated that it would produce enough food to feed the Shire if he could persuade the farmers to join with him. Many of the villages were deserted when they arrived, the inhabitants having fled when they heard of this 'large army' approaching so John sent out riders to tell the villages who he was and not to be afraid. Gradually the word spread and they were welcomed by the headman of each village and most farmers were eager to accept John's plan. The cloths and seeds were the 'icing on the cake'. John's small army were enjoying the journey too as the pace was easy and they were feeding well. He had to make sure they were watched in the villages as there were many pretty girls who were fascinated by the tough looking soldiers.

On of the scouts came back to report to John that a large number of armed men were approaching from the West. John rode out with the scouts to see for himself and sure enough they spotted them camped in a valley.

From the pennants flying they could see there were two Knights from Lincolnshire in the centre, Sir William de Falchionet and Sir Hugh Calderez, John recognised their colours from Tournaments he had been to. Riding back to his own men he called Tristan to him.

"Tristan, go as a Herald, to Sir William and enquire why has he entered my Shire with armed men?"

Tristan called two men to accompany him and rode to the encampment. Sir William himself came out to meet him and gave a reply stating that he was defending his own lands against an invasion by John as his armed excursion to the west of Norwich could only mean that John was after more territory. Tristan said this was not the case they were visiting their own villages to assist them. Sir William laughed and told Tristan to "go back to your blacksmith and tell him not to interfere with Norman Nobles." Receiving this affront John's temper rose and he called his men together.

"I want bowmen on the high ground on this side of the valley, keep out of sight until the signal. Mounted men with lance to go in on next signal, the rest will go on foot and clean up. You have all been well trained and many of you have fought with me before. This time we fight for our own homes so keep discipline and show them their mistake for challenging us."

The men responded with a cheer and captains prepared the men as John had said. John, dressed now in armour and riding Mace, rode out with Tristan and a guard. From the top of a hill he surveyed the enemy, They had assembled in battle order and were approaching the high ground. John could make out Falchionet from his colours and plumes and a little behind him came Calderez. John signalled the bowmen who stood and moved to the top of the rise, John again signalled and the bowmen loosed in one accurate volley. The front ranks of the oncoming men were decimated as the arrows struck home, the others faltered but were pushed on by those behind. Again the bowmen released their deadly rain of death and more of the front line died. Falchionet could be seen urging the men on but the line faltered again. The third volley again struck home and this time the march came to a stop. John signalled for the mounted men and led the charge down to the enemy with Tristan at his side. They rode into the mass of men like a tornado and flattened all before them until they came across the centre of the advancing army. Now it was man against man and deadly hand to hand fighting. John saw that the charge had been slowed so sounded his horn for the foot soldiers to join the melee. He forced Mace towards Falchion, the great horse even more powerful than Hammer. John dropped his spear and drew his sword and then the killing began. The glittering blade dealt death to all within its reach, Falchionet saw him coming and turned to meet him, at that moment his horse went down with a spear sticking out from it's belly Falchion was quickly on his feet and John pulled up. Two of John's guard dismounted and seized Falchionet and withdrew as John pushed on through the remainder of the fighting, he could see Calderez and went after him. Most of the men they were against were now running away but Calderez and three other Knights were still fighting. John pushed in to the fight and came face to face with Calderez.

"Yield and stop fighting," called John.

The Knights around Calderez stopped and threw down their swords but their leader just sat his horse and glared at John.

"I see no reason that I should yield. Fight me in single combat and it will be you who yields."

They both dismounted and all the rest stood back and watched. John stood ready with his sword and Calderez sprang at him with a flurry of strikes which John parried, John attacked and drove his opponent back to the men who were watching but eased as Calderez stumbled.

"You have lost the battle," said John. "Get on your horse and be gone from here."

Calderez sprang at him again and again John parried the blows and returned the attack with his sword now alive in his hands. There was a blur of shining steel and then the air around the pair was sprinkled with red, red blood from the neck of Calderez as John pressed home his advantage and Calderez fell. John pulled off the man's helm but there was no life in the Knight's body, his neck was almost severed through. Tristan had caught up with them and John said.

"Round up any prisoners Tristan and we will see if there are worthy ransoms among them."

The men who had been watching the final fight looked at one another and wondered at the display of swordsmanship they had just witnessed. One of the young Knights remarked.

“It’s true his sword has some magic about it, I have never seen speed like that before.”

There was a general nodding of heads and the vanquished trudged off to where the prisoners were being assembled. John stood, with some of his men quietly waiting, he wiped his blade and returned it to the scabbard.

“There is no magic here, just the result of much practice, “ he said.

The men said nothing and followed him up the hill. There were six junior Knights but non were from rich families, only Falchionet was worth a ransom so John had him swear to not escape and they set off back towards Wymondham. That evening around a camp fire John questioned Falchionet as to why they had attacked them.

“You must have known you were on my land, and if your spies are worth their salt you would have known that we were on a peaceful mission.”

Falchionet gave no answer and kept silent for the rest of their journey home. John despatched a messenger to Falchionet’s home for the ransom giving them forty days to raise it.

Arriving back at Wymondham, Falchionet was imprisoned in the upper room of the tower. He grumbled about the sparseness of the room and John told him he was lucky to be alive to enjoy what he had. John learned that King Edward had left for Scotland with his army and requested that John should join him at Carlisle. Tania wanted him to rest first after the last expedition and the men needed rest too, so John lingered for a few days until his men had regained their strength and he had recruited to fill the gaps made by the men he had lost. Finally he decided to start for Carlisle and on that same day the ransom for Falchionet arrived. John told him he would journey with them to Lincolnshire where he would be released. The small army moved on, the number somewhat reduced as he had left more men to guard his land since the last attack. They had reached the outskirts of Chesterfield when a messenger found them to inform them that the King had died in Carlisle on his way to Scotland. As John made camp another messenger found them with news from Sir Cedric telling him to continue on to Carlisle. When they arrived at the King's camp John looked for Sir Cedric and found him near the Royal Pavilion.

"Good to see you John," said Sir Cedric. "I came with his Majesty after all but will now go with him back to London. The Prince of Wales should be here soon and you will take your orders from him. Stay with me at the house when you come to the Capital."

John said he would. The King's body was taken south and in due course the Prince of Wales arrived and the army moved on over the boarder. After meeting supporters of the Prince in Scotland and a peace being declared, John approached the Prince and informed him that he was needed urgently in his Shire. The Prince was too busy with appeasing the Scots that he just nodded and John took that as a signal to depart. He was not pleased that the venture had been a waste of time, he wanted to get back to his home as quickly as possible so he moved his men on at a brisk pace.

After resting at home for a while John made plans to visit Peter Kortrijt and Philip de Bleese to make sure his wool trade was progressing well, he would take Harold and Tristan accompanied by just four guards. Tania was not pleased that he should be going away again so soon, Edmond pleaded to be included but John told him he was needed to protect the Castle, which he didn't believe. They went down to Yarmouth and stayed with Aelfraed until a passage was procured to take them to Flanders. It was a cold crossing and winter winds swept the decks keeping them crouched behind the small cabin where John and Harold chatted to the Captain. They reached Dunkirk and found lodgings for a while waiting to make contact with de Bleese. It was a cold wintery evening when Philip arrived to meet them in front of a roaring fire in the Inn where they were staying. After the welcomes and when they were sitting drinking warm spiced wine, Philip brought them up to date on his business. Sadly his father had died two months ago and he was still getting used to the fact he was now in sole charge. He said he was pleased with the arrangements with Peter, Count of Kortrijt, they had arranged between themselves that Philip would take a larger share as the transportation cost less.

Overall everyone was happy with the arrangements and they looked forward to a profitable few years. Harold said he would like some fresh air as the heavy wine and the long trip had made him tired. “Take a guard with you,” said John “and a cloak as it is a miserable night.”

The young man agreed and a guard got up to accompany him. They sat discussing the various happenings within the two countries and how it could affect their trade. Suddenly the Inn door burst open, Harold and his guard walked in both with blood on their clothes and hands. John quickly got to his feet and reached for his sword.

“Are you hurt, what happened, where do you feel pain?”

“It’s all right father we are not hurt, Jeffry has a small cut but nothing else. We were set upon by three men who shouted ‘this is revenge’ and then they attacked us.”

“The young master fought very well, sir, and downed one straight away. We fought off the other two and they dragged their companion away,” said the guard.

John looked at Philip, who was standing looking aghast.

“This is the work of the Hausman’s,” said John. “I shall have to visit them and stop this once and for all.” “Do you know what language they were speaking?” asked Philip.

“They shouted to us in English,” said Harold. “Between themselves I don’t know, it wasn’t French.”

“You maybe right John,” said Philip.

Harold and Jeffry went and cleaned themselves while John discussed the event with Philip.

“How did they know we were here?” pondered John.

“There are spies everywhere,” said Philip. “With the situation worsening in France we can expect more trouble. Now you have a new King maybe things will settle down.”

John said that he did not think so as there was no love lost between the King and Philip of France.

They rose early the next day and Philip gave Harold a description of the operation in Flanders and they visited his warehouse. John was pleased to see Harold take an interest in what Philip told him. Later at the Inn, after a day watching out for suspicious characters, John explained more of the trading agreement he had with his contacts in Flanders.

"Next time we come we will bring more men and pay a visit to Bruges and the Hausman family," he said. Returning to Yarmouth they visited Lowestoft and then journeyed on to Dunston. As they neared the village they stopped in a wood and John remembered the day that a man appeared out of this wood and changed his life.

Smoke was rising from the smithy fire as they rode on towards the Castle, Harold blew on his horn and the drawbridge was lowered and the gate opened. Gavin and Joan were pleased to see them and they sat down to a generous meal. They stayed overnight continuing on to Wymondham the next morning. Waiting for John was a message from Sir Cedric to come to London for Longshanks entombment and he needed to talk to him urgently. Harold and Edmond entreated with their father to take them and in the end John agreed. Harold was growing up fast and now, as a young man he wanted to be more involved in the running of the estate. John's thoughts turned to what to do with Edmond, as a second son he would not become the Earl and as Gavin was installed in Dunston it left little choice for Edmond. On the journey to London John thought of the unrest there was with the Barons and Nobles relating to their new King, meeting them in London will be very interesting.

Sir Cedric was very welcoming when they all arrived in the City, he sat for some time talking to Harold and Edmond, while Ceolwen sat on his lap. The girl could twist him around her little finger as the saying goes. The boys had always looked up to him as they knew the story of how he met their father. London appeared to be a very exciting place to the two young men, and John had to be firm in not allowing them to roam alone. After a lot of wheedling and promises of future good behaviour John agreed to take them into the City, but to make the first part of the journey by boat. They arrived at Westminster wharf and walked to the Palace, it was a hive of activity as they prepared for the Coronation. They continued on to the Abbey and paid their respects to the tomb of Edward. As it was midday they found an Inn and sat to eat and drink, the atmosphere was quite lively even at this hour. Several scruffy women approached them with offers to help them enjoy London but John sent them away, Edmond wanted the 'offers' explained and when Harold started to tell him John stopped him. They visited a number of shops and purchased a pair of shoes for each of them. John noticed there was still a number of sick people on the streets and soon shepherded them back to the boat. He had also noticed that two men had been shadowing them through the day. Arriving back at the house John spoke to Sir Cedric and told him of the men and extra guards were posted. As night fell and the moon slid behind clouds three boats drew into the bank at the foot of the gardens. Dark shadowy figures crept ashore and overpowered the guards one by one. They found the doors locked and barred but managed to scale the wall and up onto one of the balconies, quietly forcing a window the crept into the house. Harold woke with a full bladder and as he relieved himself he heard a noise, there should be no one up at this hour so he awoke Edmond and taking his sword he opened the door to his room. There stood two men, he shouted as loud as he could and backed into the room to give himself space to wield his sword. He parried and sliced at the two men as a third entered and joined the fight. Edmond was fending off an assailant as best he could when there was a roar from outside a clash of steel and John came charging into the room in his nightshirt with his sword slicing into the men. John's ferocity made his sword a blur as he despatched the men in the room he went out to assist Sir Cedric and the guards in finishing off the remaining intruders in the house. Harold looked at Edmond and he said, "Never ever make father that angry."

Candles were brought and they inspected the men who had intruded into the house. There was one still alive, but only just and as John questioned him his eyes rolled and his life ended.

"Who sent them?" questioned Sir Cedric, who had an injury to his chest. "I'm getting too old for this."

"I am not sure," said John. "We must search them and maybe

we can find out."

Most of them had money so they assumed they were paid assassins.

"What about those men who followed us," said Edmond, nursing a cut on his arm.

When dawn came they counted the cost, five of the guards in the garden were dead and two from inside the house. The boats had gone and they could find no evidence of their intruders in the grounds. The invaders in the house however did produce some clues, one man had a purse with a coat of arms and another had a scimitar instead of the usual sword. What all these clues meant John could not figure out. He went with Harold to Westminster and talked to the Master of Arms but he could throw no light on the coat of arms except that it was not English. The Palace was full of a sense of urgency as they finished the preparations for the return of the King and his new bride.

They embarked on their boat and went further down river to the Tower. The building was now finished and John went to the place where the Mint was located and showed them some of the coins they had taken from the brigands. One of the men there recognised a coin from France that was not used now and another coin that was used in Flanders. John's thoughts immediately turned to the Hausman family, but why pursue him to London, and with such force? John talked at length with Sir Cedric and felt that he should be at home in case of attack there. Sir Cedric understood and said he would represent him at any of the meetings with parliament or the King. So the Ivanson family left and went home quietly early one morning and were well clear of London before John called a halt.

"We will rest here and make an early start in the morning," he told them. "I want to be back in Wymondham as soon as possible."

They made good time back to Wymondham and once they were settled John talked with Tania about the events in London.

"I will go and talk to Aelfraed and see if he has seen much activity at the docks and people moving inland," he said. "I will take Harold and Edmond, the more experience they have of the land the better."

John's first stop on their journey to Aelfraed was at Dunston where he talked with Gavin and discussed ways they could ensure their wool reached the right hands in Flanders. Gavin told him he sent guards with every shipment and so far they had had no trouble and reached the warehouse in Flanders. Gavin wanted to accompany them to meet Aelfraed and John agreed. Aelfraed was pleased to see them but said there had been little activity from Flanders and no noticeable numbers of men coming over. His spies in Yarmouth and Lowestoft were reliable so it was unlikely any one from the Hausman family were involved. After spending the night with Aelfraed and toasting anyone and everyone, it was with heavy heads they departed the next morning. John planned to go up the coast to Shipden as he had not visited this area and was one of the far outposts of his authority. They camped near North Walsham that night and John sent Harold into the village to find out as much as he could without raising suspicion. When he returned he was able to tell them that most of the peasants were under the control of a Knight called William Baudrette whom they hated. He lived in a Castle nearer to the coast and his father had come over with William of Normandy. John had not heard of him and Sir Cedric had never spoken of him. John looked at his men, there were not enough to take on a real battle perhaps they could just call on the man in courtesy and hope he was not willing to clash with the Earl of the Shire who was under the King's protection.

The next day John dressed in the best clothes he had with him and they marched on to the Castle. As they neared it Alban blew a horn and the gates were opened, John noticed there were men on the battlements with crossbows and armed men stood around the gates. They entered a Bailey and a steward came to meet them. "Who comes unannounced with an armed escort to meet Sir William?" he asked.

"I am Sir John Ivanson, Earl of Norfolk, and I am on my way to Shipden and wanted to meet Sir William, especially as he has not accepted any of my invitations to Norwich."

The Steward bowed and asked John to follow him, John signalled for Harold, Edmond and Gavin to accompany him. They were taken to the hall where a richly dressed man rose when the Steward announced them.

"This is an unexpected visit," said Sir William.

"As I was in the vicinity I thought it would be right to call on you as we have not met," said John.

"It is true our paths have not crossed, we tend to keep to ourselves out here," went on the Knight. "I was unwell when we received the last invitation to Norwich."

"I hope you are fully recovered now as I intend to call us all together again soon."

Sir William gave a thin smile and indicated chairs for them to sit. John explained he wanted the Shire to work together so all could benefit, the Knight made no comment and asked if they would like something to drink. John could feel his coolness.

"We won't stay, as we still have some distance to travel. Perhaps I could come again on a more formal visit."

"If that is your wish, you will find our taxes are up to date. I am not sure what else we would discuss." John's temper was beginning to rise and Harold said.

"We must leave sir if we are to reach Shipden on time."

John nodded his head at Sir William and turned on his heal heading for the door. The Steward jumped out of the way and scurried after him.

"My Lord is not in good humour today but I am sure you will receive a warm welcome on your next visit sir."

John gritted his teeth and strode on.

Once they were outside and mounted John spoke to the Steward.

"You can tell your master that next time I come here I will

expect the courtesy my rank demands, and no excuses."

They rode out of the Castle and John put his horse to the gallup to ride off some of his frustration. Calming down as they reached their camp John was not sure he had handled that in the best way. This man could be an enemy and he did not want more of those in his fiefdom. They carried on to Shipden and made camp just outside the town. John and Gavin rode into town and hunted out the mayor. He was a small portly man who was more bluster than action and as soon as he knew who John was began to try and please him, offering rooms in his house for John and his sons. John said he would stay with his men but thanked him for the offer. During the conversation it was obvious that he was afraid of Sir William and tried to keep out of his way. He let slip that a lot of money went from the town to William in so called taxes. John managed to gather some detail of what was going on. That night at the camp John, Gavin and Harold discussed what should happen next. Harold was all in favour of going back to the Castle and confronting Sir William, but John and Gavin pointed out they did not have enough men. The final decision was to go back to Wymondham and organise a large force to come back and stop the finance of the town being looted and to put Sir William in his place.

From Wymondham John sent messages to the Sheriff of Norwich that he would visit the City in one month's time, this would give time to anyone who wished to petition him to be there.

Back in Wymondham John collected a large force made up with his own men and a contingent from Dunston. Gavin was to accompany him with Stephen and Tristan but Edmond was to go to Dunston and Harold to stay in Wymondham. John explained to his two sons that it would be good experience to be in charge for the time he was away.

They arrived in Norwich with rumours flying around as to why John had come with so many men. They camped near the Castle, with John and his captains accommodated within. Sheriff Edgar also was inquisitive as to why John was there, all John would tell him was that he was exercising his men to prepare them for any event that might happen and as he was making for the coast it would give them some sea air.

John stayed in Norwich for some days and received many petitions he also sent an invitation to Sir William to meet him there. They attended mass at the Abbey and by his presence made it known that as the representative of the King he demanded all their loyalty.

Leaving Norwich they marched on towards Holt where they met the son of Baron William, David. He was a pleasant young man and had taken over his fathers lands. With Alfred, son of Hugo of Fakenham, they had become prominent members of the Norwich Council. Sitting in John's pavilion the two young men reported that everything was quiet and normal up to Sheringham but beyond that towards Shipden there was unrest in the villages and the peasants were meeting in groups. Sir William was using his men at arms to try and keep order by using brute strength and stirring up more resentment. John told them he was there to put a stop to Sir William's tyrannical rule, they both wanted to go with him . John's army now increased with addition of their troops. Following the coast tracks they were soon in sight of Shipden. John turned inland and they made camp in a small forest. He sent outriders to keep watch on any activity. Sitting around the fire that evening John explained their strategy for the morrow.

"I will approach the Castle and see if we can discuss the situation with Sir William, if this fails we must cut all roads to the Castle. If he fails to meet me then we have time to lay siege to the Castle. I would rather take this strategy than an all out attack where we would lose more men."

At that moment the guards brought in four villagers who had walked into the camp. They explained to John that they were fed up with the way they were being treated by Sir William and wished to ally themselves to John.

"What do you think I am here for?" questioned John.

"Sir, with all these men I would say you are going to capture Sir William and take him to prison," said the leader of the group.

"Then you would be wrong," continued John. "I shall visit the

Knight as a matter of courtesy but we are on the way to Shipden to see if the port needs to strengthen it's defences. I am aware of the friction between you and your Lord but remember your position, he is your Lord and you toil for him. If you have a genuine grievance then make a case and bring it before the Sheriff."

The visitors stood in silence for a moment then turned and walked out.

"That was hard talk Sir," said Gavin. "I assume we are still going to capture Sir William."

"I am going to call on him, as I said, and I shall demand a change in what is going on here. If he disagrees, which I am expecting, then we shall make him see the error of his ways," answered John. "I don't want those villager to go back and tell everyone that we are attacking the Castle. Secrecy is the way."

The following day John set up a small camp not far from the Castle and sent a Herald to Sir William to come to him and discuss development of his land. The Herald was told to tell the Knight that the Earl would not take no for an answer. John and his men waited for over two hours, during this time they were spied upon by riders from the Castle. Eventually the Herald returned and reported to John that Sir William would come to him in the afternoon. While they had been waiting John had sent for his army to come nearer but to still keep in cover. Mid afternoon saw the Castle gates open and a group of horsemen appeared followed by a large troop of foot soldiers, they marched towards John's camp and as they approached a second, larger group of horsemen joined them from the other side of the Castle. John and Gavin mounted their destriers in full armour and John's mounted Knights and cavalry came out of the trees behind him. The edge of the wood also was suddenly filled with bowmen. Sir William's troops lined up opposite John's camp and a Herald approached. The message from Sir William was that this territory was his and his alone and he did not recognise the authority of John to interfere. John sent the man back with a terse reply.

'Yield to your Earl or face the consequences.' With that he signalled the bowmen to prepare. John saw the Herald reach Sir

William and then the line started to move towards them. The bowmen were given the signal to loose and the first flight hit the advancing troops and men fell. Horses fell too which caused chaos in the ranks of the advancing men. The next signal was for the mounted men to advance, there was just time enough for one more flight of death from the sky. The mounted men hit the front of Sir William's troops and the slaughter began. John rode forward with the rest of his foot soldiers and when they reached the fighting it was obvious that the battle would not last long as men at the back were already running away. Gavin was fighting Sir William and they were trading blow for blow. John pushed on towards them and just as he reached the fighting pair Sir William managed to find a gap in Gavin's armour and his sword slid in. Gavin toppled from his horse and John took advantage of Sir William's hesitation after delivering the blow and moved in to Sir William. His sword flashed in the sunlight and found its mark, Sir William's head flew into the men still fighting and suddenly the fighting stopped. John dismounted and went to Gavin who was laying still, he removed his helm and saw that there was no life in his eyes.

"Take him to my tent," said John. He remounted and called to his men to follow him to the Castle and to pick up the body of Sir William and bring it with them. They entered the Castle bearing the Knight's body, his Steward led the way to the Hall where they placed the body on a table complete with its head. Sir William was not married, which John thought probably was part of the reason he was so aggressive. The Steward said he and his wife would see to the Knight's burial.

"I shall leave my Knight, Sir Tristan, here to take charge," said John. "I expect obedience to him."

The Steward nodded and bowed and said he would serve the Knight. John left to go back to his camp making sure he had left enough of his own men to support Tristan. Gavin had been stripped of his armour and his wounds cleaned, John looked down at his friend and sorrow overcame him for a moment.

"Bring a cart to take him home," said John. "This is a sad day, let the men from Dunston escort him. Stephen, let's go home."

As they marched back towards Norwich John thought of what he would say to his sister Joan. Fortunately they had a son so she would have a reminder of her husband.

II

Tania was devastated at the news of Gavin's death and immediately made plans to go to Joan. John said he would accompany her but would have to return to Wymondham as soon as possible. There was also news from London that Sir Cedric was not well. Once Tania had comforted Joan and helped her to come to terms with Gavin's death John went back to Wymondham to formalise the plans he had been thinking of on the way home. Who should replace Gavin in Dunston? Who would replace him in Wymondham eventually?

Edmond was too young and inexperienced to control Dunston but Stephen would be the man to help and guide him, and he always had a soft spot for the home Castle. He would leave Tristan at Shipden who would soon organise the area the way he knew John would like it. John felt satisfied with his plan and turned his thoughts to his visit to London and to see Sir Cedric. They mourned Gavin and held a dinner in his memory, many of the Tennants came as Gavin had been well liked.

Arriving in London John found Sir Cedric recovering from his illness but very angry at the King's close friend, Gaveston, who had taken over the organisation of the King's coronation. The man had been banished by the King's father but Edward had reinstated him when his father died. Now he was the cause of much anger from the Barons. John listened patiently and tried to figure out the parts that would affect him and his estates. He told Sir Cedric of his plans and they sat and talked about them and John could see that the Earl missed his old home. He visited Westminster and kept out of the way of the builders as he paid his respect to Edward at his tomb in the Abbey. He was sitting quietly when two Barons approached him and asked him what he thought about the return of Gaveston.

“I think the King needs him but the country does not,” said John. “It would have been better if he had stayed away.”

The Barons looked at one another and then one of them said.

“He is in favour now but many of us feel that he should be sent away again. Will you support us when the time comes?”

John looked at them and said, “I am but a country man, I don’t think my word will carry much weight, I do not visit London or take my seat in Parliament.”

“You, together with Sir Cedric, are a powerful force and many are interested in what you do and say. We are all noticing how well your estates thrive and your men are loyal. Many here would listen to your views,” said one of the Barons.

John did not respond as he did not want to be drawn into the politics here in London. He politely excused himself saying he had to get back to Sir Cedric. Sitting in the boat on the way back he thought about what had been said, would he make a difference? That evening he discussed the subject with Sir Cedric as the Earl was used to the ways of things in London and at Court.

“There is trouble brewing in that area. I no longer advise the King as I used to do for his father. The best advise I can give you is to return to Wymondham and continue with the plans you discussed with me earlier. I am sure there will a solution to the problems here soon.” John stayed a further two days and then returned to Wymondham to his family.

Resting at home John mulled over what the Barons had said to him in Westminster Abbey. He did not want to be in London, he thought it was a dirty and dangerous place and he much preferred his country life.

John felt he was powerful enough in his Shire, he had a good number of men under arms who constantly trained and had proved themselves in battle. He decided that the politics of London could reach whatever conclusion they did, he would stay out of it. The King and all the fawning courtiers were so insincere that it made John feel sick every time he met them.

One winters evening John sat in the Wymondham library

looking at the collection that Sir Cedric had left there. He came across some old parchments written in a language he could not understand. He made a mental note to ask Sir Cedric what they were. As he was leafing through them he found one page that had strange markings illustrated that could be figures or numbers and he recognised one of them, it was the same marking that was on his ring.

II

Over their first meal of the day John suggested to Tania that they ride over to Dunston, he needed to talk to Edmond and to be brought up to date on the how he was handling his lands. When they arrived at the Castle, Edmond was at first nervous of his father's visit but after a talk with the Reeve, John relaxed and said he would ride over to the church as he had not been there for several years. "The new Priest has settled in," said Edmond. "There was no one there for a while after Father Aldred's replacement died but the Bishop has sent a new man."

John nodded and said it would be a good time to meet him. As he rode to the church he remembered the times he and Joan had made the journey and how Father Aldred had liked the barrels he brought. The church looked just the same, older and more weeds surrounding it, but the same peaceful air about it. The Priest came out to greet him and after John had told him who he was the man invited him into the church. After some polite conversation John said he would like to see anything of Father Aldred's personal effects that had been left there, if they had not been destroyed.

"Certainly Sir," aid the Priest. "I have disposed of his old clothes but all his other belongings are in a box in the Sanctuary."

John went to the small room off to the side of the altar with the priest trailing after him, there he found the box.

"I will take this with me and see if it tells me anything of his family."

"Not that I have found Sir," said the Priest. "but as you knew him you may find a clue."

John departed and went back to Dunston Castle. He searched the box and most of the contents were an odd collections of mementoes of the old man's life. Among some old parchments John found one that had been pressed between two pieces of wood. John carefully parted them and looked down at a piece of very old parchment as he looked at it he could not recognise the language, it was not Latin or Greek but the writing was very regular. The next few days he spent in the library at Wymondham searching through books trying to identify the strange writing. Nowhere could he find the information and as he sat discussing it with Tania she said.

"Why don't you ask father, he may know something, he has travelled a lot?"

John left the subject for a while but the puzzle kept coming into his mind so he decided he would visit the Earl. As he was making his mind up when to make the visit Sir Cedric arrived at the Castle. He said he was fed up with London and the way the King was acting so he had journeyed to the family he loved. One evening as he sat with John the conversation turned to the library and did the Earl want to move his books to London.

"No, I took what I wanted and the rest can stay here," he said.

"I have been trying to find out what the inscription on my ring is," said John. "I can find nothing in the books."

The Earl smiled and said that the book he needed was in London but he did not publicise the fact that he had it.

"As you know," continued Sir Cedric. "The Jews have been banished from these shores and the inscription on your ring is in Aramaic which is the basis for their ancient writings. It was widely used in the Arab lands and we came across it in our Crusades."

John showed him the ring but Sir Cedric said he could not recognise the figure but it looked similar to what he had seen when he was on his Crusade. John remembered his father had been on a Crusade and wondered if that is how he came to have the sword and the ring. John thought to himself that he had now two tasks, one to search through his father's box again and second to go to

London and look at Sir Cedric's book.

When he was practicing with his sword after Sir Cedric had returned to London, John tried to feel a connection between the ring and his sword but there was nothing, he was still fast even though he was older but nothing exceptional. John wondered why he had not linked the ring and sword together before.

Several months passed before John and Tania made their journey to London. John remarked that the outskirts were becoming as dirty as the centre and he would be pleased when they returned to the clean country air. Looking through Sir Cedric's books he found an ancient volume that had an illustration of some of the Aramaic letters but the one on his ring was not among them. Perhaps it was not an Aramaic letter at all. John returned to Wymondham and put the puzzle to the back of his mind as there were many things in the county that needed his attention, it was time to visit Norwich again.

John sent a messenger to Edgar at Norwich informing him of his intended visit and to gather together any petitioners so that they could be dealt with quickly. He would see any of the Barons on the second day.

John again made a special effort to show off his position again and journeyed in full armour, without his helm, and with a large escort. Going through the villages people came to cheer him and on entering Norwich there were large crowds gathered. The Sheriff was at the Castle to meet him and after changing out of his armour he sat down to hear what had been going on in the city since his last visit. He learnt that there was still disquiet between the French quarter and the English, some of the leaders wanted to see him on the morrow.

In the morning John sat and listened to the complaints of both sides. He made the point that Norwich was an English City and would abide by English laws as would all people in his fiefdom. His policy of all working together for the good of all and all reaping the benefit for all would continue. He said to them.

"You are all citizens of this fine city, so work together and sort out your problems, if you cannot do this then I will make the decisions for you as I see fit. You may not like that. This evening we will sit down and eat together."

The banquet went well and when the evening came to an end there seemed to be less hostility between the groups.

On the Journey back to Wymondham John thought whether it would be better to live in the Castle at Norwich and be at the centre of the Shire or stay at Wymondham where he felt comfortable and at home, he decided he would discuss it with Tania. His mind also thought about finding more information regarding his ring. As they neared their home a rider came from the Castle with news that Sir Cedric was seriously ill in London. John hurried back to the Castle and immediately prepared for Tania and himself to go with all speed to the City.

When they arrived at the London house they were met with the news that the Earl was near death. The Lady Ann was with him and when Tania rushed to her father's side she looked at John and shook her head. They stayed with Sir Cedric until he quietly passed away. Later Lady Ann said he had suddenly fallen ill and the apothecaries could do nothing for him. There were many falling sick in the City and if the Earl had not gone to a Parliament meeting he may not have caught the sickness. John made the necessary arrangements to fulfil the Earls wishes to be buried in Wymondham next to his wife. Lady Ann accompanied them on their sorrowful journey. When they arrived at Wymondham many Town's people and a few Tenants were in the Castle Bailey, as John had sent a courier to inform the Castle of Sir Cedric's death. There was a very sombre mood as the coffin was unloaded from the cart and taken in to the Great Hall. The Abbot was there to receive the Earl and then discussed the funeral arrangements to take place in four days, allowing time for all who wished to attend. Boorman and his new assistant made arrangements to accommodate as many senior Nobles as possible, the rest would find beds in the Town.

The day of the funeral was overcast with showers of rain.

"Supposed to be a good omen," said John. "It is not good for me as I shall miss him."

A tearful Tania nodded her head. All the Nobles came and the Abbey was full, just the family and a few close friends attended the entombment, John had ordered that Sir Cedric's wife should also be entombed with him and effigies of them both had been ordered to surmount the tomb which is situated in the North Transept. Later at the banquet, in his honour, many spoke of his kindness and fairness.

II

One day, after the Castle had retuned to normal, John sat relaxing in the Library, he pulled out an old book that had recorded some of the writings of Knights who had been on Crusades. Sir Cedric must have gleaned them from his friends. The Earl's writings were interesting but one parchment, written by a Sir Gregory of Pulham, whom John had never heard of, mentioned meeting an Arab Sultan on his way through France. John thought this was strange to find such a man so far from his home. Gregory befriended him and accompanied him back to the Holy Land. The Arab had been searching for items that had been stolen from him and he had traced the robber to France. He had recovered most of his possessions except a ring that was very important to him. This ring had disappeared and the Arab had given up the search as being an obvious foreigner and an enemy to some he had decided to return home. The area where the Knight met the Arab was not far from Chateaux Vent. John considered that a trip there would be better than journeying to the Holy Land, but where would he start? Maybe it would be better to let things stay as they were, he did not know if the ring would have the same effect on Harold. Now was the time to find out.

One evening after their meal, John asked Harold to come up to his room and he told him how he thought there might be some connection between the ring and the sword but only when fighting a genuine opponent, sparing had no effect at all. Harold listened and asked his father if he believed in magic.

“No, I do not but somethings are not magic yet they are hard to explain,” said John. “You will own the sword and the ring someday and I wanted you to be aware of how it feels.”

The young man looked at him.

“I think it is your skill father not any outside influence.”

John was pleased with his answer and made a decision to let him use his sword at the next opportunity.

John suggested to Tania that now everywhere was settling down it would be pleasant to take a trip abroad perhaps they could visit Chateaux Vent and stay there for a few days, she agreed and said it would be good for Harold to see the property. John wondered if there would be any chance of some information about the Arab at the Chateaux. Preparations were made and came the day, John, with the whole family, ladies in waiting and a contingent of twenty men at arms journeyed to Lowestoft. They would sail from there to St Malo and then proceed to Chateaux Vent. They spent a couple of days in Lowestoft as guests of the Mayor and finally found a ship that could take them all to the Brittany coast. As they sailed from the port John stood with Tania looking at the disappearing landscape and drew her to him, would they find the answers he wanted in France?

17451868R00162

Printed in Great Britain
by Amazon